# Tattoo the Wicked Cross

Floyd Salas

# Tattoo the Wicked Cross

Grove Press, Inc.
New York

And with him they crucify two thieves; the one on his right hand, and the other on his left.

And the scripture was fulfilled, which saith: *And with the wicked he was reputed.*

—Mark 15:27–28

For Velva

# Part One
# Dead Time

# Dead Time

## I

The gilt metal letters above the main gate, THE GOLDEN GATE INSTITUTE OF INDUSTRY & REFORM, were dull in the overcast spring morning, but they remained vivid in Aaron's mind as he stepped on short wobbly legs into the institute office.

A pungent odor of Pinesol disinfectant, laced with the smells of stale wax and worn metal furniture, had the familiar reek of the airless detention home halls he had left only two hours before; they gave him the feeling that he had dreamed of or had been in this very office before, and they reminded him that his brother John had told him to remember . . . something, but he could not recall what it was.

The long bench which stretched away from him tho length of the gray wall was familiar, too, and so were the fluorescent tubes of light burning like ribs of hot ice on the low ceiling and frosting the thick coat of varnish on the high counter which divided the room.

The big man in khaki who sat typing on the opposite side of the counter could have been any man in the detention home, and his command to sit down could have come from any of their indistinguishable mouths.

Aaron sat quickly down, but although he sat erect, with his hands clasped in the lap of the old Boy Scout pants he had

11

worn for the trip, his old gym shoes just touching the floor, his faded sweatshirt not touching the wall, all he could remember was the fat kid's joke as he left the DT.

"Give your soul to Jesus, dad, because your ass belongs to the man at the institute."

He had explained that the clothes Aaron wore would all be burned, and had warned him of vague rumors that his best friend and crime-partner, Barneyway, had been stomped soon after his arrival. This warning now flipped through Aaron's mind with Barneyway's huge luminous eyes as the probation officer entered the office carrying a large, manila envelope.

But the dull metal letters of the sign still stood like bars before him and between him and what he was supposed to remember. They had stood like giant bars across his last glimpse of the Northern California highway as the gate closed behind him. They had barred the windshield of the black state car and the blank side of the official pass that the guard had put under the wiper before the car began its slow creeping drive up the paved road, which circled like a noose through the main grounds.

They had stood like fence posts across the open fields inside the barbed-wire institute fence. They had been as tall and solemn as the ash-brown twin rows of eucalyptus trees which stood guard on opposite sides of the entrance drive. They had striped the flat, white institute buildings. They had stood as stiff and important as the flagpole in front of the office, and had spaced the sloping lawn of the hillside there with the significance of statues on graveyard plots.

The metal letters now masked the face of the close-cropped gray head, with the shaved sideburns, which was decapitated by the counter, and also replaced the metal clock hands on the wall. They sat on the floor as heavily as the steel cabinets, in which the manila envelope with his life history would be filed. They let less daylight through the windows than the Venetian blinds. The typewriter spelled them out with its distracting clack-clack instead of what he was supposed to remember, although he kept telling himself that a thousand other guys, including Barneyway, had already been through the gate.

"C'mere," the man ordered.

And Aaron forgot the letters, for the khaki bulk of the man seemed to swell with each step he took toward the counter until he was directly beneath the mountainous chest and shoulders.

"My name is Mr. Toothman," the man said and took the manila envelope from the probation officer in return for a dis- interested shake of his fingers.

"My job is to make sure you do your time here without making a nuisance of yourself. And your job is to make sure you obey all the rules, all day, every day, and you'll do your time without getting yourself hurt. Got me?" the man asked and glared at Aaron from short-lidded, dry and unblinking eyes.

"Yes . . ." Aaron said, in a thin voice.

"What?" the man asked and poked down with his blunt nose.

"Yes!" Aaron blurted out, his tongue darting out and over his full lips in a nervous action.

There was a short, welcome pause in which the man took a manila folder out of the manila envelope, flipped its cover open, and studied Aaron's record, a pause in which Aaron tried to remember again, a pause briefly interrupted by the slight monotone of the probation officer:

"He behaved himself on the way up here. Seems scared and ready to learn his lesson, and they told me he buckled down pretty quick at the detention home."

The lipless gap that served for the man's mouth opened slightly, then closed, as if taking an impatient and barely tolerant breath. The probation officer leaned on the counter with an indifferent slouch, propping his elbow on it, his soiled gray suit falling in sacklike folds to his scuffed shoes, his colorless eyes neither looking at nor avoiding the man's stare, looking nowhere, looking at nothing; but the colorless lips flickered in a smile when the man started reading again.

The smile and the timbreless voice surprised Aaron, for the probation officer had hardly spoken during the hundred-mile trip, and now to hear him speak in his defense was totally unexpected. For the first time, he saw the mild neutrality in the probation officer's face, saw a complexion neither pale nor tanned, eyes of no distinguishable color, not even a purposeful gray, but without contempt nor any desire to punish in them.

"Aaron D'Aragon . . ." the man said, commenting aloud on Aaron's crime-jacket. "Never been arrested for theft but with five arrests for fighting, and all within two years, and, in each case, involving a gang which was led by him. You're a Big Shot Instigator, huh?"

"I . . . I . . . yes," Aaron, said, submitting as he knew he had to, as he had during the long two months in the detention home; but he was ashamed of his stutter, and he felt a blush stain his cheeks.

"It's hard to believe such a little squirt could lead a gang of mostly older boys, a couple of them with records, too. You're not even five feet tall and you're fifteen, aren't chou?" the man asked, then demanded, without waiting for an answer: "Answer! It says here, you've always got an answer for everything. Answer!"

"Yes," Aaron replied, making sure he said it clearly; and the ease with which he answered under the man's pressure gave him courage, so that he stood straighter, squared his narrow shoulders, brought his legs together, and lifted his chin slightly but carefully so as not to appear defiant, not to show the slightest hint of cockiness.

Occasionally the man looked up from the folder and stared dry-eyed and unblinking at Aaron, as if for verification; and Aaron found that he could endure the stare without a shirking sideward glance, could look past the carefully curled black lock of his hair and prove that he had nothing to hide, that he was ready to do his time, do it good, get it over with, get back out on the streets, and start living again.

The man slapped the folder closed and dropped it on a desk, lifted the counter leaf, forcing the probation officer to jerk back to keep his arm from being slammed against the wall, and muttered something as he stepped past him. The colorless fingers of the probation officer snapped on the brim of the gray hat in a silent goodby, and the screen door squeaked open and clapped shut.

To catch up with the man Aaron had to skip across the room, hurry out the back door, cross a gravel clearing, his footsteps sharp as a watchdog's bark in his ears, and run up the concrete steps of another building. Here he realized he was passing through the hospital corridor, odorous with antiseptics, and was aware of a nurse's stiff white cap, the rustle of her starched uniform, and her mumbled greeting to the man. The next flight of stairs required an extra effort, for his knees were weakening and his legs were growing heavy, and he was afraid he would stumble as he walked down a dark corridor lined with wooden cell doors to a shower room at its far end.

"Get those clothes off," the man said; and Aaron scratched his chest and tore a button from his trouser fly in his nervous haste to undress quickly under the man's impatient stare.

"Alright, lift those arms."

Aaron lifted them, and the man scanned his armpits, his hairless crotch, then his head as he scraped blunt fingers through his hair.

"Turn around. Bend over and spread your cheeks. Okay, now get in that shower and make it quick, and get that stinking grease out of your hair."

Aaron stepped into the punishing sting of hot water, letting it tattoo his head, briefly rubbed soap into his scalp, turned the cold water on, and let it numb his flesh and every concern except getting out of it. Then he hurried to rub down with the towel and slip on a woolen nightgown before the man got angry, and he found himself trying to remember once again and to listen to the man, too, as he was being locked in a cell.

"You'll stay here until the doctor's examined you, until that duck's ass haircut has been clipped, and a job's been found for you. If you behave, you'll be treated square and you'll do less time. But if you act up and play the wise punk, I'll teach you something. I'll make you act like a man while you're here or break you in trying. And if you get too tough for the institute, you'll get committed to Youth Authority, and maybe those boys in the state reform schools will teach you what tough is? Got me?" the man asked in a tone as brittle as the shine of his eyes.

"Got me? I said?"

"Huh?" Aaron said, but the command sharpened his memory.

"Got me?"

"Oh, yes. Yes," Aaron said.

"Yes! Yes! Yes!" he kept repeating to the thick gray door which shut in his face, for he had finally remembered: Mother!

## II

At first Aaron's struggle to remember his mother produced only a smear of pale skin on the transparent pane of glass in the small window slot of the door. He stared harder until he forced an image to appear on the glass, forced himself to see nets of fine wrinkles about deep green eyes, and saw, without forcing, nervous pencils of cigarette smoke streaming from thin nostrils, but also saw, although he didn't want to, a stark frizz of damp black hair framing a swollen face, bloodless yellow from an enlarged and dying heart; and he threw himself at it, to see past it.

The window slot was a palm wide, and even by standing on his toes, he could only see the upper half of the gray door opposite his, its empty window slot, which mirrored and mocked his attempts to see, his attempts to forget, and a giant burnt-out bulb on the hall ceiling, caged in wire.

The light which escaped through the slots into the hall was too dim to permit more than a guess at where other cell doors might be, and a hop in the air, with his finger tips hooked in the bottom ledge of his window slot, only allowed him a glimpse of the hardwood floor and the metal banister which guarded the edge of an empty stairwell.

He then turned and leaned against the door, his eyes watering from the strain of trying to see through the thick, smudged glass, his body lost in the wide skirt of the white woolen nightgown, his bare feet flat and cool on the hardwood; and he blinked away the wavering corners of his cell.

A barred and screened window on the outside wall filtered and thinned the gray daylight so severely that it darkened the gray woolen blanket on the bed and the gray walls. It blotted the shadows in the corners and erased the edges between the walls, between the walls and the ceiling, between the walls and the floor, between the walls and the baseboard, between the walls and the metal cot, between the metal cot and the metal radiator, between the cot frame and the cot blanket, between the cot frame and the cot legs, between the cot legs and the floor, between the boards of the floor, between the floor and the side wall, between the side wall and the ceiling, between the ceiling and the back wall, between the back wall and the window frame, between the window frame and the barred and screened window itself; and he leaped on the cot and bounded to the window, touched a bare toe to the radiator, balanced on it with one foot, and stared out.

But the window square of bars and wire screen limited his view to the top of the hill and the gray sky, and he jumped from the cot and ran to the door, but he could only see the opposite door and the caged and burnt-out bulb; and he turned and stared at the walls, but their edges were blurred; and he leaped on the cot and bounded to the window again and leaned on the radiator and stared out once more.

Sun spots moved slowly across the matted side of the hill as the morning clouds began to break, and for a moment, a beam, which had penetrated the bunching mass of clouds, illuminated the red bark of a manzanita branch and captured his attention, held it, then vanished; and he watched the subtle play and variation of other sun spots until his foot began to ache.

He then lifted his foot from its uncomfortable position between the metal humps, stepped back on the cot, and tried watching from a more relaxed position. But he could only see a patch of scrub brush, and the screen and bars obscured that too badly, so he sat down on the cot.

The silence in the isolation cell rang in his ears. There was a sour taste in his dry mouth. He wiggled his toes and flattened his feet against the floor. He shook his head hard, and the damp curling hair fell into his eyes. He pushed it back by running his fingers through it. This gave the tips of his fingers a faint shine, and he stared at his fingers until they were dull again. Then he stood and began to pace the narrow path between the cot and the wall. Then he measured the distance heel-to-toe from the door to the back wall and counted twelve bare feet. Then he guessed the distance of the cell's width as six or seven bare feet. Then he stood on the cot and bounced and touched the ceiling with his fingers and guessed that it was eight feet high. Then he began to pace the narrow path between the cot and the wall again. He paced from the door and its window slot to the back wall. Then he paced from the back wall and its barred window to the door. Then he paced to the back wall. Then he paced to the door. Then he paced to the back wall. Then he paced to the door and stopped. Then he paced to the back wall and stopped. Then he spun around so swiftly that his nightgown billowed but was stopped on his first step by the punishing sight of the cell door.

He was stopped by the cell door. He was stopped absolutely by the cell door. The cell door stopped him because the patrol car had stopped him. The patrol car had stopped him because its red dome of frightening light had stopped him, and had kept him from running by flashing the weird glow of panic over Barneyway's smooth cheeks, over the cheeks of three other zoot-suited buddies, over the cheeks of the bloody-nosed kid they had slugged.

The glass slot in the cell door stopped him, too, stopped him like a blank and unblinking accusation, as damning and accusing as the kid's pointing hand, as punishing as the stinging slap of the cop's fat palm, as the instant ringing in his ears, as bright as the current of lightning that had numbed his brain and had petrified into the curved bar of light on the pistol handle, and as taunting as the cop's snarling challenge:

"Go 'head, punk,

"Run!

"Run!

"Punk!

"Run!"

He clapped his hands to his face to shut out the blank accusation, to squeeze the snarling challenge out of his mind, and squeezed until he heard a noise, the jangle of keys, the slide of footsteps on a floor, and voices.

He threw himself against the door again and stood on tiptoe to see out the slotted window, hoping to see Barneyway, picturing a small bony figure in detention home dungarees, slumped and hunched in a futile attempt at a pachuco slouch.

But he could only see the door opposite his, the staircase banister and the wall; and he hooked his fingers in the bottom of the slot and hopped up twice, hoping to spot somebody coming up the stairs, somebody who might know Barneyway, at least, somebody who would know that . . . the . . . rumor . . .

The noises stopped, the voices receded; and although he hugged the door and stayed on his toes until they hurt and stared at the banister until his eyes watered, he could neither hear nor see anyone; and he dropped down on his heels and stepped back from the glass with aching eyes.

He glared at the glass slot until it seemed to glare back at him, to return his glare with a mocking promise of nothing, to beckon him to see not Barneyway's gaze, a gaze made deep and luminous by the curving concentration of heavy eyebrows, but the vacant, transparent edge of his own freedom, to taunt him toward that brittle but unbreakable edge, to prompt him into violent useless anger; and he leaned toward it, wanting to leap at it, smash it, splinter it, tear it and his fingers apart in a fit of screaming, sobbing rage, suffer from its slicing glass slivers, but suffer with courage and revenge, suffer but suffer hating.

Hating, he sat on the cot. Hating, he tried not to hate. Hating, he tried to forget the glass slot and the rumor. Hating, he tried to do something to forget, and, hating, he dropped his hands between his legs, pushed past the skirt of the nightgown, and, still hating, pressed his sweating palms against the varnished floor.

He pressed really hard, really trying to forget and not hate, and found, when he lifted his palms, that the sweat made moist islands of dampness. He pressed his palms down again and again, and filled in the spaces between the dark blots, and began to forget.

The pattern grew until he had made a thick line from the cot to the wall and had forgotten. But the end of the line below him was fading away, and his hands were dry, so he gave it a hurried stamp with his foot, and stood next to it, and saw a sign of the cross, with a twisted horizontal beam.

The heel print formed the high end of the beam, but because the toe print wasn't large enough to really weigh its end down, it tilted the beam off balance, and made him dislike the sign. He then tried to ignore the sign by pacing the narrow path between the cot and the wall again, by counting and recounting the twelve step distance from the door to the back wall, from the back wall to the door.

But each time he reached the spot where the cross had been, he'd see its dark outline, although he knew it had already evaporated, and he'd try to step over it and lose his step count.

Then he'd start over again and see the outline again and try to step over it again and lose his step count again.

Then he'd start new from the other direction and see the outline once more and try to step over it and skip a number and lose his count again.

Then, trying to make sure he didn't lose count, he stepped on it, and then started stamping on it and cursing too, until his heels hurt and he heard himself shouting.

Then he dropped on his knees and made the sign of the cross and tried to pray.

"Hail, Mary, full of grace . . ." The doll's face of a blue-hooded Madonna suddenly appeared before him, as he smelled wisps of candle smoke, the sooty odor of burnt kitchen matches, and saw the bent slot of a brass coin box. ". . . Blessed art thou amongst women. . . ." The Madonna vanished and he saw his mother at prayer, saw her in a simple white nightgown, her hands clasped tightly between the slopes of her ongging breasts, her rapidly praying lips fluttering, almost kissing the large-mooned fingernails, standing because kneeling might cause a heart flutter and a faint.

She vanished, too, with the first sag in his back, and he shifted his weight from one pained knee to the other and tried to say the rosary. He tried to visualize the words of the Lord's Prayer in block letters in his mind, because his lips made only mechanical motions, but he couldn't see the letters although he forced himself to pray until the sag in his back became an ache.

He quit trying to pray but stayed on his knees, his face

resting against the coarse wool of the blanket, his arms on the cot, too, his narrow buttocks leaning on his small heels, hardly aware of the chill in his bare feet, no sight in his open eyes, wishing that prayer would transform him now as it had before her death, when it wasn't a discipline that he used to control himself, to make himself behave, to keep himself out of trouble, when it filled his mind with pictures of a soft-eyed Jesus, a blissful Mary, and a grandfatherly, white-bearded God, when it was a joy that numbed his body so that he didn't even feel his arms and legs.

His first Holy Communion was still a vivid memory of untroubled grace, of a paper-dry wafer host melting upon the spoon tip of his tongue, leaving a taste of white bread and a breath of Christ. But it was a grace banished forever by the death of that ninety-pound sack of wrinkled flesh and bone in the bright hospital room his twelfth summer. It was a grace banished by the uneaten box of stale chocolates on the enamel bedstand, by the dark, wilted edges of roses, by the wheeze of those last breaths, by those unbearable moments of hesitation in which her heart seemed to stop before the pitifully brief wind of exhale fluttered from her chest. It was a grace banished forever by the reassuring smile she kept turning upon him, a smile that seemed all teeth, that seemed to ripple the transparent skin back in a revelation of bone socket and skull. It was a grace banished once and for all by that crucified Christ on the stained-glass window of the hospital chapel, by that Christ who flooded the altar with an orange and sulphurous glow, by that Man-God on the window who denied the rush of hoarse prayers and hoarse pleas, who refused the promise of a lifetime of penance for the continued thump of that soft muscle in her breast, a grace banished forever by Him! that Christ! that God!

A sob croaked in his throat. There was a wet spot on the blanket from his open mouth. He rubbed at the tears which filled his eyes, cursed himself, jumped to his feet, smashed his fist against the door, moaned, and cradled the burning knuckles of his right hand in the damp of his left palm, but glad, glad of the pain, wishing only that he had hurt somebody else, too.

He sucked the blood from his torn knuckles and liked the nail taste. Then he cocked his left hand to slam it, too, against the door. But a long, quavering breath escaped from him, and he dropped his clenched hands to his sides, rubbed his sweating palms against the thick nap of the nightgown, made an about-face, and the soles of his feet squeaked with friction.

He gazed absent-mindedly about the cell until he noticed a gray brush stroke on the hardwood floor, where a careless painter had run off the baseboard. He fixed his eyes hypnotically upon it for some time. The stroke would blur occasionally, come into focus, and blur again.

He shook his head to clear it and, looking for more defects, let his sight follow the baseboard to the back corner of the cell, let it turn there and follow the board along the back wall into the film of dust and darkness under the radiator, let it glide up to the top of the radiator's accordion ridges, when he noticed odd traces of shadow on the wall above that suggested letters.

He squinted his eyes and tried to decipher them without moving from his position, but he was unable to, and he began to take slow steps toward them, trying to discover at what distance he could.

By the third lagging step, he felt his pulse quicken, for he could distinguish a cross with three rays above it; and another step brought the numbers 1 and, possibly, a 5 of a date into view; and with another step, he guessed that a circled indentation was in reality a twisted heart, with a pachuco cross planted into the cleft between the lobes and the year 1945 scratched below the tip. But the faint hollows within the clumsy heart remained obscure until he reached the wall and ran his finger slowly over the thick coat of gray paint.

He felt his sense of triumph grow into admiration as he

traced the name RICKY DE LA CRUZ across both lobes of the heart, made out a plus mark, and spelled out the EVA that was wedged into the heart's point. For the guy must have spent days of stolen spoon-handle labor carving that five-inch heart into the bare institute wall, and he had to be full of guts and love to do it, because he knew he was going to have to suffer for it. Yet he had so much guts he carved it in the most conspicuous spot in the cell, where it could be seen by anyone and everyone who looked through the glass slot, and *so that* it would be seen by anyone and everyone.

Aaron wished he had a spoon, too, to prove *he* had the guts to love, to prove that neither the man nor the cell nor dead time could kill either his guts or his love, to prove what the thick, useless paint and the year that had passed had proved for Ricky De La Cruz, to prove that he, like Ricky De La Cruz, was greater than the cell!

The loud blast of a whistle reverberated in the cell, blurred the faint outlines of the heart, and echoed for seconds after it had stopped; and, curious, Aaron hopped on the cot and looked out the screened window.

The portion of sky framed by the window was cloudless, and the green scrub and wild grass on the hill glimmered in a full sun. The shadow of the building divided the clump of red-branched manzanita exactly in half, and he guessed that it was noon and lunch time.

He heard the shout of distant voices, the tramp of marching feet, and he tried to picture Barneyway marching in a moving column under a wide sky, but he could imagine nothing more than the small figure he had seen shuffling down a detention home hall in a crooked line.

The marching stopped. Silence, and then the dim metallic click of silverware, of tin cups and pitchers, the slap of trays, of pans, and the hum of voices.

He leaned the side of his head against the bars until the upper tip of his ear touched the outside screen and tried to distinguish the individual sounds. But the pleasure he felt when he was able to pick out footsteps changed to fright when he heard the jangle of keys and realized that both sounds were coming from the stairs behind him. He hopped off the cot, ran to the door, caught a glimpse of an approaching guard, dropped on the cot, and waited, as innocently still as possible, for the door to open.

A pink-faced man peeked through the glass slot and smiled with crooked teeth. His khaki shoulder then replaced his face as a key tinkled, metal scratched on metal, and he swung the door open wide enough for a pudgy, light-skinned colored boy to hand Aaron a metal food tray, and then quickly closed it.

Aaron took the tray but was more interested in the boy, who had vanished, for he had no appetite and he wanted to ask the boy, especially since there was no hostility in the pale-brown eyes, if he knew Barneyway. But he let the tray settle on his thighs, scanned it, and began to pick at his food as he did when he ate at home alone.

The brown gravy had a good flavor but the mashed potatoes were lumpy, and two spoonfuls were enough for his stomach tightened. He forced himself to take a bite of the crusted fish patty, and it flaked apart in his mouth. It was strong but tasty and he mechanically ate half of it, although he had to tense his stomach muscles with every swallow. He skipped the table-spoon of peas in its shallow crater but drank all of the milk because it was easy. Then, remembering the hungry hours be-tween meals at the DT, he spread the applesauce on one slice of bread, folded it, folded the rest of the fish patty into the other slice, placed both of them under the foot of the mattress, and tried to relax his stomach by stretching out on the cot.

His breath got so short he had to raise himself up on one elbow and take long, lungful swallows of air. He then dropped back on the cot, his head in the pillow, and tried to lay abso-lutely motionless, tried to prevent even the slightest quiver of an eyelash. He tried to stop all thought, too, and with deliberate blinks of his eyes he succeeded in blotting out all painful pictures which came into his mind.

He succeeded so well and for so long a while in preventing any single memory or daydream from developing into anything remotely unhappy, there was no longer any need to try and control his motions and thoughts; and his mind idled, his unseeing eyes filled with the neutral gray of the ceiling, a color he didn't notice again until he heard the sound of keys and footsteps on the stairs.

He threw his legs off the cot and raised himself to a sitting position as the door opened, then snatched the tray from the floor, and stood and switched his weight nervously from foot to foot as the man took the tray and asked if he wanted to go to the toilet.

When the man's toothy smile sagged with his jowls Aaron feared he might be forced to eat the rest of the food or be punished.

"You don't seem to have eaten much . . . Patty's gone, though, and the applesauce . . . bread. . . ."

The man's smile reappeared and without the teeth it was thin-lipped and weak, but he laid the tray next to the stair banister, motioned to Aaron to follow him, and started down the dim hall.

Aaron hurried after him as if he had been set free, springing with each step, reaching with each leg, and slapping each foot against the cool floor, for he was out of the cell, on the other side of the locked door, away from the solitude and the enforced thinking. But the walk was too short and he did not get to see a single other prisoner, although he still had the walk back, and he counted on the noise of his first trip to bring faces to the window slots for the second.

The white tile of the toilet floor was a cold thrill to the soles of his bare feet, too, and just standing next to the enameled trough was a pleasure, let alone the relief his shrinking bladder gave him, and the fun he had aiming the stream of colorless urine which spurted out of him. The strong soapy odor of a yellow bar of disinfectant by the center drain even smelled good, and he sprayed the bar and started to wash the wall of the trough, when he noticed that the man was standing next to him.

Then, discreetly lowering the stream to a point directly below him so he wouldn't get bawled out for playing around, he tried to sneak a glance at the man without stopping. But he stopped the trickle with a pinch and dropped the nightgown. For the balding head was cocked to one side! The thin lips were tucked into the pink cheeks in an inquisitive smile! And the eyes were glazed!

The eyes blinked, switched toward Aaron's concealed crotch, blinked again, switched back to the trough, blinked again, switched toward Aaron's face and blinked again, blinked the glaze away, then vanished as the man turned abruptly away and led Aaron quickly back to the cell, smiled as he closed the door, peeked through the slot, and disappeared.

But his dreamy gaze lingered in front of Aaron with the transparent reality of the window glass. For Aaron could both see through it and it completely stopped him. He knew the man was a queer, but he couldn't figure out what kind. The man had taken advantage of him but hadn't touched him. The man had tricked him but was nice to him, and Aaron now feared his kind and unpredictable gaze as much or more than Mr. Toothman's cruel stare.

The man had watched him piss!

The man was a queer!

For one vigorous moment Aaron wished he were his brother Stanley so he could break the queer man's crooked teeth, and for one vigorous moment he *was* Stanley, facing himself in the courtroom, feinting at himself, sticking out a slow-motion jab, thick upper lip curling over two big winking teeth, thick hair waving back from a broad, boxer's brow, then straightening out of that crouch with the limber, muscular movements of a professional fighter with a string of kayos to his credit, but a fighter who had lost his most important fight by weakening himself with a whore; and Aaron straightened out of his crouch, and rubbed his palms on his thighs, wrinkled and bunched the nightgown, lifted its skirt, and realized how helpless he was.

He wasn't a former All Army Lightweight Boxing Champion at all, nor an arrogant naval officer, in a grave black and white uniform, like his brother John, who scared away the girls as much as he did the guys with the stern orders and the snapping replies that seemed to make the taut skin of his cheeks vibrate and his eyes glint.

He was a small kid locked in an isolation cell, doing dead time on his very first day in a reform school. He was a small kid who not only could not slug the man like Stanley nor cow him into submission like John; he could not even tell on the man.

Who would believe him? Not other men. Not anybody in his family. Not his fat bald-headed father for sure, who was so huge and powerful he couldn't imagine being molested. His dull-brown eyes couldn't be convinced of anything that might cause them discomfort. Even his tie knot looped out like a crooked, impatient finger demanding a simple explanation when he was told something too important to be simple. Yet his blunt face could not explain either when, while putting on a coat to go out, a packet of rubbers dropped onto the floor.

Aaron slapped his hands against his thighs and spun around in a meaningless circle to whirl the thoughts out of his mind. The wind from the turn rose with a swirl up his naked body, ballooned the nightgown, and he came to a stop facing the screened window. He concentrated on it to clear his dizziness and get his balance, then climbed on the cot, rested a foot on the cold metal of the radiator, and leaned his forehead against the bars.

The clump of manzanita was completely in the shadow of the building and it was cooler now. Some time had gone by anyway, and he guessed that it might be two o'clock. He stayed stretched from the cot to the window for many minutes, trying to forget the queer man, trying to occupy his mind by making phantom figures out of the shapes of the bushes, the mounds of earth, the bare irregular patches in the knee-high grass. But it didn't work because he was too conscious of what he was trying to do, that he was stretched from the cot to the window, trying but unable to escape the man or his isolation or the time before him.

The bars before him blocked all escape, and the screen before him even checked what he saw. Two ways. It actually checked the hill, too. It checked the sky. Three ways. Or more? For it checked . . . yes. . . . It even checked his memory.

The small squares of the screen loomed as big and black as those in the courtroom windows, which had checked his sister Nora's bare arm when she tried to console him after his sentence. But he tried to keep from weakening, for all his memories of her were checked: the view of the corner from his bedroom window, the dark shaft of the Lutheran church steeple, the street light, his thoughts of her while waiting for her, his belief in her, and her lies!

Small screen squares had checked her pale complexion as she had combed her hair by sunlight before going out, as they had checked the vow she made that she never dated sailors, never went to the USO, never did anything their mother wouldn't have liked, and checked his wish to believe when the comb's teeth had pulled at her long black hair, tilted her head, turned the perfect oval of her face into profile in the mirror, stressed the straight bridge of her nose, but could not conceal the dark eye which glowed in a long-lashed corner watching him, and had checked his wish to believe when the comb had twirled free, and she had turned full face to the mirror but did not look in her own eyes.

Small screen squares had checked his wish to believe when, late at night, an electric train finally screeched to a stop at the corner, and he held his breath, still needing to believe, still wanting to believe, only to see her silhouette round the sharp edge of the church steeple, with a staccato tap of high heels, accompanied by the checked cutout of a long-stepping, trouser-flapping, round-capped sailor!

Small screen squares checked his past, would check his future for an unknown time, and checked him now, stretched from the cot to the window in an uncomfortable position. His hands were checked. His nightgown was checked. His heart was probably checked. His—he heard footsteps again, and he jumped down and sat on the cot, afraid to peek out the door because of the loud, close sound of the noise.

There was a jangle of keys and the khaki shoulder of a man at the window. The door opened and the queer man beckoned to Aaron, who rose warily, trying to decipher the mild expression on the pink face for a possible trick; and he continued to watch the man closely as he followed him down the hall.

He noticed how the man's feet struck the hall floor in a short-stepped sliding manner, like a girl in sandals. He noticed the soft, khaki hip swells that hung over the belt, the bald spot, silver-dollar size, at the back of the skull, the round-shouldered slope; and stopped, apprehensively, when the man stopped at the last cell in the hall, across from the toilet, and waited by its open door for him to enter.

He forgot his apprehension when he saw a small elderly man in a brown suit, with a neat silver mustache and silvery hair, sitting behind a wide table, writing. The man looked like a portrait of an old-fashioned, kindly doctor Aaron had seen in prints and how he imagined his brother John would look some day, long after he had started his own medical practice.

The man raised his head, glanced at Aaron, gave no greeting, and concentrated once more upon his writing. But a yellowed eye chart with faded letters and a small scale with a height measurement attached to it convinced Aaron that he was going to be examined.

"Take off your nightgown," the doctor said, without looking up; and Aaron grabbed the shirt but hesitated, remembering the man behind him, turned and saw only the empty space of the doorway, the cell across the hall, and wondered why he hadn't heard the man leave nor why he hadn't heard the doctor come up the stairs and pass his cell.

"Take it off!"

A strand of Aaron's hair caught on the neck button of the nightgown. He pulled. The strand held. He pulled again. It held. He tried to unloosen it with his fingers but saw the impatient expression on the doctor's face, so he gave the nightgown a jerk and it came free with two or three hairs still entwined about the button, and left a smarting sensation on his scalp.

"Put it on the table," the doctor said, rising, taking a stethoscope out of his bag, stepping around the table, and placing the rim of cold metal against Aaron's chest. He then listened, as Aaron breathed deeply, with bored indifference written on his face by the countless wrinkles and the tiny frozen trickles of blue and red veins which lay beneath the surface of his transparent skin, a skin smelling of shaving lotion and powder.

"How old are you?" he asked, his breath bitter with coffee, taking the black knobs out of his ears, reaching behind him for Aaron's folder.

"Fifteen," Aaron answered, bracing himself for the familiar insult.

"Why you're just a peanut," the doctor said and, checking the folder, asked again:

"Are you sure you're fifteen?"

"Yes," Aaron answered. "Yes, I'm fifteen!" he repeated, biting his lower lip with the front teeth as he said the number, trying to pronounce it as rudely as possible, making it ring like a curse, while his left nostril rose and quivered and pulled the left side of his upper lip into a peak of sarcasm.

"Boy," the doctor said and looked pointedly at Aaron's groin, "you don't have the body of a fifteen-year-old. I'd say thirteen, at most."

A hot blush darkened Aaron's face, for a bald groin and a scrotum which was as shriveled as a walnut caused him unrelieved shame whenever he took showers in front of other boys his age. All his friends were more physically developed, not just taller, and their scrotums hung loose and grapelike between their legs, under beards of pubic hair.

The doctor was apparently satisfied with the score of their brief contest, and he weighed Aaron with indifferent movements, measured his height, said, "Four-feet-ten," in a matter-of-fact tone, checked him out on the eye chart, made him cough twice while he hooked one finger under each of his testicles, tossed his nightgown to him, wrote the results of the examination down in the folder, said, "Your body structure is husky enough, but you don't have an ounce of definition to your muscles," and marched Aaron, in silence, back to his cell.

Aaron had kept his lips tight to keep from speaking and betraying the humiliation he felt, but when the doctor was closing the cell door and he knew he was going to be locked in once again, he asked, in a polite voice:

"How long will it be before I get put in a company? Don't have to stay locked up in here anymore?"

The doctor held the door open for a moment as if he were surprised at the break in Aaron's defense, but made no answer, shut the door, looked through the glass slot, shook his head in a noncommittal manner, his lips sealed by his silver mustache, and disappeared down the hall.

"You son of a . . ." Aaron said, but not loud enough to be heard beyond the walls of the cell, angry with himself for comparing the doctor to John, trying, as he climbed on the cot again, to justify his dislike for the doctor, telling himself, as he searched for the shadow of the building, that the doctor had exaggerated, that lots of guys his age were small and didn't have hairs, and that size and hairs didn't stop him from being considered manly by the rest of the guys or from getting girls either, from having more girls than most guys.

He lay down on the cot and touched his hairless groin through the nightgown and fingered his soft penis, fingered it idly and without any interest or thrill. For he had only masturbated two or three times in his life and had failed to come to a climax: once while crouched with a bunch of boys in a boxcar, having a contest, unable to have come anyway, because of his laughter.

He pressed the soft, ridged sack of his scrotum and then removed his hand. It wasn't not having a long one to screw girls with. It wasn't that, for none of his buddies screwed girls yet. They only talked about it. It was sitting on the edge of a wicker seat on a slow-moving bell-clanging streetcar, approaching the end of the line deep in West Oakland at two o'clock in the morning, and staring out the window to hide his embarrassment because his toes wouldn't touch the floor if he sat back and because Judith was afraid to be with him so far down in West Oakland so late at night.

It was the anguish the forced giggles that shivered up from her double chin caused him, frightened giggles that blanched the color out of the faint freckles scattered over her nose, that faded the blue in her eyes, that bleached the sunny warmth out of her dark blond hair, guilty giggles, too, over the lie she had told her mother so she could stay out late, giggles whose fear was not concealed by the chuckles of Barneyway and his girl, whom they were taking home, giggles that were tight with assumed nonchalance, that rippled above the whine of the streetcar, above the white caps of the sailors, the frowzy hair styles of sailor-bait girls, the pomaded heads of stray pachucos, the nifty-brimmed hats of colored zoot-suiters, and the safety helmets of night-shift shipyard workers, men and women, white and colored, young and very old.

It was the sight of stars glittering far beyond the dirty window, a window bleared by city scum, clouded by the smoky breaths of people, streaked by fingerprints and rivulets of damp bay dew, but stars so far, far beyond the window that they seemed to both magnify and make meaningless his embarrassed anguish over the length of his legs and her guilty, scared, and too loud giggles.

That was it! That was having no hairs! That was only being four-foot-ten!

The hoarse blare of the whistle blew his thoughts away, and he sat up, relieved but confused, for he was sure it couldn't be the dinner whistle. He stood on the cot and looked for the line of shadow. It stretched away from the building in a forty-five degree angle and was some twenty feet beyond the clump of manzanita. He checked the shadow again, trying to figure out how time had passed so quickly, when he heard foot-steps on the stairs again, and he jumped to the floor and ran to the slotted window just as the colored boy and the man stepped out of the stairwell into the hall.

The door opened without the sound of keys and almost hit him he was so unprepared for it. The colored boy jammed the tray into his chest while he was still confused, and he didn't realize the boy had winked until the door had closed and he had a tray full of macaroni and cheese in his hands, which he had to eat (although he had food stashed under the mattress and less appetite than he had at noon) or get in trouble.

He picked a spoonful and let the melting lump lie on his tongue for a moment, savoring the tang, trying to get some pleasure out of it before he swallowed it, without biting it. Then he tried to see if he could suck the cheese taste out of each lump until it melted and, in that way, get every minute particle of pleasure from each mouthful, while using the pleasure of each mouthful to revive the memories and pleasures of past meals, also make each mouthful last longer than the previous one. But when the cheese taste weakened and the macaroni tasted too doughy, he swallowed the pulpy lump.

He continued this game long after he felt any enjoyment in it, and he stopped only when it occurred to him that he was eating to keep the queer man from punishing him. He then tried to clean the cheese off each individual macaroni with his spoon and put the nibbles of cheese he had gathered on his tongue. But this was too much work; he slid the tray under the cot and sat in motionless boredom until he realized that he was watching the dark window slot for the queer man's pink face, fearful of a forced feeding.

But the macaroni was too cold to eat now, and he considered smashing it with the spoon and hiding it under the white bread. But this didn't seem practical. And he began to worry about getting put on bread and water for not eating. Or maybe kept in isolation longer? Or made to see the doctor again? Or maybe . . . ?

The door began to open slowly, and his first impulse was to kick the tray farther under the cot with his heel, but the colored boy appeared, with his finger held to his lips, and his voice, when he spoke, was as soft as his pale-brown eyes.

"Buckshot's my name, dad. Yours?"

He stood in the doorway, left foot in the cell, right foot in the hall, leaned his chubby shoulder against the door frame, and held his pink palm out before him.

"Some skin, man."

"Aaron, man. Glad to meet yuh." Aaron slapped the palm with his fingers. "You don't have a key? Do you?"

"No, man. This door's been open since you seen the doctor. Doc always does that. He's a good guy. He forgets to lock it."

"The doctor?"

"No, man. Doc is the tall man who came on duty after breakfast. You know, the guy with the crooked teeth."

"He's a good guy?"

"Yeah," Buckshot said, his pale eyes questioning the question. Then he smiled and the bulge of his big upper lip leveled with his teeth. "Don't worry about him, man. He watched yuh take a leak, huh?"

"Yeah."

"Listen, man. Doc won't bother yuh. And if yuh want a favor, he'll do it for yuh. He's one of the best men here. He won't touch yuh. Just stare. And he only does that to new guys, anyway. It'd be great if that was all yuh had to worry about."

"What a ya mean?" Aaron asked, suddenly worried about Barneyway, afraid to ask Buckshot now if he knew him.

Buckshot leaned back and looked down the hall, pulled on his bottom lip with his pink finger tips, cleared his throat, dragged the rubber edge of his shoe sole against the hardwood floor until it squeaked, and stalled so long that Aaron lost his fear of the warning. His own lips then spread slightly and hinted at his loss of respect for Buckshot, his belief that Buckshot was falling into the common jail habit of storytelling: the very habit that made him doubt the rumor about Barneyway, a habit in which each guy was the big hero of his own big dream, and the dream so big it was unbelievable.

"It ain't no lie. There's things here to worry about," Buckshot said and added, quickly, as if trying to recover his lost face:

"You might even get put in the dairy. And in the dairy, the big, bad guys give it to the little guys."

He stopped, apparently trying to see if his words had any effect on Aaron and to give them, by stopping, more mystery.

"You mean they stomp 'um, man?" Aaron asked, but this was no big mystery, for getting stomped was an accepted part of just being around bad guys and jailbirds, everybody stomped.

"That's not news," he said, but without scorn, for it was a real danger, and he could imagine big muscular guys, eighteen-year-old guys with men's bodies, powerful biceps and shoulders, hairy chests, guys who *might have* stomped Barneyway.

"No, man. I don't mean stomp," Buckshot said, his tan face seeming to swell with superiority.

"What do you mean?" Aaron asked, more suspicious of a lie than scared.

Buckshot lowered his head and its mass of auburn-colored, wiry curls; he was obviously stalling for dramatic effect, and he lifted his full, round face to Aaron before he said, "They beat 'em up, first, and, then . . . gang-bang 'um . . . man!"

"Gang-bang 'em?" Aaron blurted out, and the tip of his tongue glided slowly out between dry lips, moved up the chapped slope of the top lip, and eased back into his mouth on the lower, like a receding wave tucking its edge into its own backward roll along the sand.

"Gang-bang 'um, dad. Make queens out of 'em forever."

"Queens?" Aaron said and licked his lips again.

"Do you know what a queen is?" Buckshot asked, his voice sharpened by confidence.

"Yeah," Aaron said. "Yeah, I know what a queen is."

He spoke loudly, embarrassed by the cool way Buckshot was studying him, as if he, Aaron, didn't really know what a queen was, as if he might be one himself!

"I know what a queen is," he said and sat up and looked squarely into Buckshot's eyes so as to stop any wrong ideas that Buckshot might get about him.

"Well, that's the way it is in the dairy," Buckshot said, and squeaked his sole against the floor again, cleared his throat again, and leaned back and looked down the hall again. His full neck was a smooth expanse of tanned skin. He then leaned back in the cell and although he appeared relieved that Aaron had stopped staring at him, neither he nor Aaron attempted to carry on the conversation.

"I'd better go. The man might come," Buckshot said and pulled the tray out from beneath the cot. He then stepped into the hall and started to close the door, but just before it had eased shut, when only the width of his fingers prevented its closing, he glanced sympathetically at Aaron, and flicked his fingers in a salute.

"See yuh," he said softly and left.

The sound of his receding footsteps accentuated the silence in the cell, Aaron's lonely isolation, the danger in the warning, and Aaron's fear that the dirty stories were almost bound to be true. And if they were true, the rumor then . . . about Barneyway . . . was . . . ? But he couldn't allow himself to admit this possibility. He couldn't allow it to be true. He'd have to hear it from his buddy's lips first, before he'd accept one word of it, and he jumped to his feet and doubled his fists and shook them in front of his face. He studied them and gingerly touched the torn skin of his knuckles, swearing that it couldn't be true, that it would never happen, and that even if it were possible. . . . ?

Gray walls surrounded him. His fists were trembling with tension. He dropped into a boxing stance, weaved to his side, and threw a steaming right hand at the guy who might have slugged Barneyway. He set his jaw and then shuffled forward as if he were stalking the guy, fists clenched, ready to counter-punch at the guy's first move, which would be his last mistake, all of his fear ready to explode in thrilling anger. He was determined to drop the guy right away, make the guy pay for punching his best buddy, his crime partner, make somebody pay for the misery he felt; and he punched, dropped the guy, but had gained so much momentum with the quick, angry flurry of punches that he had to block his fall against the door with his arms. He shuffled back toward the barred window, feeling mean, the nightgown swaying, fists up, set, ready to punch again, determined, full of guts and confidence, but the cell lights came on and his eyes fell on the heart.

He took another shuffling step forward, then stopped and studied the heart until he could make out the letters spelling RICKY DE LA CRUZ, the plus below, and EVA wedged into the heart's point. Then he dropped his fists and ran his finger over the cross and the three rays above it. Then he took a deep breath, let it out in a long sigh, and saw darkness through the screen. Then he climbed on the cot, leaned a foot on the radiator, and looked out the window.

The whole hill was the shade of dusk. The bleat of crickets rose like a hum from the darkened grass. The manzanita was a clump of blue shade, and the sky was a patch of violet, darkening to a cloudy purple in the east. His feet began to get cold. He grabbed the bars and tried to shake them. He felt chilled inside, too, but he told himself he didn't care. No isolation cell. . . . Dairy or no dairy. . . . Not a single rumor . . . mattered. . . .

He shoved his face against the bars so that the edges of two made indentations in his cheeks and his nose touched the screen beyond. He pressed harder and then harder, trying to see how much pain he could take. His eyebrows and cheekbones took the brunt of the punishment, and he imagined that his brother Stanley was watching him, and soon he was straining with all the strength he could muster in his off-balance position, the stretch of his body across the open space between the cot and the window, making himself take the pain for long seconds, long, long seconds, until it began to hurt too badly and he quit.

The bars left tight creases on his cheekbones for a moment and his eyebrows burned, but warm blood quickly flooded the creases and the brows and brought him an intense satisfaction. He grabbed the bars again and leaned his face against them in exactly the same position again, so that their touch was harsh to his tender skin, and he tensed himself and got ready to test himself again. But his grip relaxed, and he leaned his forehead against them instead.

A long intake of breath then whistled against the roof of his mouth, held for a moment in his chest, was expelled in a broken cough, and his shoulders jerked as if a chill had passed over him, and he began to cry with low, muted, but quivering sobs.

# Part Two

# Buddies and Bad Actors

# Buddies and Bad Actors

The black skin fold which creased the base of the big colored guy's skull seemed wrist thick in the afternoon glare to Aaron, who followed him across the hospital lawn.

The low wooden building to the left of the walk loomed too large, too, for eyes accustomed to the close, boxed walls of the isolation cell; and the range of high hills across the vague green of the valley, along which a diesel truck groaned lonely and unseen, seemed only five or ten miles away, although Aaron knew it was a good fifty.

His blue shirt, stiff and still creased with fold lines, fit like armor too big for him to fill. The breast pocket took up the entire left side of his chest, and the shoulders stuck out beyond his arms and made him feel small and defenseless when he compared them to the colored guy's bulging arms and back.

Even the cheeks of the guy's lumpy butt seemed powerful, for they packed the back pockets of his dungarees and appeared to shuffle along as far behind him as the protrusion of the bedroll he carried so easily under one arm. Each separate buttock muscle popped into tension and relaxed, and both swelled out below his sway back as if they were flexed when he halted at the road to wait for Aaron, who approached with Buckshot's tan face in his mind and the fat kid's warning in his ears.

"You don' have to be sad, ma-han. That dead time past. Ev-ry day count now. You get used to the insti-toot quick.

43

An', besides, I your cadet captain, an' I here to be you friend. Call me the Buzzer," the guy said and patted Aaron's back.

"Take a look aroun'. You cun almost see all the may-in buildings from here. That building on you right the gym. The roof point on the other side the chapel wing. This here to you left the dining roo-oom. The office just on the other side of it, by the flag pole. The li-brar-ryy one long room between 'um. They all three in the same building. You see now on the way to the dor-mi-tory. It in the last compoun' on the other side o' the hill. Passed it on the way from the may-in gate. Last compound. See?"

Following the black finger, Aaron could see the black dormitory roofs of three of the compounds beyond the large lawn on the slope of the hill. Uncultivated grounds stretched from the foot of the hill before him, around a baseball diamond, to a high barbed-wire fence by the highway, where cars passed small and noiseless and free in the distance. A light breeze brought a refreshing country smell of turned earth and alfalfa and he grew curious and did look around him, but chiefly with the hope of seeing Barneyway.

"What's that building to the left, the big one on the hill behind the dining room?" he asked, for he could see the upper portion of a flat-roofed white building above.

"That the schoo-ool."

Aaron turned in the other direction, scanned the grounds and saw no one, but noticed the wide peak of another white wooden building about half a mile beyond the steeple of the chapel, toward the sea, with a weather vane cock upon it, and he pointed at it and asked, "What's that building over the hill with just the tip showing?"

"Oh, that the dairy, ma-han. That where you going to work," the Buzzer replied with enthusiasm, gold-capped teeth glinting between the thick puffs of his lips.

Aaron dropped his hand with a slap against his trouser leg

and turned and then shielded his eyes with the brim of his hand as if the sun still hurt them. His trembling stomach bunched into a knot, and the next and most important question about Barneyway was smothered inside him, unasked, by Buckshot's warning.

"You like it there, ma-han," the Buzzer said and started walking along the paved road toward the office. "A good place to work. Plen'y of milk to drink. You get strong fast. Get tough. Nobody mess with you then. An' better, no man aroun' all thuh time."

Aaron scanned the wide double doors of the dining hall as he passed them, with the vague hope of detecting something familiar about them which would reassure him. All he could see through the library's bay window was the disheartening sight of empty tables and chairs and bookshelves standing like strangers against the walls. He cast a searching glance through the screen door of the office when he passed it, hoping to see some kind of authority, of protection, even Mr. Toothman, but saw only the outline of the counter. The first sight of the compounds made him stop and shudder, and he then sank further into fear with every step that took him down the hill toward the square pens. For he couldn't see a single person in any of the asphalt courtyards, which were barricaded on three sides by long dormitories and on the road side, facing him, by link-iron wire fences, topped by barbed wire.

There was no one inside the courtyard of the first compound, and no one in the second nor in the third nor in the fourth, and no one in the fields between the compounds, and Buckshot's brown face became more persistent and, finally, as warped and as tall and as sharp-tipped as the fences.

It seemed to discolor the plain white of the dormitory walls and dull the black of the dormitory roofs. The iron hinges of the heavy gate in the last compound creaked with its warning, which the soft thud of Aaron's rubber heels on the asphalt courtyard repeated with slow, counting measures. And when he entered the dormitory and saw only two rows of metal beds against bare white walls, gray lockers at rigid attention between the beds, a yellowed urinal in the doorless toilet at the far end, and not one person, Buckshot's voice was as distinct to him as if it had just spoken.

The Buzzer had to call him away from the door to help make his own bed, and slightly ashamed but still scared, he approached with his weight balanced well enough on his toes to start running on the first impulse.

But the Buzzer nonchalantly snapped the sheet open, and as Aaron caught it and they drew it taut between them, tight along the mattress, Buckshot's face began to fade. With the second sheet, Aaron couldn't see it at all, and the two gray blankets muted the last of the isolation cell murmurs. For it occurred to Aaron that he was fixing a place for himself in the institute and that he was bound to contact Barneyway in a day or two, and when he had folded and tucked the last blanket corner under the mattress, he felt relaxed enough to hope he might see Barneyway before the day was over. He then slipped the pillow case over the pillow himself, smoothed the wrinkles out of it, and sat on his own bed without waiting for permission when the Buzzer sat down.

The Buzzer offered him a cigarette, and he shook his head but carefully watched the Buzzer light one.

The struck match hissed across the rough dungaree of the buttock and thigh, smoked and burst into full flame as the swipe of the Buzzer's hand reached the level of the cigarette in his lips. He held the match below the paper tip as if it were standing on end, and only the point of the flame reached the cigarette. He then took a deep drag, let his cheeks puff out with the smoke, held it for a moment, then blew the flame out with the exhale, without moving the match or the cigarette.

"Don' smoke, huh?" he asked, the words smoking with the remnants of the deep drag coming out of his mouth.

"No," Aaron said, almost hypnotized by the ritual, having to remind himself to stay on guard.

"Now you jus' take it easy aroun' here at first," the Buzzer explained, sliding the cigarette into the side of his mouth, and tilting his head so that the spiral of smoke missed his squinting eye.

"I the cadet captain of the com-pa-ny an' the duke of this com-pound, an' I goin' to take care o' you. If any-bo-dy mess with you, they messin' with me. Hear?"

He withdrew the cigarette and straightened his head.

"Hear?"

"Uh-huh," Aaron replied, leaning back, propping his hands on the bed behind him, the toes of his brogans just touching the floor, watching the Buzzer scheme, feeling grateful, for the first time, for Buckshot's warning.

"Say? You hungry or somethin'? I got a candy bar."

The Buzzer stood and started toward the screen door.

"No," Aaron replied, but the Buzzer kept walking and Aaron called after him: "I'm not hungry."

A metal hinge squeaked in reply, for the Buzzer stuck his hand into his locker anyway, rummaged around, and returned with a bright red- and white-wrapped Baby Ruth, which he held out to Aaron.

"Go ahead, lit-tel buddy. That what a friend for, to be good to his friends. Share with 'um. Go ahead."

"No," Aaron said curtly, unwilling to let the Buzzer do him any favors, favors which would obligate him. For although he didn't want to get the Buzzer mad at him and he didn't know if the favor was a trick, he wasn't taking any chances.

"No, I'm not hungry. I don't want a candy bar," he added, and he didn't waver at the sullen shutting of the thick lips nor in the tense pause which followed.

"That okay," the Buzzer finally said, grinning. "If you ain' hungry don' eat. Ev-vur-rything okay. Fine. Now, I tell you what we goin' to do."

He sat next to Aaron.

"I goin' to fix it with the man so that you get to work with me. You an' me we be work buddies. Pautnas! How that soun'?"

Aaron turned his face away from the sour odor of stale tobacco, and sat up and rested his hands in his lap. But the Buzzer leaned so close their shoulders touched, and Aaron then stood and stretched his arms, pretending they were stiff.

"Sounds okay," he said, stepping into the center aisle of the dormitory, kicking his legs as if they, too, were stiff, managing to move away while making it seem a natural desire to loosen up. He wanted to go outside where the Buzzer couldn't try anything, but he didn't want to appear scared.

The ash of the cigarette was a half an inch long. The Buzzer was eying him as if he couldn't figure him out. Finally, the Buzzer took a drag, noticed the ash, flicked it to the floor, asked, "How old are you?" blinked at Aaron's clipped answer, and took another drag; and Aaron was grateful, for a second time, for the warning which had caused him so much misery.

"Done time before?" the Buzzer asked, tapping the cigarette several times with his little finger, although it had no dead ash.

Aaron swung one leg back and forth, pretending to be preoccupied with loosening it, but trying to gain time to think. For it was a crucial question, and he thought of lying, but he was afraid to risk losing the advantage he had gained.

"No," he said. "But I was head monitor of the DT the two months I was there," and he was convinced that he had scored well with his truthful answer, although he had only been head monitor of the home group, the boys under sixteen, by the quick drag the Buzzer took and the long moment that passed before he exhaled it.

The exhaled smoke then faded into blue shadow before the Buzzer asked another question, and he asked it with his sway-back as stiffly curved as a bow and from a mouth that was set in a thick puff:

"What was your beef?"

"Stomping . . . man," Aaron said, speaking slowly for greater strength. "Stomping . . . I got busted with my gang for stomping a bunch of paddies."

Circles of bright white flashed in the Buzzer's eyes, and joy surged through Aaron, and he shuffled forward and snapped his arms and shrugged his shoulders in the loose, disjointed exercise of a boxer warming up. But glancing back, he saw the sly spreading of the thick lips and the caps of gold teeth again, and realized that he had overplayed it. He stopped exercising as the Buzzer stood, took a drag, dropped the butt, crushed it with a twist of his brogan, and shuffled toward him.

"Le' me show yuh aroun' the dorm, ma-han," the Buzzer said. "I'll show yuh where the washroom is."

"I can see it from here," Aaron said, glancing back at the urinal, mentally kicking himself for ruining his one small victory.

"I'll show yuh where thuh soap is."

"I don't need to wash."

"Come own. Ain' nothin' goinna happen. Jus' show yuh aroun', ma-han. So you don' have to fight that line at dinna-time an' in the maunin'," the Buzzer said, trying to guide Aaron toward the washroom by pressing against the small of his back.

It was a light touch but Aaron's skin twitched, and he moved quickly away, trying to gain distance and time to think, Buckshot's warning in his mind again, but determined to pro-tect himself, heartening, too, at the sound of the iron gate banging against the fence.

Voices. Footsteps crossed the courtyard and more could be heard on the pavement of the road.

The Buzzer stopped and listened, and Aaron hurried to the washroom, where he waited in the doorway, feeling much better and safer.

"Yuh see the soap in that locka' in the corna'," the Buzzer said, shuffling to the screen door, and slamming it, without another word, behind him.

Aaron sighed with relief and used the urinal, but quickly so he wouldn't be noticed by the guys entering the dorm. For although Buckshot seemed more like a buddy than a bragger now, the Buzzer had unnerved him, and he stalled in the toilet, trying to compose himself.

He washed his hands carefully with warm water and soap, and rewashed them, and rewashed them, but his nerve decreased the longer he stalled. Approaching sounds put him on edge. The toilet became a trap from which there was no escape. It then took the chill of the rinse water to convince him that he should go into the dorm, where he had a chance to run, at least, and where he had already managed to scrape through one encounter, but keep to himself until he found Barneyway.

He went directly to his locker, without allowing himself to look at anyone, and took out his towel and dried each finger slowly and separately in order to occupy himself and avoid the stares. But a tall blond kid, with a hooked nose, entered, who made all the stories seem possible and made him wonder if he *could* hold out long enough to contact Barneyway.

For the big guy dropped on his bed in the opposite row, jerked a comic book out of his locker, banged the door shut, crushed his pillow, kicked his legs out on his bed and began to read. But he kept glancing at Aaron through hooded eyelids with such cold and astonishingly bright blue eyes and with a small mouth so pursed with disapproval on a heavy chin that Aaron caught himself twisting the towel around a single finger long after it was dry.

Aaron then put the towel away, lay down, too, and self-consciously pretended to examine the ceiling. The ceiling slant on his side of the dividing beam appeared longer than that on the blond kid's side, and he was not sure whether this was an optical illusion caused by his peculiar view of the ceiling, the constant shifting of his gaze from the ceiling to the blond kid and back again, whether it was his worry, or whether the slant on his side was actually longer—when the Buzzer entered with a Mexican kid, who had a tattooed cross in the middle of his forehead, just above his eyebrows.

The Mexican let the screen door fall against his heel and stood in the doorway staring at Aaron, who watched him in return, without looking away from the ceiling, and who, while wondering if the guy might try anything, began to really doubt whether he would be able to play it safe.

The Mexican then sat down and Aaron relaxed a little. For his new enemy's backbone was a knobbed ridge between bony shoulder blades, and skinny guys, even if they were tall and he wasn't, usually weren't a match for his boxing skill. It took weight and strength to bully him to the ground, and although he had no intention of fighting, he planned how he would slip under the long arms, get inside them, and connect with his own punches in case a fight did start, when another guy came into the dorm, who made him so apprehensive he didn't even pretend to look at the ceiling.

This guy's sharp, almost pretty features were drawn together in a scowl, as if he were trying to see Aaron better as he approached and disliked the little he saw, and his rolled-up sleeves banded swollen biceps, which seemed to swell bigger as he drew nearer. He then sat on the bed next to Aaron's and immediately demanded:

"What's your name, kid?"

Aaron answered him in a level tone, trying not to show fear or act bad, and trying, also, in his predetermined caution, not to stare at the tattooed beauty mark on the guy's cheekbone nor at the black whisker stubble on the guy's chin.

"D'Aragon?" the guy said, repeating the name to himself. His torso was so big-boned and long that sitting down he seemed taller than his five and a half feet.

"From Oakland?" he asked, his lips lifting, almost snarling, revealing a row of square teeth, but the scowling furrow stayed between his fine eyes.

"Yes," Aaron answered softly, anxiously, realizing that the guy had heard of him and that if the information was not good, his chances of avoiding trouble in the dorm would shrink to nothing.

"Are you the little guy who got cornered by the beans from Santa Clara about a year ago and fought so hard losing they gave you a free pass?"

"Yeah," Aaron replied, and encouraged by the implied compliment in the question, he sat up and hung his leg jauntily over the side of the bed, keeping to himself that he had fought with panic after his gang had scattered and couldn't remember any of the details of the actual fight.

"You're pretty small, man. Wouldn't have believed you were so little. My name's Dominic Franklin."

The grudging tone of the self-introduction kept Aaron cautious and prevented him from asking about Barneyway, although he placed both feet on the floor and faced Dominic.

"Would'a never believed you were so small, for the rep you got out in East Oakland, even though I heard it."

"Thanks," Aaron said, but he couldn't tell whether the statement was a compliment or a complaint; and trying to avoid the stern face, he stared at the tattooed hands, which gripped the knee-caps of the short legs.

Dominic doubled his right fist and jabbed out with it so Aaron could more clearly see the HATE tattooed in india ink across its fingers, a letter to a finger. He then jabbed with his left fist and LOVE was tattooed across its fingers in the same manner, and a small pachuco cross, with three rays, filled the hollow between its thumb and forefinger. Then he smiled and proudly flexed his right biceps and surprised Aaron with the professional tattoo of a rose which popped into a firm petaled bloom upon it.

A banner beneath the rose, with a blood-red **MOTHER** written across it in ornate letters, billowed with tension, too, and they both smiled; and Dominic asked, "How come no tattoos, man? A little dude with your rep oughtta have a tattoo."

Aaron shrugged in reply, although Stanley had made him scrub a fountain pen cross off his hand with the warning that he could only have one when he could whip his big brother. But there was more respect than criticism in the question, and Aaron felt the tattoos had given them something in common. The dinner whistle then brought the possibility of seeing Barneyway in the dining room, and Dominic's beckoning nod was so friendly that Aaron eagerly followed his example and stood at the foot of his own bed for count.

The Buzzer shuffled down the aisle, checking the count, and smiled at Aaron as he passed. Aaron answered with a cool nod, which, although not hostile, came from a growing sense of safety and his success, so far, in keeping his distance from the guy until he could defend himself. The Buzzer kept smiling but also kept the thick skin fold at the back of his neck to Aaron when he returned, checking the other row.

"You're sharp, man, for not trusting that guy," Dominic said; and Aaron nodded again, with gratitude and increasing confidence, and he snapped smartly to attention when the Buzzer called count, and, without turning his head, watched the man come striding through the doorway and complete the count with such efficiency it seemed a lucky sign.

The man marched down the bed row, tanned and wiry in his khaki uniform, pad and pencil in hand, mumbling, lips twitching, eyes two boys ahead of the boy he was passing, counting the second row before he had finished the first row and even started back toward the door, jotting down his total while he walked, three beds before he reached the last boy, his footsteps then thumping across the courtyard before the screen door even started to swing shut or the Buzzer began to lead a single file line out onto the porch.

The smack of rubber-soled brogans marking time until the command to move out the gate echoed under the porch roof and was as invigorating as a drum beat to Aaron, who stood next to Dominic like a buddy now, who bent his knees and placed his feet with the cleanly coordinated movements he had learned in the Scouts, who felt a part of the beat, who moved with a fluid motion out the gate on the Buzzer's command, who made a flawless column right on the paved road, who marched briskly to the smacking rhythm of shoe rubber on asphalt and to a meeting with his best buddy.

He marched in a blue two-man column a city block long, beneath the mild rays of the late afternoon sun, a clear sky, with a spine stiffened by confidence and pride and Dominic's critical but approving stare, sure now the rumor was a shuck story, sure he'd be able to handle the Buzzer, sure he was making an impression on all the guys in the dorm, sure he'd get a good institute rep soon, and sure, he kept his shoulders back, his chin high, and swung his arms smartly in time to the slap of rubber soles.

He marched nimbly up the hill that he had slunk fearfully down only a short time before and leveled off at its top without a perceptible backward jerk of his trunk, and marching sharply, he began to look for Barneyway before he reached the mess hall, and marching sharply, still looking, he passed through the wide doorway of the dining room, where the column split into two single file lines, which moved down opposite walls, and in which the boys no longer marched but walked, although he marched, still looking, until the slow shuffle of the jammed line, moving forward to the food counter, brought him to a halt.

Then he began to look around the large room for Barneyway. He scanned the white-uniformed kitchen crew at the counter, who filled each pocket of his tray with large servings of food: a tin bowl of beans with its savory aroma, shredded cabbage moist with vinegar and oil, syrupy plums, a slab of cake, and two slices of bread; then he searched the tables as he accompanied Dominic down the center aisle to a long table near the entrance.

He scanned the entire room again before he sat down: the dwindling lines at the food counters and the tables now nearly filled with boys; and the familiar scrape and click of metal spoons on metal trays, the clink of tin cups and metal pitchers filled with milk and steaming coffee, and the noisy drone of voices made him feel he understood them. He knew what they were thinking, for this was the same experience on a large scale that he had known at the detention home. Dinner time was one of the best times of the day, better than lunch because another day was almost whipped and because everybody, including himself, could cross off another day, yet, each boy telling himself that he really couldn't count the day yet, at least not until lights out, but counting it as finished anyway, though not admitting it to himself, but knowing he could legally three-quarters count it, and, then, forgetting to count it, finally, in the pleasure of the meal, of filling his belly, of doing something he liked in a world he hated.

And then he, too, sat down to do something he liked, and he shoveled the beans and their tasty brown soup into his mouth steadily until he had eaten half his portion.

He looked around the hall once more, still without luck, but still optimistic, still sure he would see Barneyway before the day was over. Then, still searching, he washed down the salty taste of the beans with a full cup of milk and was lowering the cup from his lips and could still taste its metal when he heard the sound of marching feet on the pavement behind him. He turned around as a short column of boys entered and hurried down to the food counter, and his heart jumped in his chest, for Barneyway was among them, his crewcut head almost lost between the shoulders of two taller boys.

Aaron struggled with his urge to jump up and shout. But when the first boys in the column reached the table opposite his and walked to its far end to sit down, and Barneyway started to follow them, his tray balanced in his hands, his huge eyes already concentrated upon the section of the table where he would sit, Aaron could not control himself any longer, and he raised up from the bench and waved his arm.

But he was too late, for Barneyway turned without noticing him, and a man, who was standing by the food counter, looked curiously at him, and, afraid to call out, he dropped back on the bench, under Dominic's inquisitive frown.

"Who you waving at, man?"

"That guy! Barneyway! The little guy with the big eyes, who's just sitting down. See him? Know him?"

Dominic's upper lip lifted into a contemptuous curve and Aaron's next question dropped to a whisper.

"What compa-ny . . . are . . . those . . . guys . . . in . . . ?"

"Those guys," Dominic said, "are from the hospital. Some are walking cases who come down to the dining room so they won't have to take a lot of trays up there, and the rest of them, most of them, are protected punks on Queens' Row."

He broke his bread and sopped up the brown bean juice with it as if the subject were beneath him, then bit down hard on the bread with his square teeth, ripped it away with his tattooed fingers, and turned his frown on Aaron.

"Barneyway?" Aaron asked, putting everything he meant in pronouncing his name.

The scowl on Dominic's face made it appear as if chewing his bread was hard work. He swallowed, then turned to his food again, raised the cup of milk to his mouth, and, just before drinking, said, "He's in the dairy dorm with us."

Aaron was partially relieved by the answer, but Dominic's attitude left the question about the rumor more in doubt than ever, and he began to worry about *why* Barneyway was in the hospital. He left his cabbage untouched, the beans half-eaten, picked at the plum, and ate all the cake with another cup of milk, without gaining the nerve to ask another question, afraid that Barneyway had been stomped and that Dominic was involved in some way.

"You gonna wait for that guy?" Dominic asked when he had finished.

A mouth full of milk and cake gave Aaron an excuse to nod, but he regretted it as he watched Dominic turn away, drop his tray on the scullery counter with a clatter, toss his silverware, his cup, and his bowl into wire racks, and walk out the door without him, for it seemed an unhappy foreboding.

Perspiration dampened his forehead as he stalled at the table, for in addition to the warmth his worry produced, the dining room was hot from the heat of the ovens, the steamtables, the food, and the closely quartered bodies. Soon, he was the only one left at his table and one of the few people, besides those from the hospital, still in the dining room, and the contrast between its deserted appearance and how it had seemed when he had first entered, when it was crowded and he was happy, was depressingly apparent to him.

The kitchen crew, moving swiftly in white uniforms, began to clear the tables and wipe up the last traces of what had been, for him, the very best moments of the week's time he had done in the institute. The glances of a curly-haired blond kid, whose cheeks expanded like bellows with each shouted order and whose mouth wheezed into a sneer when it was completed, made him feel so conspicuous he went outside to wait, for he was afraid there might be some rule about visiting other tables.

The sun was only a foot above the blue rim of the distant coastal hills, and he waited in the long wall shadow next to the doors, reminding himself that getting placed in the same dormitory with Barneyway was a lot to be thankful for, something he couldn't have planned, and tried to convince himself that a few quick words from Barneyway would take care of all his doubts about the rumor and the hospital.

There was a loud clatter of several trays, voices, and footsteps; and anticipating the pleasure of the greeting, he flattened himself against the wall and prepared to surprise his friend.

Several pink-faced, meek-appearing boys came through the doors, and the blond kid closest to Aaron jumped with fright when he saw him. But Aaron put his forefinger to his lips for silence, and the boys moved away, some smiling at the blond's fright. The blond himself stayed in front of them, putting as much distance between himself and Aaron as he could without attracting attention.

Punk! Aaron thought. Queen! Sissy! Broad! The sneer on his face chilled the smiles, and only the blond bothered to peek back before disappearing with the group around the corner of the mess hall.

When Aaron turned once more to his watch, Barneyway had already stepped out of the doorway and was making a wide right turn in an obvious effort to keep a safe distance away from the boy flattened so mysteriously against the wall, although there was curiosity and even some humor in his large eyes.

"Barneyway!" Aaron yelled and jumped at him, and saw recognition of himself in his friend's face the instant the arms were thrown up in protection and locked with his own arms in mock combat.

But the momentum of the leap drove Barneyway back until, with a scraping of his shoes and a deep flushing of his face, he managed to hold his ground. Then Aaron laughed and Barneyway laughed, and Aaron let go and Barneyway let go. Aaron could then see his own tight smile in Barneyway's tight smile, his own tense, crouched body in Barneyway's tense, crouched body. He popped his fist against Barneyway's shoulder and Barneyway hit him. He reached out and Barneyway reached out, and they clasped hands and squeezed until white tension framed their fingernails.

"When did you get here, Aaron?" Barneyway asked and released his grip.

"Last Friday. Just got out of isolation this afternoon."

"Man! Boy! Man! Is it good to see you."

"Good to see you, buddy," Aaron said, forgetting, in his pleasure, all about the rumor which had bothered him so much in the detention home, which had tortured him so badly the long lonely week in isolation, which had seemed so unescapable and true only a few minutes earlier, and he asked, out of nothing more than a desire to talk:

"What are you doing in the hospital?" and caught his breath at the importance of the answer.

But Barneyway began to walk at a nonchalant pace toward the hospital and answered, casually:

"I had a fever yesterday. Felt weak. So I checked into the hospital. I'll probably stay a couple more days."

And Aaron breathed again and noticed the heavy baritone of Barneyway's voice, for it seemed to have deepened in the month since they had seen each other, and his own voice was still a piping tenor.

"Hope you get out soon," he said, too pleased by the answer to mention the rumor, and noticed also that while Barneyway's eyes were still large and soft, his smooth, unblemished skin now stretched over a bony prominence: twin ridged cheekbones and a jutting clefted chin, in particular.

"I'll probably get out quick. Not any fever now. Just a little weak still," Barneyway said, and the black and heavy down, thickening on his upper lip, slightly strengthened the weak smile he gave to discount his illness. Although the smile appeared as shallow to Aaron as the reflection of the setting sun on the hospital windows, he tried to make Barneyway feel better.

"Guess what? I'm in the dairy company with you, and we'll

get to buddy up all the time we're here, all the time, Barney,"
he said, expecting a wide grin, but a blank expression dropped
over Barneyway's face like a window shade, drawing the
rumor down between them.

Barneyway then started quickly up the hospital walk, jerking his wiry body with each swift step, swinging his arms as
if the elbows were locked and he could not bend them, and
making a frustrated fist of each hand by tucking his thumbs
under clenched fingers.

Aaron rushed after him to keep him from going inside the
hospital and grabbed his arm at the foot of the stairs and
stopped him; but Barneyway pulled his arm free with such
a violent wrench that Aaron motioned to him to sit down
rather than risk a question.

They sat in silence on the hospital steps as the sun set beyond the coast range, while Aaron tried to think of a way to
find out what was wrong without starting an unpleasant conversation; but the low streak of clouds which hung over the
ocean burned with the deep red of the vanishing sun for such
a brief while before smoldering out, and the lawn, the steps,
the hospital windows all took on the dark tones of dusk with
such dispiriting speed that he surrendered to the melancholy
within him, to the dying day about him, and made no attempt
to speak.

There was no breeze but the air was cool. Crickets began
to chirrup with a loud volume that Aaron could not help but
compare to the muted and more lonely chirruping which he
had heard from his isolation cell, but which, although less
lonely, saddened him, too, and made him want to break the
depressing mood that had come over himself and his friend
on their very first meeting, a meeting which had meant so
much to him, a meeting he considered trying to improve by
telling Barneyway he had heard lies about him but didn't
believe them, and that. . . .

But Barneyway sat too morose and too silent to speak to,

staring out over the grounds into the quickly settling night; his face wounded and yet very manly in profile against the final red glow of the horizon, contoured like an athlete's from the crewcut to the clefted chin; his small mouth a bare line.

The strong cast of the features caused Aaron to recall the stubborn, almost Indian set they took on when Barneyway was forced into a corner: a withdrawn expression which showed a willingness to suffer as long as it could hate, and Aaron often wanted to smash it off the face with his fist. But there was no hate in the features now, only the impression of a disquieting pain, an impression which Aaron was afraid to question through fear of hurting himself as well as Barneyway.

The glow from the unseen compound lights gradually outlined the gray block of the mess hall and the sloping hill before them. A large globed night light burned brightly above the sloping ramp of the gym now, too, and the floodlights on the watchtower at the main gate were severely visible in the distance.

Dots of light from scattered cars moved slowly and freely across the darkened landscape, while dark knots of boys moved slowly up and down the sloping ramp in front of the gym as if they were caged there, talking in low voices which were not decipherable but were depressing to Aaron: for he knew the boys were telling each other stories about the "outs."

He knew that each guy would take a turn and try to make his story good enough, exciting enough, and brave enough to capture the imagination of the others, and convince them of how heroic and beautiful and true his dream world was, and share it with them. He knew that the other guys were listening patiently, trying to get in contact with the story so they could really experience it, really become buddies with the guy telling it, and through it escape the jail in which they were trapped. He knew that while they were listening, they were trying to get ideas on the same subject for stories of their own, which they could tell when their turns came.

He knew what was happening on the ramp, although it was his very first day on the institute grounds, because he had seen a hundred guys do the same thing in the detention home. Every reform school graduate he had ever met had the same storytelling habit or didn't talk at all, and this was the reason he had doubted the fat kid's story. He did listen to the good talkers, including the fat kid, and he even enjoyed the stories, encouraged them to tell others, but he snubbed the bad liars into silence by withholding all comments when they had finished, by his failure to say, "Gee! Yeah! No lie? Mother's Honor?"

Nightfall soon diffused the outlines of the separate groups on the ramp, and Aaron could see only a mass of indistinct heads under the night light. The storytelling now seemed so wasted and futile to him, he wanted to shout at them that they were all bad liars, that they were all locked in jail, that they weren't great gangster heroes or movie-star lovers, and that no lie would ever set them free; and he turned to Barneyway, unable to contain himself any longer, needing to hear the clear sound of his own voice in order to rid himself of the depressing sound of the voices on the ramp.

Barneyway turned to him at the same moment and both spoke at once. Each asked about the other's family, stopped to let the other speak, and then broke into laughter at the confusion and the abrupt silence.

"You first," Aaron said, more than willing to listen to anything that the smooth plane, which composed Barneyway's face in the faint light from the hospital entrance behind them, wished to say.

"How's your family?"

"Everybody's pretty good," Aaron replied, answering a polite question in a polite way, but since it was an attempt at reconciliation by his best friend, he then tried to give an honest answer.

"My old man is still as big and fat and healthy as ever and

talks about this place as if it's for summer vacations. Nora's prettier than she ever was, I think, but after a visit from her it takes me a couple of days to get back my guts. And Stanley's the opposite. He pretends being locked up's a joke, but he's supposed to fight for the state title in a month or two, knocked a guy out last month. John's an intern at UC Hospital now, and even though he tries to be nice to me, he always makes me feel like I'm on trial. You know. All the things I'm supposed to do and that."

"Yeah, I know. You got Stanley though, Aaron, and he'll probably be champion of the world," Barneyway said, and he seemed to mean it, for Aaron noticed the note of idolatry and envy of himself, too, for having a main-event fighter as a brother, in the wistful way in which it was spoken, and he asked, "How's your mother? She been to see you here, yet?"

"Once. Probably again soon though. I sure need the visit when she comes. But, then, she's the only person who does visit me."

"You've got a pretty mother, Barney," Aaron said, then realized the compliment had touched a tender spot, and appreciated the night which masked Barneyway's face and helped him hide his painful memories. For he was reminded of how welcome the darkness of the hall had been on a Sunday evening a year before when they returned from a movie and started up the stairs to his bedroom as a woman's cry of "Someone's there!" made them pause, then pad up the carpeted stairs, without comment, although they both recognized the voice, for Barneyway's mother had been drinking in the now darkened front parlor with his own father, and her auburn hair was mussed and her gray-green eyes were fuzzy with gin.

"She's a good mother, Barney," Aaron said, trying to apologize, knowing it still hurt Barneyway to catch her, although he had already had three stepfathers and a dozen "uncles." "She tries to take care of you. You live good. Have plenty of money. All the clothes and everything else you want. A mother can't be everything. She's no man, and she's young and pretty. She's supposed to live, too."

"I know," Barneyway said, accepting the apology. "Yet, I can't help but wish she was like your mother. A real mother. But, then, you might be even worse off. Your mother might have been great but she's dead. In a way, neither of us have the mother we want . . . . Huh, Aaron?"

"Yeah, that's the truth, Barney," Aaron replied, aware that Barneyway was asking him to agree so *he* could apologize for stepping on hallowed ground. "Neither of us actually has the mother he wants."

"Any more letters from Judith since DT?" Barneyway asked, trying to change the subject.

"Two," Aaron answered, but without any desire to elaborate, and the squeak of bats grew louder and closer, almost sinister as the conversation stopped altogether, killed by the unpleasant turn it had taken.

Aaron looked nervously about, and the cold glitter of the stars, unblurred by the dense city atmosphere to which he was accustomed, increased his melancholy. He started to speak but heard the distant bellow of a diesel truck passing along the highway and folded his arms, instead. Then he felt chilled and sought the warmth of his armpits with his fingers.

He then began to feel surrounded by crickets which muttered incomprehensible rumors about mysterious and unsolvable problems, and each time he decided to say something, he became distracted by them. Finally, the night and his thoughts became so oppressive that he couldn't bear them any longer, and he slapped Barneyway on the back and jumped to his feet.

"Come on, Barneyway," he said. "We don't have to be sad, man. We might be in jail but we're together just like we been for three years. Hell. We'll make it here like every place else. We been through a lot together. This ain't nothin'!"

"We've been like brothers, huh!" Barneyway said and jumped to his feet, too.

"We're like brothers now," Aaron said, still more enthusiastic.

"We have almost the same last name," Barneyway said.

"We've cut school together."

"Got suspended together."

"Had our first gang fight together."

"Got put in the DT together."

"Got sent away together."

"We're better than brothers because we don't have to be together and do."

"We're bad-acting brothers, and we're going to let every guy in the dormitory and every guy in the whole institute know it. Ain't that right, Barneyway?" Aaron cried.

"Ain't that right?" he repeated when Barneyway didn't answer, but his tenor voice lingered in the night air, the boast sounding forced, needing Barneyway's baritone to confirm it, and his enthusiastic attempts to talk the mysterious problem away had brought him full circle back to it.

"Why don't you tell me, Barneyway? We're buddies. We're not supposed to keep anything from each other. We're supposed to help each other," Aaron said, and could sense that Barneyway wanted to speak but needed support, badly.

Dominic's contempt was like a shadow in Aaron's mind, which kept prompting him and prompting him until, in an intuitive vision, he saw the perpetual gold-toothed smile of the Buzzer.

"It's the Buzzer, huh? Tell me about it, Barney. So I can help you. Tell me!" he said.

"I'd . . . I'd . . . I'd like to kill 'im! Kill 'im! Aaron!" Barneyway shouted and frightened Aaron so badly he remained silent and stunned until the act of reaching out for his friend helped him regain his speech.

"What for? What did he do? Tell me! Tell me, Barneyway!"

"I caaan't. I caaan't, Aaron," Barneyway cried and ran up the steps, his figure a flicker of shadow in the doorway, through the screen door, and gone more quickly than the slap of the door itself as it slammed behind him.

Aaron then stood alone at the foot of the stairs, with the fat kid's warning and Buckshot's warning echoing and intermingling in his mind, and with the answer to the question that his life, at least his happiness and his future, seemed to depend upon as brittle and as fragile and as untouchable to him as the question made by the dim light bulb on the high ceiling of the hospital hall.

# Part Three
# Schoolin'

# Schoolin'

## I

The long hollow blast of the morning get-up whistle boomed deep into Aaron's sleep, disturbed the peaceful night in which he had escaped from his troubles, and he pulled the covers over his head without opening his eyes and wiggled farther into the snug, warm oblivion of the pillow.

But the whistle blasted for a full minute and blew like a shrieking wind and blew into Barneyway's scream and blew all sleep away.

He opened his eyes to escape the image and lay without moving, staring at the crumpled sheet which covered his head like a shroud, listening to the muffled tones of sleepy voices, the steps of rubber-soled shoes on the concrete floor, knowing he was back in jail, knowing he would have to get up, but clinging to one more moment of rest, although that rest was troubled, too, until the Buzzer scared him completely awake.

"Outta the sack, you lazy punks, or I throw you out."

He threw the covers back and sat up and his pillow fell to the floor, but he snatched it up before the Buzzer could say anything, and hopped out of bed, and toes curling away from cold concrete, pulled his nightgown down from his hips with a long shiver just as the Buzzer shuffled by.

"Fix your bed quick. Then wash up," Dominic said, tucking his own blankets under the mattress, looking strangely stump-

69

legged in the long nightgown; and Aaron began to fix his bed with practiced but automatic movements in the weak burn of yellow bulbs, the dismal semidarkness of an overcast morning.

He made a tight stretch of the sheet and blankets and folded the top part of the sheet back over the blanket to frame it neatly, but his eyes and thoughts were on the Buzzer, who shuffled back and forth, rushing the boys, trying to get the dormitory ready in time for count.

He watched the weird waddling of the powerful figure while he tucked both sides of the covers under the mattress so that no fold or crease marred the blanket surface. He noticed how the light spread shadows on the black face that pulled the coarse features into swollen distortion while he smoothed the pillow with careful strokes. He watched the busy figure with such intense and constant preoccupation that when it moved down the aisle toward him it swelled to gigantic proportions, and he had to thrust his hand into his locker for his towel to clear his sight.

With his towel hooked around his neck and nausea in the empty pit of his stomach, he then followed Dominic to the washroom, where he stood in dejected silence, staring at the floor, moving a step forward every couple of minutes when the skirt of the nightgown in front of him left an absent space, space he had to fill, space as empty as Barneyway's face at the "good news" the night before, space—

Hot water splashed, steaming, to the concrete, and he jerked his foot back, and escaped the stinging sprinkle as he recognized the kid bent over the washbasin by his knobby backbone as Tommy Rodriguez, "Rattler," the guy with the cross on his forehead.

The thin back made Aaron wish that it was Rattler, instead of the Buzzer, who was bothering Barneyway, and he let himself take offense at the spilled water, for he was certain he could take Rattler in a fair fight. He wouldn't even have to box. He could just charge a skinny guy like that and either punch him or throw him to the ground, then stand victorious as the thin arms and legs flailed wildly in the air, stand—

Black and stiff-lashed eyes, cold with the tattooed cross between them, the snow-white nap of the towel below them, banished the picture as Rattler turned away from the wash-basin, drying himself, rudely shoved by Aaron, and began combing his hair in the long mirror above the urinal.

An angry heat filled Aaron's head, but a weakening nausea rose from his stomach, too, and he kept his temper. For in spite of his thoughts about whipping Rattler, he didn't have one buddy he could depend upon in a fight, and he concentrated upon the hollow cavity of the bowl before him in order to avoid trouble with a buddy of the Buzzer's, trouble he couldn't possibly handle by himself.

Water freshened his face but the nausea stayed in his belly, and seemed to be the cause of the strange presence and the severe outlines that permeated and framed everything. The foot railings of the beds he passed on the way back to his own bed fenced off a path for him as rigid as guard rails set there for that purpose. His locker was like a squat sentry standing against the wall, and he hesitated for an anxious moment before he put his towel in it and took out his clothing. His shorts and his trousers, his shirt and his nightgown could have been the belongings of a stranger. His brogans fit like wooden shoes, and he clumped back to the washroom in them while button-ing his shirt, rocked before the mirror in them while combing his clipped hair, and was having trouble patting his short hair into place when Dominic entered.

"The first days are the hardest," Dominic said, winking at Aaron in the mirror, getting the sides of his unruly hair first with fast sweeps of the comb, pressing a finger in them to even the waves. "I'm gonna talk to the man as soon as we get to the dairy and ask him if you can work with me before the Buzzer gets any ideas. I've had one of his punks picking up the garbage with me for the last week or so, and he ain't shit, and the man knows it."

The word sounded odd coming from Dominic's fine-featured face. Yet the vulgar sound of the word, the contempt with which he used it, and the snarl of his lips seemed to enhance his good looks. He shook the locks above his forehead and they fell into a mass of curls upon it, then, misunderstanding Aaron's stare, he stepped away from the mirror, explaining:

"Your hair will be as long as mine again, fast, man, and I'm giving you a hand because I like you. You got guts. Come on."

Aaron followed him, but the nausea was worse. He felt lightheaded and high. He floated back to his bed and stood for count. And when he filed out onto the porch and fell into march formation, his legs appeared and disappeared below the white buttons of his blue shirt as if they were disconnected from him.

Yet, he was aware of everything. He watched his body walk, saw his legs, saw the buttons, saw the Buzzer and knew where *he* was at all times. He kept himself paired with Dominic, began marching on order, kept step, but didn't feel the rhythm. And when the column turned right on the road, under an overcast sky just beginning to clear, under low clouds whipped along by a strong wind, the full force of the institute's cold, impersonal routine, a routine he was now entering completely for the first time, seemed to sweep over him with the bleak glow cast by the pale sun, chill his queasy guts, swamp all hope, and promise a future as ashen-hued as the black face of the Buzzer.

"That's the way to march. That's the way," Dominic said, and Aaron arched his back and raised his chin and tried to get some snap into his marching.

But his movements were listless. It took work to plod up the hill, to move his cumbersome legs, and the patch of weak sunlight which filtered through the clouds onto the white watch-tower at the main gate quickened his nauseous fear; and he marched into the heat and roar and steam of the dining room as if he were totally alone and Dominic did not exist.

A row of heads stretched before him, shortened, then vanished abruptly, and he was at the food counter. He took his tray and slid it down the wooden tracks, put a tin bowl of oatmeal in a scratched crater, accepted two slices of raisin bread at the end of the counter, turned into the uproar of the tables, took several steps, and found himself at the dairy table.

He picked at the thick, pasty food until its shallow pool of milk was gone, without once rousing himself to ask Dominic a single question about the proposed job or the day before him. He then began to dip his bread into a cup of hot chocolate but paused to lift it in a feeble wave when Barneyway appeared through hovering mist of chocolate-and-coffee steam, tray held high before him.

The cleft in Barneyway's chin flicked up and down in a semaphoric greeting, but his face was expressionless; and Aaron nipped without appetite at his bread, hurt by the snub, in spite of his own slight greeting, feeling it was undeserved because Barneyway seemed to be the cause of his misery.

He raised the cup to wash the bread down but sensed something, hesitated, with the tip of his tongue tasting the tin lip, kept his head still, let his eyes roll into the Y'd corners of his lids and into direct focus with the Buzzer's eyes, then looked quickly down his nose into the moist heat of his cup. He sympathized with Barneyway, but was so impaled by the Buzzer's pointed stare himself that he was unable to move until Dominic stood up to leave.

Dominic first wiped the muddy streaks of oatmeal out of the tin hollows of his bowl with his last crust of raisin bread, then stood, and with what appeared as a mighty flourish to Aaron, reached for the ceiling with a cup of chocolate held like a gun, emptied the cup, aimed it at Aaron, beckoned with it, and left the table before anyone else in the dormitory had finished breakfast.

Aaron was quick to follow and drop his tray upon Dominic's at the scullery counter, his bowl in Dominic's, his spoon upon Dominic's spoon, but almost carried his cup out the door with him, and he had to lean back and toss it into a rack, then rush to catch up. He followed Dominic around the corner of the dining room to a wooden annex, waited while Dominic went into the officers' dining room, marveled at Dominic's courage, and credited Dominic with freeing him from the Buzzer's stare.

But the gravel pebbles along the walk soon took on the color and distinction of the Buzzer's eyes, and the walk itself offered the doubtful safety of a concrete platform elevated only a single inch above them. He began to wonder if the pebbles endangered him *only* because Barneyway was his buddy, and this was such a disloyal and fearful thought that he skipped away from it and went to meet Dominic when he reappeared with the man.

"Aaron's your name?" the man asked, holding out a tanned hand, looking curiously, kindly at Aaron through a lock of light-brown hair which had evaded his khaki cap and streaked across a smooth brow.

"I'm Mr. Handy. Think you're strong enough to lift those garbage cans onto that wagon?"

"Yes," Aaron said and tightened his grip, although he didn't know what wagon. He held onto the man's hand as much for the safety it promised as to prove his strength, and he held onto it until the man pulled free.

"Got a shake alright. Okay, give 'im a try, Dominic, and if he ain't worth a shit, fire 'im, and I'll put him to work shoveling road apples. You can start now if you want to. I'll include you in count."

Aaron followed Dominic again, and he stepped in each of Dominic's steps, stepped on a line if Dominic stepped on a line, drifted near the edge if Dominic drifted near the edge, although with misgivings and was careful not to let a shoe stick over, but he had to walk next to Dominic along the road and was no longer safe; and while the bleak glow that had chilled him before breakfast was now gone, his vision was so excessively clear that every object before him had a peculiar and unsettling illumination.

He tried to blame this on the still overcast sky, and the chalk white of the gym seemed to verify this. But the chapel wing adjoining the gym was in sunlight and the sky that framed it was a clear patch of blue and yet its outline was as emphatic as an engraving. The front walls of the trade shops lined the sloping hill below the gym like shields, and the dirt road that he and Dominic took at the bottom of the hill stretched straight across the untilled fields to the dairy in the distance as if it had been machine graded and lacked only pavement.

He walked in a wheel rut to limit his view and refused to lift his head when Dominic spoke to him, but the trudging sound of his shoes lingered in his ears with an evasive yet distinct overtone which was as disheartening and mysterious as Barneyway's cry on the hospital steps. And an occasional and isolated track of a single iron wagon wheel in the soft earth of a rut had an effect upon his emotions as great as the flick of Barneyway's chin at breakfast.

When they entered a big wooden building next to the dairy, its darkness and the strange strong smells of horseflesh, hay, and manure were too overwhelming for any type of reflection, and he had trouble just following Dominic about. But when Dominic grabbed a halter off a hook and threw open a stall door and an old horse lifted its bony head out of a hay trough and glared at them with one filmed eye, that eye reminded him of the Buzzer.

"You better watch how I do this," Dominic said and threw a halter over its head, laughed at Aaron's timid distance, and led the horse to an old wagon, with an iron-plated bed, fenced by a short plank railing.

"You gotta learn how to do this yourself or I'll fire yuh," he said and chuckled again and hooked the halter to the wagon forks and hopped onto the wagon with a one-handed easy spring, saying, "Let's go, daddy-o!"

Aaron had to use both hands and two tries to get onto the wagon, and Dominic commented:

"You'll be making it quicker than that before the morning's through," and he clucked his tongue against the roof of his mouth and rippled the slack in the reins and started the old horse at a wooden-jointed clopping walk through the open doors of the building and onto the packed dirt of the yard.

Aaron stepped backward and then forward on the wagon, with his arms outspread to keep from falling, too concerned with keeping his balance to worry, and although he wavered unsteadily, he kept his feet as the wagon cleared the dairy gate and turned onto the dirt road toward the main grounds.

But once on the road, Dominic called out a loud "Hah!" and slapped the reins against the bony haunches of the horse, and it lunged into a trot, jerking the wagon after it, and Aaron threw himself forward, bending into a jackknife, hands slapping against the rusted metal to keep from falling on his face, then dropped back onto his butt with a plop, more startled than hurt.

Dominic chuckled and peeked slyly down at him before Aaron caught the joke and saw himself: still scared, still surprised, but unhurt and safely seated, seated as stiffly as a doll, and he saw the humor in his comic fright, and began to laugh, and laughed for a full minute. He laughed until Dominic turned away with distaste at the hysteria in it.

Yet the joke had relieved his feelings and he now, happily, saw things so much less clearly, and his buttocks cushioned the jolts of the wagon, and occasional giggles broke from his lips all along the road, past the fields, so easily and thankfully blurred by a simple recollection of his comic fright, past the struggling line of inmates on their way to work at the dairy, which the eruption of a giggle caused to blend into the landscape, and all the way to the paved road, at the bottom of the main hill, where the sight of the Buzzer and Rattler crossing the lawn from the compound killed the last giggle in his throat.

"You'll like the job, man," Dominic said, noticing the approaching figures when Aaron stopped giggling, and he snapped the reins against the dry-hide haunches of the horse and hustled it up the hill.

"Some guys get up at five in the morning to milk the cows. The rest of the guys have to be around the man all the time. We boss ourselves and don't have to get up until the morning whistle, have fun reining the horse, have lots of free time," Dominic said, and Aaron, to whom his chin was a massive whiskered stubble, heard him speak, saw the mouth shape the words, saw the pucker of the lips with "You'll," the tongue's tip touch the square teeth with "like," and the final compression of the mouth with "time," and nodded politely in reply.

But neither Dominic's attempts to help him nor the compulsive attention he paid to the metallic clip-clop of the tired hooves on the pavement, to the creaking wooden frame and rattling plates of the wagon could relieve the anxiety that the appearance of the Buzzer had rekindled within him.

Although Dominic kept trying. He talked as they passed the trade shops, the chapel, the gym, the mess hall, the library, and the office. He talked as he reined the horse around the office and into the gravel yard, crisscrossed by countless wagon tracks. He talked right up to the back door of the kitchen, where six large garbage cans awaited them on the concrete porch. He talked as he backed the horse, talked when the rear wagon wheels bumped the concrete, and talked when he hopped down, tilted a can, and rolled it next to the wagon bed.

"The kitchen is one load in itself, man. After this, we'll hit the rest of the main buildings, and then the compounds. Last, the officers' cottages. Best of all there because they're always half empty and light. Let you rein the horse then. Okay?"

"Sure," Aaron answered, jumping down to help him and seizing the garbage can handle in order to fight the wave of self-pity that Dominic's concern produced in his chest. He ignored the pulpy odor of the spoiled food by refusing to turn his head, and he squeezed the handle so tightly that the heat of his hand warmed it.

"One! . . . Two! . . . Threeeeee!" Dominic called out and Aaron, welcoming a task that required the combined efforts of both his body and mind, leaned, braced, heaved, and grunted, unconcerned by the sharp wet ring of the can's bottom against his left palm, was proud as the ring caught on the wagon, proud of its screech against the iron plates as they shoved the can back, and flattered by Dominic's fist of approval when he stepped back to tilt and roll another can toward the wagon.

"You're a bitch for yourself. Ain't you?" Dominic said, after they had loaded the last can and begun the slow creaking pull across the crunching gravel.

"I try."

"You do more than try. You do." Dominic wiped his forehead. "Little man, iron hard. You'll make it, dad. And you can quit worrying about the Buzzer 'cause you're gonna make it. Hey! Don't lean against those cans. You don't need 'um. Stand like a boxer. Left foot forward. I know you can box. Bet on it. I bet. . . ."

Dominic's encouragement was offset by the Buzzer's name, and his voice drifted into the background as the slow clop, creak, and grind of the horse and wagon began to pound out the passage of idle time and promise ages of monotony, in which each second would be crammed with images of the Buzzer and Barneyway; and an agitated Aaron, searching for some aid, remembered his advice to himself, and braced his arms against his thighs with sweating palms as he tried to concentrate.

Mother! he thought, rocking with the wagon as it rounded the office.

Mother! Mother! And rimless glasses microscoped pale-green eyes.

MOTHER! spelled out in block letters in front of the library.

Mother! Oh, Mother! recited like the beginning of a prayer as they passed the chapel.

Mother-Mother! Mother-Mother! to the rhythm of the wagon sway and the hum of the metal-rimmed wheels on the asphalt when they started downhill and picked up speed.

Mother-Mother! Mother-Mother! Mother-Mother! Mother-Mother! he recited until it became an internal chant which deadened all sound and curtailed all sight; and the world about him gave him no misery, the figures he saw had no significance, the boys sweeping sidewalks in front of the trade shops and the boys picking rubbish off the grounds and the boys in the field crews and in the dairy yards could have all exchanged places with each other and with all the objects of the landscape, with all the buildings, with all the trees, with all the fields, with all the hills, and—when the road dipped into a ravine—with the grassy walls of the ravine, with the clumps of short willow trees, and even with the blue sky, spotted now with tiny cloud puffs.

Mother-Mother! Mother-Mother! Mother-Mother! Mother-Mother! he recited until they reached a dump at the end of the deep ravine, and he felt so good that he was eager to help Dominic tip, lift, and empty the cans down the slope of trash into the ditch. The work so warmed his body and occupied his mind and made him so energetic that he completed it too quickly, and Dominic had to stop him when he tilted a can of garbage.

"Not those, man. We drop those off at the pig shed. Slop, man, that'll turn out good bacon. Let's rest now. Have a smoke."

Dominic hopped down from the wagon, offered Aaron a cigarette, lit one for himself, and squatted on his haunches. He took deep drags of smoke and rested his arm on his thigh. His bicep flexed, stretched the rolled shirt sleeve into a tight band, and the blossomed rose of his tattoo impressed Aaron once more, and he squatted down, too, sensing that Dominic wanted to talk and "buddy up."

"How long you know Barneyway?" Dominic asked, watching Aaron carefully, as if he expected a lie and wanted to be able to detect it.

"Three years," Aaron answered, fatigue spreading through his limbs, expecting an unpleasant conversation, and positive that the one eye which stared at him, while the other squinted to shut out a pillar of smoke, was searching for a way to plot its next move. But the work and the chant had been effective: the extraordinary vision was gone and he didn't feel over-whelmed by anxiety.

"You guys good friends, huh?" Dominic asked, and the beauty mark seemed to contract with his intense contemplation.

"He's my best friend," Aaron said. "We're practically brothers. We're cousins," he added, lying, but it was an old lie and he felt justified in making it, for even the guys in the gang thought they were cousins.

Smoke seeped slowly out of Dominic's mouth with his next question.

"On what side of your family? Your mother's or your father's?"

He caught Aaron with an open mouth, for nobody had ever questioned the lie before, and he chuckled.

"Cousins don't ask other guys if they 'know the little guy

with the big eyes?' or only know their cousins for three years," he said and added:

"But that's okay, man. I know by the lie that you really like him. You must feel for him like a brother or you'd never try to make a cousin out of him."

"We have almost the same last name," Aaron said, trying to salvage some of his lost face. "My name's D'Aragon and his is Aragon, and his family's from Colorado just like mine, and he even lives across the street, and he eats dinner with us all the time, and his family gives mine presents for Christmas, and so do we, and—"

"You don't have to justify it, man. Like I say, you must like the guy a whole lot or you'd never try to make a cousin out of him."

"He's like a real brother. He spends most of his time at my house. He—"

"I know. I know, maaan," Dominic said, getting irritated, and he took several more drags on his cigarette without speaking, letting his irritation dissipate with the exhaled smoke.

"Do you shave every day, Dominic?" Aaron asked, after the smoke had faded, trying to make up, and struck once again by how big Dominic looked sitting down.

"On the outs I do. I been shaving since I was fourteen. You probably won't start until you're twenty or twenty-one."

"How come so late?" Aaron asked, hurt by Dominic's proud comparison, trying to conceal his wounded feelings with another question, running his hand over his smooth cheeks.

"Because you're so undeveloped, man. You hardly have any hair on your legs. How are you going to start shaving before you're twenty?"

"Barneyway was like me only last year and he's starting to shave now," Aaron replied, forgetting Barneyway was an uncomfortable subject. "He gets a stubble on his chin about every three weeks."

"That's about all the man he's got in him," Dominic said,

standing, dropping the butt on the packed earth, grinding it out with a twist of his brogan. "Let's move, dad."

"Barneyway's no chicken," Aaron retorted, using the wagon tongue as a step, but Dominic cracked the reins and startled the horse into a quick walk without answering.

"Why ain't Barneyway a man?" Aaron insisted, standing like a boxer, facing Dominic, rocking with the wagon, trying not to sound too demanding but determined to get an answer.

"Oh, you're gonna make me tell you, huh?" Dominic said and chuckled with such genuine humor that Aaron smiled, but Dominic added: "He just ain't, man. That's all."

"You can't say that unless you got proof," Aaron said, but he was afraid Dominic had proof, and an image of the Buzzer froze briefly, like a silent movie still, in his mind.

"Nobody's on trial, man. I don't have to convict anybody. I can think any goddamned thing I want to, about anybody— you, too."

"What'd ya bring it up for, if you didn't wantta talk about it then?"

Dominic smoothed and evened the reins with elaborate motions and only allowed Aaron to see his profile as he spoke:

"You're a salty little guy, huh?"

"I saw Barneyway choose a six-foot, twenty-year-old guy at a beach party a year ago," Aaron said, ignoring both the compliment and the attempt at humor, "and all the other bad actors I was with were too scared to fight him, and all Barneyway had was an empty wine bottle in his hand, and he stomped across the sand, right into the middle of the guy's gang, and the guy backed out, too. Now tell me that ain't straight?"

"It's straight, alright," Dominic conceded, holding the reins casually with one hand while he fished for a cigarette in his shirt pocket with the hooked forefinger of the other. "But guys change, too, and he had all his buddies with 'im. *You* said they were bad actors. And he was probably loaded on wine besides. Lots of guys got guts loaded."

"But most of the guys—except me and one other who wanted to be a pro fighter, too—were loaded, and we were all hanky of the guy."

"That might be so." Dominic quit pretending to look for a cigarette. "But guys still change."

"Tell me how you're so sure then. Tell me," Aaron insisted, but a dry rainwater gully in the road gave Dominic an excuse to stall.

He slowed the horse almost to a stop, and when the wagon dipped forward, he reached behind him with one hand and held it against an empty can to prevent it from sliding, then motioned to Aaron to do the same.

Aaron knew he was being stalled, and he waited patiently for Dominic to answer after they had crossed the gully. He waited until he could wait no longer and was going to demand an answer when Dominic suddenly shouted, "All the guys in the dairy think he's pussyyyyyyyyyy!"

And he slapped the reins against the bony haunches, and yelled the horse into a can-rattling trot, closing the subject, drowning out by sheer noise any attempt of Aaron's to continue the conversation, and thus forced Aaron to grab the rim of a full can and hang on as he rushed the horse around a curve and out of the ravine.

## II

The edge of the chapel door was as flat and even as a yardstick which measured off, at an oblique angle, exactly half of Aaron's peeking head, and he allowed only his pompadour, his left eye, his nose, a corner of his mouth to show beyond the edge until he was satisfied that no one was inside the chapel and slipped past the door and leaned against it.

He was displeased. For although small cell-like windows of stained glass cast a lead-toned hue throughout the narrow room, there were no shadowy corners that promised sanctity, and the doubts with which he entered were intensified.

The varnished benches had no backs and were as exposed as the bleachers of a baseball field. The simple Christ upon the cross had the blocky, unexpressive outlines of a carving that had not been carried past a rough-hewn preliminary stage. A red velvet cloth covered a wooden table to one side below the cross, and both the cross and the table sat upon an altar which was as plain and uncluttered as a bare scaffold and fenced by a wooden railing. He could see no other place to kneel, and he considered leaving.

But it was cool inside, at least, and outside there was the noon heat and that black face, with its dispiriting grin; and he began to walk lightly down the aisle to keep his footsteps from resounding on the pine floor, still hoping for a private place to pray until he reached the railing, although prayer had become a drudgery which only old habits sustained.

He needed the familiar atmosphere of a Catholic church now. He was certain of that. He needed its somber, penitent interior. He needed the stylized agony of a Christ at fourteen stations of the Cross, offering fourteen separate spaces in which to pray. He needed that old dusty sadness, as if sifted by stained glass, which made the plaster statues seem as hallowed as solid marble.

He stepped to one side—for there was a gap in the railing before the cross—looked about and behind him in a final check, still hoping to spot some special praying nook or an overlooked confessional booth, but saw only walls as bare and unconcealing as those of any army barracks.

He genuflected: knocked his kneecap once, softly, on the floor, and knelt at the railing, only to hear the rattle of the garbage cans all over again, and he leaned against a full one and braced his foot against the side plank of the wagon as they trotted around the curve, and Dominic's mouthful of contemptuous teeth dragged out the ending of that terrible word: "Pussyyyyyyyyyyy!"

He crossed himself and bowed his head and tried to begin praying, hoping to get some relief from the tormenting problem through the performance of a dutiful act, hoping that the sacrifice involved in forcing himself to perform the act would bring such satisfaction that a spirit of sanctified grace would settle upon him and he would have no problems of any kind. But no prayers came. He felt as if he were kneeling down in a courtroom. The chapel was constructed and furnished with the bare efficiency of a jail.

He pressed his palms tightly together, trying to compress all motion and all thought into the first act of praying, but the cynical dot of Dominic's beauty mark held his attention; a mark which had punctuated with a decisive period all of his attempts throughout the morning to get Dominic to explain; a mark which had ended Dominic's warning outside the dining room to be out of the chapel by one o'clock and on time for school; a mark which . . .

Aaron's palms relaxed, the cupped air between them popped with suction, and he let his hands fall, fingers entwined, to the railing, disappointed because he had made the discipline of prayer work in the detention home in spite of the bars, and in spite of . . . the . . . . Prayer seemed so useless now, but without it. . .? without it. . .?

"Touch your middle finger to your forehead," he said aloud, and did it, "then to the white button in the middle of your chest, then to the left shoulder, then to the right, then start praying: Our Father, Who art in Heaven, hallowed be Thy . . ."

*Pussy* was the dirtiest name a guy could be called. *Pussy* was the . . .

He made the sign of the cross again, pressed his hands together, made the fingers and the palm heels perfectly even, and began a Hail Mary, hopeful that the whispered rhythm of this prayer would rock him into a state of dutiful contentment, hopeful that the waves of recitation would take effect as they had in the detention home, when they had helped him behave, when prayer was the only habit he could depend upon, the only thing he had left of his mother, the only thing that everybody, including the man, thought was right, when—although neither it nor behaving gave him any joy—it kept him out of trouble, and was . . . the only thing. . . .

The prayer had passed swiftly out of his mouth in a mumble, and he stopped himself and closed his eyes and lifted his face toward the Christ and tried again:

"Hail, Mary, full of grace, the Lord is with . . ."

But he heard the rattle of the cans again, and he grabbed the railing, opening his eyes to keep his balance, and gasped at the sight of two large angels, with swords in their hands, hovering in the clouds of a mural on the ceiling.

Coarse layers of house paint had been brushed on by an inmate artist who, in an attempt to make them pretty, had made them look like old whores. They reminded Aaron of police matrons, too, for the harsh, manly angles of their faces were stressed by the thick smears of bright lipstick and heavy rouge; and the eyelashes, which were supposed to be pretty, were so long and thick they encircled the bulging eyes like the masks of assassins, and their busts were so large and heavily outlined in black paint that, although the angels wore flowing white robes, they gave the impression of chest armor.

Guards not guardians, he thought with disgust, and then felt guilty for thinking about angels in that way, and he tried to discover good things in the mural. But a closer inspection only made the grotesque leers on their faces more obvious and reminded him of Dominic's when he had shouted: "Pussyyyyy-yyyyyy!"

He lowered his head and rested it on the cool smooth railing to get the angels out of his sight and the thought of

Dominic and that word out of his mind. But the confused feelings that the mural had aroused stayed with him, for the angels seemed a perfect example of all the confusion in his life.

Church on Sundays and prayers every night didn't do any good against guys like the Buzzer. He had fought enough bullies to know that, and he had stomped enough guys himself to know that no sign of the cross could stop an excited gang. And when was it all right to fight and even kill? He had become hysterical when he had seen a wild-haired girl slap Judith's face into a splotch of red, and he had thrown the girl to the ground and had started pounding on her back and didn't know he was under arrest until the cops fingerprinted him at the city hall. And why get a Medal of Honor for machine-gunning thirty-five yellow Japs and jail for breaking a guy's nose who messed with your girl? Cops never put Stanley in jail during the war for street fighting. They patted him on the back, called him a good soldier, told him to move on, and picked up his victim. The men in the DT didn't like sissies either. No sissy ever became a monitor. Yet the man would toss a guy in the hole for fighting, put it down on his record, and make his sentence longer. A guy couldn't win for losing: if he fought, he got a good rep, the man might make him a monitor, but kept him locked up. If he didn't fight, he got beat up and put down by all the guys, the man didn't respect him but let him go home sooner. It didn't figure out. Nothing was what it seemed to be. Everything was like the mural.

The fingerprint grain of the wood hurt his cheekbone and distracted him, but it was just another example, like the mural, of how displeasing prayer had become since. . . ? since. . . ?

Mother! He could try that! It had worked on the garbage wagon! He chanted:

Mother-Mother! Mother-Mother! Mother-Mother! Mother-Mother!

But the chant sounded so ironic coming from him in church, kneeling in front of an altar that his unspoken, unadmitted, undigested grudge against God for killing her erupted inside him like the discomfort of heartburn.

The chant was as futile as that chant to Him for her at that last rosary. That futile chant had floated like swamp scum upon the sweet, sick smell of scores of wreaths of flowers in the funeral home. That futile chant had rippled like sluggish waves in the oppressive, stagnant heat from a hundred bodies. That futile chant had been chanted by a hundred mourners and chanted to the monotonous thudding beat of a hundred fists on a hundred breastbones:

"Oh, my God, I am most heartily sorry.

"Oh, my God, I am most heartily sorry.

"Oh, my God, I am most heartily sorry."

He still hated that chant. He hated— He hated— He— He was afraid to admit to himself that he loved his mother more than God. But his mother would never have killed anybody. His mother would never have let anybody die at all, if she could help it, not even . . . not . . . even . . . the Buzzer!

His cheek still hurt. He laid the other side of his face against the railing, searched for the warm spot his cheek had made on the wood, found it, rested his head, and regretted coming to the chapel. For he was afraid that prayer would never work for him again. He was afraid he had lost the only control he had over his life. He was afraid that the tool he had used to keep himself from hating a man who had left slap prints striped across his face for half an hour afterwards was gone. It was a tool that had helped him apologize to the man for talking back to the monitor who had whacked him with a paddle, a tool he had learned to use so well that *he* had become a monitor, and then head monitor, and *he* wielded the paddle, and *he* . . . ? he . . . ? he . . . ?

He lifted his head as he realized why prayer had worked so well in the DT. He had prayed there, in barred light, with only one thought: to behave, to behave, to behave, because that was what was wrong. He had to pray *only* for what was wrong.

He had to pray for *one* particular thing. He had to pray for the *help* to do that one thing. He had to pray for the *will power* to do it. He had to pray for the will power to *do* some thing, as he had there.

He straightened into a good kneeling position, determined to pray for help in finding out what was wrong between Barneyway and the Buzzer. He knocked his knees together, his anklebones, his feet, and checking behind him to see if he was still alone, he noticed the awry hang of his new shoes below him; and he tried, before praying, to make a roughly even line of determination out of the twin strips of clean orange leather between their dirty soles and heels.

Sore knees and a pain between his shoulder blades would be part of his sacrificial payment of God for His help, for the will power to seek out the cause and find an answer to the problem.

The words came haltingly at first and then began to slide with a whisper's ease from his mouth as the discipline of recitation took effect. And although he did not expect to feel the presence of God like his mother's hand upon his neck nor his chest to swell with an exalted sense of a purified soul, the humble habit of confession was still strong, and if he had admitted to himself his own fault in incidents which he thought were unjust in the DT, he could discover the cause of the trouble involving his best friend no matter how badly it might make him feel, and for a brief unhappy moment, he thought of Buckshot.

He stopped, and straightened his back, and decided to recite his rosary all the way through from the beginning, and he began with the conviction of a normal speaking voice:

"I believe in God, the Father almigh—"

"Jesus Christ, man! What the hell's the matter with you?" Dominic yelled, standing silhouetted and stump-legged in the doorway. "Come on! The guys are lined up for count outside the school. Run! or you'll spend your whole goddamned day praying in the hole. Run!"

# III

Sunrays, magnified by a wall of windows, spilled in puddles off brown desks, heated and lit every corner of the schoolroom, but converged on Aaron, who unbuttoned his shirt to the middle of his chest and spread his damp collar to cool his neck.

The scrambled conversations of the boys irritated him, too, for he was still breathing hard from the run from the chapel, and he would have liked to have rested in the shade. But there wasn't a shady spot in the school room, and Dominic had sat down directly in front of the teacher's empty desk, placed his books, with their worn jackets in the pool of light on his desk, and motioned to Aaron to sit next to him.

"This is the twelfth grade in here. Don't worry!" Dominic said, stopping Aaron's protest. "You can do the work. You watch. Math, English, History all going on at different speeds. You'll see."

Every other seat in the front row was an empty, waving rib of dark, trouser-polished wood, and Aaron's desk was so completely isolated that he was afraid to take advantage of a room filled with guys and with possible hints which might solve his problem. But the desire for a less conspicuous seat, and one from which he could pursue his intentions, proved stronger than his shyness, and he tried to find one.

All the other desks were taken, perhaps fifty in all, but once he had turned and had seen that he was not the center of attention, he began to study the room from his seat.

The guys were big and many showed blue stubble on their cheeks. This was important because Barneyway was smart in school and the big guys might pick on him for it, call him a show-off. Just as he, himself, didn't like to use the paddle to keep the home group quiet when the big guys were in the DT dayroom for movies, because he didn't want them to consider him a smart punk.

There were a few white shirts in the back rows, too, and he recognized the blond guy who had shouted orders in the dining room and whose weasel expression made him a natural suspect as an accomplice to the Buzzer. The guy's drooping eyelids twisted slyly at the corners and his lips had the same droop and twist to them and contrasted sharply with the square brown features of the big Mexican in white kitchen uniform who sat next to him.

Aaron was then surprised to see the Buzzer sitting in the very last row, the black skin fold corkscrewed on his twisted neck, speaking to Rattler, who was across the aisle from him.

"What's the Buzzer doing here?" he asked, curious, but hoping that the answer would provide some kind of a clue, although conscious, also, of a vague sense of deceit.

"Still worrying about him, huh? Forget the dude and, anyway, after you're sixteen, if you don't go to school, you either got to work or learn a trade, and the Buzzer don't like those dirty shops any more than I do. He don't do nothing here. Pretty quick, he'll have a reason for going out and he won't come back. Wait and see."

Conversation dropped to a low hum as a young dark-haired man came into the room, strolled up the center aisle with casual steps, leaned one hand upon his desk, seemingly pivoted upon his long fingers toward the class, and waited for silence.

Full cheeks, closely shaved and pale-sheened, seemed to swell with impatience. A thick eyebrow arched into a tight curl on his forehead, wavered, but the conversation continued and the soft body sagged visibly within the blue suit and the eyebrow drooped and a soft voice said, "All right, boys. All right, boys."

Small black hairs quilled the tattooed H of hate on Dominic's crooked right pinkie, and he smirked so Aaron would understand the signal; and Aaron sat up, attentive, certain this meant something, searching the man's soft face for further signs.

The conversation hummed indifferently on.

"All right, boys," the man said.

Hum of conversation.

"Boys!" the man yelled, and his voice squeaked. "Let's begin with English!"

There was a resentful hush in the room, and the resentment, the heat, the glare, the odor of crowded sweating flesh made Aaron wish he was outside, where he could find some tranquil place in which to figure out some type of plan. He despised the man for not making the boys respect him, blamed the man for not protecting Barneyway, and disliked the man even more because his own resentment found expression in the word "pussy," which was loaded with the incriminations about Barneyway he hoped to disprove.

"Which of you boys in the top group have finished reading the story about Joan of Arc?"

The man's voice grated upon Aaron's nerves like the squeak of chalk on a blackboard.

"And who knows who condemned her and where?"

Dominic raised his hand.

A quick leveling of the arched brow acknowledged the hand, but the brow arched again, touched the tip of the curl as the man looked around the room seeking the answer elsewhere. He repeated the question, and Dominic slid down on his seat into an indifferent slouch and stared arrogantly at the ceiling as if he were sure he would be called upon. Aaron was amused by his conceit, especially since it was intended to offend the man, but he didn't risk a smile, which would have relieved his own feelings, because Dominic looked too touchy.

"Well, what's the answer, Dominic?" the man asked, wearily.

"A council of French churchmen at Rouen," Dominic said, speaking to the ceiling, raising his voice with the Rouen to prove how easy it all was. He then bore down on the seat with his hands, and let his body swing free between his arms, his legs together, his toes sticking out beyond the desk, pointed like a gymnast's, before dropping down again, with a thump, upon the seat, massive chin at desk level, and he so filled Aaron with admiration for him, for a guy so tough he wasn't ashamed to be smart, to be single-o, to pick and choose his own way, that it took an upward tilt of the chin to alert Aaron to the man.

"Your name, please?"

"Huh?"

"Your name?" the man asked again, smiling, and someone snickered from the back of the room, and Aaron blushed and appreciated Dominic's quick rescue:

"Are we going to discuss the battles Joan of Arc fought?"

"I'm not sure yet," the man said, the arched eyebrow quavering with annoyance.

"I'm ready to now," Dominic said. "You said to have it done."

"We'll get to that," the man said. "Now just keep your pants on, Dominic. There's—"

A snicker cut him off. He dropped his arms, stood stiffly, and tried to threaten the class with a no-nonsense stare. But his eyebrows were too finely plucked, his cheeks too smooth and pale, and his eyes too soft to scare. There was silence, though, and he began to question Aaron again, but with a persistence that made Aaron feel as if he were on the witness stand, with the whole courtroom watching for a mistake.

"What grade are you in?"

"The tenth."

"Do you know your grammar?"

"Pretty good," Aaron answered, wishing he were on the garbage wagon, wishing the man weren't so friendly with him, beginning to fear now that the guys might compare him with the man, that the guys might think he, too, was pussy.

"Ha-ha!"

"What's a noun?" the man asked, pretending he didn't hear the laugh.

"The . . . the name of something."

"Very good," a voice said and the class giggled.

The man slapped his arms to his side and stared at the class until the giggling stopped. Then he asked, in a very dignified tone:

"What's the subject of a sentence?"

"It's . . . it's . . . it's what's being talked about," Aaron answered, cringing as he waited for the next smart remark to explode in his ears, all thought of solving Barneyway's problems gone.

"Very good," someone said.

"Very good," said someone else.

"Verrr-ryyy goooood," added another voice, and Aaron recognized the Buzzer's drawl as the class started laughing, and recognition sapped the last shreds of his confidence, and he sank down, his thin body huddled into his big shirt, his face enflamed by a hot blush.

"I see no reason for any wisecracks," the man said, putting his hands on his hips, pursing his mouth, trying to present a grim appearance, but he was so ineffectual he made Aaron feel worse.

"This boy is only answering my questions and very well, too. We'll have no more smart-ass remarks," he said, primly, brushing at the curl on his forehead, and he waited until the class had become quiet before he asked another question.

"What is a verb? I mean, give me an example of one."

Aaron was positive that the grins were as sharp and poised as knife blades behind him.

"A verb?" the man asked, and Aaron, ears ringing, dreading the next remark, but wanting to get the ordeal over with, tried to answer:

"It's . . . uh . . . It's, uh. . . . An example is . . ."

He peered at the man from below his flushed brow, feeling disgraced forever in front of Dominic, sure that Dominic would think he was pussy, too, now.

"Come ownnnnn, kisssss-aaasssss, what's thuh ansuh?" the Buzzer cried, and the class burst into laughter again.

"All right . . . that's enough," the man said. "That's enough! That's enough!"

But the laughter only became louder, and the man sat down in disgust, pouting, eyebrow sagging, and Dominic shook his head with a contempt which Aaron felt was meant for him, too.

"Come-ownnn, kisss-aaasssss," the Buzzer said, and Dominic's irises sliced to quarter-moons in the corners of his glancing eyes, and the glance triggered Aaron into action, and he sat up, jammed his chest against the desk edge, stuttered as he tried to answer, and then shouted his answer, shouted it as loud as he could, to prove *he* wasn't pussy:

"Scare is a verb. Pray is a verb. And love is a verb."

"Verrr-ryyy good. Verrrrr-ryyyy goooooooooood," the Buzzer said.

"Very good," Rattler said.

"Very good," said another guy.

"Very good," said another guy and another guy and another guy.

And Aaron snapped his seat against the backrest and jumped up and shouted:

"Fight is a verb!"

Then he twisted around at his desk and faced the blue and white blur of uniforms, and all the laughing faces, and kept shouting:

"Fight is a verb! Fight is a verb! Fight is a verb! Fight! Fight! Fight! Fight! Fight! Fight! Fight! Fight! Fight!"


## IV


The smooth envelope, yellow-tinged by electric light on the thick nap of the blanket, lifted Aaron somewhat out of the belligerent depression caused by the classroom scene and intensified by nightfall. But the finger he hooked in a corner pocket of the sealed flap was barbed by his sense of failure, and he made a ragged tear the entire length of the letter before examining the return address to see who had written to him. He noticed that one end of the letter had already been neatly sliced open and rubber-stamped by a censor. His clumsy, useless tear then seemed like an unlucky omen of how his attempts to solve the problem might turn out, and he was convinced he was some kind of a jinx when he saw that the fuzzy edges of the rip had separated the first name Judith from the last name Prize and had mutilated the return address.

The blue-black censor's mark became an unlucky sign, too, which meant that some man had stamped with ink upon his private thoughts even before he thought them and had already ruined them, and the letter was almost certain to carry bad news. The censor's mark then stood out like a token of some strange and unknown and perfect thing, and yet, at the same time, was a brand of his bad luck and his guilt and his punishment. And he was afraid to open the letter and, then, ashamed of his fear.

He jerked the folded pages out, snapped them open, and sat at the foot of his bed, close to the bulb which hung from the center beam of the dormitory ceiling, eager to lose himself in the letter, and hoping that every word was going to be a sign of affection. But as insurance against bad news, he looked around him to remind himself of where he was before he began to read.

Mail call had made the dormitory quiet. Most of the boys sat alone on their beds. Those without mail kept to themselves, obviously respecting the privacy of the lucky guys with the sheets of paper in their hands, which was completely unlike the congregation of loud groups the previous night. Dominic, too, lay on his bed, blocking the light with his letter, reading from the shadowed side.

Hi, Aaron.
Just a note. I'm writing in the kitchen. Mom is in bed and

I just finished some homework. I had planned to write to you at school tomorrow because Mom has been complaining about your letters, but this is better.

She found out about the candy I left for you at the detention home—Remember?—from one of my *good* friends. Some friend! It upset her so much she used it as an excuse for one of her periodical Lost Weekends. That way it's my fault, not hers. You know. What burns me up is that she wouldn't let me go visit you on regular visiting days and then she complains when I do it my own way. Maybe if she got married, she wouldn't have to work, and we could get along? I don't know?

But don't worry, I'll manage some way to get permission to go visit you up there. She tried to use the excuse that the institute was too far away from the Bay Area when I first mentioned it to her. Then she said the coast highway was bad, and that I couldn't make it up there and back on the bus before dark, and everything else she could think of.

She just doesn't understand. But when I can convince her that you're not just a pachuco who spends all his time walking around in black drapes, with a silver cross hanging from his neck, she'll let me. I know, because she was real surprised when I told her you had never stolen anything, and I'll be able to write longer letters then, too.

So be good, and think about *all* the people who care for you, and all the kids, and remember that I'll get there as soon as I can. So expect me and say hello to Barneyway for me and please write to me.

Your good friend,<br>JUDITH

P.S. I get home before Mom does and I'll be sure and get the letter.

He laid the sheets down on the blanket, smoothed them flat with only the slightest crackling and leaned so close to reread the last, "good" page that his head almost touched the foot railing. His chest swelled with the phrase: ". . . think about *all* the people who care for you. . . ."

He pictured the cheek lines that winged out from her pert nose as if she had spoken it and then pictured the pucker of her full lips with the ". . . you . . ."

He then reread the entire letter from the beginning, skimming over the unhappy facts, searching for hints of praise and affection, and attached himself, like a leech that could survive on the ink it sucked from the paper, to the statement: "But when I can convince her that you're not just a pachuco. . . ."

He was astounded by how much her letters could mean to him. And he regretted now that he had treated her more like a friend than a girl, and he tried to pretend that there had been a real romance between them.

But the greeting for Barneyway punctured the daydream, deflated the expansive feeling that the letter had produced, and left him locked in the real world of the institute, with real problems, a naked bulb above him and undeniable concrete below him.

"Trying to memorize that page, man? Got camera eyes or somethin'?"

Aaron fumbled with the pages. Dominic moved to the foot of his bed opposite Aaron, but his frown made the joke sound bitter.

"I was . . . just looking at it."

"Don't apologize, man. It must be a good letter. And the chick must like you a lot or she wouldn't write so quick. You only been in the institute a week."

"We're not going steady or nothin'," Aaron said, honestly, but he was flattered, for getting mail from a girl gave a guy prestige. He picked up the pages, held them self-consciously, folded them once, and shoved them into his back pocket to get them out of sight.

"Who wrote to you?" he asked, trying to change the subject.

"Just my mother, man."

"I wish I could say 'Just my mother.' If I had a mother, I probably wouldn't even be here, wouldn't have to take a lot of crap off a bunch of rats just because I can answer the teacher's questions, and wouldn't even know the goddamned Buzzer. They don't mess with you that way."

"I'm bigger, man." Dominic flexed his muscle. The rose bloomed. "And you're doing okay. All new guys get messed with. You let 'em know today, they'd have to *try you* to beat you, and that's a lot. Just wait until you get a rep and you'll be fine. The Buzzer won't mess with you then. You'll see. Besides, you wouldn't want a letter from my mother even if she was *your* mother."

Aaron picked his envelope off the blanket to avoid having to answer Dominic's uncomfortable comment, and he busied himself by folding and refolding it until the 'Judith Prize' was a torn heading on a postage stamp size packet squeezed between his fingers.

"You know what's in that letter, man?" Dominic said, crushing the letter in his tattooed fist and throwing it with such force to the floor that it bounced as high as his bed frame and, then, rolled with a flutter under his bed.

"Misery, man. Woman misery. Complaints. My mother's got everything wrong with her that she can have wrong with her: liver, kidneys, heart, womb, low blood pressure, no blood pressure. If you don't believe it, ask her. But you won't have to because she'll tell you all about it, anyway. She makes me do *her* time as well as *my* time. She wishes something was wrong with me so I could feel bad and we could share it together. Then we'd have something in common. She only comes to see me about every three months, twice since I been here. And that's too often as far as I'm concerned. It's just sickbed talk, anyway. She can stay home and keep her goddamned Jesus with her, too."

Fragile spears of light and shadow gave the crumpled surface of the letter a suspicious appearance to Aaron. For although he believed that Dominic was showing off a little bit, especially the part about Jesus, a guy didn't say things like that unless he felt pretty bad, and Aaron felt sorry for him.

"You know what's really wrong with my mother?"

Aaron pretended to be preoccupied with folding the envelope a final time and making a thick roll of it between his fingers, but Dominic kept talking.

"You know what's really wrong with her? She can't chippy like she used to. Men don't give her the play anymore. Those that do, get a piece of ass and split on her. She's too fat now, too old, fifty, wrinkles from all that lush and party-time during the war. She been screwing like a young whore since my father died six years ago. . . ."

Aaron wanted to slap his hands over his ears, scream out a halt, jam a towel into Dominic's mouth, do something, anything, to stop him. It was sacrilege to talk about your mother that way, and he was sure Dominic's heart was vibrating with each syllable, while he, himself, couldn't prevent glimpses of his own mother's wrinkles, her tired eyes from appearing before him.

"She used to try and get me on her side as a kid. But I'll take my old man's beatings before her whimpering any day. He was a man, daaad," Dominic said, dragging the corners of his mouth down, smashing his fist into his palm. "He was what he said he was, all the time. She even lies to herself. She goes out and gets laid and, then, goes to church, goes out and gets laid and, then, goes to church. She even chippied on him when he was alive. Finally, I told on her. He kicked her ass. Kneeled her down and stripped her dress off, made me watch. Her big tits hung down onto bellyrolls of soft fat, and he beat her with his belt. The dimples on her ass jerked like jelly with each whack and she screamed and said she wouldn't do it no more, just like the sniveling bitch. And she didn't, either, because he kept her in the house until he died a couple of years later. My old man was a mean old dago, built just like me. He was a cold-blooded dude. But he was a man, and everything he said he was, he was. Man, dad, maaannn!"

Dominic reached down and under the bed as he finished, grabbed the wadded letter and threw it, floating, into the center of the aisle by the washroom door, then stood defiantly, daring anyone to complain about it. But no one noticed and he sat down heavily upon his bed, slumped forward, and seemed drained of energy.

Aaron could have thanked him for stopping, but he, himself, was comforted by the memory of a slightly plump mother in a print-flowered dress, a good mother in a warm kitchen, and for the first time, he felt superior enough to Dominic to want to help him.

"I hate women, man," Dominic said, after a few minutes. "They're all weak bitches. I hate 'em just like I hate gutless punks and niggers. I hate niggers because they're gutless unless they're in a mob. I ain't seen one yet that would stand up against a gang by hisself. They won't even fight single-o if they figure they might get whipped. The Buzzer knows I hate 'um. He stays away from me. Big Stoop asked me if I wanted to be a cadet captain right after I first got here. But I turned it down. I don't want nothin' to do with niggers, even bossing those black, stinking punks. And I'll take Big Stoop, hisself, any day, over nearly all the guys here at the institute, even the supposed-to-be-bad guys. He's as bad as he acts."

"Big Stoop? Who's Big Stoop?" Aaron asked, and the constant stress that Dominic, with his explosive speech, kept him under was heightened by the image of a giant Chinese walking out of a comic strip into real life.

"Who's Big Stoop?" Dominic mocked, his mouth curving as thin and viciously as a scimitar blade. "He ain't in *Terry and the Pirates,* dad. He's that big, giant, deputy-cop sonofabitch that checked you in. Mr. Toothman, man."

"Wow! Big Stoop! That's a good nickname for him."

"Damn good. But don't sell him short. He's a big man and he's a good man. Broke a guy's arm about three months ago when he caught the guy with a chicken sandwich from the kitchen. A Mexican dude and game, game. He even took a bite when he got caught and tried to swallow it. But Big Stoop grabbed him and bent his arm behind him until it snapped trying to make him spit the bite out. Then he smeared the 'lump' in the guy's face. Spread mayonnaise all over that brown skin, made the game Mex whimper. Big Stoop is a cop and a bad one, and he runs his institute like he knows how. I respect the dude for what he is, me."

"I won't sell him short," Aaron said and felt the guy's fear when he got caught, the horrible pain of the broken arm, and the humiliation of having the sandwich smeared over his own face.

"I hate gutless punks," Dominic said.

A slight stiffening of Aaron's shoulders and a spreading of his elbows betrayed his inner tension, his fear that Dominic might include him, and his fear that in some future conflict with the Buzzer, he might not prove manly enough, hard and tough and game enough, but fear he was distracted from by the clash of the compound gate. And he listened, curious as to why the man would be coming in before count.

Wide-spaced footsteps and lighter, quicker ones sounded on the asphalt, and he could tell that some boy was rushing to keep up with the man. The door opened, a deep voice said something, and Barneyway stepped into the dormitory. And Aaron didn't know whether to be happy or sad.

His first impulse was to call out. But Barneyway stood with his back to the door as if he were ready to turn and run: a small thin figure, almost comic; and Aaron found himself faced with the problem and all its complications, when he didn't feel prepared for it, when he was afraid he couldn't be hard and tough and game enough to fight it. But when Barney-way walked down the aisle with such timid steps it looked as if he had blistered feet, Aaron was moved, and he stood and cried:

"Barneyway! Me! Barneyway!" with such enthusiasm that a wary smile split Barneyway's compressed lips.

"Man, I'm glad you're better," Aaron said, leaving Dominic behind him, discounting everything, once he had spoken, except his best friend. "But how come you came in so late at night?"

"Big Stoop ran . . ." Barneyway sat on his bed. "Big Stoop . . . Mr. Toothman, ran . . . ran me out of the hospital, ran some other walking cases out, too. He said we were gold-bricking . . . said. . . ."

The large moist eyes looked beyond Aaron and the explanation stopped. The sallow complexion had a gray hue. Aaron started to ask him if he was still sick when the cleft in the chin quivered with fright, and he spun his own head around with such force that a muscle snapped and burned in his neck. He hunched his shoulder against it to ease the pain, but the pain subsided into insignificance at the sight of the Buzzer shuffling toward them, at the fearful impact he felt as he realized that he was about to see for himself!

"How my little pautna' Air-ron?" the Buzzer asked, reaching out; but Aaron had no intention of forgetting the wise-cracks in school nor was he going to let himself be conned in any way when he might have to fight, and he evaded the hand with a slight twist of his torso.

Shallow glints of humor showed in the Buzzer's eyes, and he pushed by Aaron and massaged Barneyway's hairline.

"How my little pautna' Bau-nii-wayyyyy?"

Barneyway stared meekly at the half moon of concrete floor between his feet.

"Bau-ni-wayyy my best little buddy, Air-ron. An' I glad you his buddy."

He leaned his head back on the fulcrum roll of flesh at the base of his skull and looked down his flat nose at Aaron, sighting between the shotgun barrel holes of his flaring nostrils, as if he were farsighted.

"We be threee buddies, mus-ka-teeers. Threeeee mus-ka-teeeeers. You . . . an' me . . . an' Bau-niiiii," he said.

And the hair on Aaron's arms rose with a goose-pimpling chill, a chill which trickled across his skull as the Buzzer sat down, leaned back, and propped his arm on the blanket behind Barneyway. For the Buzzer did it in a deliberately dainty manner, and the dormitory was so quiet that the mattress crunched slowly and loudly beneath his weight.

"Ain't nothin' shakin', Bau-niii," the Buzzer drawled and rocked sidewards, touching Barneyway with his chest, making him flinch. "I always take care o' my little buddies. I fi-gur a little ma-han who don' have no eee-kuaaa-li-za need some kine o' pro-tec-shun, bein' as there ain't no blades nor no blooo-bar-rulled pistols aroun' to warn big cats away. You know, by bustin' off a few caps. You know, for my ownnn gooooood bee-have-vurrr. Help these little cats out. You know."

His thick grinning mouth stretched widely and slowly for the benefit of his friends, but an expression of mock seriousness dropped like a hood over his face when the lights blinked off and on, off and on, warning of bedtime, count, and lights out.


V


Occasional barks of laughter, comments, and hoo-rahs disturbed the darkened dormitory for some time. But eventually the joke of Barneyway's fright wore out for the Buzzer and his boys, and the sleepy mumble of a word, the rustle of sheets, the heave and sigh of deep breathing and the drone of someone snoring down by the washroom were all Aaron could hear.

The exposed rafters of the ceiling formed faint lunar bridges of light across a smooth expanse of darkness, and Aaron traced the thin beam above him across the dormitory into the wall of shadow over Barneyway's bed, and the bond of their friendship seemed as thin and tenuous, seemed to disappear like the beam in the dark fear which hovered over Barneyway and which he would not illuminate.

A chill trickled across Aaron's skull at the thought of the nostrils which had flared above him, and he dreaded an illumination now as much as the unexplained fright. For Barneyway's poor performance was the clinching lesson in his first day's schooling: he didn't know if he could take care of himself yet, let alone be hard and tough enough to help Barneyway, even with all the answers.

He started to make the sign of the cross but got no farther than the touch of his finger to his forehead, for Barneyway *had* acted like pussy! And Buckshot's tan cheeks puffed with the pride and importance of his warning! And Aaron covered his eyes with his hand to hide from both sights, then turned over on his side, pulled the covers up to his ears, pressed his head into the pillow, and tried to smother with sleep all the unhappy bits and impressionistic memories of his first full day on the grounds.

He tried to relax and let the fatigue of his body seep into and still the crowding turmoil in his brain, while he focused all his thoughts upon the figure of his mother, hoping that the strong haloed glow which surrounded it would settle over everything nearby. For the standard he needed was there in her person: she was kind but her sons had to be brave, and she had insisted that he live up to the examples set by his father and his brothers.

But the glow around Barneyway's mother came from a jukebox in a downtown bar, filled with loud music and sailors. Its gaudy lights painted her drunken face with shifting colors, smeared her lipstick, spread her hair into wild tangles, and

Aaron had to force his eyes open and keep them open in order
to make the picture go away.

Sleep and sounds then began to fuse together: snores
groaned with the weight of his worries, then all ground together in his head with the slow revolutions of a concrete
mixer, then spilled with the pressure of sliding mud down the
chute of his throat into his body, smothered the beat of his
heart, spread in a swelling mass into his aching stomach, sunk
with expanding pressure into his bowels, and put such a con-
tinuing and uncomfortable strain upon his sphincter muscle
that he finally had to force himself to get out of bed, while still
asleep, and stagger down the dormitory to the toilet, only to
stop and stagger back, like a cripple from the contracted
muscle, at a dark shape which loomed in the faint light ahead
and leered at him with eyes as vacant as mask slits.

The toilet was such a long block behind it that Aaron kept
backing up, for he couldn't run because of the pressure and
he was afraid to turn his back to the shape, until he was able
to escape by a flight of stairs. He managed to climb its tor-
tuous steps without losing control by keeping his legs together,
and he reached a toilet on its top landing with the swinging,
slatted doors of old-fashioned saloons he had seen in cowboy
movies.

A shape lingered inside but the cramps were too dreadful
for him to care, and he pushed through the slatted doors only
to stagger back from the stench of stale urine and dry clots
of human stools which were scattered about the floor. His
stomach retched. His eyes smarted and watered. And he feared
he might have to squat and relieve himself on the landing,
but, luckily, he saw another toilet at the far end of a long hall
with a man inside it.

He started toward it but each heel step against the hall floor
was a sharp rectal pain, and yet his legs floated as if he did
not touch the floor, and there was no sound to his steps, and
he walked for blocks and blocks and it took him hours and

hours, and the gas writhed in his bowels, and his sphincter muscle was cramped, and he could not wake up, and he began to doubt that he would ever reach it and then reached it, but there was no sound in it either, although he rushed in and staggered over a drunken man on the dirty floor, who had unbelted pants, a ghastly white complexion, and looked as if he had been knocked down, for there was a scratch of blood by his mouth.

Shadows sat on bright enamel bowls, too, and Aaron backed out. He backed all the blocks to the other toilet, and it again took him hours and hours, and he began to doubt that he would ever reach it and then reached it, and the stench was gone, and business-suited men loitered inside, and a hand pointed to an empty booth, and a voice warned him to stay away from the other toilet.

He unhooked his belt and started to unbutton his fly when veined hands grabbed for him. He slapped the hands and jumped out of the booth and knocked the charging shadow out with a smashing right cross and felt its powerful jolt in the bone socket of his shoulder.

A rose bloomed on his flexed bicep, but none of the shadows on the bowls accepted his challenge, and he turned to leave.

Several pairs of violently swinging doors blocked him and the shadow was behind him again. But he was no longer afraid, and he timed the doors, jumped through them with neat co-ordination, and climbed another flight of stairs.

Splinters from the rough flooring of an old stage hurt his bare feet, and he discovered that a nude boy sat on a toilet seat upon the stage, facing a dark auditorium, with an older woman, whose naked breasts sagged down to her stomach, on one side of him and a teen-age girl, with pale nipples, on the other.

Shrieking laughter.

Rows of teeth fenced the ridged roofs of their gaping mouths.

The wooden toilet partitions were only waist high and the three nudes could see each other. The water closets were suspended in the air above the seats, and rusty chains with wooden handles hung down by each sitter and were connected to a green, corroded wire, which connected all of the water closets and they could all be flushed together.

All of the seats in the theater were empty, then suddenly filled with naked teen-age boys and girls. The boys' laughter, counterpointed by the shrieks of the girls, exploded in the huge hall and waves of air pressure buffeted Aaron's nude body. He saw that an extension wire ran from the water closets out above the audience, and a toilet chain hung low enough from it for members of the audience to reach up and flush the toilets.

A hoarse chanting then rose from the audience and began to increase in noise and tempo like a football yell, and it took him a while to get accustomed to the sounds and to grasp that the nudes on the stage were having a contest and that he could look at the girl when she went but not at the older woman, for she was a mother.

He tried to make out the features of the girl and the woman, for they were vaguely familiar. But they both turned their faces away from him, and he started to tiptoe out in front to get a better look at them when he stopped in horrified shame.

Hideous grunts came from the woman's twisted mouth, and she strained so harshly that all the muscles in her body swelled, her face turned a livid red, and her eyes bulged out. Finally, she farted, let go with a loud splash, and gave a deep, baying moan of relief.

The entire audience clapped their hands over their heads and ducked their heads between their knees, then sat up with the synchronized movement of a formation of soldiers, and began to giggle.

The giggling grew louder and louder and louder until it

reached the roar of hysterical laughter, and at its very peak, a thin wan-fleshed boy jumped up and grabbed the handle of the toilet chain.

He lifted it high in his clenched fist with an exaggerated, slow movement of his arm, gritted his teeth in a struggle to control either laughter or sobs, jerked the handle down, and snapped the chain and the extension wire into a loud rattle and a vibrating hum—a hum which sounded above the wild laughter and above the crash of water in the flushed toilets.

# Part Four
# King's X

# King's X

## I

Rushing water crashed on Aaron's skull and pounded into a laughing, shrieking, whistling, constantly increasing crescendo until he awoke, threshing about, to the get-up whistle, threw the covers back, hurried to the washroom, lifted his nightgown, and dropped upon the cold horseshoe of a toilet seat.

He sat with the skirt of his nightgown hoisted around his waist, bunched in his lap, his feet chilled by concrete, and his sight swimming with sleep. He relieved his aching bowels and relaxed, but the rising fumes revived the nightmare, that baying moan of relief, that mother who sat as he sat, who . . .

Stall walls shut him into his own stink.

Light winked from a porcelain washbasin.

He wiped himself with disgust and did not look in the toilet when he flushed it.

He would not look in the steamed mirror above the washbasin, either. He even avoided the misty reflection of the nude light bulb in it, and tried to splash the memory of the grunting mother out of his head with cold water. He failed and stared at the running water as it whirlpooled to the top of the bowl, rather than look at any of the boys who were crowding into the washroom around him. But the animal sounds of blown noses, the trickle of urine in the trough, the flushed toilets, the growl of a mouth getting ready to spit out a lunger were so nauseatingly real that he took a deep breath, held it, and plunged his head into the water.

The cold shock tightened his skin. He opened his eyes and rolled them. The white basin tilted and waved. His eyeballs chilled, smarted, and warmed with their own moisture when he closed his lids. Water sighed, sleepily, in his ears. But his ears popped with suction when he straightened up and the bellow of noise woke him completely.

He ran his fingers through his hair, still staring at the bowl, grasping why people chose suicide by drowning, then pulled the rubber plug, stepped away from the washbasin, bumped into the first boy in line behind him, and walked with a dripping face and a haunted mind into the dormitory, where he was repelled by each nervous tic of Barneyway's wiry body as it dressed facing the locker, by each quick peek over the shoulder of the timid eyes, by the fingers that worried so hopelessly over a single button, by a toe that took two, *two,* worthless tries to slip into a sock.

At his own locker, he tried to rub the memory of the squatting mother away with his towel and rubbed so hard his face burned. But she sat on the bed when he fixed it, although she left no imprint. She sat close to the locker when he put his uniform on, and she sat next to him when he put on his shoes. She was in the mirror when he combed his hair. And she was in his head when he stood for count. She sat there, grunting, straining in his brain. Mothers did . . . they did . . . Mothers did . . . shit! And he winced and ducked his head, flattening his foreneck with his chin.

"What's the matter, man?" Dominic asked.

"Nothing. Nothing," Aaron answered, and held tightly to the foot railing of his bed for count.

"Don't let the Buzzer's show last night throw yuh," Dominic said, and Aaron didn't reply, for he was quite willing to let Dominic believe anything in order to avoid an explanation of what was really wrong.

And although furrows of concern creased Dominic's brow, he kept the festering cause of his anguish to himself throughout the march to the mess hall, through the gantlet of the food counter, with its irritating clash of trays, pans and silverware, and safely into the obnoxious slurping sounds of a small army of boys at breakfast.

"Look, man. I know you're bumkicked over your buddy. But you gotta have something in your belly. You can die in a place like this. Nobody'll notice. Drink some chocolate, anyway."

Aaron picked up the cup and let a mouthful of the warm slightly-bitter liquid glove his tongue, swallowed it, and then repeated the useless act. But he let a swallow linger and cool in his mouth once, started to consider why, and the mother took shape again. He then set the cup down and tried to respond to Dominic's attempts to cheer him up.

He heard Dominic say that it was Saturday, that there was no work, and that they were free to enjoy themselves. But his eye kept drifting back to the cup, back to the cup, back to the cup until he noticed a small piece of cooled chocolate clinging to its lip like coughed-up phlegm.

The piece was nauseating and yet he kept looking at it.

He listened to Dominic and still he looked at it.

He turned his head and looked back at it.

He turned his body and sneaked a glance at it over his shoulder.

Finally, he forced himself to pick up the cup and drink the piece down to get it out of his sight, but shook his head with distaste when it slid down his throat.

"I told yuh to *forget* the Buzzer and your buddy," Dominic said. "Now, let's get out of here."

Chocolate drowned the words of denial in Aaron's mouth, but still willing to let Dominic misunderstand, he swallowed and, without speaking, followed Dominic outside, only to be confronted by the timid hump of Barneyway's back a few feet from the doors.

He guessed that Barneyway had not eaten, since he and Dominic were the first to leave the table, and heedless of Dominic's well-meant but misconceived instructions, he tried to care about Barneyway's plight, and think about the danger-ous cost of caring.

He tried to imagine a broken nose, black eyes, maybe a gang stomping, maybe a . . .

But the coarse hairs which V'd, imperfectly, down the back of the neck into the blue collar struck him as being such a pitiful sign of weakness, of . . . the squatting mother reap-peared with Barneyway's face.

"There's gonna be boxing matches behind the gym quick, *Aaron*," Dominic said, with unmistakable meaning.

The clear blue of the morning sky heightened the luster of Barneyway's eyes.

"Let's me and you kill time till then walking around, *Aaron*," Dominic said and walked a few steps in the direction of the gym.

"Let's go, Barneyway," Aaron said, looking squarely into his eyes, ignoring Dominic, trying to prove to himself that he did care.

"I gotta get a book outta the library," Barneyway said, squinting at Aaron, but glancing at Dominic. The lie as obvious as the groove the squint made in the bridge of his thick nose.

"Come on, man. Come on with me."

"I gotta get a book."

"I want 'cha to go, man."

Barneyway plucked at the front of his shirt as if there were lint on it and ignored the plea.

"Let's make it," Dominic said, and Aaron hesitated, feel-ing that he had a right to leave because he asked Barneyway to go with him, yet wanting to support his friend, even if he could see no worthwhile reason for either fighting or winning, and he stalled, hoping for some alternative to occur, for some kind of compromise to present itself.

But Barneyway picked a piece of lint from his shirt and pretended to study it, and, as the woman reappeared, Aaron started after Dominic.

"Yuh gotta forget about that guy's problems," Dominic said, "and start thinking about the good things that are happening. Think about those good bouts that are gonna go on real quick."

Dominic's descriptions of the great fights he had seen behind the gym, and the buildings and trees and figures they passed, and the paths they followed on a long, rambling walk around the main grounds were no more than background for Aaron's recurring nightmare visions—visions which fused with the background into that final, horrifying scene on the old wooden stage, with that mother grunting and straining and turning a livid red.

He also found, as they walked, that whenever he let his gaze rest on a particular spot, a tree trunk, a bleacher, a compound bench, his idling mind conjured up a picture of the mother that was hard to shake because it in turn affected the rest of his thinking and his body, too, and his chest felt as empty as his stomach, and not one of the things he thought he believed in seemed worth a kicked-in rib.

Groups of boys all rushing in the same direction disturbed him as badly as the shadowy shapes of the nightmare, and he tried to blame the phenomenon on his imagination when Dominic suggested they cut across the visitors' lawn for the fights at the gym.

He then attempted to rush away from his tortured thoughts, caught himself, and tried to pace himself, but it was difficult for him to make each step reach only as far and take only as much time as Dominic's steps because Dominic leaned back as if someone were pushing at his waist and kicked his feet forward with a loose-ankled and confident nonchalance.

The pace grew harder to control as they drew nearer to the gym and his desire grew to forget all his problems in the excitement of a boxing match; it became almost impossible to control when he glimpsed the white ring apron, a corner post, and the bristling yellow ropes. And the sight of a hundred or more boys standing around the ring behind the gym, shouting for two colored boys, who were stripped to the waist and who pounded away at each other in a wild slugging match, so excited him that his yells of encouragement, his shouted instructions to the fighters attracted attention even before he and Dominic reached the top of a hillock.

"Right hand 'im! Right hand 'im! he yelled to the crouching boy because the tall guy carried his left hand low.

"Jab-jab-jab! Machinegun 'im!" he called to the tall guy because the shorter boy charged in and didn't punch until he had rammed his shoulder into the tall guy's stomach.

Throughout the round he wanted to jab for one and throw the overhand right for the other, and only the ring of a rusty bell and the crowd's applause quieted his cries and caused him to notice the humorous shake of Dominic's head.

The sweating black bodies of the two boys disappeared below the ring in a blanket of blue dungaree, patched here and there by the white uniform of a guy from the kitchen crew. There was an anxious lull as the crowd waited for the next bout to begin. Faces tilted toward the empty ring, patient, quiet. But when several minutes passed and no boxers climbed through the ropes, a restless milling began, and the squatting figure reappeared in the very center of the ring, the sun spotlighting her sagging, tremulous breasts, her straining attempts to win the contest, and Aaron turned to Dominic, trying to rid himself of it.

"Everything's okay, man," Dominic said. "Enjoy yourself."

But his face wrinkled into a perplexed scowl and Aaron had to turn away to hide his self-pity.

"Be back," Dominic said, and, without explanation, he began to push through the crowd. His curly head threaded its way to the ring apron, talked to the khaki cap of a man there. A tattooed arm reached up and dropped a blue shirt upon the apron. Both of Dominic's arms reached back, elbows uppermost, and his T-shirt waved like a flag. Then he climbed up the steps, through the ropes, and frowned as the man tied his gloves.

Feathers of anxiety for Dominic fluttered in Aaron's stomach as a stringy-muscled colored guy, stripped to the waist, black flesh rippling with highlights, climbed into the ring and waited for the man. But Aaron was more scared by the large audience, by the risk of getting badly whipped in front of so many people than by the colored guy, a beating itself, or the fact that there was no matching of weights between the boxers.

The bell rang and the two boys circled each other. Aaron crouched with Dominic, head down, heavy chin tucked into the thick mat of hair on his chest, massive shoulders and arms covering his face and belly, built of stone.

The colored guy moved in and jabbed twice. The second jab caught Dominic with a soft pat on the forehead, and he charged like a street fighter, with little strategy, but so carefully concealed behind his guard that all of the guy's punches bounced harmlessly off him.

In close, he threw a barrage of roundhouse hooks with blurring speed and drove the guy, staggering, toward the ropes. But the guy kept sticking out a long jab, gamely trying to keep Dominic away, trying to get enough room between them to use his long arms to advantage. But Dominic kept driving inside, and, in anger, the guy tried to shove him back with both of his gloves, pushed at the charging body, exposed his head, caught three punches in succession, fell **back** against the ropes and dropped to his knees.

Aaron cheered with the crowd until his voice was hoarse, cheered until the half-conscious boy was helped down the stairs and until the last of the applause finally trailed off, then clapped by himself for a few seconds, and then stalked around the ring with Dominic, shared the victory of that indifferent conqueror, who waited for a challenger, while taking deep breaths to catch his wind, sweat glistening in a knobby line down his backbone and sheening the matted hair on his chest.

Occasional shouts and claps of admiration broke the slow passage of the accumulating minutes until Dominic, well rested, stopped by a red post, and placed his gloves on the upper rope, as if offering proof they were only gloves.

But nobody challenged him.

He stalked about the ring once more, swinging his arms, loosening up, and stopped by the red post again.

Nobody challenged him.

He placed his gloves on his hips and shook his handsome head in amused disgust.

Still nobody challenged him, and Aaron was proud, for Dominic was a duke and they were buddies.

But a beckoning, curving gesture of Dominic's arm bewildered him. Dominic then lifted the top strand of the ropes and beckoned again, and all faces turned toward the hillock and a murmur of disbelief and amusement arose from them and rippled over Aaron in embarrassing waves.

Dominic beckoned again, smiled, and Aaron, with his eyes fixed on the ring post, started down the hillock. Boys fell back and made a straight path to the ringside for him, where— dwarfed by the khaki figure of the man—he took off his dungaree shirt and climbed up the steps and through the ropes with trembling legs.

He shoved his hand into the padded tunnel of a glove, but he was so nervous his thumb caught in a wrist fold and he had to withdraw his hand and reinsert it. He dug down into the glove's folds again until his fingers pressed against its tip and curved around a bar of padding. The familiar smell of sweat-worn leather soothed him a little, and when the laces were tied on both gloves, his wrists bound, and his fists snugged into compact balls, he was able to fall, without thought, into his habit of loosening up before the bell.

He hopped up and down on the canvas mats, conscious of their seamed dips and creases, dropped into a squat and bounced up, did it again, kicked his legs, cracked his knee joints, shuffled around the ring throwing mock punches, walked around swinging first one arm and then the other in windmill motions, stopped and spun his head in dizzy circles on the ball socket of his neck, reversed the spin, stood stock-still for a moment to allow his head to clear, and got stage fright all over again.

"Take it easy, champ," Dominic said, walking past, speaking out of the corner of his mouth. "Just a workout. Just a workout."

But the bell turned him around with his guard up and froze Aaron's attempt at a smile. He couldn't even feel his legs, didn't know if he moved, saw a formidable shape shuffle toward him, saw a purple glove reach out . . . but tap his glove in a symbolic handshake, and all his fear was gone.

He circled Dominic without a trace of stage fright, with confidence in his classical boxing style, with his trunk erect, elbows against his midriff, upper arms hugging and protecting his body, forearms two parallel gateposts, knobbed by clenched gloves, face a beveled incline from his brow to his chin, hidden between his chest and left shoulder.

He shuffled forward gracefully, feinted a jab at Dominic's head, dropped into a jackknife over his right hip, stuck the jab with a "pat-pat" into Dominic's gut, and skipped lightly backwards on his toes, easily evading Dominic's ponderous, tanklike shuffle. He heard the crowd murmur and knew he looked good, for countless afternoons in a professional gym watching Stanley and other fighters train and the experience of boys' club bouts had produced what the pros called "class." He felt good, too. The man approved. Stanley would approve. John and his father and even his mother would have approved.

Two light jabs slapped against his gloves, told him the bout was really for fun, and he took advantage of the slow withdrawal of the last jab and jabbed quickly back, alternated with a jab to the face and a second jab to the stomach again, which went way in, surprised.

Dominic smiled.

Aaron smiled.

They circled.

He moved around until his face and body were in shadow and the sun was in Dominic's eyes.

They circled again, and Dominic bore in behind a spearing jab, throwing it three, four, five times, trying to corner Aaron, catching him twice with glancing blows to the head, missing the rest, but forcing Aaron to dance away.

He zigzagged to confuse Dominic. His brogans barked against the mat. The crowd murmured again.

Moving in, he feinted a jab at Dominic's face and sunk a hard right hand under the heart. It popped when it connected and Dominic's elbow slapped in a reflex action against his side.

He nodded in approval, bore in again, caught Aaron against the ropes, and rallied with four, five, six, seven punches, wouldn't let up, forced Aaron to fall inside the punches, forehead against the matted chest, leather burning one eye, nose stinging, the copper taste of blood on his lip, the shouts of the crowd in his ears.

He shoved with all his strength until he felt Dominic start pushing back. Then, with one movement, he leaned to his side, hooked a glove under Dominic's left elbow, pulled Dominic toward him, and spun the husky body past him into the ropes, jabbed to keep Dominic off balance, and skipped out into the middle of the ring.

But Dominic came on, caught Aaron with a jab again and went into another rally: no bombs, just grazing punches. The smacking leather didn't hurt and Aaron liked the burning contact.

He fell into a huddle again, and when the rally slowed and stopped, he cut loose with both hands to Dominic's belly and a left hook around Dominic's guard to the chin, jarred it, twisted the mouth open.

Dominic shoved him back, held him at arm's length, caught him with a good right hand to the head and forced him to fall inside, where he clinched by pinning Dominic's gloves under his arms.

Dominic tried to pull them free, couldn't, smiled.

"Hah!" Aaron said, victoriously, and let go.

They broke, circled each other for long seconds, each trying to figure a way to pierce the other's guard. Aaron knew Dominic was too tired from the two rallies to try bulldozing right away, but he, himself, was too tired and wise to risk slugging. He knew what Dominic's superior weapons were and respected them. The job of the mock warfare was to use his own weapons to Dominic's disadvantage, without any attempt to hurt and with no expectation of getting hurt.

He hopped in with a left jab to the face and a hook to the ear, skipped back out again, smiling, and danced around the ring as Dominic, smiling, chased him.

Feet scraped loudly against the mats. Breath was heavy. Gloves weights. Aaron's T-shirt was damp and clinging to him, but they kept stalking each other. Aaron connected with the cleaner, snapping punches, and Dominic caught him in close with more clubbing, inaccurate punches.

They both showed their fatigue and threw fewer and fewer punches, and they were in the middle of an exchange, in which they more mauled and shoved each other than punched, when the bell rang, and they threw their arms around each other's shoulders and circled the ring to catch their breaths, to the prolonged clapping of the crowd.

Sweat streaked down Aaron's winded body. He wanted to throw the heavy gloves down and jerk his hot T-shirt off. But he felt good, really good, for the first time since he had been in the institute.

A swell of clapping greeted him at every corner and carried him to the next corner and to the next swell of clapping. And when they had circled the ring once, Dominic raised Aaron's arm as the winner. And the clapping exploded with cheering yells. And there was no longer any mother, no nightmare, no Buzzer, no, not even Barneyway.

## II

The phonograph on the chapel porch played a swing band accompaniment to Aaron's swaggering march through the crowd on the chapel lawn, to the nods of respect from colored guys, the grinning hellos from Mexicans, and the waves of white hands. But unlike Dominic, whom he followed and whose powerful shoulders served as a natural ballast for a muscular torso, his shoulders jerked and floated like half-inflated balloons upon the strings of his arms, and his swagger was a twisting motion of his body alone.

"This is Jenson, man," Dominic shouted over the blare of the loud-speaker, propped on the top porch step. "This is Aaron, Jenson," introducing him to the blond guy from the dorm with the hooded eyes.

"Champ, you mean," Jenson said without warmth, although the slitted mouth suggested a sullen compliment.

He lifted the speaker to the porch, turned it, muting the blare of the music, stepped down the stairs and reached for Aaron's hand.

"Champ! Kicked Dominic's ass today."

The twinge of pain from his bunched knuckles reminded Aaron that Jenson got up at five in the morning to milk cows, and that he didn't see Jenson until they had lined up for lunchtime count at the dairy.

Frosted blue eyes glanced approval to Dominic.

"He goes," Dominic said, and Aaron was too flattered to work his numbed fingers.

"What-a-ya wantta hear? Pick it, man," Jenson said and stepped back up the stairs to the record's final strains.

"Some jazz, man. Something that jumps. I don't wantta be sad."

"Go ahead, Tiger," Dominic said and chuckled, and the scowling furrows and lines of his face softened, and Aaron wished it could always look as relaxed and then began to believe that this was possible.

For he was getting a rep. Guys treated him with respect. Every word was a tribute and sounded like fine jazz. The grunting mother in the nightmare was like a scene in a black-and-white movie that he had already seen twice and no longer scared him. And neither the Buzzer nor Barneyway seemed much of a problem since Dominic had consented to let Barneyway play shadow to them, for Dominic was a duke, and when you ran with a duke, guys treated you good.

"Hey, man. How about 'The Seventh Street Boogie'?" Jenson asked, slipping the record onto the felted pad of the turntable, and he began to snap his fingers in two-beat time before the solitary bass of the piano began its climbing roll.

A solo left hand straddled the keys, took a key's step with the thumb, followed by the ring finger, and made its rocking way up and then down the bass, once, and, then, twice before Ivory Joe Hunter's black right hand began to pick with one finger at the keyboard in a counterpointing melody, played coquette with it for a couple of bars or so and jumped into the music with all five fingers, followed by the brass, rhythm, and strings of the whole rocking band.

Aaron's response was a tap of his foot to the solo left hand, the nodding of his head to the climbing bass, the snapping of his fingers as the left hand started up for the second time, and then the swaying of his entire body in accompaniment to the counterpointing melody; and when the whole rocking band joined in and started blowing away at the repeated, pulsating, vibrating, beating melody, he thanked Jenson with the vital, charging heat of his blood, with the rhythmical sway of all his loosened bones, with the tingling energy that swept over his entire body, with joyous visions of a hundred spontaneous dance floors, between the counter stools and the tables in a hundred cafés, in which a hundred tight-skirted girls boogied toward him through the shimmering colors of jukebox rainbows with snapping hips and shaking breasts.

"Go, Joe, go!" he shouted, and Barneyway started clapping his hands in time from his seat on the bottom stair. Several boys joined him. More boys stood and started tapping their feet. The boogie got louder and more wicked. A couple of guys started snapping their hips. Soon, all the guys were standing, tapping, shuffling, rocking, and Aaron was surrounded by a rhythmic bobbing of heads, a blue sway of bodies. Everybody was great, was a superman, a great pachuco, a boogie-woogie rocker, a King Kong Duke, with a thousand broads waiting for him at the gate, and there wasn't no man, no institute, no mothers, no fathers, no outs, no misery, no blues, nothing but boogie, boogie, boogie!

"It's 'The Seventh Street Boogie.' Yeah! Yeah!

"It's 'The Seventh Street Boogie.' Yeah! Yeah!"

A chubby colored kid began to soft-shoe down the sidewalk toward the porch, sanding his rubber soles upon the concrete with the easy swish of wire brushes on a snare drum. The sound captured Aaron and held his inspired attention before the swaying boys cleared the walk and he recognized Buckshot.

Buckshot's fat body rolled forward with effortless steps, fat belly and plump butt quivering with dancing jazz. He hopped into the air when the bass of the piano neared its lowest depth, seemed to hang suspended for a moment with one knee bent against his chest, balanced on the toe's tip of the outstretched leg, then stomped his foot in mock anger right on time with the final bass note.

"Yeeeeeeeeeaaaaaaaaaah!" the crowd chorused.

"Yeah! Yeah! Yeah!" Aaron cried, dancing every step with Buckshot, anticipating every graceful quiver and effortless roll; and when Buckshot raised up, with an arrogant expression on his face, one eyebrow arched in a mocking, feminine manner, tan cheeks sucked in, lips pursed in a cupid-bow kiss, little pinkie beckoning, beckoning, the back of a hand on the hump of an out-flung hip, a sardonic smile playing over his pursed lips, brightening the brown eyes, he jelly-assed with him in a mincing, knock-kneed gait closer to the porch and called out:

"Boogie, baby, boogie!

"Boogie, boogie, boogie."

The piano rolled down deep again, and when it reached its lowest notes, Buckshot hopped into the air again, brought his right foot down with terrific force, but stopped it a scant inch from the walk, and gently tapped his toe.

"Go ahead, baby! Go ahead! Go ahead!" Aaron cried, sharing that immense and beautifully controlled power.

And as the brass joined in again, and a wild trumpet began to solo with shrill authority, Buckshot threw his hands in the air, scattered his fingers, and rocked up the walk with tight legs, top-heavy in the head, still sanding, his whole body quivering with exalted joy, his eyes as moist as melting chocolate, his mouth open in a silent cry of ecstasy.

"Take us with you, Buckshot! Take us with you!"

But when the band settled down to a journeyman's beat, he began to sand like a train chugging up a track: bent back, bent kneed, head down, and double fisted. His lips puffed out. His eyes chinked. He became the man!

"Ooooooooooooh, Buckshot! Ooooooooooooh, Buckshot! Tell us like it is! Tell us! Tell us!"

He hopped into the air again and came down on the sidewalk with a loud smack, hopped up again, and came down harder, and as the band swung into a roaring, rocking jazz climax, he did it again and again, his face a mask of brutal anger and confident, self-righteous power.

"Kill those punks, Buckshot! Kill 'um! Kill 'um!"

Buckshot then jumped high in the air with the final, blaring measure, inspired by the cries, both knees tucked, and came down on the bottom step with all his weight and the explosive force of his heavy brogans in perfect time with the final beat.

"Yeah! Yeah! Yeeeeeeeeeeaaaaaaaaaaah!"

Hand clapping smothered the final yells and pattered off in the upsurge of happy conversation, the shifting of the pleased crowd toward the porch, and a melancholy blues number. And, panting, tan cheeks balls of sweat, Buckshot sat down on the stair between Barneyway and Aaron.

"You were great," Aaron said.

"Thanks, man," Buckshot said and, turning to see who had spoken, recognized Aaron. "Say, man, you were pretty great yourself this morning. I wouldn't have believed you could go like *that!* You're a future pro champ, man. You made this bad Dominic look easy."

He jabbed a finger at Dominic, who leaned against the banister.

"Little man make you go, huh?"

"Go-go!" Dominic said.

"Little man make your broad, too, if you ain't sharp," Buckshot warned.

"I'll make your mama, if you ain't careful," Dominic countered, but without anger.

"I'd make your mama, but you ain't got no mama," Buckshot said, leaning back on the stairs, exposing a sweat line under the gleeful expanse of his double chin, and thin slashes of facial shadow made Dominic's silence seem threatening until he rhymed his challenge:

"Now if you wantta play the dozens / let's have some fun. / But I gotta dozen caps / for just your one."

"You can't cap me," Buckshot said, " 'cause I come from way down West, / down by Third and Pine, / just as close as I can get / to the railroad line."

Aaron saw yellow SP buildings, rusty tracks, and the soot and grime that coated the old wooden houses at the foot of Pine Street in West Oakland. But although the cap was good and made him want to join the fun, he couldn't help thinking that Pine Street, which was the roughest, toughest borderline by the bay among pachucos, was a good street to be *from* not to live *on*.

Dominic had evidently expected a cap on his mama and he hesitated, and Aaron joined the contest, proud that his own neighborhood was on the opposite side of West Oakland, near town, proud that the tall, old buildings were owned and cared for by the people who lived in them, proud, too, that there was only a scattering of colored people, none of them poor.

"I do my living up on Fourteenth Street, / on the corner of the block where the best streets meet."

Buckshot offered Aaron some skin, and Dominic leaned down and slapped his palm to welcome him into the game, and Jenson joined in from the porch with a singsong bass: "Now you cats act / like a bunch of paddies, / got no mamas, nor daddies, / yeah!"

"Yeah! yourself, Big Jenson, / go hide your head / 'cause

your mama's getting laid / on top your bed," Dominic countered, and they all laughed as Jenson covered his face.

Two boys on opposite sides of the porch fired a volley of their own partly memorized, partly ad-libbed caps at each other, and Aaron ducked his head and covered his ears and pretended he didn't want to get caught in it, but he hoped somebody would throw a cap at him so he could get back in the game.

A small crowd began to gather as Jenson spun the record into a revolving wheel above his head, caught it without touching its grooves, put a longer playing disk on the turntable, turned the volume of the speaker down to background level, and took up Dominic's taunt.

They exchanged caps two or three times until they ran out of verses, and Buckshot, with his twisted copper curls, chose Aaron; but before Aaron could answer, the slurred drawl of a colored kid from the South put Buckshot down, and a pockmarked white kid put him down, and another boy put him down, and the lawn became a no man's land of dirty caps. The crowd shouted at good caps, laughed at funny ones, and jeered and moaned at poor ones.

A nudge of Buckshot's knee at a cap made Aaron laugh. He'd laugh at a poor cap, although he might moan, too. He'd laugh and shout at a good cap, and he'd laugh in expectation before a cap was finished. For the dozens was dirty kicks, nothing counted, nothing was sacred, nobody had to be afraid or get mad, everything was for fun, for freezies: king's X and kick right back.

The free-for-all was at its peak—guys were interrupting each other, guys were speaking at the same time, trying to finish a cap which another guy had started, stopping, laughing at their own attempts—when the Buzzer and Rattler appeared on the outskirts of the crowd with two guys from the kitchen.

The weasel-faced blond guy was slouched over in a pachuco pose, pretending he was tough. Aaron despised him, suspecting him of joining in the classroom taunts. He had learned his name was Bobby Shuck and that the big Mexican guy with him was called Boomby and was duke of the kitchen. Dark pimple specks spread over Boomby's brown cheeks as if he were smiling, but his mouth was set and mean; and although Aaron was sure he was involved in the classroom hassle, too, he feared him.

The Buzzer rested his knuckles on the humps of his butt, and Rattler's mouth was a sharp crescent beneath the tattooed cross.

Words dribbled slowly to a stop. There was a long pause in which all heads turned toward them, in which Jenson picked up the phonograph arm, held it between his fingers, and which he finally ended by setting the arm down on another record.

The music began with the low, harmonious and consoling orchestrations of Glenn Miller, but Rattler broke into it with his throaty voice, pointed a knobby finger at Barneyway, and used a stock verse known by everyone:

"I saw your mutha down on Seventh and Pine / selling her pussy for a bottle of wine."

Saxophones throbbed to the pulses of Aaron's heart, and no one spoke, for Rattler was playing dirty—not by what he said but how he said it. Aaron then leaned forward to see around Buckshot's plump body and to prompt Barneyway to come back with a happy cap, save the game, and put Rattler down by treating the attack as a joke.

He was certain the large eye in profile could see him. But Barneyway only rubbed his hands on his dungarees, and Aaron slid to the very edge of the step, trying to force an answer, for his own prestige was at stake, too. Any cap would do for answer. But Barneyway had to answer!

"Hee-hee! This boy can't talk. Hee-hee!"

Rattler posed in an exaggerated slouch, dungarees pulled down below his hips, baggy seated, shirt unbuttoned.

"Maybe he ain't got no mama?" the Buzzer said. "Now a

man that'll run when his mama is called, / will suck on a dick if its balls are bald."

A blush ballooned Barneyway's face, seemed to set it afloat, rising and lifting his body with it into an erect position. He stuttered, stopped, mouth open, struggled to answer, stuttered again, and closed his mouth, and Aaron declared: "The Buzzer and Rattler think they're bad. / Good in a gang but alone they're had."

The figures of his enemies shimmered in the hot sun before him. Tiny wrinkles wormed over his tight chin. He heard the needle scratch as Jenson picked up the phonograph arm, getting ready for action, and in the quiet, he could feel the support of the crowd. It was a battle for himself alone now.

A confused babble broke from Rattler and the Buzzer, both speaking at the same time. Rattler stopped and the Buzzer repeated his verse: "Some little boys think they keen. / A bust in the mouth decide who mean."

Rattler added: "Some little boys need to be schooled. / If they keep actin' up, they gonna get cooled."

Arms loose and ready, they challenged Aaron and all eyes watched him. The whole scene flashed before him. He saw himself battling, throwing punches from a gang-fight crouch, maybe losing, maybe getting lots of help, maybe getting to see the Buzzer and Rattler and their two buddies smothered under an angry storm of boys. But he also saw the gray misery of the isolation cell, Big Stoop, and his own puffed face in the mirror. He saw himself as a loser, falling off the perch which he had climbed that morning and which was above most of his problems, and he said, coolly, trying to keep the battle on a speaking level:

"Everybody got a right to rhyme if he wants to. We were having fun until you guys got into it."

Worms wrinkled over his chin again as he tried to keep his face from showing fear. He didn't think he sounded chicken, although he was trying to keep out of a fight. But the Buzzer thought he was scared and called:

"Stand up, if you ain't a punk like you friend," and Aaron jumped to his feet, shouting:

"Don't call me no punk, Buzzer."

He shouted it again when the Buzzer started toward him, side-stepping and hopping with quick, broken movements through and over the squatting boys, unable to make progress because no one would make room, but advancing with the slow, unreal, and unescapable force of a phantom in a nightmare.

The muscles in Aaron's legs collapsed and he caught his breath, but in the catching found the courage to fall into a fighting crouch, and heard before the Buzzer had covered six feet—though he almost couldn't believe it—Jenson's deep voice, warning, ironic:

"Now you ain't going to try and punch on that boy? Are you, Buzzer? I thought the dozens were supposed to be fun? You ain't actin' like you're enjoying yourself."

The Buzzer slowed but kept moving, and Dominic said, "Lay off him, Buzzer. You started playing rough and he just gave you some rough talk back."

The Buzzer stopped, pink gums exposed by the angry working of his jaw, and Aaron felt the strength come back into his legs.

"Leave the little guy alone," someone said, and the Buzzer turned to see who it was, and Buckshot sang out: "Now let's have some dozens with plenty of rhyme, / 'cause we gotta do something to kill this time."

And all the boys started throwing caps at the Buzzer. He sneered as he tried to answer the first one, but another was thrown at him before he could get to the rhyme; he tried to repeat it but forgot the rhyme when a third cap was thrown at him; he tried a new cap but stuttered with a new challenge;

he didn't get to begin again before another cap hit him and another and another and another, and he finally gave up under a bombardment of taunts and jeers and laughter, and Jenson put on another jumping record, and Aaron spit at Barneyway's feet.

# Part Five
# Every Mutha's Son

# Every Mutha's Son

## I

Static crackled from the office loud-speaker and all conversation in every dorm, in every courtyard stopped. Jenson's eyes were bright blue and anxious. The shadow of the wire fence links made lopsided squares on his tense face. Dominic sat quiet and unconcerned on the compound bench. Aaron, between them, couldn't help an intake of breath as the loud-speaker squawked the lucky inmate's name, but he wasn't expecting a visit, for Sunday was a busy day in his father's restaurant, and he didn't freeze with hope as Jenson did. Nor could he sit with Dominic's stoic detachment, for he longed for the relief a visit could give him from his hatred of the Buzzer, which soured his stomach like heavy, undigested curds.

The warm afternoon air relaxed into waves of noise again, until the next announcement would stop all sound in the compounds and charge the atmosphere with expectation. But the placid blue of the sky was splotched with hatred for Aaron and even Jenson's excited talking failed to clear it.

"Now what would you guys be doing if it weren't for me?" Jenson said, not asking, telling, and boasting because he was happy, but reminding Aaron of his own attempts to sleep the idle morning away; to evade, in sleep, the Buzzer's constant threatening stare and the unhappy sight of Barneyway's morose solitude; to rid himself, in sleep, of that word that perfectly described Barneyway's failure in the dozens and the discomfort his own hatred of the Buzzer caused him.

"Both of you guys would be laying inside, bumkicked, if it weren't for me. Go on, admit it! Admit it!" Jenson said and thumped a short, chopping right hook into Aaron's ribs.

"Owww, man!" Aaron complained, hugging his side. "Alright, I admit it! I admit it!" he repeated, for Jenson had helped with his surprising and noisy enthusiasm, with his: "Come on, man, get pretty, get pretty. Shoes shined! Hair curled! Get those nasty duds off and put on your bonerues!"

Jenson had helped by pushing him, Aaron, off the bed, by shoving him to the washroom, by getting a clean uniform for him, by shining his shoes for him, and by singing in a bass voice, while keeping time with the shoe brush: "Gettin' pretty! Gettin' pretty!"

And Jenson had prodded Dominic into dropping the Sunday paper and changing clothes by punctuating his song with shouts of: "Come on, ugly. Join the party. Join the party, ugly."

Jenson had helped by exciting all the guys, and the smell of shoe polish had pervaded the dormitory, and Aaron had to see it to believe that boys in jail could get so concerned about their appearance: see them lined two and three deep in front of the washroom mirrors, combing and recombing their hair: see them pose for each other after they had finished dressing and ask each other for comments, their faces painful barometers of the criticism and approval: see them run nervous fingers down the makeshift pleats of their dungaree pants, smooth the blue wrinkles out of their shirt sleeves, and try not to bend their arms or sit down until they had met their visitors in their unblemished best.

Jenson had helped, but it was past, and he added now: "Be laying inside like that punk, Barneyway," and held his fist up, ready to punch again, and Aaron's ribs throbbed as guilt clamped like a tight cap on his skull.

For he sat on a bench in the sunshine between two bad-acting dudes, watching the Sunday visitors, while his best buddy, Barneyway, sat by himself in the dormitory, pretending to read a comic book, unwelcome, unable to join him, put down by everybody after the dozens. But inside his skull, guilt had a black face, guilt dragged out Dominic's word with gold teeth, drawled Buckshot's warning, and grunted like the mother; and Aaron wanted to smash it away but got hit by Jenson, instead, caught by surprise.

"Come on, man, get that sourpuss look off your pale face."

He sprang up and shot a right cross into Jenson's arm, and Jenson cocked his big fist at Dominic, held it for the preliminary squawk of the loud-speaker, and snapped it into Dominic's shoulder as the name crackled out; and Dominic jabbed Aaron in the thigh, while Aaron hammered Jenson just above the knee.

"Better, better, betterrrr. Jesus, look at that broad!"

A teen-age girl walked by with small steps, knees bound by a short, tight skirt with side splits, breasts poking to perfect points in a bright red sweater.

"Hello, baby," Jenson said, and her lipstick flared like shoestring bows over the corners of her smiling mouth. Penciled lines arched high over her shaved eyebrows, slanting her eyes and her coquettish glance, accentuating the tattooed beauty mark on her cheek. Her brown hair was a wild halo of fuzzy ringlets.

"Tell me that ain't sweet?" Jenson said, and Aaron dodged his next punch, disliking her beauty mark and shaved eyebrows, considering her and all the girls who swayed by in tight skirts and sweaters, with thick rolls of bobby-sox around their ankles, cheap. Girls were supposed to be sweet and cherry, not sharp and hard.

He resented the guys who swaggered by in finger-tip coats,

baggy-kneed drape pants, thick-soled stomping shoes, and duck-tailed Hollywood haircuts, too, for his own zoot suits hung unused in a dark closet.

The parents, who looked so poor, so washed out and gray, depressed him most of all, for all the men seemed to have on thin gabardine pants and cotton sportshirts, with wide collars winging over cheap sportcoats, and all the women seemed to wear flimsy dresses, which billowed shapelessly upon them.

The loud-speaker squawked more often and irritated him, also, for although he wasn't expecting and didn't want to expect a visit and could see most of the visitors as they arrived, he listened for the sound of his name with every announcement.

He searched for his father's Studebaker among the battered pre-war Fords and Chevies, which began to form an unbroken fence around the visitors' lawn on the hill, was disappointed, and shared a bitter and envious conspiratorial smile with Dominic and Jenson, when the Buzzer's real name, Oliver Wiley, was announced, and the Buzzer rushed out of the dormitory and across the courtyard with short, waddling steps.

Condemned to sit on a bench, while the guy he blamed for ruining even that small pleasure enjoyed a visit, Aaron made fun of the Buzzer's ugly walk, which was more of a waddle than a walk, and which, with the almost deformed protrusion of his buttocks and his efforts to hurry, made it appear as if he were wading through knee-high water instead of skimming over the hard surface of concrete and asphalt.

Aaron watched him until he disappeared in a crowd of visitors by the office, waited for him to reappear, worried that he had been lost, and, finally, caught sight of him among the groups on the lawn, leading a Negro couple dressed in black and a zoot-suited kid to a redwood table not far from the compound fence, where his mother's appearance fulfilled Aaron's most malicious hopes.

"Amen, boy, a-men," Mrs. Wiley said in a hoarse voice,

as she stepped nervously about, flapping the full sleeves of the black coat which overlapped her fat body to her thin shins.

"Praise thee Lord. Praise thee Lord," she said, fanning the air with a thick Bible, her puffy mumbling lips nearly touching the tip of her broad nose.

"Praise thee Lord," she said; and only the memory of his own mother, in a white cotton nightgown, standing in solitude and prayer, prayers which had a private meaning, kept Aaron from making sarcastic comments to Dominic and Jenson.

"Bless this boy, Lord. Bless this boy. Bless this boy," she said, her big wobbling buttocks swelling like pillows beneath the coat with her shuffling steps, yet steps which had a bird's quickness, steps which Aaron thought were weird and disliked and yet liked because the Buzzer's mother took them.

"Hush!" she said when Mr. Wiley reached out to restrain her, and the worn wrinkling highlights of his black sleeve vanished at her command, his bony face sagging down so that only the burrs of his hair showed.

"Hush!" she repeated, and the Buzzer's brother stopped preening, a smoothing finger pressed against an eyebrow, until he seemed sure she didn't mean him, then he pressed at his stiff, pomaded hair, brushed down the lapels of his fingertip coat, and searched for lint along the yellow pinstripes of his baggy knees.

"Hush!" she said again, although no one had spoken; and Aaron shared a wise glance with Dominic and Jenson: as bad as the Buzzer acted, his mother was the man!

"The Buzzer looks more like her than his skinny father, except she's fat," Dominic said and nudged Aaron, who joyfully punched Jenson, who nodded in agreement, then stood on the bench, stretched his long frame, stared for a moment, and smiled.

"I think I see my old man's Chevy," he said and pointed to a battered gray car, with a twisted front bumper, parked the wrong way in front of the office. "How'd he get up there?

Must be drunk? Probably is. Goes to bed with a bottle of whisky. Know he couldn't make it all the way up here from Frisco without stopping for a couple of drinks or a pint."

He started to say more but the loud-speaker crackled his name, and he jumped off the bench, into the air, shouting, "Go! Go! Daddy-o!" and trotted across the courtyard, slammed the gate, and made it up the hill within a minute, to the envious grins of both Dominic and Aaron.

Aaron grinned less with envy than distaste when he saw Jenson leading his parents about, searching for a place to sit down. Aaron grinned to pretend that he thought it was funny that Mrs. Jenson was drunk and had to keep one fleshless arm around Jenson's waist to keep her flat body from toppling over with every lock-kneed step. He grinned to hide his impatience with Jenson for not stopping in one of the clear lawn spaces and sitting her down. Then he grinned to hide his shock when Mrs. Jenson's clumsy steps made him realize she was lame, that she leaned on Jenson for support, and that they needed to find a bench for her.

He grinned to hide his shame for thinking the worst of a buddy's mother, and he grinned throughout the minutes it took her to reach the redwood table, where the Buzzer and his family sat. He grinned to hide his annoyance that they had picked a place where he could see her so well: the chopped edge of her straight blond hair, her heavy jaw, Jenson's nose hooking out from her gaunt face; and that the Buzzer was staring at her.

He grinned to pretend that he enjoyed Mr. Jenson's good humor, the sunburned cheeks flushed with booze and laughter, the open mouth, but he then grinned because he couldn't hear the laughter, although he leaned forward on the edge of the bench and tried to hear, and was going to blame the Buzzer and Mrs. Wiley for making too much noise, when he noticed that they were quietly watching Mr. Jenson laugh, too, and laugh silently, his limp red hair flattened over his broad forehead like a cap brim, while he filled two paper cups from a bottle in a brown bag. Aaron grinned readily then because Mr. Jenson was getting away with such an act and because he still couldn't hear any laughter when Mr. Jenson handed the cup to his son, although the solid belly swelled drum tight within the sport shirt and shook as if it would burst free from the wide leather belt.

Aaron grinned quickly at Jenson's guttural laughter, which carried over the cup into the compound, which stopped when Jenson took a tasting swallow, smacked his lips, and gulped down the drink, but which started again when he handed the cup back to his father, who filled it again and laughed without sound and kept laughing, without sound, as the paper cup passed back and forth between them several times, but only Jenson could be heard.

Aaron grinned, also, when he caught himself hunched over on the bench, peering through the wire links of the fence like a monkey watching the spectators at a zoo, but he was so embarrassed—for Jenson was his buddy and there could be no critical staring—that he avoided Dominic's eyes, and sat back, and started watching the other visitors again, and quit grinning altogether.

But the sun got hot, the waiting tiresome, and as the arriving visitors thinned to a trickle they began to look more and more alike; and his eyes began to drift back toward the Buzzer, toward his homely mother, his skinny father in his old-fashioned black suit, his flashy, zoot-suited brother; and he began to believe that the Buzzer had chosen that spot in front of the compound just to show off a visit and irritate him.

Yet, when Dominic announced that he was going inside and read the Sunday papers and waited for a reply, Aaron didn't answer and didn't move. For the thought of Barneyway lying inside on his bed, where there weren't even any visitors to offer a distraction from him, was more unwelcome than the presence of the Buzzer, who could also be hated. And Dominic gave a tired sigh and continued to sit, sleepy-eyed, upon the bench. And Aaron, screened by the fence and warmed by the sun, felt a drowsy melancholy settle, gradually, over him, too.

The squawk of the loud-speaker became distant and lonely, and the figures on the lawn took on the appearance of cutouts. He found that if he allowed his imagination to drift into fantasies in which the arriving visitors were coming to see him, the happiness of the greeting helped him to forget the presence of the Buzzer before him. But he discovered that this only worked if he concentrated upon his own feelings and thought of how happy he, himself, acted. For when he tried to imagine how his visitors would act, he only saw strangers through a wire fence and, immediately after, the Buzzer and his family, too, and, then, he had to wait for new visitors to pass by before he could make the attempt again.

A plump girl, in the crisp folds of a blue summer dress, who was drifting slowly into his fence-obstructed view, gave him a chance to pretend he was getting a visit from a girl. Then he pretended it was Judith and tried to picture himself embracing her, without really looking at her so as not to ruin his daydream. But her blond hair and straight legs looked familiar, and he sat up and, cupping his right eye with a fence link, tried to make out the girl's features and quiet the hope that fluttered in him.

But she walked with her head down, leaning slightly forward, one arm cradling a purse below her breast, the other drooping into the wide skirt as if the long walk from the main gate had tired her; and it wasn't until she looked up at the office and he saw the fine tip of her nose, as sharp as a pointing finger, and the delicate chin, nearly lost in plump flesh, that he called to her.

"Judith! Over here!"

Her features flattened as she turned from profile to full face, searching for him, and gave him such an immensely different impression of her that he had an unhappy intuition of disappointment, which became stronger as she walked toward him, with her head tilted, still unsure, although she grabbed impulsively at his fingers and hooked them in hers when she reached the fence.

"Go to the office," he said. "I can't leave the compound until they call my name."

She withdrew her fingers in a slow protest at his solemn greeting, but there was no question in the calm acceptance of her blue eyes, and she turned and walked away, without answering, but with a determined step and speed so out of character with her small size it pained him.

"She's pretty. She looks like a sweet chick, too," Dominic said.

Aaron nodded, but the compliment only heightened his sense of a contradiction in her features, and he kept her in sight, trying to detect something attractive about her figure, until she disappeared behind the screen door.

"Thanks," he replied after the door had closed, but kept it framed by a fence link, unwilling to consider anything but the unexpected and strangely saddening visit, waiting for her to reappear again.

"That's the kind of a girl to have. Most of these guys have broads that look like lays. I can see you don't go for flashy chicks."

"She's not my girl," Aaron said and, resenting the insinuation, he risked a glance over his shoulder at Dominic, but quickly framed the door in the link again, then, ashamed of his ingratitude, added, "But I like her a lot."

"You'd better *make* her your girl then," Dominic said in a voice so compelling that Aaron turned, truly astonished, and Dominic stepped to the fence and continued in a clipped tone:

"She only wears enough lipstick to pink her mouth. Don't wear no tight sex clothes either. That's a lot, man. She sure don't look like no bitch to me. Hold onto that girl, man. I wish I had one like her."

The static of the speaker gave Aaron an excuse not to answer, for no words could repay such a high compliment from Dominic; and his own feelings about the compliment were too mixed and confused to permit an honest reply, even thanks, so he tapped Dominic's stomach and started toward the gate before his name was announced, flattered, but also resentful over being told what to do.

Still, the compliment gave him a buoyant step, and he glanced through the gate with unconcealed conceit at the Buzzer, who, unhappily, didn't notice him, then increased his speed and walked with a still lighter step the closer he got to the office, where she waited for him, and where her appearance seemed all out of proportion to the neighborhood girl he had known and to the girl he had just seen in such a critical light.

He recognized the pale freckles scattered over her nose, but her hair curled into a page-boy on her shoulders, which disconcerted him, for it made her seem older and prettier; and he wondered if her beauty was caused by jail or Dominic's compliment or both, then discounted it to prevent more disappointment.

He did return her smile and he did take her hand when she held it out, but he didn't hold it too tightly for fear its warmth would have an effect on him, and he was tempted to touch the freckles and put his finger on a flaw he was certain of and, therefore, couldn't possibly hurt him.

Her voice had a tremor in it, too, which he tried to blame on his own nervousness and, thereby, deny the emotion it caused in him; and he became angry at Dominic for influencing him when they began to stroll along the road and he noticed that her breasts were larger, for he was sure two months could not make such a difference.

But a single glance at the small double chin, which propped up the fragile point of her real chin, was so vivid and so familiar, such proof that he wasn't imagining or exaggerating the appearance of her features, or their beauty, he became self-conscious about how *he* must look to others.

He saw himself, unhappily, as a thin black-haired boy in reform school dungarees, shorter than this pretty girl by an inch or two, yet her boyfriend to anyone who might notice, and, embarrassed, he saw that she was embarrassed, too, and he feared for the same reason. For they walked along the road like sweethearts when they were only good friends, and he almost let go of her hand but discovered a private space on the lawn and led her quickly to it.

The wide skirt of her dress belled over her tucked legs. She waited for him to speak as if she could sense the strain he was under. He plucked at the strands of grass that formed the shadowed outline of his crossed legs, getting a secret if slight satisfaction from his polished brogans and his clean gray socks, but so thoroughly confused he couldn't think of anything to say. For Dominic's compliment had undermined his critical view of her and made him vulnerable to her. And she would sit on the lawn before him for only a short time, and the small imprint she would leave on the grass would ripple quickly out of existence, and he hated the Buzzer with all the suffering that was in him for an intense moment.

He snapped the moment with a strand of grass. He bit on the strand. He ground it between his teeth. He sucked the bitter juice and tasted it as he asked:

"How's your mother? She let you come, huh?"

The color which glowed in Judith's cheeks pleased him as much as it hurt him, for it confirmed his expectations and guaranteed that they would not become too inflated.

"No?"

"I didn't tell her," she said. "You know how she is, Aaron."

"Do I!" he said, smirking, swallowing the grass juice, unable to forget the haughty greetings given the Spanish boy in the black drapes who dared to visit her daughter, by the handsome woman with the sharp features and the severe gray bun at the back of her head, and he added, trying to make a joke out of it:

"My name's a bad word at your house, huh?"

"Oh, it's not that bad, Aaron," Judith said, laying plump fingers on his hand.

"I told you in my letter that she went on one of her binges when she found out about my hiding the candy in the drain pipe at the detention home. She kept saying I was lucky the police hadn't picked me up and put me there, too. Then she said the whole neighborhood was talking about me and you, and that I'd not only ruin my reputation but drag her down, too, and if I didn't behave, she'd put me in the detention home herself. She got so carried away she had a drink and then started drinking and got so drunk I had to stay home from school for two days to take care of her. And now she's so ashamed of that she hasn't said anything at all about you. So it's not bad, but I can't bring it up now. I'll have to wait for the right chance."

"I don't blame her though," he said, awkwardly, but honestly, for his own family had stopped him from writing to a buddy who had been committed to Youth Authority, and he added and meant it: "I wouldn't want my daughter seeing some guy in a reform school."

"I blame her. But she'll come around as soon as she sees I really mean it and I can convince her that it was silly to send you away just because you got in a fight."

"Get her permission before you come again, huh?" he said, passing over the present but unspoken fact that his very first arrest had been for fighting over her, Judith. But his reasons included more than respect for a mother. He wanted to enjoy a visit that was really his. Whispered shouts through the yard cage at the DT were no fun, and the fear of withdrawal that plagued this visit kept him from believing in it and aggravated instead of soothed his deep resentment toward the Buzzer.

"Okay," she said, her bust rising with relief and reaching,

he believed, a remarkable size. "I promise. But what about you? Be real good, Aaron, so they'll let you come home quick."

"I'm trying to. I want to. But there's guys here that bother you," he said and stared down the sloping hill, searching for his enemy, and saw Mrs. Wiley waving her Bible over her head, and could distinguish her hoarse voice from the crowd's chatter, but couldn't see the Buzzer.

"Ignore them. You're smart enough. You've never let anybody lead you around, Aaron, or shove you around either."

"Nobody's shoving me around," he said, and found himself looking for the Buzzer again, and added, defensively: "Barneyway's here, too, you know."

"How's he? He's not hurt, is he?" she asked, her features puckering with concern, seeming to gather into the point of her nose, and he lied quickly:

"No!"

But he lied because of *her* worry and because the subject of the Buzzer could ruin his visit, and he purposely turned his back to the redwood bench.

"No, he's okay," he said, but her face grew piquant with disbelief, and he could see a question taking shape upon it, and he tore a handful of grass from the lawn and flicked the fluttering strands at her, whining: "Okayyyyy, little mother. Okayyyy. Okayyyyy."

She fell back, startled by his change of mood, then wiped the strands from her face and threw them at him. But they fell in his lap and she ripped some from the lawn and rubbed them in his face.

He ducked his head but let her do it, then grabbed her wrists, forced her hands back, and struggled with her to control them. He struggled with her until the seesawing tension of their arms brought his eyes into direct focus with the plain blue of hers, then held her wrists taut but motionless for one utterly simple moment, a moment in which he was conscious of her direct gaze, of the blond glint of her lashes and nothing more, then held onto her wrists to perpetuate that moment, held onto them as the moment began to dissipate with a commotion from behind him, held onto them as the moment gave way to dread, until the blue of her eyes quickened with curiosity and wavered toward the commotion, then dropped her wrists as the moment vanished, and turned around, guessing that the Buzzer was somehow involved, tasting the bitter grass, hating Mrs. Wiley with all his disappointment as soon as he saw her pacing the lawn with nimble steps, flapping her sleeves like a gigantic crow, dragging the Buzzer, who was trying to stop her by hanging onto the tail of her coat, and shouting in a croaking voice:

"Amen, amen, amen. Listen to thuh Word o' thee Lord. A-a-a-a-a-men! Amen, amen, amen!"

The sight sparked like flint in his brain and the angry twist of his trunk tightened with excitement, and he jumped to his feet, and, trying to see better, took one step, then another and another, until he was several feet away from Judith before he remembered her and called to her, but he couldn't wait for her, and he began to drift toward the joyous spectacle of a humiliated Buzzer, with his excitement growing into malicious proportions within him.

"Don't, Mama, don't," the Buzzer pleaded.

"Shame! Shame!" she said and slapped his hand down, ruffled her Bible's pages, and darted about on her stem-thin legs.

"Shame! Shame! That what wrong with all these peoples here. They 'shamed o' thee Lord's Word. Listen to thuh teechin' o' men instead o' Jesus. We all in trouble here, muthas an' fathas an' sons, 'cause we payin' heed to mens instead o' Jesus. What wrong with us is we doin' what the man say not Jesus. What wrong with us is men. Men, men, men, me————ennnnnnnnnn!"

"Mama! Mama!" the Buzzer cried, and reaching out to

her with one arm and reaching back to his father for help with the other, he looked as if he were being ripped apart between them.

But Mr. Wiley only opened his hands and showed his palms, and the Buzzer's brother started edging away, his bright suit clashing with a clump of bushes behind him; and Aaron grabbed Judith's hand to hurry her, afraid the growing circle of visitors around the Buzzer would become too thick for a good view, for the flap of Mrs. Wiley's sleeves and her raucous voice carried over the lawn, over the heads of all the now standing visitors and those who drifted in slow but increasing numbers toward her.

"Men! Men! Men put you boy here, mutha!" Mrs. Wiley said and stabbed her fingers at Mrs. Jenson, who curtained her lowered face with her straight hair.

"Men put both ah boys here, mutha. Both!" Mrs. Wiley said and thumbed the pages of her Bible, opened it, scanned its pages, but clapped it closed and, arms spread like great wings, began turning in a slow circle.

"Until mans who run thuh world take thuh Word o' thee gentle Jesus to heart an' beat their swor-ords into plowshares, an' stop this fightin' an' killin' an' sinnin' an' beatin' on each utha, thuh jails be full o' ah boys. Listen peoples, white folks, too. Listin! Listin! to thuh Word o' thee gentle Jesus. Amen, amen, amen, amen. Listen to what I say-yinnnnnnnnnnnnnnn-nnnn!"

The circle of people around her flapping preaching figure became so dense and Judith was such a hindrance to Aaron, who didn't want to miss anything, he quit trying to make his way through it, and stood on tiptoe to see better, aided by the downward slant of the hill. He hoped Mrs. Wiley would put on a spectacle so wild that the Buzzer would be humiliated forever, and he tried to deny the pity he felt when he saw the anguished edge of the Buzzer's teeth and the late but consoling touch of Mr. Wiley.

But the Buzzer spun savagely around, ready to attack his father; and Aaron rejoiced when Mr. Wiley stepped quickly back, limp-wristed, taking the crowd's attention with him, and Mrs. Wiley turned and shouted:

"See? See, muthas? See what ah mean? See my boy ready to strike his fatha? An' his fatha ready to strike him? See? Man agin' man. Fatha agin' son. Hate in thuh fam-ly. Ev-vurry-bawdy full o' sin. Sin, sin, sin, sin ev-vurry-where. Ow-wa time sinful as So-dummmmm, 'cause no-bawdy heedin' thuh Word o' thee Lord Jeeeeeeeesus!

"Jeeeeeeeeeesus!" she repeated with squinting eyes, purple gums, and a row of big yellow teeth, and a chuckle rumbled over the crowd, and Aaron squeezed Judith's hand and she pinched him with glee, and Mr. Jenson stood and taunted:

"Tell us all about it, muthaaaaa!" and his big face swelled with silent laughter.

"Ah will! Ah will! White man!" Mrs. Wiley said, slapping her Bible. "White folk drunk an' foolish, laugh at uh wooman full o' thee Jesus, laugh at gentle Jesus an' wooman, thuh only peoples who partake o' Him."

"You big, gentle wooooooman, give us thuh Word," Mr. Jenson said and laughed until his belly shook but made no sound, although the crowd's laughter was loud; and Aaron laughed the loudest, both from amusement and to hide from himself his own special motives and the truth he heard in her sermon.

He then began to force his way through the crowd, sensing that he was taking a chance on making a fool of himself but yielding to his excitement and to his desire to hurt the Buzzer, slipping around larger people, using his small size to advantage, pulling Judith along with him, willing to risk missing some fun for a chance to get into the fun, and reaching the cleared circle with the next taunt.

"Come on, big, gentle wooooooman, save us, save our souls, make us gentle and *you* tell us what to do instead of men,"

Mr. Jenson said, the sun spinning off his red hair as he turned and waited for the crowd's laughter.

There were a few smiles, but shadows hollowed Mrs. Jenson's face and she held tightly to Jenson, who raised his cup and took a very long drink; and only Aaron laughed and, laughing, caught Mr. Jenson's attention, and Mr. Jenson said it again, and Aaron laughed again, laughed to enjoy himself, laughed with the expectation that he would get a chance to say something, too, laughed until the Buzzer, sputtering with anger, shouted:

"Shut up! Youuuuuu white trash bastaud!"

Mr. Jenson cleared the circle before him with a swift spread of his arms and stepped into it with a soundless laugh, seemingly frozen and silenced by the same cruelty which frosted his blue eyes.

But Mrs. Wiley hopped in front of the Buzzer and stopped him on his first step, poked her face to within an inch of his, mirrored his widely spaced eyes with hers, and spoke to him with his mouth:

"Undouble you fist, boy. You doin' like he doin', an' you both wrong. Both meeen an' cruuu-el. Meeen an' cruuu-el like all men, wantin' to strike out . . . strike!"

"Stop 'im or I spank 'im!" Mr. Jenson taunted, his belly shaking, and spittle foamed on the Buzzer's lips as he tried to step around his mother; and Jenson shoved through the circle, next to his father, crushing the paper cup in his fist; and a thrill coursed through Aaron, for he hoped Jenson would slug the Buzzer and start a fight which would spread all over the lawn and involve all the visitors and all the boys; but Mrs. Wiley threatened to stop it before it started for she shook the Buzzer's shirt and warned him:

"Did you hear what I say, boy? Boy, get that meen-ness out o' you heart an' stop starin' at that man or I whip on you an' I whip on you now!"

Her fingers dug furrows in the Buzzer's cheeks as she

twisted his head around and forced him to look at her, while Aaron watched the duel of eyes in a fascinated hush.

The Buzzer blinked . . . blinked again. Rings of white turned bloodshot.

His eyelids closed and she let him lower his head, and the ridge of muscular flesh at the base of his skull spread into his arched neck; and Judith's held breath blew over Aaron with warm relief but caught again at Mrs. Wiley's new command:

"Kneel down!"

The Buzzer's body snapped into rigid attention and began to tremble, but he wouldn't obey, but so thoroughly transfixed Aaron that Judith couldn't turn him aside, although she dug her nails into his arm.

"Kneel!"

The trembling became worse.

"Kneel, I say," Mrs. Wiley said and pursed her lips.

"I say kneel!" she said and slapped the Buzzer, and the sound seemed to ricochet off every wincing face around Aaron and lingered in his ears even as the Buzzer let out a long groan of misery and anger but let himself be shoved to his knees, let his lumped buttocks rest upon his heels, let his chin lean upon his chest.

Aaron began to weave from side to side and shift his weight with little half-steps, as if he were searching for an opening in the circle through which he could leave, but unable to spare a second's attention from what was occurring before him, found himself hemmed in, trapped by his own gluttony, trapped by Mrs. Wiley, who placed her hand upon the Buzzer's head and closed her eyes and began to pray.

"Gentle Jesus, fo'give this here boy fo' his tra-gre-shun agin' his mutha. Fo-give 'im. He be filled with the hate an' meeen-ness o' men, an' he not strong enough to o-va-whe-elm his mos' sinful heart. Fo'give 'im, Lord. Fo'give 'im. Fo'give 'im. Fo'give 'im. Fo'give 'im."

She kept repeating the phrase to the sky above her, swaying

backward and forward and forward and backward, blubbery-necked, bristly-haired, but lulling Aaron, with her rising and falling and mumbling chant, into a hypnotic trance, in which he was not aware that he was swaying with her and that his lips were working as if he were chanting, too.

"Fo'give 'im—Fo'give 'im—Fo'give 'im—Fo'give 'im—Fo'give 'im—Fo'—"

"Heyyy!" Big Stoop bellowed across the lawn, and Aaron ducked, then backed into Judith as the big man strode to the crowd, followed by two suntanned guards.

"What the hell's going on here?"

"Mista' Po-leese, we prayin'. Ev-vury-bawdy prayin' fo' thee Lord to fo'give mah son his cruu-el an' meeen-ness heart. We prayin' fo' you, too, Mista' Po-leese."

"You're what? Praying for me? Break it up!" Big Stoop said and began shoving people aside, forcing his way through the crowd to her, to Aaron, who cringed, sure to be blamed, too, and who became totally bewildered when Big Stoop reached the clearing and was blocked by the Buzzer. For he was both for and against Big Stoop and for and against the Buzzer. He wanted both of them to win and both of them to lose.

"Back to your dormitory," Big Stoop said; and the Buzzer's face became a mournful black, but he refused to move; and Big Stoop shoved him and made him stumble, but he recovered his balance and stopped.

"Move!" Big Stoop commanded.

And the Buzzer took spiritless, waddling steps through the crowd, between two parked cars, across the road, and into the compound, where he looked out through the fence, almost lost in the line of curious boys who were pressing against it.

"Now on your way, lady, and if you want to see your son again, there won't be any more of this prayer meeting stuff. Get moving."

But Mrs. Wiley, who was shorter and squatter but almost as

heavy as Big Stoop, ignored the order and her husband's tugs at her coat, and gave her own warning:

"You better har-kun to thuh Word, Mista' Po-leese, or you end up burnt black as Hell."

"Get out of here," Big Stoop ordered again.

But Mrs. Wiley knocked her husband's hand away and closed her eyes and uptilted her face and cried out:

"Lord! Gentle Jesus, give me thuh pow-wa to suffa' this fo' you," then dropped heavily on her knees and pleaded: "Kneel. Kneel down, Mista' Po-leese, while you still got time. Don' end in thuh flames o' Hell. Kneel an' pray. Kneel an' pray."

And Aaron began to side-step around her, his eyes fixed on the deep ruts which circled her black eyes, the cheek lines grooved into her sweating face, and the heavy lips which cried:

"Kneel. Kneel down, Mista' Po-leese-man, or thuh Dev-vil get you soul, get you soul, get you soul."

Aaron then covered his mouth with trembling hands to stifle his laughter while Judith giggled and Mr. Jenson's belly shook with silent mirth and Jenson grinned with the crowd.

"I'm warning you lady," Big Stoop warned but his voice died away:

"Get . . . out . . . of . . . here. . . ."

Splotches of tiny veins spread over his cheeks and cap brims cast masking shadows over the tense eyes of the two guards, and the boys in the compounds climbed the fences and stood on benches and porch roofs for a better view.

Aaron thrilled as her voice rose into a long, moaning wail:

"Ooooooooooooooooooooooh!" then broke with a staccato shout:

"Jesus is dead! Jesus is dead! Jesus is dead! Kneel-kneel-kneel!" to her tugs at Big Stoop's trouser leg and, then, rose again: "Ooooooooooooooooooooooh!"

And Aaron sneezed laughs through his cupped hands and Judith giggled and Mr. Jenson laughed soundlessly and laughter rumbled up from the compounds and over the crowd and

Big Stoop grabbed Mrs. Wiley under an arm and tried to lift her.

"Goddamnit! Get out of here!"

But she held on to his trouser leg, crouched into a black hump, and Big Stoop couldn't lift her and all the guys in the compounds cheered and kept on cheering.

A guard wrapped his tan fingers around her hand and tried to pull it away from Big Stoop's khakis, and failed, and tried to jerk it loose, and failed, then started twisting her wrist, bunching the khakis over her hand, pulling them so far down that Big Stoop had to hitch them up by the belt once and then twice again; he waved irritably at the guard to stop, hitched his pants up a final time with brisk dignity, and motioned to the guard to help him.

But she squatted down when both men grabbed her under the arms and lifted together, straining until their faces were red, but failed to move her and gave up; and Aaron joined in the tremendous cheer that went up from all the boys in all the compounds and from all the boys and most of the visitors on the lawn. And he cheered louder when Big Stoop poked a long arm at the compounds and started to shout an order, but she suddenly straightened out of her crouch and screamed:

"Yi-yi-yi-yi-yi! Jesus is dead-dead-dead! Yi! Jesus! Yi-yi-yi!" and threw her Bible at the guard and grabbed Big Stoop's crotch with both hands and kept shouting: "Jesus is dead! Jesus is dead! Jesus is dead!"

And Big Stoop yelled: "Jesus Keeeeeeeeeerist!" and clamped his legs together and dropped into a semi-squat and staggered backward, clawing at her fingers, and the guard threw his arms around her waist and tugged on her and the other guard started shoving the crush of people back.

Then Aaron leaped and cheered when Big Stoop, trying to get free, pulled one way and the guard pulled the other way and her huge black body was stretched between them, but still moaning:

"Ooooooooooh! Jesus! Jesus! Jesus!" while Big Stoop shouted:

"Jesus—Christ—let—go!" and she repeated:

"Ooooooooooh! Jesus! Jesus! Jesus!" and Big Stoop yelled:

"Jesus—letgo—letgo!"

But Aaron stopped cheering when she kicked the guard away, sent him stumbling backward into the other guard, and jerked down on Big Stoop's crotch and dropped him to his knees and stunned the crowd into total silence, for in that incredible moment, Aaron saw himself standing above both the hated man and the Buzzer's mother, saw them below him, locked in combat, wrestling on the lawn in front of all the boys in the institute and all their visitors.

Big Stoop broke the silence with a yelping cry: "Yi-yi-yi-yi-yi!" and threw himself backward and dug his heels into the grass, trying to scoot away, but dragged her huge body between his legs and anchored himself and thrashed about with a purple face and then screamed:

"Jeeeeeeeesus! Keeeeeeeeeeeeeeeeeeerist! Leggo-leggo-leggo!" and she moaned:

"Ooooooooooooooooooooooh!" and rocked between his thrashing legs and held on and gripped tighter, although both guards pulled at her arms; and when the crowd began to shout and all the boys in the compounds cheered, Aaron began to hop and dance and clap his hands and shout encouragement and instructions to her; and when the tangle of khaki backs and black patches and arms and legs and gaping mouths got so entangled he couldn't tell who was who and who was where, he began to shout and scream for all of them and for none of them, just to shout and just to scream; but Judith appeared and her arms kept trying to hold him still and her hand kept trying to shut his mouth and her voice kept trying to calm him and her face kept trying to block his view; and he pushed her out of the way, while still hopping and still screaming, so he could search for Big Stoop in the heap below him, and see him shout:

"Goddamnit! Jesus Christ! Goddamnit! Jesus Christ!" and see Mrs. Wiley while she moaned:

"Ooooooooooooooooooooooh!" and see Big Stoop shout: "Yi-yi-yi-yi-yi-yi-yi!"

Then Big Stoop swung one hand high behind him and brought it down across her face with a slap that catapulted her completely over his leg and onto her back, a slap that echoed into the courtyards of the compounds and silenced them, a slap that petrified Aaron with disappointed shock, his mouth still open but silent, his arms still in the air but motionless, arms that drooped slowly down to his sides with the long rising disappointed "Awwwwwwwwwwwwwwwwwwwww" from the compounds.

Then Aaron saw, or thought he saw, Mrs. Wiley lift her sweating head like a decked fighter, jaw slack, eyes spinning, and rock helplessly from side to side, trying to get to her feet.

And Aaron thought he saw Big Stoop, plum-colored with humiliation, stand, straighten painfully out of a crouch, brush off his khakis with two simultaneous swipes of his hands, erase the pain from his face with a stern expression, point at the screen door and command:

"To the office, Goddamnit! To the office! The office!"

"Mama! Mama! Oh, Mama!" cried the Buzzer and he ran out of the compound, jumped the fender of a car, charged across the lawn, pushed through the crowd, tried to throw himself at Big Stoop and, then, struggled with both guards, who locked his arms behind him and marched him to the office behind a limping Big Stoop and Mrs. Wiley, supported between her husband and her zoot-suited son.

Aaron thought he heard hushed laughter spreading over the lawn after the group had passed into the office, and thought he saw all the arms waving as the boys in the compounds formed cheering circles around other boys wrestling mock battles; and the noise grew louder and louder and louder, but he stayed in the very center of the circle as the sounds and sights whirlpooled around him, alone in his hysteria as Judith shook him by his arm, her lips making sounds he couldn't hear, her eyes growing murky and dark as a storm sky, then, suddenly, brightening into wide scared circles with the prolonged blast of the whistle.

## II

Heat hung like an unhappy memory of the hot day about Aaron and all the quiet boys in the darkened courtyard. It dimmed the glitter of stars above him, clouded the color of the dormitory walls, dulled the black asphalt, blurred the cricket chant, and deadened the few dormitory sounds which filtered with weak light through the screen door onto the porch where he stood between Dominic and Jenson. For there were no noisy circles of conversation behind him. There was no laughter, no click of dominoes, and little movement.

It seemed to Aaron that each boy, whether standing, sitting, or lying on his bed, was as worn out by the wild scene on the lawn as he, himself, was. And it seemed to him that each boy was locked in his own skull, reliving, like himself, the memories of his visit: the good greeting, which hurt, was bad because it was lost and only a memory now; the bad moment of goodby, which was good because it was a memory of a visit which could now be relived; or, wishing, maybe like Dominic, that he had enjoyed a visit; still suffering over the wasted day, which could have been the best day, a suffering doubled because he could not blot out the visits of the lucky guys, or suffering, maybe, like himself, because he had *wasted* his lucky visit on the wild scene.

The whistle's blast had blown away his bewilderment and

the stark blue of the eyes before him had revived him, but they had to part. For Big Stoop had cut short the visiting hours with the shattering static of the loud-speaker, with his rush from the office, with his stalking about, with his shouting, with his shoving, and with his shooing away of the visitors.

In the confusion of that mass departure—the slamming of car doors, the roaring of motors, the thin clouds and harsh smells of exhaust fumes, the grinding of gears, the shouts of farewell—Aaron had walked with Judith down to the compound gate, where, regretting the blurred and wasted minutes lost on the lawn battle, he had tried to prolong each final moment, tried to notice and drain it of every possible sensation: the moisture of her hand, the pressure of her bust against the blouse, the faint odor of her face cream when he leaned forward and kissed her lightly on the lips, too shy to embrace her since there was no declaration of love between them, but tried to stretch out, relish, and even show off for the guys watching this visit, his visit, a visit from a pretty girl, which was only a second from being over.

Barbed wire and watchtowers trapped him on the institute grounds now. Low compound buildings surrounded him. Jenson and Dominic stood on both sides of him. He was in jail, and he had wasted in hysterical excitement a visit from a girl who liked him and who was his only touch with the outs. He had wasted the only proof he really had that the outs was there, did exist, streets and buildings, family and friends, and that it included some space, some thoughts, some feelings, and even love for him. It was a waste which tortured his pride and tainted with shame and regret what should have been pleasant if nostalgic thoughts.

"She looked pretty in that blue outfit, didn't she?" Dominic said, guessing Aaron's thoughts, speaking to the courtyard, his cheek as smooth and soft as Aaron's in the soft light from the screen door.

"Yeah," Aaron answered, distracted by Dominic's perception, noticing for the first time how many shadowy figures stood quietly along the horseshoe-shaped porch, but convinced that she *had* become prettier.

"You're lucky. Hold onto that girl. She's gonna help you do this time."

"Huh?"

"She's gonna help you do this time, *man,*" Dominic said, irritably. "When it gets so bad, when you feel so miserable, beaten down and lonely you wantta commit suicide, she's gonna be the reason you won't. She's gonna come and see you, maybe write a letter, just plain be outside there, waiting, and you're gonna be able to make it. Pay attention to me, man. You know I don't like broads. But I've had a few, a few too many, and I figure I know a good one when I see her."

There was a sharp pitch of resentment in Dominic's voice, sharpened, it seemed to Aaron, by the rim of light that edged his collar and cut across his darkened throat. But Aaron was grateful to Dominic for dropping his bitter pose and for the words, which created an image of Judith that was etched in flawless outlines: the plump face became a perfect oval. Plain blue eyes glowed like luminous orbs. Surprisingly full breasts topped a curvaceous figure, and the straight legs swelled from slim ankles into graceful calves.

"Everybody should have a good broad. If every guy had a good broad, he wouldn't end up in a joint like this."

"I guess that's true," Aaron said, agreeing both because he believed it and to soften Dominic's tone, and he tried to bring Jenson into the conversation:

"Every guy should have a girl alright."

The blond hair at the back of Jenson's head blocked the dormitory light, but Aaron, because of the difference in their heights, the distance between their faces, could distinguish the angry curve of his nose, his sharp mouth and jawbone, and could still smell the whisky.

Jenson didn't answer, and Aaron, trying to disregard the

snub, turned past him, looked into the dormitory, and a warm smile spread up his own face like the first sputtering flare of a match flame.

"Look! I never thought I'd ever see a resemblance between the Buzzer and Barneyway."

The Buzzer lay with his hands clasped beneath his head, elbows protruding, a few feet from the screen door, and across the aisle, down a row of legs, Barneyway lay with his hands clasped beneath his head, gazing at the ceiling.

"Even those guys need broads," Dominic said.

"Yeah, even them," said Jenson.

"Yeah," Aaron said, keeping his voice low, feeling guilty because he had avoided Barneyway all day and because he had enjoyed himself so much at the Buzzer's expense.

"It sure surprised me the way the Buzzer let his mother slap him around today. Man, I even felt a little sorry for him, and I never thought that would be possible."

"The dude was even humble when Big Stoop let him come back to the dormitory before dinner," Dominic added and turned to the courtyard again, followed by Jenson.

Aaron turned, too, but the night throbbed with his guilt now, as gentle as the bleat of the crickets but as persistent and aching, for the Buzzer *had* been humble when he had returned to the dormitory, and he *had* been humble and obedient to his mother, while his own behavior, in which he lost his head like a madman over another's suffering, would have shocked his mother.

"Looked like he was just waiting for somebody to say something about his mother, though, to forget how ashamed he was," Dominic said.

"Don't blame him," Aaron said, trying to ease his conscience a little. "A mother means a lot to a guy." He was thankful they couldn't see the twinge of self-pity he felt cross his face.

"She means everything, man," Jenson said, in a low, growling tone. "I'd kill for my mother."

Dominic's cheek wrinkled in disbelief.

"Mother's Honor!" Jenson said, defending himself against their unspoken doubt. "I was gonna kill my old man for her only about a month before I got busted and sent here."

Dominic's cheek smoothed into a tolerant shield, obviously waiting for the *story*, willing to listen only because Jenson was going to tell it.

"It's the truth, man," Jenson said, speaking to Aaron to get his support and so determined that he convinced Aaron, who wanted to believe him and who nodded, listening.

"One night when I came home late from the show, my old man was beatin' on my Mom. You guys saw her today. She has trouble just walking, and every time he'd slap her with his big hand, she'd drop. He smelled like a brewery. I could smell his drunken, stinking breath when I walked in the kitchen. My Mom was on the floor. I had heard her scream when I walked down the driveway to the back of the house. I didn't wantta go in. Knew what I'd see. But she wasn't hurt. Just a little blood tricklin' out of her nose, and her face was all red from where his big paw had left its mark.

"You know my Ma ain't pretty, you guys," Jenson stopped as if to make sure he had their attention; but to Aaron, the explanation and the pause were as poignant and as delicately futile as the soft pat of a moth's body and the flutter of its wings as it hit the screen behind him, for Jenson had his attention and his sympathy.

"My Ma don't even set her hair and it hangs stringy and straight as a horse's down her head, and she ain't too smart, either, can barely read." His voice twanged with the stress of explaining these uncomfortable facts. "She ain't the cleanest housewife I ever saw in my life, and she looks in her forties and she's only in her early thirties. But she's my Mom. You know what I mean?"

"Yeah, I know," Aaron said.

"Yeah . . . I know, too," Dominic said, as if he really knew.

"Well, man, she's layin' on the floor, whimperin', and I can see the gap where he knocked out two teeth before. Her eye is bloodshot, too, and he's giving her hell because she didn't wash the dishes or somethin'—I don't know—but really because he came home drunk and wants to take his crummy misery out on somebody else. Man, I wantta bawl. But I go into my room and undress to my shorts, climb under the blankets, don't have no sheets, and try to go to sleep. But he keeps picking on her and there ain't no door between my room and the kitchen. So, I got the light in my face and his loud, drunken voice in my ears, and the army blankets scratchin' against my skin, and about every five minutes or so, in between yells, he hits her again and down she goes.

"This goes on for about an hour and I'm so mad I can't help cryin' to myself. I want to jump out of bed and strangle him shut. But he finally runs out of lush, gets too loaded to argue, gets sleepy, and staggers off to his room. I hear the springs when he flops down. My Mom stays in the kitchen and washes her face off in the sink. I can hear her sort of whimperin' to herself. It sounds like a little kid in a corner. I'm hatin' so bad that I jump up, walk into the kitchen in my shorts, jerk open the drawer with a rattle of spoons and stuff, and grab a butcher knife, and I ask her, man, and I'm cryin' hot tears, man, but I'm not sobbin', and she's cryin' tears and whimperin', too, and her nose is swollen and turning blue all over one side, and I ask her if she wants me to kill 'im. I tell her if she wants me to, I'll do it right then. I'll go into the bedroom and stick that blade in up to my fist. I tell her that. But she says no. She says that it's okay. That he don't really hurt her, anyway. And she says that though he's a mean bastard, she don't want 'im dead. Then I ask her if I can kill 'im for me! So *I* won't have to listen to 'im beat on her anymore. And she says no, she don't want me to. And she wipes her face and quits cryin', except for a hiccup or two, and tells me to go to bed. And I do. But when I'm goin' through the doorway, she calls my name.

" 'Bob-by,' she says, real slow and soft, like it's hard to say. 'Bob-by.'

"And when I turn around, she hobbles across the floor toward me so fast that I'm afraid she'll fall, and she does fall, but I catch her by her skinny arms, and stand her up, and she squeezes me, and I hug her so tight I almost break her bony back.

"I woulda killed 'im for her," Jenson said.

"I would've, too," Aaron said, believing it at that moment.

"Some women need . . ." Dominic spaced his words so that they were emphatic and cruel. "Some women need . . . a . . . good ass-whippin'. . . . But if I was Jenson . . . I would've killed 'im . . . with*out* asking her."

Silence sealed the pact between them, and Aaron was sure he had discovered what it was made the night both so sad and so sweet: a bond of love greater than themselves, greater than the institute or any jail, a bond he wanted to share with all the boys, a bond which could bring a peaceful truce to all their differences and all their battles. For it seemed to him that he even knew what each boy was thinking about, dreaming about, even if he didn't know his exact thoughts.

He was with Jenson and his love for his lame mother. He was with Dominic and his love for a mother he also hated. He was with Barneyway, behind him, in the dormitory, alone, staring at the ceiling, thinking of a mother who didn't visit him that day. He was with the Buzzer, sullen and black, shamed by his love for his mother, a mother that he, himself, had wronged. And he was with every boy in every dormitory whether standing or sitting or lying with his face buried in his pillow. He was with them all in their love for their mothers, their sweethearts, their sisters, and all the women who made up the best part of their jailed lives.

Love seemed to hang in the night air like the leftover

warmth from the hot day, settle like starlight over the forbidding watchtowers, the locked gates and high wire fences, the flat, white, iron-barred buildings. It seemed to revive the chirruping of the crickets, the flutter of insects, the rustle of animal noises, and fill Aaron with such a supreme, almost unbearable feeling that he turned to Dominic, needing proof that this feeling existed, that they shared this communion, and he found proof, suddenly, in the rose tattoo.

The delicate petals of ink seemed to bloom with Dominic's frustrated, unfulfilled love for his mother, and it struck Aaron that the rose was an emblem of this unfulfilled love, an ornamental, bittersweet emblem, an emblem which would never wilt but which would never really blossom, and an emblem which he would carry to the grave with him . . . carry all . . . the way . . . to his grave. . . .

# Part Six
# Lights Out

# Lights Out

Tooth-powder flecks polka-dotted the washbasin mirror and a reflection of Aaron, with his chin lifted, brushing his teeth, he rarely saw: his jaw was square, his upper lip as puffed as the Buzzer's, his nostrils unsightly holes, his eyes chinked, and only the widow's peak of his hair showed on the short bulb-lighted brow.

He didn't consider himself good looking, but the person in the mirror was a homely stranger, who was as disappointing and hard to look at, after the softening starlight of Sunday, as the hard-edged objects in the washroom and the institute buildings by daylight.

His busy movements streaked the spots on the mirror, for he made an elaborate Monday-night ritual out of getting ready for bed, and he concentrated upon the act of brushing his teeth with such thorough precision that he whipped the tooth powder into a lather that foamed over his full lips and spilled down the corners of his mouth and dripped on his nightgown.

It was as if he were unable to break the grueling routine of the day, a day dominated on the surface by Big Stoop, who called out the numbers of the morning count in a rasping voice and made an inspection out of it. Who marched them to the mess hall and set the pace with his long legs. Who stood between the food lines and checked each tray and no boy got more or less than standard servings. Who counted them in the dairy yard. Who was an overseer at work. Who patrolled the grounds like a traffic cop and whose station wagon intersected with the garbage wagon on every trip to the dump. Who made lunch a quiet meal. Who made school a study period. Who haunted the free hours of the late afternoon with his long shadow. Who regulated the evening hours with his rattling keys.

Checkers clicked loudly on the board between Dominic and Jenson, and Aaron listened carefully for the Buzzer's drawl or any commotion that would announce his entrance into the dormitory. For the Buzzer and Big Stoop had divided the day between them and nobody seemed to care. Dominic and Jenson acted as if there was nothing special about Sunday night, and whenever Aaron had mentioned the lawn scene to any of the other guys, they had laughed it off very lightly. There was only a light hum of conversation in the dormitory now and there had been nothing louder all day.

Many of the guys were already in bed and most of the others were in their nightgowns, waiting for lights out. Only Barneyway was fully dressed, lying on his bed now, hiding his face behind a paperback book, hoping, Aaron knew, that the Buzzer, who had picked on him all day, would not bother him tonight.

At the blast of that morning's whistle, Aaron had heard iron bed legs scratch on concrete and a cry and Rattler's throaty laugh; he sat up in bed to see the Buzzer standing over Barneyway's rusty-springed bedframe and Barneyway climbing out from under his overturned mattress, pulling his legs free of the entangling blankets, one sheet trailing from him like a fallen white flag; and the lull-in-the-battle of Sunday night, which Aaron had hoped would become a permanent truce, had been broken on Monday morning.

He stopped brushing, lifted his lips, exposed his teeth, studied them, and then carefully labored over the back teeth, the front teeth, teeth which were set on edge at breakfast by the presence of Big Stoop and the Buzzer. For the Buzzer was determined to prove what a bad duke he was while the man was standing over him, and he courteously poured the last muddy drizzle of the breakfast chocolate into Barneyway's half-full cup. But he drank the chocolate down in big gulps, belched, and slapped the cup down in Barneyway's tray, splashing dregs of chocolate onto Barneyway's chin.

Aaron cupped his mouth under the cold water tap, filled it, raised up, checked the doorway again and began to gargle, fish-mouthed, before the mirror, trying to keep in mind, although he was preoccupied with his present thoughts, Dominic's advice in the morning darkness of the wagon shed:

"There never was no buddy-up last night. Don't you know that?" He had shaken the halter at Aaron. "Take care of yourself, man. Yourself! You can't expect guys to stay buddies just because they were all homesick on Sunday night. The Buzzer was just bumkicked over his mother's bad scene, that's all. He ain't no different now, and he ain't about to be. Maybe even meaner. Wants to even things up. Don't want his rep ruined. And Barneyway ain't no different, either. Maybe more gutless." He had poked Aaron in the chest. "I'm your friend. Jenson's your friend. You're our friend. We're all friends. You know why? Because we'll fight for each other, that's why. Barneyway won't even fight for himself."

Aaron spit the water out, rinsed his mouth, pushed the soft rubber stopper into the drain, turned the hot water tap on and ran it full power until the basin filled and a mist rose up. He lifted small palmfuls of water and patted his face gently with them, disappointed because the magic of Sunday night was gone, because feeling only came through touch and because it went no deeper than skin. He was disappointed, too, because Barneyway didn't protest when the Buzzer shuffled around the table at lunch and switched his empty for Barneyway's full tray. And he was disappointed and confused because his attempts to pray under the upraised swords of the angels afterward had all ended in daydreams of Judith, which had nothing to do with Barneyway or the Buzzer.

The hot water ran out of the basin, and he wasn't confused about that, he knew that. He then let the cold water run without plugging the drain, and when he splashed it over him, it made his skin feel tight. He knew that. He also knew that Barneyway's cry in the schoolroom, immediately after Big Stoop had left, had tightened his skin, too, and that the teacher's useless protest and his useless spitcurl had not relaxed it. But why had Barneyway hidden when he searched for him after school? Why did Barneyway snub him when he tried to offer support?

The corded nap of the towel soaked up the dampness from the outside of his face and warmed it. He knew that. He also knew the towel did not warm the memory of the chill that had streaked over him at dinner when Barneyway had let the Buzzer pour milk into his bowl. But why had Barneyway then eaten the beans, puddle of milk and all? He had given up hope then that the memory of Sunday would or could change any of the guys. He had lost faith then that there even *was* a memory to anybody but himself, for Dominic was probably right: there never was no buddy-up. And Dominic had congratulated him when he did not go in search of Barneyway after dinner:

"Now you're solid. Now you're taking care of yourself."

He braced himself against the solid door frame—something he could depend upon and believe in, as long as he didn't try to see too much in it—and prepared to enter the dormitory, determined not to look at Barneyway, determined to take care of himself.

But he glanced at Barneyway with the very first step, saw him pretend to be engrossed in his book, and in anger at the snub, he fixed his eyes on the checkerboard, on Dominic and Jenson hunched in T-shirts over it, and pattered with tiny slaps of his bare feet to his locker.

The game gave him an excuse to snub the snub, to prove

that he was solid, as solid as Dominic and as solid as Jenson, a guy who could take care of himself. And he watched the game carefully, concentrated upon it as if he were playing, and tried to keep himself from seeing or feeling anything except the actual moves of the game.

Dominic took two triumphant hops with his black king over Jenson's red men, lifted the red discs with exaggerated daintiness, shook them like dice by his ear, as if he really enjoyed their soft clicking, rocked back and, then, forward again from Jenson's straight-arm in the chest. The friendly rivalry between the two solid buddies only made Aaron feel, more acutely, the confusion and disappointment in his own friendship with Barneyway; and he opened his locker, hoping to find a distraction there.

It was as cold and dead and disappointing as the whole day had been. But he tried to occupy himself. He put his toothbrush on the metal shelf, exactly parallel with its edge. He hung the folded towel over the iron rung below the shelf. Then he straightened and evened the towel so that it neatly curtained the empty space between his dungaree shirt and pants, which hung on opposite hooks. Then he straightened his brogans. Then he pulled the gray socks out of the brogans and covered the laces with them. Then he searched for something else to do, anything to keep any thought of Barneyway from seeping into his mind. But he could see nothing which might occupy him, and he began to wonder what he was doing crouched down, hiding from a guy everybody else thought was pussy; and he realized that he was "thinking of Barneyway," so he grabbed his brogans out of desperation, deciding to polish them as he picked them up and heard the screen door slam and Rattler make some comment.

He kept his crouched position, the brogans in one hand, feigning indifference; but he knew that if the Buzzer was with Rattler, which he took for granted, Barneyway was going to suffer, and if Big Stoop came by, it would only be worse.

He listened for the Buzzer's voice, expecting Barneyway's cry, but heard a strange sound, instead, and dropped the brogans and straightened up.

The Buzzer's blue shirt was caught on his wrist by a buttoned cuff, and it ruffled and whooped with wind as he swung it around and around with swooping, fancy gestures and danced on his toes by his bed in an awkward parody of a ballet dancer. He hopped and swayed from side to side, forward and backward, with sinuous twists of his swaybacked body, and, finally, snapped the shirt free, then bunched it and tossed it gently as a bouquet of flowers onto his bed, but held his position, arms extended, balanced on one leg, the other jutting out behind him, and got a loud laugh from the guys around him.

"Chudini! Chudini!" Rattler shouted in pachuco slang, meaning pussy, and he pointed at Barneyway and began to undress for bed. He limited himself to peering over his skinny shoulder, laughing with a husky, rattling wheeze, and making encouraging motions; and Aaron believed he was too ashamed of his bony build to show off. Barneyway kept his face completely covered by the book and only allowed his eyes to skim over it when he turned a page.

Yet checkers clicked on the plywood board with an unbroken, indifferent regularity. An occasional grin of satisfaction would crease either Dominic's or Jenson's face when an opponent's man was taken, and Aaron began to doubt his own impressions. He wondered if he was making the same mistake, but in a different way, he had made the night before. He decided to play it safe and stay by Dominic and Jenson, and suffered over a decision that shriveled all his fine hopes down to a "safety-first" in just one day, when a burst of laughter stopped the game.

The Buzzer was stripped down to his white boxer shorts, posing with flexed muscles. He stuck his chest out, sucked his stomach in, and twisted his upper body into profile, so that

with his tiny waist and deeply swayed back, he looked deformed. His biceps popped up like eight balls on his arms and
the black dress gloves he had put on made glistening leather
fists.

Gold sparkled between his black lips with a chanting, rolling song. But guffaws and laughter drowned out the sound,
and he had to begin again:

"Now thee Buzza' is bigga' than thuh bee,

                                  **e-ven**

thee hor-net is smalla' than he.
So, tonight,
thee Buzza'
          sting a lit-tel.
Tonight,
      he
bee-wrap a lit-tel
               punk-honey,
bee-wrap a flaow-wa,
get him some
            punk-honcy."

He kept singing as he shuffled down the dormitory on the
swollen, knotted thighs and thin crooked calves of drumstick-
shaped legs, slowed the shuffle to a slow dance, swayed his
muscle-banded body in time to short steps, skipped a step
sometimes and gave the shuffle a sort of contrapuntal rhythm,
posed for every boy he passed, with his head stiffly upright,
corded muscles fanning down his swollen neck into his trunk
like thick roots, posed and leered at Aaron, who dared to
stare back from his safe place, then stopped and posed at
Barneyway's bed, where he did a circling dance.

Guffaws and laughter applauded him.

The paperback was lowered with fearful slowness.

A bloodless face, with compressed lips and eyes as glazed
as porcelain was propped against the pillow, and Aaron told

himself it wasn't true, that it didn't look like that, that he was
just . . . seeing. . . .

"Get me some
>    some
>        punk-honey,
>    bee-wrap some
>        some
>        punk-honey."

The Buzzer shuffled around the aisle as he sang, then
stopped singing and began to boogie: snapped his pelvis as if
he were screwing, cupped his gloved hands over his groin,
narrowed his eyes, and sucked in his breath as if he were at
the peak of a come.

"Chudini! Chudini!"

"Pussy! Pussy!"

And Rattler's husky, wheezing laugh reverberated in
Aaron's head like Buckshot's warning in the isolation cell,
which he denied because it couldn't be: not that! and not in
front of everybody!

But the boogie in front of Barneyway's bed and the cries
of pussy continued until the lights blinked mercifully off,
back on, off, on, and the Buzzer shuffled down the dormitory
to his bed, still dancing and smoothing his black gloves.

Then his low wailing chant floated into the ceiling rafters
as all the guys got into bed. It became staccato barks when
Barneyway took off his clothes:

"Punk-punk-punk-punk-honey!" It stopped long enough for
the man to count, started again with the clash of the gate, the
rattle of keys, increased in volume, floated eerily in the
darkened dormitory, until Aaron imagined he could see the
white snapping banner of the shorts and the ghostly black
body performing its macabre dance against the faint white wall
behind it.

Bare feet began to shuffle again and the moaning chant
broke into song:

"Get me some,
            some, some, some . . ."
And white shorts took shape before Aaron's eyes.

The shuffling steps came closer.

The song stopped.

A black body loomed as vaguely as a specter in the aisle, and Aaron got ready to kick, but it floated past him, no longer dancing, crossed the aisle, and disappeared in one swift motion into Barneyway's bed.

"Hey!" Barneyway cried, but it was too feeble and Aaron had no hope.

Blankets rustled.

"Get out!"

The words hissed as if coming from between clenched teeth, and Aaron heartened at the sound, doubled his fists for Barneyway, and fought the battle from his own bed, for he was afraid to help, and afraid he couldn't help.

"Get out!" Barneyway cried again, and Aaron propped himself on his elbows, aware of an audience of blurred faces, and whispered to Barneyway to fight.

"Get away! Get away!"

The bed skidded, blankets thrashed, the struggling increased, and Aaron began to hope that Barneyway might hold him off.

But a gloved fist connected with a muffled smash, and Barneyway yelped and, then, pleaded:

"Oh, leave me alonnnnnnnnnnnnnne."

The gloved fist struck again and again, thudded, thudded, thudded; and Aaron lifted his blankets, held them, trying to get the nerve to throw them back and jump up; but Barneyway cried out:

"Please! Oh, pleeeease!" and Aaron dropped them back upon himself, tears burning his eyes, but without the courage to lower even one foot from the safe comfort of his bed to the cold floor.

"Shut up!" the Buzzer said and struck once, twice again, and the struggling stopped.

Whimpering.

Stifled sobs.

A grunt that ended in a shriek.

Another guttural warning.

A big hump in the dull light from the screened window high above Barneyway's bed.

A final useless screech, and Aaron ducked under the covers, packed the pillow around his ears and tried to deafen himself to the terrible mechanical creak and pause of the bedsprings, which kept growing louder and more furious, louder and more furious, louder and more furious, until it reached the pitch of a laboring, broken, ear-shattering scream!

# Part Seven
# Pledge for a Crime Partner

# Pledge for a Crime Partner

## I

After-lunch chatter on the visitors' lawn had faded into garble when Aaron saw Barneyway stop by the white ribs of the baseball bleachers, swing his arm in his stiff-elbowed way, as if to occupy himself, then look toward the fields across the road from him, where the wild grass and the clumps of trees were hot and still under a noon sun.

The slant of the hill lengthened Aaron's steps, increased the pace he had kept since he left his warm spot against the mess hall wall, without any comment to Dominic or Jenson, and started following Barneyway, who now, as Aaron drew closer and the noises grew fainter, strayed over to the home plate backstop, apparently unable to decide what to do, then swung his arm again, but held it out behind him, and spun around with fright.

The purple bruise on the swollen cheekbone was frightening to Aaron, but he was determined to fulfill the penance he had promised in the cool atmosphere of the chapel, a promise as hard to make as the prayers were to say, a promise made to the memory of his mother but now to the image of Judith, a promise it had taken a whole Tuesday to make, a promise he was going to keep, and he kept walking at the same speed until he saw how the bruise edges had yellowed like a wilting blossom, then faltered, took a long, slow step, raised his eyes,

183

concentrated on the bristle tips of Barneyway's crewcut, and kept moving.

"Hi!" he said, trying to appear casual, yet unable to keep from glancing at the pale currents of discoloration running through the bruise, which then disappeared behind an evasive profile.

The profile itself had such a strong brow and such a powerful, clefted chin, it was hard for him to associate it with the cries and the whimpering of Monday night, and when he stopped, the brow, the whimpering, the screech of springs, the drudgery of praying, the image of Judith hooded by long hair, all clashed and tangled within him so that the intended vow couldn't take form in his mind.

His tongue felt tightened by the shame that paralyzed his good intentions within him and charged the very air between them.

Traffic noises filtered through the wire backstop and by their faintness intensified the silence:

Thin cry of a car horn.

Truck drone.

Tire ripple on hot asphalt.

Distant hoot of a train whistle.

The tiny tick, tick, tick, tick of boxcars on railroad tracks.

"Hot today . . . huh?" Aaron said, finally.

". . . Yeah . . ."

"I been thinking, Barney . . ."

"Yeah . . ."

"We been . . . we been buddies a long time . . ."

Humped blanket in dim light. He heard his voice begin again.

"We been best friends for three years."

Facts were the way. They didn't take thought. Mouth open, but he couldn't think of any more facts, and he started over again.

"Three years. Three years is too long, too long not to stand by each other when one guy needs help."

He stopped, needing help to continue, and a discolored, wilting bruise came slowly into his view. But a close sight of the bruise shocked him as badly as his first sight of it on Tuesday morning, and it took his speech away again. Then, only the moist gratitude in Barneyway's eyes gave him the courage to finish.

"I'm sorry, Barneyway, for not being your friend. If I'd 'uve stuck by you, he might not even . . . have tried," he said and watched the slow rise of Barneyway's arm bridge what had seemed an unspannable distance between them, and he grabbed its wrist, declaring:

"I'll stick by you, Barney. To hell with the Buzzer. I promise on my Mother's Honor. I . . . promise!"

Boxcars ticked slowly out of hearing, leaving a moment of silence in which he stood locked to his friend by an arm, a hand, and a promise, but a moment which the movement of Barneyway's finger, lifting, pointing at the bruise, threatened to destroy, a moment in which Barneyway's optimistic voice saying, "Look! It's going down," did not destroy, but Aaron's too quick reply of: "Yeah! It's almost gone!" did destroy.

He felt foolish, caged by the backstop, and afraid he had ruined everything, for Barneyway pulled free, turned away from him, hiding the bruise, and crossed the road, but then stepped into the field and stopped, plucked a long strand of grass, and held it up for admiration.

Aaron hurried across the road and, in his enthusiasm, called to Barneyway to follow him, and forced a path through the fields, his pant legs swishing through the tall grass, whipping past the stiff branches of stunted manzanita, scraping against the rough trunks of tall oak trees, and led his friend on an unplanned noisy course into a small secluded meadow, where the musky odor of untilled earth blended with the mint-sharp grass smell, the dusty reek of weeds and bushes, and hung motionless in the warm air like a pleasant, intoxicating ether.

In the meadow, far from the danger of the Buzzer, the contempt of Dominic, and the sullen dislike of Jenson, he began to feel as if they were old friends again. And he forgot all unpleasant memories, forgot the fact that barbed wire and a watchtower were near by. He forgot that they were doing time. He forgot Judith, too, and when he heard the song of a meadow lark, he called to Barneyway to help him find it, and they searched for it, with what he was certain was a shared delight, until Barneyway spotted it on a high oak branch, then squatted together in the shade at the base of the tree to listen to it.

The song kept reverberating in the bellows of the bird's throat as if the bird were swallowing the notes, but increased steadily in volume and wind until the throat swelled and seemed about to burst, then rolled out of the open beak in a mocking higher-toned, note-swallowing echo of itself.

The notes kept repeating, repeating, one beginning before the other had ended, sounding off across the meadow, lulling Aaron into a complacent peace, in which only the song and the meadow and Barneyway existed, in which the supreme pleasure he felt, the beauty which seemed to envelop him convinced him that he had made his pledge as much for him-self as for Barneyway, as much for his own sense of well-being as for Barneyway's safety or for his need to prove that friend-ship did, really, exist.

But when the lark had reached and swallowed the final and weakest echoing note, it paused, as if it were through, and both Aaron and Barneyway waited anxiously until the throat swelled again, the gulped note reverberated in the throat, gathered in volume, intensity, and burst out of the open beak into a rolling echo of itself all over again, and they relaxed again, but it was short-lived, for the lark stopped singing abruptly, ruffled its feathers, and sprang from the branch into flight, accompanied by their long disappointed moan.

But the bold flutter and chatter of a flock of blackbirds caught their attention next, and they watched with eager amusement until they were distracted by the scratch and scurrying of a small gray squirrel, which vanished as quickly as it appeared. A rustling of leaves above them failed to produce anything, and trying to find something to share together and keep their happy mood, they tried to follow a trail of nervous ants up and around the broad trunk of the tree, each pretending to see the trail a branch higher than the other, higher than the other, until they reached the tip of the tree, laughed, and finally agreed on an area of rough bark where they really lost it.

"How would you like to be an ant?" Aaron asked, with a blade of grass between his grinning teeth.

"And climb trees?" Barneyway asked, being equally ridiculous. "No thanks. But if I was. . . . If I was," he said, the bruise making his expression serious, "I'd like to be a biiiiig red one and sting the Buzzer right on his big black ass," and with a smirk at Aaron's laughter, he stretched out on the ground and lapsed into a self-possessed silence.

Aaron watched him for a few minutes, pleased that after the turbulent events of the past week they could relax together, and chuckling to himself at the joke, he, too, stretched out and used a thick root as a pillow.

He stared through the slightly shifting branches and leaves at a peaceful blue sky, pleased by his pledge, too, satisfied that the past mistakes of both of them no longer counted, and that together, they could make sure they both did good time the rest of their stay in the institute.

But the sky seethed with obscure movement. One moment, he was sure it was the quivering of the leaves. The next moment, the blue seemed to swell and come alive with swimming indistinct worms of white. He tried to blink them away. But each blink only increased them. And they began to bristle like sparks between the branches and the thorny leaves of the tree. He was suddenly seized with fear. And he sat up, feeling very, very small.

# II

The shadow of a tall eucalyptus tree leaned out of the gully between the schoolhouse and the main office, spread over Aaron and Barneyway, who were standing on the walk below the school steps, zigzagging up the steps, into the entrance of the school, out again, and cut its peak off at a sharp angle on the edge of the flat roof.

As if it had reached too far, Aaron thought, zigzagged under the strain and lost its head, but he replied:

"Let's go to the library then. I'm tired of walking around, tired of—" He almost said *talking*. "We been walking around since school let out."

"Okay!" Barneyway said, enthusiastically, and his wiry body kept up an electric, restless movement as they started down the walk and moved out of the tree's shadow.

Three days had dried the bruised petal of ruptured blood vessels on Barneyway's cheekbone to the color of a wilted violet, and the swelling was gone; and Aaron was more affected now by the pocked texture of the sidewalk which reminded him of the tiny pimple craters, with the whiskers sprouting out of them, in the hollow of Dominic's cheek, playing him for shine, the most he had seen of *that* friend's face the past day.

"In a week or two, she wrote," Barneyway said, when they reached the paved road and started up the hill. "As soon as she gets somebody to drive her. I hope Stanley does so we can have a visit together."

The letter and the proposed visit were all Barneyway had talked about for the past day, while Aaron had been concerned with the snub Dominic had given him when he ran up the walk with Barneyway to get into line for school, with

Dominic's change of seats in the classroom, and with the beauty mark that had been turned to him and stopped him at every approach.

"It'll be good to be with her. A guy don't have to put on a show with his mother. You know. Act rough. Talk bad. Don't have to pretend he likes to play ball or box. I can talk about music to her, and Carmen Cavallero, too. Boy, I wish I could practice on a piano."

The sun sliced Aaron's legs across the knees, and shortened the shadow on each leg with each of his steps up a hill on which Jenson's legs had marched into tall shadows with each step down it and away from him that very day.

"Carmen Cavallero is a bitch on the piano, Aaron. No jive. Mother's Honor. Oh! Sorry!"

He paused and with his sleeve brushed off the spit he had sprayed on Aaron's shirt.

"Carried away," he explained, but talked on. "You oughtta hear him on Polonaise. Man! I'm telling youuu, he's a bitch!"

Waves of hill shadow splashed against Aaron's ankles as he waded upward into the sun, wondering if he and Barneyway would reach a point where they'd be respected, where Barneyway's speaking voice wouldn't sound like a solitary shriek in the dormitory, and if his own support would give Barneyway the guts to fight the Buzzer. For everything depended upon that. That would bring them respect. That would revive his dying friendships and only that would justify his pledge.

The scuffed toes of his brogans looked as ragged in the full sun at the top of the hill as he felt. He promised himself to shine them after work the following day, Friday, the last day of the week that he would get to spend his morning with Dominic, who had only talked to give instructions this morning, the only morning Aaron had been sorry to hear the lunch whistle blow. For Dominic had stood closer to the Buzzer than himself for noon count. Closer to the Buzzer. . . .

"The Buzzer," he said to himself but aloud.

"Huh?" Barneyway said, stopping, his face blanched. "Where? What's the matter?"

"We're real friends, aren't we, Barneyway?" Aaron said. "Real friends, huh? Aren't we?"

"Real friends. . . ?" Barneyway asked, and the color came back to his face and the corners of his mouth curled up, like the tips of a long mustache, in a wry, tolerant smile.

"Sure!" he said, flippantly, and began walking again, talking: "And when she gets here, Stanley and you and me, we'll all three of us. . . ."

The mud and garbage grime dried like dirty putty on the edges of Aaron's brogans would have to be cleaned off with a stick before they were polished, in case he got a visit from Judith, whose past visit now seemed full of subtle gestures of affection for him, gestures which were—as in the simple laying of her plump fingers upon his hand—so completely different in attitude from Barneyway's nonchalance: as if it were easy to give up all your buddies and get played for shine.

He twisted his ankle in the middle of a step for a glance at the dirtiest brogan and realized he was walking alone before he set his foot down. His head swung in one swiveling motion toward Barneyway behind him and back again in the opposite direction toward the Buzzer, who was tapping a roll of comic-books against his leg, and Rattler, who was closing the library door.

"Come on," Aaron whispered, but loud enough for Barneyway, who couldn't see him speak, to hear him, and took two careful steps toward the threatening figures, but he didn't hear any movement behind him.

"Come on," he said and waited, without turning, for the swipe of rough pant legs brushing past each other, for a rubber heel against the paving.

No sound.

"Come on," he said, still whispering.

Nothing.

He turned as Barneyway began to rush away, swinging arms pumping elbows high in a comic motion.

"You gotta stand up to 'um! Don't let 'em scare you! Barneyway!"

The blue shirt rippled between the shoulder blades and the buttocks gave a quivering jerk with every anxious step that carried Barneyway past the office and over the hill.

"Barneyway!"

"Punk!" the Buzzer said.

"Punk!" said Rattler.

The library's bay window provided a fluctuating transparent frame for their torsos. And Aaron had an urge to say something nasty to them or go into the library, anyway, to prove to himself and them that he didn't fear them. And he stalled, trying to make up his mind, then trotted after Barneyway. He didn't run too fast for they'd think he was scared, but he didn't run too slow for they'd think he was trying to convince them he wasn't scared.

"Wait!" he called as he passed the office, and Barneyway, who had already reached the first compound, slowed and waited by the second.

A group of boys stopped playing net-ball in the courtyard and watched Aaron run down the hill. They made him feel so conspicuous that, by the time he reached the compound fence, he was not only panting with exertion and anger at Barneyway for backing down on his first test but also rage over finding himself in such a foolish position.

"Goddamnit! Why didn't you keep moving?"

Barneyway started walking again.

"Answer me!" Aaron commanded, as much for the boys watching as himself, trying to cover his embarrassment by showing off, by acting bad, by trying to make his superiority to Barneyway obvious to them, and taking advantage of his legitimate anger to be insincere, but so conscious of it that once out of the boys' view, his tone was softened by guilt and relief.

"Don't you see that if you act afraid, he'll try it again?" he said, and asked his question of the white wall, for Barneyway had stepped past him. Then the honest sound of his own voice, mentioning Monday night for the first time between them, gave him the nerve to get tougher: "If you keep acting like a punk, they'll keep messing with you."

But Barneyway screamed: "You never had it happen to you!" and shocked all the toughness out of him.

"It hurts. I shit clots of blood the next day. I could hardly touch my butt with toilet paper. It stung. The paper was spotted with blood. I could hardly sit down all day. Do you hear?" Barneyway cried, his eyes filmed with anger; and a shiver seemed to ripple from Aaron over the field of weeds and grass between the compounds, and he thanked God there were no witnesses.

"And who are they? I'm scared, yeah. I'm scared. But who are they?" Barneyway demanded. "The Buzzer ain't so bad. I saw his mother slap his face and make him kneel down like a cocksucker on the lawn, in front of everybody. Yeah, I saw his mother do that to him. And I was glad, glad! Do you hear?"

Aaron tried to slow down and stay between the compounds, but Barneyway began to hurry, as if the excited anger within him pumped his body into faster motion.

"And Rattler? He ain't nothin' but a kiss-ass punk himself. He does everything the Buzzer says. I could whip him if I didn't have to fight the Buzzer, too. I could whip his skinny Mexican ass. I could whip him if he'd fight fair, by himself," Barneyway shouted, and only his hysterical screech kept Aaron from admiring him.

For Barneyway had a terrific punch for his size, and Aaron believed he meant what he said, and he liked the superiority he showed by calling Rattler a Mexican, meaning a guy browned by Indian blood and not of pure Spanish descent like themselves.

"And your friend Dominic? He don't even have anybody come to see him but a fat old woman painted up like an old whore. He don't even have a girl. Why does he act so tough? so mean all the time? if he's so sure he's tough?"

The shrill whistle in Barneyway's voice caused heads to lift on a porch bench at the far end of the next compound they passed, and Aaron hoped none of the guys could understand the words.

"And how about your friend Jenson? If I had an ugly mother like his, I'd go kill myself. I heard about him, too. He punked a guy in the Frisco DT. I heard about it. Why is he acting so proud? Anybody that'll pitch'll catch. That's right!" he shouted and hurried, elbows pumping, buttocks jerking, past the next compound, toward theirs, where dormitory windows loomed like huge eyes; and Aaron held a finger to his lips.

"You, too!" Barneyway said, throwing his hands in the air. "What do you care what all those guys think? When you were in the DT, you wouldn't let anybody make you fight. You didn't *have* to fight, and you got to be head monitor. You told me not to fight because it would be bad on my record. I saw you cry when that ugly nigger Hubert tried to fight you. And you weren't afraid of him. You know you weren't. You didn't want to get in trouble. You said so and everybody believed you. You're not a bad actor like them. You like to draw and read and dance and listen to music by yourself like I do. We were in glee club together, remember? Who's doing wrong by not wanting to fight? Do you want me to fight and get in trouble?"

"No," Aaron said, stopping by the compound gate, conceding in order to stop the argument before they entered the courtyard, relieved that no one was in it. "No, I don't want you to get in trouble."

"I'll get in trouble if I fight . . . Aaron," Barneyway said, and it sounded like such a weak excuse that Aaron was angered and his first impulse was to point out that "not fighting" had got them *both* in plenty of trouble already, and although he contained that, he couldn't keep himself from risking another noisy argument.

"Barneyway? Do you want it to happen again?"

The cleft in Barneyway's chin lifted and stretched thinly toward the licking tip of his tongue, dropped into position as the tongue disappeared, and he tried to answer. But he stuttered, gave up, and stalked through the gateway, with Aaron following him, persisting:

"Do you want it to happen again?"

Barneyway stepped off the porch and started across the courtyard.

"Do you want it to happen again?" Aaron said, trying to catch up with him. "Goddamnit! Answer! Do you want it to happen again?"

But Barneyway didn't answer until he reached the screen door, where he said, curtly: "I don't have to ask for trouble," and let it slam behind him.

"I don't have—" Aaron said, flipping the door open, ready to finish shouting out that he didn't have to either, but he saw Dominic look up from a book, and he slammed the door so hard the screen buckled, and marched with hard-heeled steps along the porch to the fence, which he hooked his fingers into, shook and, then, leaned his forehead against.

The ridged fence links formed an unbroken wall of metal from his matted pompadour straight down to his brogans, something he could lean on and depend upon. He was beginning to doubt if Barneyway would ever fight back, and, much worse, the strain of trying to support both of them was draining his own strength and made him feel like quitting. If he hadn't given his word. . . . He tried to shake the thought out of his head.

"I'd shake it, too, man," Dominic said, stepping out of the

dormitory. "That punk Barneyway will not only drive you batty, he'll make you weak as him."

The sun slanted like a sash from his shoulder to his hip as he approached, still talking.

"You gotta get more choosy and pick your friends. Protect yourself. Run with buddies as strong as you. You hear what I'm saying? And you better start now because Big Stoop told me I'm leaving within a couple of weeks. Got my release."

"What?"

"Got my go-home, within two weeks. Get busy or you'll get done in when I leave."

Aaron's quick smile sagged with the warning.

"I can't just give him up, man. I gave him my word I'd stick by him."

"You better break it then. He just let you down, didn't he? I don't know what happened, but I'll bet, risk some goodies that he just folded on you when the cross came down. Didn't he?"

Dominic waited for an answer.

"I knew it," he said. "Listen, man. Two weeks isn't long. If you don't have any strong buddies like Jenson to help you, the Buzzer and Rattler are gonna do you in. No tellin' what'll happen. Got me?"

The insinuation was discouraging, but it only reminded Aaron of what had happened to Barneyway, and he said, "I can't give him up just because he can't whip the Buzzer, man."

"I'm not telling you to do that. It's because he don't fight the Buzzer. You know he'd fight if he thought he could win. He's a quitter and that's why you better put him down. He's gonna make you so weak, you're gonna end up like him. You better listen to what I say. You better give up that Sunday school stuff, that do unto others bullshit, all that fairy-tale shuck."

Strands of pompadour, flattened over Aaron's lowered forehead by the fence, veiled his expression of disagreement, and he didn't argue; but the tattooed rose burst into full bloom as Dominic still insisted:

"See? See this, man? Only broads are weak, man, don't fight. Only broads believe that Jesus talk. Look what happened to the guy? He went around preaching all that love-shit and ended up with his hands nailed to a cross. You only got two choices in this world. You can be weak like a broad or strong and cold and bad like a man. There ain't no in-between. You got to take care of yourself, be cold, back away from a guy who gets hurt because he won't even try and protect himself.

"Hear me?" he asked, and Aaron was weakened by an urge to play it safe and put Barneyway down. For he doubted if Judith would expect his pledge from him under the changing circumstances. And he held tightly to the fence, and used it, with the strength he drew from his belief that Dominic was wrong about Jesus, to help him reply:

"He needs me, man."

"You mean he uses you," Dominic countered; and Aaron grabbed the fence with his other hand, needing all the support his hooked fingers could give him, as he tried to remember how good his pledge in the chapel had made him feel.

Staring through the links, he then saw Barneyway's comic walk, the bruise, the blood-spotted toilet paper, the Buzzer's dirty boogie, and he could have sworn he heard Barneyway's voice in the dormitory. He listened, trying to verify it, heard nothing, but let his fingers ripple down the fence, and said, with quiet conviction:

"He's my friend. Barneyway . . . is my friend."

## III

Mr. Handy counted aloud the double line of boys in the dairy yard for the third time, a thick lock of brown hair escaping his cap and curtaining the eye he sighted down his finger. But

Aaron knew the count was one short, and he knew that Jenson was missing because he had been watching for him, hoping to notice some change in his attitude, some sign that he might help in a battle with the Buzzer after Dominic left.

The blast of the noon whistle was due, and Aaron shifted with an impatient hunger, a hunger made more acute by Dominic's imminent go-home and his growing concern over Jenson's whereabouts. He wanted to start marching immediately toward the mess hall, which was situated, with its heat and tantalizing food smells, but unseen, in the inch of space between the white top of the gym and the barred second-story hospital windows on the hill beyond the fields.

"Damn," Mr. Handy said and brushed irritably at the lock of hair, which might have amused Aaron if he weren't so worried. For Mr. Handy was as kind as he was soft brown all over, told the guys dirty jokes, teased them about their girls, and threatened, in fun, to throw them in the hole. But Aaron wanted to jam the hair lock under the cap himself now, as badly as he wanted to tell Mr. Handy that it was Jenson who was missing.

"You better get the list, Buzzer," Mr. Handy said. "Hurry. We're already late."

The Buzzer ran into the office and returned at a trot, carrying a clipboard with fluttering pages, and playing such a conscientious part that he annoyed Aaron, who compared it to his bully role during last evening's lockup, where he had taken the opportunity, because Dominic read and Jenson didn't appear until the gates were locked, to be obnoxious and loud.

Jenson had been so tight-lipped, tall and sullen when he had fumbled in his locker, took things out, put things in, made little noise, got into bed before lights out, and poked his toes into twin blanket peaks against the foot railing, without even a good night to Dominic, that Aaron had considered replying to one of the Buzzer's wisecracks, in order to start a fight and force Jenson into taking his side for him. It was a big risk, but it seemed small next to a certain beating and maybe worse, after Dominic left.

"Jenson!" Mr. Handy called out, holding the clipboard up so the boys could see the page, as if they could read the name. "Who knows where Jenson is?"

Nobody answered, but Dominic flattened his hands in his back pockets, hunched his shoulders, and leaned his head far back on the wings of his neck muscles; and Aaron tried to read the expression on his face.

"Mr. Dixon hasn't been around either . . . ?" Mr. Handy said, asking, searching for an answer with a sweeping glance along the line. "Must be together?" He brushed nervously, futilely, at the lock of hair. "Buzzer, you run up to the loft and see if you can spot the truck. I'll call the main office."

He went into the dairy talking to himself as Barneyway's disembodied head poked out of the wall of blue uniforms and switched its eyes from side to side to share its curiosity with Aaron, who flicked his eyebrows in a flippant answer that belied the concern he felt, for he had no confidence, at all, in Barneyway. Dominic's good-natured wink was not only surprising but discouraging, too, for he usually cursed when somebody kept him waiting.

"Mr. Dixon hasn't checked in all morning," Mr. Handy said, returning, brushing at the lock. "Listen you guys. You better tell me if you know where Jenson is. If I don't count him, it's an escape. He'll hit the hole, get some more time, maybe, might even get Youth Authority. Goddamnit, you guys, you better help me. Jenson's a good man, works hard."

The empty hollow of Aaron's stomach rumbled with hunger and foreboding. If Jenson had escaped. . . ? Then, after Dominic went home. . . ? Aaron tried to read the answer he feared in Dominic's unconcerned slouch, got his answer with another wink, and lost all doubt when he saw the sun flash on a station wagon windshield, heard the whine of its motor, and knew it was Big Stoop. The blast of the noon whistle then blew away the last of his hopes: Jenson was gone.

The sight of the station wagon spun Mr. Handy in nervous circles: from the line to the station wagon, to the line, to the station wagon. He sent the two boys nearest him to help search the dairy, and when the Buzzer reappeared, he sent the Buzzer and another boy to search the sheds, started to send another boy, also, but called the boy back, and was so obviously afraid of Big Stoop that when the station wagon pulled into the dairy yard with a rasp of rubber tires and soft billows of dust, Aaron's apprehension had reached a fearful pitch.

"Search the buildings?" Big Stoop asked, throwing the door open and crossing the yard with heavy steps.

"Four still searching," Mr. Handy added to his eager nod. Apparently satisfied, Big Stoop turned to the count lines, and Aaron watched the big man while standing at perfect attention.

Big Stoop rested his big hands on his big hips, leaned forward from his thick waist, poked his bull's head down, sighted with the stiff brim of his khaki cap, and moved along the front line at a slow menacing pace, never breaking his step or allowing his gaze to waver, as if he could peer into the brain of each boy he passed with one glance of his glass-hard, lashless, unblinking eyes.

Slow crunching steps drew nearer to Aaron, and he held his breath to keep from flinching when the eyes reached him, succeeded, breathed again when they passed, and watched, without moving, the huge bulk of khaki crunch out of the corner of his eye in its search for the one boy who couldn't look back.

The crunching stopped.

Aaron turned slightly and saw enough khaki to guess where: Barneyway!

"Out of line, you."

A tiny half-step put Barneyway into view beyond Dominic's chest, where he stood under Big Stoop's stare for such long silent seconds, Aaron began to hope that Big Stoop would realize his mistake.

"How did he get away?"

Thin fingers tried to shape an answer out of a mumble.

"Speak out!" Big Stoop demanded, and everyone snapped to attention again.

"I . . . I don't know," Barneyway said, the fingers moving, shaping again, then spreading and stiffening with the shock of a slap that sent him staggering down the line as far as Aaron, whose heart shriveled with shared humiliation and their lost last chances for respect.

Big Stoop stalked Barneyway, but every feature on the wide, bovine face: the slitted mouth, the broad-bridged nose, the tiny red and blue veins that mapped the dry skin—was as clear to Aaron as to Barneyway, and he felt as threatened as Barneyway by the crooked finger and the command:

"Ca-mirrrrr!"

Trembling spread from Barneyway's hands up his arms and over his body, but he didn't move; and Big Stoop grabbed him, so that he stumbled and almost fell as an ankle twisted and a knee bent close to the ground.

"Gonna tell how he got away?"

"I don't knooooooow," Barneyway moaned, and a sob caught in his throat as he coughed out: "Don't know—don't know."

"Mr. Dixon?" Big Stoop then asked and wobbled Barneyway's head with a backhand.

"I don't know," Barneyway said and started crying; and the huge cupped palm clapped in Aaron's ears with the next slap, and clashed like cymbals in them with the next one, which spun Barneyway's head around with its force, blood spurting from his nose, streaking across his cheek; and anticipating still another slap, unable to control himself any longer, Aaron yelled:

"He don't know! He couldn't know! He don't know—He don't know—He don't know—He don't know—He—"

He kept yelling as Big Stoop flung Barneyway aside and charged into him, but he was too mad to be scared, too mad to fear the red face, the cruel eyes, the blow that rang gongs in his ears, numbed his face, and knocked him to the ground, too numb then to care that he was jerked to his feet, knocked down again, jerked to his feet, and knocked down again, and too deafened by his own anger and the numbing slaps to care or understand what the shouting voice was saying.

Then, suddenly, no slaps, no gongs, no shouting, only the woozy comfort of the ground.

A long blue smear with many heads fenced one side of him and the other was a blend of blue and khaki posts, moving, connected by a stretcher of khaki.

Skinned elbows propped him up.

Big Stoop's bark cleared his mind a little, and he saw the Buzzer and Mr. Handy carry the limp body of Mr. Dixon, bald head covered with blood, past him and put it into the back seat of the station wagon.

Big Stoop's voice again.

The shift of gears.

A rasp of tires.

The sun shimmering like a silver bar on the station wagon bumper.

A smell of exhaust fumes.

And the slow settling of dust about him.


# IV


Phosphorous burns of wooden kitchen matches striped the warm steam pipe Aaron sat on in the brushy hide-out behind the compound, and the headless stubs of the matches lay scattered and barely visible in a litter of cigarette butts, wadded candy wrappers, and empty cigarette packs, cellophane, and open-flapped matchbooks on the gully floor, for it was darkening rapidly with twilight under the leafy tent of the manzanita tree.

Willow and scrub branches thickened the tent wall and prevented anyone from seeing Aaron, from seeing the hide-out, a hide-out which only a search for total seclusion had led him to discover, a hide-out so filled with worthless trash that only his desire to avoid the disgusting sight of Barneyway, whose friendship seemed as worthless, allowed him to tolerate it.

A sigh of long grass disturbed the hush. Someone was forcing his way through the field between the compounds, and Aaron sat up and listened, unwilling to let anyone see his reddened eyes, eyes whose impressions of people, of best friends, especially, he no longer trusted.

Soup and milk for Friday's late lunch and again for dinner, chocolate and cold toast for Saturday's breakfast, and soup and milk for lunch and dinner again had been the only food he could make himself swallow; and his belly was as tight as a fist from it and he felt as mean.

He hated everybody and everything with the exception of Judith, whose image had been as fleeting but as sparkling as the sunlight which had skimmed off the shiny leaves and penetrated the gloom in the hide-out; an image of a sweet, true cherry, which had appeared to him with Dominic's prophetic words:

"When it gets so bad, when you feel so miserable, beaten down, and lonely you wantta commit suicide, she's gonna be the reason you won't," and which the intruding sound prevented from reappearing.

Tall grass fenced the back wall of the compound, told him where the now darkened trail was and where he could expect to see the noisemaker. But the figure which appeared by the corner of the compound was too dark for its features to be distinguishable and was, also, partially blocked from view by an old comic book, stiff and browned by exposure, which was jammed into the crutch of a limb.

He peered through a leaf-free spot below the book, recognized the thin shape and short height of the figure as Barneyway, spit a bitter taste out of his mouth, and regretted it. For Barneyway heard the sound, edged closer on the narrow trail to the hide-out, waited, listening, then jumped from the path into the gully, stumbled upon the rocks, and while trying to see through the thick branches, began to feel about for the entrance with the clumsiness of a blind man. Aaron couldn't repress a snort of humor.

"Duck down, you'll see it," he said, evenly, coldly, and snorted again as Barneyway flinched.

"That figures," he said to himself, but aloud, unable to keep himself from striking at a guy who couldn't tell the truth without getting done in, a guy who couldn't get done in in a gutty way, who had to go down like pussy, and who had to get them both, and their chances, slapped down by that giant bastard.

"Stand up. You been inside for three feet now," Aaron said, forgetting in his bad mood that Barneyway, who was still crawling, had not yet adjusted his eyes to the hide-out's darkness.

For all of the men were bastards. Even Mr. Handy, who was as afraid of Big Stoop as an inmate, was a bastard; and Mr. Dixon was a bastard with a fractured skull. And Jenson was a mighty avenger who did more than slap, who busted Mr. Dixon's bald head with one blow of a pick handle at five-thirty in the morning, who stole Mr. Dixon's pickup truck, who drove it to the blind end of a back road and over the open fields like a tank, who smashed it against a tree stump twenty miles away, who escaped, and who was as bad as Dillinger for his age, and bound to be one, all the guys said.

Barneyway hit his head on a branch with a knock and a shiver of leaves as he stood and instinctively touched the sore spot.

"Don't cry now," Aaron said.

Big eyes had the dull shine of the leaves around them.

"What's on your mind?"

"We can't go into the dorm, Aaron," Barneyway said in a voice so mournful that a pulse of fear quickened in Aaron; and he drummed on the pipe to show he was not concerned and mocked:

"And why can't we go into the dorm?"

"The Buzzer and Rattler are bragging how they're gonna finish the job for Big Stoop on both of us."

Hollow beats dribbled to a stop.

"Did they say tonight?"

"They didn't say."

"What the hell yuh scared about then?" Aaron said, beating on the pipe again, harder, faster, stopped, and dropped to the ground, shocking his sleeping feet with the impact.

"Let's go in right away," he said and grabbed Barneyway's shirt sleeve.

"Let's go in and get our ass kicked. We're used to it. Come on. Let's go. Can the Buzzer hit harder than Big Stoop?"

"I thought you'd be glad I told you," Barneyway said, trying to pull free; and Aaron sighed and released the sleeve, feeling sorry for both of them.

"I am glad," he said. "But I'm sick of the whole thing, sick of getting bullied, sick of being scared, of getting whacked, sick of crying . . . of . . ." he almost said *you*, ". . . of praying even, sick of the whole goddamned place. I hate that goddamn chapel. I hate those ugly angels in it. They look like bull dikes."

He pounded on the pipe with both fists but couldn't make it echo, and a kick to its underside only produced a dispiriting thud. He turned and leaned against it but got no comfort from its mild warmth, and the strain of trying to see in the hide-out irritated him.

"What are we gonna do, Aaron?"

"How in the hell do I know?" he yelled and noticed the oblong rectangles of orange light high in the back wall of the compound, which meant they'd have to go inside for lockup soon.

"How could I know, Barney?" he said, trying to apologize, sorry, but disgusted, and with little hope. "Jenson's gone. Dominic ain't about to risk his go-home. I don't know. Just don't know. I'll tell yuh the truth, too. I stayed away from those bouts this morning not only because I was bumkicked but because I was leery the Buzzer would choose me with the gloves, and I heard he ain't nothin' in the ring, stays away from the gym because of that. I figured him for getting meaner now that Jenson's gone and after what Big Stoop did."

"Let's go tell Big Stoop then."

"Go to hell. I'd rather get whipped. I ain't that scared. Besides, what makes you think he'd believe us? He just beat us both up, remember? And the Buzzer's a cadet captain, man, no matter what his mother did.

"I should'a gone with Jenson," he added, pretending that he could have escaped the trap, without expecting Barneyway to believe him, and then admitting that he was trapped, but in the only way he could: by hurting both of them: "There's nothing we can do, man, nothing. We're gonna get whipped on again, just like before, worse than before, whether we deserve it or not. Whipped on, man. Whipped on."

"Let's go to the hospital, then, Aaron. Tell 'em we're sick. They'll let us in. They'll have to if we—"

"Sick? . . . Sick?" Aaron said. ". . . Sick?" And he was suddenly ashamed of himself, ashamed of what Stanley would think, and Judith, too, ashamed of wanting to quit, ashamed because he knew there would have to be a showdown when he made his pledge.

"Goddamnit, Barneyway," he said, "we're going in that dormitory. You understand? And if we get messed with, we're gonna fight. You understand? And if you don't fight, I'm gonna put you down. Got me?"

He pushed Barneyway into a squat and into a duckwalk through the branches ahead of him.

"Got me?" he said for his own benefit, too, as they climbed out of the gully and started inching their way along the dirt ledge behind the compound.

"Got me?" he kept repeating, but with decreasing power on the walk through the field.

"Got me?" he said, without force, when they reached the compound gate; and he did not lift the iron latch, for his knees had the peculiar weakness in them that always gripped them when he had time to think before a fight, time to consider his reasons for fighting, the consequences, and to doubt his own courage.

"Is Dominic in there?" he asked, trying to cover up his stall.

"Yeah, but he's not gonna—"

"I didn't ask you that. Don't forget what I told you," he said, severely, and felt his own courage come back to him. "If you get picked on, fight! Don't take it or it'll only get worse later, maybe even. . . ." He paused in order to sound more cruel. "Maybe both of them will try and give it to yuh, if you act scared."

He then shoved the gate open, strong again, strong enough to cross the courtyard with determined steps, to reach the screen door, to strike a fighting stance with his commands:

"Fight! Sunday 'um! Hit first!" and, stiff and poised as a short fuse, he threw the door open and marched into the dormitory, ready to spring on the Buzzer.

But soft light, soft talk, stale, undisturbed air, and no Buzzer unnerved him; and midway through the dorm, he began to lose his driving tension. He decided to ask for the Buzzer, which was the same as starting the fight himself, but which would, at least, guarantee that he would not be relaxed and unprepared for it and would also get the nervous strain of waiting over with; and he felt satisfied and almost relieved when the Buzzer walked out of the washroom with Rattler, both with towels and toothbrushes in their hands.

"Hah!" the Buzzer said.

"Hah!" Rattler repeated and popped his towel with a whipping snap of his thin arm; and Aaron stepped forward to meet them, but was stopped by a warning cough and Dominic's beauty mark, which was switching back and forth in a signal of caution.

He didn't expect Dominic to risk a go-home for him, but the concern shown for him by the only person he trusted calmed him, and he took the advice and sat on his bed rail, waiting to pick his best shot, ready to fight still, but only if he had to, more than willing to get by without a fight if he didn't get ranked as pussy.

"Rattler, ole buddy, ole shuck, tell me what come down when I out pickin' up Mis-tuh Dixon's busted he-ed? Gimme some ins, ma-han."

"Mistuh Big Stoop," Rattler said, waving his towel and reciting to the dormitory, "he whip on some paddy boys, pale-skinned Spanish boys. Ring some bells in their heads."

"Is that a fack?" the Buzzer said, scratching the thick fold of his neck in a dumb pretense at ignorance. "Who is they? Hip me to it, daddy."

"Punks," Rattler said. "Paddy boy punks. Buddy-up punks."

Aaron was annoyed, but he kept his temper, for his initial momentum was gone, the insults were still indirect, and the odds were too great to risk a battle unless he was chosen or was really angry. Also, Barneyway was hiding behind a book again and Dominic's lips twisted in such a pronounced leer of contempt that only the earlier signal convinced Aaron the leer wasn't meant for himself.

"Ain't you gonna tell me what hap-pen, ma-han?"

"Sure, man. Big Stoop scare a little punk half to death by giving him the bad eye. Then slap him around a little to help

him make up a good enough story," Rattler answered and began to snap his towel and side-step toward Barneyway, popping the towel with every phrase, singing:
"Beat on the punk,
knock him around,
bloody him up,
make him bawl like a broke-dick-dog,
like pussy,
punk-punk-punk."
He drove Barneyway, hands half-lifted, back up the bed to the wall with the stinging snap. And a snort of contempt from Dominic brought Aaron to his feet, his throat tight with an angry, disgusted, barely contained scream at Barneyway.

"Oow!" Barneyway said, not loud, flinching from the sting on his chest.

"Ow!" Barneyway said again, standing, and trying to flatten himself, with spread arms, against the wall between his locker and his bed.

"Ow!" Barneyway said again, and Rattler's laugh rattled like phlegm in his throat and he snapped the towel into Barneyway's crotch, and snapped Barneyway's hands when Barneyway tried to cover himself, and snapped Barneyway's butt when Barneyway turned, and raised the towel to snap it again.

"Stop!" Aaron yelled. "Stop!"

Rattler aimed the towel at Aaron.

"This ain't hurtin' you none. You better stay out of it."

"Quit torturing him," Aaron said, and disregarding the warning which pulsed in the vein at his temple, challenged:

"How would you like it, if I did it to you?"

"How did you like it when Big Stoop slapped your silly head around for butting in on somebody else's business?" Rattler drew his arms back to snap the towel. "And how would you like me to—"

"Find out! You sonofabitch!" Aaron yelled and threw himself at Rattler's throat, locked his fingers on the Adam's apple, and knocked Rattler backwards, over Barneyway's bed, and down to the floor.

"Yaaaaagh," Rattler groaned, trying to get his breath, prying at the fingers, struggling and kicking, knocking first against Barneyway's bed and then the adjoining bed, sending both of them skidding, and still groaning: "Yaaaaaaaaagh."

But the ridges of the Adam's apple helped Aaron hold his death grip, and Rattler's weak punches to his forehead and jabbing thumb to his eye only forced him to duck his head down between his stiffened arms and helped him to squeeze tighter, and he squeezed tighter, squeezed until Rattler's eyes popped out of their lids, squeezed until the groan became a wheeze, squeezed until a blow caught him in the ribs, knocked his breath out of him, doubled him into a ball, and sent him sprawling into the aisle, gasping for breath, fighting the faint that swept over him.

Another kick caught him in the back and knocked him farther, and he kept rolling, rolling instinctively, rolling to evade the next kick; and he rolled into a bed, rolled under it, rolled while trying to get his breath, rolled while watching for another kick, rolled while nausea knotted his belly and voices rose and fell like echoes in an empty auditorium.

Two pairs of pant legs and heavy brogans did a crazy dance by the bed, scuffled, skidded on the concrete.

A toothbrush fell to the floor and was crushed by a brogan.

One pair of legs began to back up under the flatfooted, driving advance of the other pair.

Fists thumped solidly against a grunting body, squashed against soft facial skin, and the Buzzer landed on his back and his feet flew up and dropped, and he cradled his jaw with one hand and raised the other in surrender; and Aaron knew that Dominic had saved him from a stomping.

Aaron then, while still gasping for breath and still nauseated, slid out from under the bed and, holding his side, got to his feet, determined to stand above his enemies and enjoy the victory, regardless of the discomfort.

"Don't ever mess with my boy while I'm here, or go-home or no go-home, I'll kill you," Dominic said, crouched above the Buzzer, who kept his palm up, his mouth shut, and stayed down.

Rattler sat on the floor between the beds, taking deep breaths, caressing his scratched throat; and Barneyway stood flattened against the wall, as if petrified with fear.

"You okay, little buddy?" Dominic asked, helping Aaron to his bed.

"Good. Real good," Aaron replied, gratitude making him discount the pain, noticing how very, very fine Dominic's features were for such a square and heavy head; and this seemed to mean something important, although he didn't care to think about it.

"I feel real good. Those two rats are on the floor, and my side don't even hurt."

He straightened up to prove it and caught his breath.

"Don't huh? You bad little mutha," Dominic said. "Jumping the dude when you knew you'd have to fight the Buzzer if you started winning. Me with my go-home and all, too. You're too bad to run with a punk like that."

He pointed at Barneyway against the wall.

"Look at him? You took his battle for him twice now. Got hurt both times, and he still ain't helped yuh. I just risked my go-home for you because I care what happens to you. That punk's gonna get you killed when I leave, and *he'll* live through it. Put him down, man. I'm telling you, Aaron. Put him down."

Barneyway's thin lips compressed into a straight line and he stopped trembling, moved away from the wall, pulled his bed into place, fixed its covers, and handed Rattler the towel, without once looking at Aaron.

"See what I mean?" Dominic said. "Look at the punk. He

acts like nothing happened, and you might have got your teeth kicked out and some busted ribs, if I hadn't been here."

"Barneyway," Aaron said, softly, too satisfied with the outcome of the fight to be angry, willing to listen to an explanation.

Barneyway smoothed the pillow with elaborate motions and Aaron raised his voice:

"Barneyway!"

Barneyway blocked the smoothed pillow very carefully and placed it exactly even with the head railing, totally ignoring Aaron, whose ribs began to ache at the busy movements which, committed in silence, admitted betrayal.

"Barneyway," he said and remembered his threat in the hide-out.

"Why didn't you help me, Barneyway?"

The pillow was smoothed, blocked, placed, and the motions had stopped, but there was no answer.

"Answer me!"

A stiff face turned slowly, finally, almost defiantly, toward Aaron, but did not speak.

"Why didn't you help me?"

The luminous eyes were willed into indifference.

"You dirty coward! You yellow, rotten coward! We'll never be friends again. Do you understand? Never! Never! I don't care if every nigger in the institute screws you. Do you understand? Do you? Do you?"

The eyes never wavered, never blinked.


## V


Thin, transparent clouds veiled the sun, streaked the sky, spread fleeting shadows over the scattered groups on the visitors' lawn, diffused outlines, highlighted some persons and special groups, then blotted them out, and created such a wavering, sporadically patched, darkened and lightened landscape that Aaron concentrated only on the subdued groups by the office for Judith, when the compound gate clicked behind him.

He scanned the office area as he walked, expecting to see warmth and sunshine on a gray day where she stood, as if she were enveloped in her own aura, like the image that he had depended upon throughout the week, and could warm him with it. He wanted her to soften the disappointment that had settled over him after the fight. He wanted her to soothe the hurt of the betrayal. He wanted her to salve the bruises from the kicks, kicks that gave him an unhappy taste of what he could expect when Dominic went home, kicks that made her visit not just important but urgent.

The pastel green of her skirt and sweater was gray-toned from a distance and her hair seemed ash blond in the overcast light, which was a mild let-down he took in stride, with a warning to himself that he must not expect too much from her visit. But when he started up the hill, her hair looked so very different, he slowed his pace with a premonition and lowered his gaze to the pavement, trying to deaden his feelings to correspond to the asphalt's dead color. He tried until he reached the top of the hill, then looked up, and let himself hurt.

A tattooed dot sat on the highest point of her cheekbone. A hard dot that drew all the rosy sweetness he had pictured in her cheeks into a point of blue corruption. A blatant dot on a little girl's face that advertised a rogue beauty. A dot that served as the center of attraction for a wild halo of ringlets, that set off the sharply tipped breasts of a very tight sweater, that suited too well the short skirt with the side splits, which made her hips lumpy and exposed the bulky caps of her knees. A dot that could not prevent a diverting glance at her legs, now thickened and straightened by bobby-sox bunched into thick rolls at her ankles.

"Hi!" she said weakly.

"What did you do?" he asked, unable to return her greeting or her smile.

She fumbled with her purse and smoothed her skirt, and the blue of her eyes was plaintive when she looked up, almost pathetic, but sensitive, and ready to respond, as if she were both shamed and shielded by the tattoo.

"What did you do?" he asked again, unwilling to go near her; and when she fumbled with her purse again, he strode past her.

She caught up with him, but her tight skirt bound her knees, and she wobbled, taking two steps for every one of his, and grabbed his hand to slow him down, but he jerked it free with an angry snap of his wrist, and kept walking.

"Aaron," she called, falling behind.

"Aaron, wait for me! Let me explain."

He stopped by the chapel and waited, without watching her, until she had almost reached him, then turned, and saw the beauty mark again.

"It looks cheap," he said, and the mark seemed to wither and draw all the color out of her face into its tiny blue peak.

"Look at you," he said. "You look fat in that tight skirt. You wobble when you walk. And what did you do to your hair? You look like a pachuca. You'll have a cross on your hand next."

The pouting thrust of her lips was counterpointed and made more emphatic by the tattoo, but the tiny patch of skin, as transparent as cellophane, which covered it, made him angrier.

"What'd you do that for? You look . . . you look like a . . . you look . . ."

But the beauty mark disappeared with her lowered face and the additional disappointment of wild light-colored ringlets made him pause, then demand:

"Tell me what you did it for? Tell me! Tell me!" but with decreasing power, for her lifting eyes were a surprisingly calm blue, and her dispirited voice was almost glacial in tone:

"All the girls have them now, Aaron."

"All what girls?" he asked, unable to believe she could defend herself.

"Our crowd."

"That's not saying anything."

"You wear drapes, don't you?"

"I'm a guy, Judith. You're a girl. Do you fight? Do you go to jail?"

She clamped her upper lip between her teeth and pulled her nostrils down into distortion, but he persisted:

"My sister would rather die than tattoo herself."

"Your sister!" she said and her voice was a high, weird tone of resentment and dismay.

"My sister!" he repeated, striking her with it for fighting back, and she lowered her face again. But he was too disappointed to stop, too conscious of betrayal, and he asked, "You didn't get permission to come, did you?"

She lifted her face with the question and bit her lip again. Her eyes appealed to him for a moment, then clouded over, and she shook her head once, stiffly, and did not look away.

"It doesn't matter," he said, disappointed because she did not break down in some way under a charge that hurt him so badly; and he started back toward the gym, swearing he would never have faith in anyone again.

"Aaron," she said, but he kept walking.

"Aaron," she called, raising her voice. "Aaron, maybe I can take it off?"

He weakened but wouldn't turn around, and she ran after him and grabbed his hand, and although he didn't return her grip or comment on her suggestion, he didn't try to pull free.

"Canned milk might take it off, Aaron. That's what I heard."

"It doesn't—"

"I won't dress like this anymore," she interrupted. "I'll wash my hair when I get home and set it like I used to. I'll—"

"It doesn't matter," he said again, but more weakly and stopped by the gym ramp.

"Aaron, I'm sorry that I put it on."

"I just said—"

"I thought you'd like it, Aaron," she said.

And he let his arm relax. And he let himself look past the tattoo. He let himself see the little girl's pure blue eyes. He let himself see the cherry he knew in those chippy's clothes, the cherry he had gone to jail a first time for, who had written to him this time since his arrest, who had come to see him a second time without permission, and he said, regretting it as he said it, knowing it would only lead to more disappointment:

"I'm sorry. I'm sorry I yelled at you."

"I did it after an argument with Mom. She wouldn't let me come. She said she'd never let me come. She said—"

"Judith! Don't explain! You're here!" he said, trying to stop her, for her appearance was completely transformed by his admiration, and the tattoo was now a badge she could be proud of, a mark of distinction, of guts. But the alteration followed too swiftly upon and was too contradictory to the cherry he had seen with the previous glance and confused him. And he waved his hand at her, as if to dismiss her and her hair-do and her tight skirt and her bobby sox, and he didn't know what he thought of her.

"It's not just the tattoo or the way you look."

"What else did I—"

"It's not the tattoo! It's not you!" he said, irritably, blaming her for making things so complicated and confusing.

"You're sure?" she asked.

"I'm sure," he said and turned his back on her again and stared out over the visitors' lawn.

"You won't be here long, Aaron," she said, after a quiet pause, and slipped her hand into his. "Keep being good and you'll get to go home. You will. I know it."

"Good?" he said and a glimpse of her hair set off a wave of resentment in him.

"Good?" he repeated and turned so he couldn't see any part of her.

"Just be good and it won't be long."

"Good?" he said again and the word had a bad taste. He wrung his fingers free of hers and stared over the lawn again, seeing, without noticing, the small number of family groups sitting in scattered picnic circles. *Good* seemed especially ironic coming from a girl who had tattooed herself, who seemed a good example of Dominic's advice, and he wondered what Dominic would say about her beauty mark: a bitch? a lay?

"What else is wrong, Aaron?"

"I-can't-be-good," he said, meaning to mock her but heard a spoiled-brat sound instead, which irritated him because he felt it could be justified.

"Why can't you?" she asked, and she seemed to hover skin-close without touching him, without interfering with an answer.

"It's not for schoolgirls to hear," he said, being cruel but truthful, and her beauty mark faded into inconsequence next to Barneyway's rape.

"Why not? I've seen the guys fight. I've seen them stomp," she said, and he started to deny he could tell her again, although she had guessed well, when he saw Rattler sitting on a bench with an old woman dressed completely in black, and he said, excitedly:

"That's why! See that skinny rat sitting with that old lady? That's why I can't be good."

"The Mexican woman with the shawl over her head?"

"That's why!" Aaron said, triumphantly, as if no further explanation were needed, and turned to face her as she leaned around him to see better and asked, with disbelief:

"Does he have a cross tattooed between his eyes?" but added

with Aaron's nod: "He seems awfully quiet and behaved with her. Why is he keeping you from being good?"

"He just does," Aaron said, disliking the weak evasion in his answer but unhappy over her failure to accept his word without an explanation; and because he couldn't think of a way to explain what was really wrong and justify his accusation without embarrassing both of them, he repeated, feeling like a martyr: "He just does, that's all."

"Come on," she said, "let's go sit on the chapel lawn there and talk."

"Not there," he said, quickly, wanting to respond to this familiar Judith, who could act like a full-grown woman at critical moments, but he dreaded the chapel with its deadwood Christ.

"I'd rather sit on that bench by the gym," he said and led her up the ramp, trying to think of some way to explain without mentioning the filthy details. But on the bench, it was her tattoo which kept him from speaking because he couldn't relate her motherly concern with its brazen sexuality.

She, herself, guessed what was wrong, for she began to gaze at the concrete ramp before her as if she were interested in how the sun, which had pierced the veil of clouds, glistened upon it, and this gave him an opportunity to start.

"You know Barneyway's in my dorm, right?"

He paused for she began to look at him again, and he had to look away in order to continue.

"Well, he got himself beat up by that big colored guy, called the Buzzer, whose mother put on that wild show last Sunday. You know," he said and stopped again, remembering his own hysteria.

"Well, the Buzzer hangs around with that tattooed guy and they both pick on Barneyway, and the colored guy, he even . . . He even. . . ."

"Yes," she said, peering closely at him, trying to keep him

from stopping, but distracting him with the tattoo and he couldn't speak again until she had leaned back.

"He . . . he beat him up real bad," he said, skipping that untellable part, the worst part, too bad and unbelievable for her ears, something he wouldn't have quite believed himself before the institute.

"Poor Barneyway," she said. "Poor guy."

"You seen the guy," Aaron said, getting excited by her response. "You seen how big he is, and he's a dog-bully, too. I fought that dirty Mexican rat with the cross over Barneyway, and the colored guy jumped me. My ribs and back still ache where he kicked me."

"They tried to stomp you?" she asked, turning a full face toward him, forgetting her tattoo.

"Tried, but that's okay," he said, pleased by her concern, pleased because the victory would sound better, more heroic, when she had heard how he suffered first. "A buddy of mine, Dominic, great guy, tough, tough guy, jumped in and made him quit, and I almost killed that rat on the bench."

"No, Aaron, don't talk about stomping or killing. Be good."

She pulled his hand into her lap and began stroking his knuckles.

"Don't mess yourself up, Aaron. Stay away from them now. With your friend to help you, you don't have to worry. Be good."

"Dominic's leaving and when he does, they're gonna try and get me. They're gonna get me," he said, melodramatically, and saying it gave him strength, but it was also an appeal for consolation, for he did not expect advice nor a solution from her. He only wanted the sympathy which the tiny beige freckles sprinkled across her nose seemed to promise, in spite of the distracting blue dot.

"You're giving up," she said and pressed his hand against her cheek, unconsciously covering the beauty mark, and he could feel her jaw move and the vibration of her voice in his knuckles when she spoke. "You can't quit like this. The Aaron I know will find something to do about it. You go tell that big guard. He'll do something about it for you."

"That big guard beat me and Barneyway up just a day before I fought that rat. That's what's wrong," he said and his voice squeaked with a self-pitying rush of words. "There's nothing I can do. I can't beat those two guys myself. I got no one to help me after Dominic leaves. I can't tell. That would make me a fink and, besides, he wouldn't believe me. And I can't run away. That's trouble even if I get away."

"Aaron, Aaron," she said, but he started again.

"I can't win if I fight. I get in trouble if I fight. Barneyway won't even help. I fought those two guys over him and it was all for nothing. I told him I'd stick by him and I had to break my Mother's Honor because he let me do it for him. He didn't even help me when they jumped me. I lost a friend. I broke my word. I got beat up for nothing twice. There's nothing I can do—nothing, not a thing. How can I be good? Good's a joke. . . ."

"Joke," he said, for he had heard the whine in his voice.

"Joke," he said again and tried to laugh, but only hacked.

"Aaron, listen to me. I don't know what to do. I really don't. But I do know that you've got your family and they care and they can do something. I don't know what, but they can. And you can write to me. I'll get the letters, don't worry. I'll do anything you want. You ask me. But don't give up trying to be good. I'll help you, Aaron. You're not alone. I'll prove that you're not. I'll get rid of this beauty mark. I'll. . . . Believe me," she said and sucked in her breath and squeezed his hand until her finger tips reddened and rimmed white, suffering with such tenderness for him that he resisted an urge to console her in order to prolong it; and he wished that Dominic or some of the guys, even the Buzzer, especially the Buzzer, could see her, could see how much he was cared for by a girl, by a pretty girl with a beauty mark, for she *was* pretty, even with the beauty mark.

You're not alone, Aaron. I'll find some way. . . . I'll. . . ."

She drew in her breath and didn't finish, for she realized that he was staring at the tattoo, and she lowered her head, self-consciously, but in such a way that to him, above her, the pale lashes of her lowered eyes swept out to the rims of her cheeks, and the tattooed dot was like a dark tear clinging to the tips of long curling strands.

He became convinced that it was a tear, a dark pathetic tear of a little girl who didn't even know how to double her fists, but who had fought back at her mother for him with it, and who had ruined her face for him with it, and it shamed him and his self-pity and the pleasure he had enjoyed at her suffering.

"I'll find a way, Aaron," she said, but was unwilling to look at him.

"I know you will," he said, trying to make her feel better. "But forget about it now."

"I'll find a way."

"Forget about it," he said, loosening his hand, wanting to caress the tattoo, but he said, instead: "Say? I thought visits were supposed to be happy?"

"Huh?" she said, looking at him but covering the beauty mark with her fingers.

"Huh, what?" he said and touched the top button of her sweater.

"Huh?" she said again, confused, and looked down, and he flicked her nose with his finger tip, and her head jerked up, eyes wide-circled with surprise, then chinked with a smile, and she pretended to slap him, but tapped his cheek, and he clapped his hand against it and fell back against the gym wall, and they both began to laugh.

He noticed the cute quiver her small double chin had when she giggled and this increased his pleasure, and he said to hell with the beauty mark and the Buzzer and Rattler and Barney-way and Big Stoop, too. To hell with everything that might ruin his visit, the only chance in the week that he got to be with someone of his own choosing, who chose him. He loved her and that was all that counted.

Love?

The warm oval of her laughing face had strange, yet familiar highlights to it; and he thought that they might be caused by the tattoo. But he stopped laughing and stared at her.

Giggles bubbled up from her double chin more slowly and trailed off as she began to return his gaze with a curiosity that quickened the blue in her eyes, a blue that seemed to turn, gradually, to the warm shade of coral with her discovery, and then quickly vanished as she looked away.

The word love embarrassed him, for kids didn't love each other. But the piquant face lifted slowly toward him, and the blue eyes, the pale freckles, the beauty mark came slowly into his view, as if confirming his thoughts, the important word he was trying to make himself believe. And the closed lips spread softly, in the faintest hint of a smile, and he knew that she had said yes, yes, she did . . . love . . . him. . . .

# Part Eight
# On Each Fist

# On Each Fist

## I

Mirage pools of light shimmered on the varnished hardwood surface of the gym floor, giving it an appearance to Aaron, with the heedless and heavy bouncing of the many boys who boxed, shadowboxed, did calisthenics and jumped rope upon it, as transparent and treacherous as thin ice.

"Punch, punch," Dominic said, joking, for Aaron's shoulders twitched defensively, as if slipping the sloppy, roundhouse punches of a colored guy who boxed near him; but Dominic added, seriously: "A little blond guy, Aaron, called Skip. He can get you a blade if anybody can."

"What's the guy's name?" Aaron asked, without smiling at the joke, wishing he could forget the whole project, not just the name.

"I've told you twice, man, twice! I know you ain't hot for this idea yet," Dominic said, leading Aaron past two boys working out with a medicine ball; and Aaron winced when the heavy ball thudded into one kid's tensed stomach muscles and buckled slightly when it was snapped back into the other guy's walled belly.

"But hot or not, you gotta have an equalizer after I go home. A long blade will keep that nigger at a distance."

"I don't wantta cut nobody, man," Aaron replied, hoping the colored guy who shadowboxed by them with sharp smooth

225

movements and whose body tapered from wide shoulders to a tiny waist hadn't heard Dominic.

His own admiration for the guy's skill and build was quickly stifled by the stink of the body and the T-shirt, which was yellowed stiff with sweat, and he feared that a blade would put him in the same class. For most of the colored guys from way down West Oakland carried them, and the Mexican guys from Seventh Street had blades in their black zoot suits, and the Okies in Government Village had them, too, while nobody in his gang had one.

"Would you rather be stomped? Punked like Barneyway?"

"Would you rather be dead?" Aaron asked, annoyed by the stupid question. "I'm here, aren't I? We're looking for the goddamned guy."

But sweat hung in the still air, smelled warm, smelled stale, smelled like old leather boxing gloves, punching bags, smelled like all the black and worn equipment of crushed and scarred old pros, smelled like the old pros, too, and smelled like the sweaty tales they told in the battered locker rooms of dark gyms, for the victorious battles were just as gone and just as forgotten to everyone but themselves as all the lost decisions, the TKOs, and the never heard ten-counts.

He then stalled by watching a boy do sit-ups, still searching for some way out, but only saw a body coil painfully off the floor like a slowly wrapping spring, squeeze into a jackknife against the stiffened knees of outstretched legs, then uncoil slowly, punishingly, and become one trembling, suffering band from the toes to the sweat-limp hair of the scalp.

"Come on," Dominic said, impatiently, and almost walked into a Mexican kid jumping rope, who seemed to hover an inch off the shiny floor with the easy grace of a hummingbird: skip-tap, skip-tap, skip-tap, skip-tap, but whose teeth were gritted with strain.

Dominic stepped around him and continued toward the open door of an adjoining room, from where the rhythmic pop of punching bags grew increasingly louder, and through which he led Aaron to a shirtless blond kid, who was punching a heavy bag.

"This is Skip, man," Dominic said and the boy stopped punching, but breathed heavily, every muscle in his long trunk pinked with sweat and exertion.

"This is my boy, Aaron, Skip. He's gonna need an equalizer to handle the Buzzer and Rattler with when I leave the end of this week."

Skip popped a final, lazy punch solidly against the bag and turned a broad-cheeked, fist-flattened face to Aaron, squinting at him with eyes almost level with his own, but as if measuring him for a right cross. His blond hair was wild with pomade and exercise, and his voice, although congenial, sounded as if it honked through his crushed nose:

"Say! Isn't this the little guy who kicked your butt a couple of weeks ago? and right after you stopped that spook?"

"The one," Dominic said, "and the same little dude who battled against all those beans from Santa Clara. Remember we talked about that?"

"Yeah. Damn right, I remember," Skip said and, pulling off his bag glove, he shook Aaron's hand with a hot, slippery palm.

"Small man, bad man. Come on, let's go somewhere where we can talk private." He waved his glove at a boy who was punching a light speedbag, with a loud racket, against a top board, and added: "Wait for me in the gym."

The seconds of the short wait were pounded out by punching bags, the minutes punctuated by the body thuds and head smashes of boxing gloves, filled with the busy sight of many boys sharpening their bodies to hurt each other, while Aaron waited for a blade which could kill; and he was not pleased when Skip swaggered across the gym floor, his face washed, his shirt on but still unbuttoned, its tails hanging to his knees, and twirling a black comb through his blond hair, led them out a side exit into the sunlight, midway between the chapel annex and the empty ring, opposite the caged windows of the metal shop.

"Now, what's coming down?" Skip asked, buttoning his shirt.

"Yeah," he said, listening intently, tucking it into his pants.

"Yeah, yeah," he answered when Dominic had finished.

"Yeah, I'll get him a blade. Take time and work. But when I do, he's gotta forget where he got it, and I hope he sticks it up that nigger's ass," and he cinched his leather belt and hooked his thumbs in it, while waiting for Aaron to speak.

The weather vane cock on the dairy roof glinted brightly in the distance, caught Aaron's attention, and remained fixed in his mind as he sat heavily down upon the stairs without speaking, although he was aware that he should thank Skip, that making a blade was not only work but dangerous, that Skip could get the hole for it at the very least, and that it was a great favor for a guy you didn't know, even if *he* didn't want it!

Wrinkles of annoyance lifted the swollen tip of Skip's nose, and he unhooked his thumbs to say something, but Dominic motioned to him to keep quiet and said to Aaron:

"If you got it, you might not have to use it, Aaron. The Buzzer is a real hound when it comes to giving up some of his black booty for a bully job. Ain't that right, Skip?"

"He's a dog. He'll run before he'll risk a blade on his leathery rump," Skip replied, and the colored glass in the chapel windows glowed with Aaron's rising hope. But the weathercock was as thin and sharp as a blade, and Judith's smile spread softly, subtly in his mind. *Good* was not a knife in his pocket or hidden under his shirt.

"Look," Dominic said, sitting next to Aaron on the stairs. "You like seeing the little chick, right?"

"Yeah, and that's the trouble." Aaron wasn't even surprised that Dominic had guessed his thoughts. "How'm I gonna face her with an equalizer under my shirt? Tell her I'm playing it cool when I'm ready to risk killing a guy?"

"Now, listen," Dominic said, as Skip walked down the stairs and stood in front of them, his nose wrinkled with perplexed curiosity. "Now, didn't I tell yuh once that you should hang onto that little chick because she was gonna help you do this time? Especially when it got so bad you felt like dying?"

"Yeah."

"You know what I think about bitches that make you weak, right?"

"Yeah."

"Have I ever bumrapped your little girl in any way?"

"No."

"Read then," Dominic said and stuck out both of his clenched, tattooed fists.

"Read!" he said.

"Love and Hate. One on each fist. Both! It takes both, Aaron. It takes your little girl. But it takes this bad-acting right fist of hate, too, and first! You can't make it in this institute or anywhere without both. Somebody's gotta care for you and you for them. But you gotta keep yourself strong enough to be *able* to care. A guy who's not strong can't really care. Look at Barneyway! Look at that punk! So weak, he has to use up all his caring on himself. He wouldn't even help you when you were fighting for *him!* Can't you see?"

Barneyway's opaque, indifferent eyes and his crucified stand against the dormitory wall seemed to Aaron to make visual sense of Dominic's words, and his own mother's skull-like face in the hospital bed was the worst proof in a different way: caring without being strong got you done in young. Judith didn't really know what he was fighting against, either, and how about her dot? It was a beauty mark and for pretty, but gutty, too: sort of a sign of good and bad, like Dominic's two fists.

"How do I scare 'im?" he asked.

"Warn 'im," Dominic said, but added hastily: "don't tell him what you got for him. Then he can figure out a way to handle it, if he wants to bad enough. Just tell him you got an equalizer. That oughtta throw a scare in 'im."

"But what if I don't scare 'im?"

"Flash it on 'im. Let him see its metal."

Click of a springblade knife, a sharp-edged shine, and Aaron could picture himself threatening the Buzzer with a push button.

"But what if that don't scare 'im?"

"Then you gotta stick 'im, or he'll take it away and stick you, screw you like he screwed your buddy," Skip said, but calmed Aaron's quick anger by the matter-of-fact tone in which he spoke, for it was apparent that he wasn't trying to show off.

"You'd have to stick 'im," Dominic said, reluctantly.

"Wow! I got no choice, do I?"

"If you act like you ain't shuckin', you do," Dominic replied. "If he sees that you mean it, he won't risk jumping you."

"And if he does? Jumps me with Rattler and some of his boys, because he knows I've got the blade?"

A circle of guys surrounded Aaron, closed slowly in upon him, and he looked carefully into Dominic's face to make sure he wasn't kidded, and the weather vane poked like a thin horn tip above the curly head.

"Get the closest one, then," Dominic said and jabbed with an imaginary blade and jumped off the stairs and jabbed again.

"Get him bad. Make him drop it goes in so far. And when the others see this, it'll stall 'em. Then run, man. Get out in the open where you got lots of room, where you can do something. Move, use your speed, if they got the guts to try you some more."

"How do I hold it?" Aaron asked, captured by Dominic's dramatization.

"Underhanded, man. Like this." Dominic held his hand with

the fingers up and the knuckles down. "Just like a hook to the belly. They can't block it easy or slip it without getting hurt, and yuh got control that way. Try it."

Aaron jumped off the stairs and threw a hook to the belly, and Skip danced back, holding a blade in his hand, too.

"You can jab, jab, jab like you're boxing, too," he said, spearing at Aaron with his left hand, and Aaron danced back, and Dominic danced back, and they made a tense triangle: each with a blade, each poised on his toes, each ready to fight and die.

"And if he goes down?" Aaron cried. "Tries to get up?"

"Don't change your grip. Jump in and poke down, that's all. Like this!" Dominic shouted and hopped forward and jabbed down, grunting with each slow and deliberate cork-screw motion of his entire arm.

"But he's getting up! Get 'im! Get 'im!"

"He's tough," Aaron cried and hopped in and jabbed, and then jabbed again.

"He's tough! He's tough! Help us, Skip! Help us! Help us!"

"I'll kill that mutha'," Skip said and hopped in and jabbed once, twice, and, face flattened with aggression, kept jabbing and jabbing and jabbing and jabbing and jabbing. . . .

## II

Reflections wavered and stretched and distorted in the clash of glass and afternoon sunlight on the library's bay window, yet heightened the contrast between Aaron's wrinkled and soiled dungarees and Dominic's immaculate steel-gray suit.

Aaron, too, while dreading the arrival of the man who would take Dominic home and Skip, who might arrive with bad news or too late or both, kept adding to the distortion and the contrast by constantly glancing at the window, wiping his hands on his thighs, sticking them in his back pockets, lifting his legs and pulling up his stockings, and kicking at the tiny blackened pebbles embedded along the edges of the asphalt road.

"Skip'll be here, just like he promised, and he'll bring good news about the blade. You can count on the guy. It takes time. The metal shop ain't no knife factory, you know," Dominic said, but Aaron couldn't make himself respond.

For Dominic was going home and he wore his semidrape go-home suit with the casual ease of a guy who knows he looks good, and who can afford to ignore the envious stares of the passing guys and the boys in the library, whereas he, Aaron, still had to do his time, had to do it alone, had a for-sure battle coming up, still didn't have an equalizer, and felt dirty and small as he looked in the window.

"Look, man," Dominic said, explaining all over again, but without heat, without exasperation. "He stole the file Tuesday, right?"

Aaron didn't answer, for going over the facts only made them more painful, and only to stand where Dominic was standing, and have that sharkskin suit fit himself with such good taste—the fingertip coat was buttoned on the inside of the double-breast and the fold which flapped free gave the coat a tapering, casual cut—would truly console him.

"Right?"

Aaron nodded but judged the knees of the slacks as twenty-eights, the cuffs as fifteens and compared them to the smaller knees and twelve-inch cuffs of most of his own drapes.

"Then he didn't get to grind it down until Wednesday, right? Right?" Dominic insisted until Aaron had to look at him, but Dominic's ruddy complexion and his black pomaded hair went so handsomely with the black knit tie and the wide white lapels of the spread collar, Aaron felt worse.

"He didn't get to finish it yesterday. Ain't that right now?"

Aaron nodded again, but it was useless, and he only longed for a pair of his own stompers, with their toes polished into as brightly burnished half-moons of dark cordovan as Dominic's.

"He figured he'd get it done today if everything worked out, and he promised he'd come and tell us about it here, now, before I left. Now ain't that right? Ain't it? Ain't it?"

"Yeah, yeah, I know. I'm not saying anything, am I?"

"You ain't saying nothing at all, and I'm going home for good in a few minutes. Half hour at most. You oughtta be saying something," Dominic said and jabbed Aaron's arm hard, knocked him off balance, hurt him, and Aaron fell into a crouch and feinted, but did not punch, and tried to apologize:

"I'm sorry, Dominic. I don't want yuh to go, but I am glad you're getting set free, and that's the truth."

"I'm glad you're glad," Dominic chuckled, " 'cause if you weren't, I'd swear you were going to a funeral, for sure."

"It's the truth, Dominic," Aaron said and, trying to prove it to himself as well as to Dominic, he scanned the tree-lined main road below them for the black car which would take Dominic to the Oakland Detention Home before setting him free. He then searched the highway and the trickle of cars and trucks along it, but felt as if he *were* counting the cars at his own funeral, couldn't continue, and tried to prove he cared with words.

"Man, I wantcha to know . . . that . . . I am glad that my buddy is getting out . . . out! away from here!" He stood at attention to keep his face stern and free of self-pity, which was a battle he had been fighting and losing all day.

"I wantcha to know that . . . it ain't just because I gotta stand alone against the Buzzer. It's mostly because my friend's going away and I can't go with him. That's it, mostly, I guess?"

"I wish you were my brother, man," Dominic said, obviously moved. "I was waiting for some shuck talk: some good guy stuff and this and that. But you came out straight, man, like always. Now, I'll tell you something, man, and I mean this. You know how bad I wantta go home? Well, I'm sorry

I'm leaving you here and that's no lie. I swear on my Mother's Honor, and not just because you're going to have to tangle with those two dogs, but because you got the guts to tangle with 'em alone, as little as you are, too. I've only known you two weeks and it seems like two years. Heard about you long before I met you. Had to meet you and see you in a cross to really believe it. You got everything, dad: guts, smarts, honor. You make being little seem big. On my Mother's Honor!"

"We'll be buddies when I get out," Aaron said, fully meaning it in his flattered enthusiam, believing it himself. "And Skip's gonna get that blade and I'm gonna stick it into that black baboon's belly. I'm going to send him straight to hell."

"Now you're with it. And send him some of that salvation steel for me, too, buddy-o."

"Salvation steel? Good name! I hope it's pretty. I hope it shines like a star."

"Ain't gonna be no factory-made blade. Gonna be home-made and ugly, but good, good."

Aaron's enthusiasm was a little deflated, for he had imagined a jeweled scabbard, a velvet hilt, and a blade whose surface was a grained network of dull brilliance. He had never seen a home made blade before and "ugly" would be a disappointment.

"A blade's a blade, dad. Remember that. Pretty ain't nothin'. Sharp is," Dominic said and added:

"See? What'd I tell yuh? Here comes Skip."

They watched him leave the metal shop, pass the chapel, and approach them with a slow-stepping walk, which was maddening to Aaron because it could conceal good news or be the dispirited result of bad news, and because Skip kept the pace and the secret throughout the slow trip to them.

"I almost got caught," he began, honking through the crushed bones of his nose, aggravating Aaron's impatience by explaining first. "I was grinding it down when the man came in and I had to drop it in a trash can and split. When I came back later, it was gone. Somebody must've swiped it. I was almost through, too, just making the point a little smoother. I'm sorry, man."

The dented bridge of his nose was all Aaron could see of his face, for he lowered it in such a guilty manner and seemed so genuinely sorry that Aaron, who was still enthused by Dominic's compliments, threw his hands up.

"Guess I got no blade, Dominic, ugly or not."

"Ugly?" Skip said.

"When can you get another one?" Dominic asked, words streaming through his lips, making no attempt to explain.

"I got to play it cool," Skip said, quick with his answer. "Two files missing one right after the other might be noticed, make the man suspicious. But. . . . Next week. Yeah, one week at most. And if I can't get a file, I can make a pitchfork out of a dinner fork in five minutes. In that case, by Tuesday afternoon, at the latest, he'll have something to fight with."

"That oughtta hold you, Aaron."

"Ought to," Aaron said, allowing himself to feel optimistic.

"Run with Skip, man," Dominic advised. "He's as bad as you. And stay away from the dorm and out of the Buzzer's way. Whatever you do, *don't* let the dude loud-talk you into fighting until you got the blade. Remember that. Don't fight until you got the blade, unless he tries to manhandle you. Then, little buddy, go! But otherwise, words won't hurt when you're working on a battle plan. Got me?"

"I got yuh. I'll play it cool until I got my blade. I'll even run, if I have to, and I'll make him run when I get it."

"Good! You'll make it with Skip's help. I know you will," Dominic said, optimistically; and the black car coming through the gate, creeping up the road, changing shades as it passed through the bars of shadow cast by the tall eucalyptus trees, did not destroy Aaron's anxious optimism.

His optimism lasted through the arrival of the car, the appearance of the probation officer, his reappearance from the office with Dominic's folder, the final handshake, the aching moment when Dominic climbed into the car, the cough and hum of the motor, the growl of the exhaust pipes, the car's cruise past the gym, the chapel, the trade shops, the open fields, the baseball field, the boys playing on it, and back through the bars of shadow to the main gate.

It lasted through the sad, tiptoeing, palm-brimming, eye-shielding minute or two of the car's passage from the gate to the gap in the green hills, and it lasted through the sun-setting, moon-rising unhappy hours between Dominic's departure, dinner and lockup time, and it even lasted into the lonely hour Aaron spent in the darkened courtyard, where Dominic's tattooed fists and Judith's beauty mark kept his courage up; and although he wasn't optimistic when he walked into the dormitory, he had prepared himself for whatever and whoever he had to face, and he was scared, but he was not afraid.

A sudden hush rushed like a suffocating wave away from him with the slam of the screen door, spread thinly over the final whispers of two boys by the washroom, who were the last to notice him, then backwashed over them.

He forced himself through the dense silence to his bed, where he considered entering the washroom, but guessed that he wouldn't undress the entire night, and sat down with his back to the wall, so he could see in all directions.

He saw the Buzzer, already stripped down to his white shorts, whisper to Rattler. He saw Rattler, the pink skirt of his nightgown belling above big dark feet, go to his locker, take out a pair of black dress gloves, and dangle them from his hand like two prize fish. But he could see no trace of the friend he needed so badly in the folded mattress and exposed iron springs next to him.

A murmur rippled across the engulfing tide of silence.

The back of Rattler's pink skirt lifted with a bow. And the Buzzer bowed as he took the gloves, with a very dainty clasp of thumb and forefinger, bowed again for thanks, then bowed twice to the dormitory, once toward Aaron and once toward Barneyway.

Crisp laughter followed each bow, and only Barneyway, who lay on his bed, staring at the ceiling, and Aaron, who took a comic book off the top of his locker and tried to read, did not laugh. But the pages rustled so loudly in his trembling hands, Aaron dropped the book on the bed, hoping no one had noticed, and tried to read without touching it, only to start at the sound of the Buzzer's song and realize by the quick, trailing laughter that everybody had been watching him.

A hopeless wish then hurt in his chest. But no wish could conjure a Dominic from the folded mattress, nor from its iron buttoned navels, nor from the checkerboard of wire links and springs below it, although the Buzzer kept singing his rolling monosyllabic tune:

"Gonna get me some
                  punk-honey.
Bee-wrap a flao-wa,
              me.
Get me some
              punk-honey."

His feet brushed in a splay-toed but rhythmic shuffle down the dormitory. His arms and hands twisted in sinuous exaggerations of glove fitting. His muscles tensed as if they flooded with black blood. His jutting rump switched easily from side to side, each buttock popping out in turn with the shifting weight of the slow beat. His head swayed in half-time, and all the muscular angles of his body swayed in loose-limbed pattern to the rhythm of his song.

"Have you heard the news?" Rattler sang out.

"Everybody's rocking tonight."

And was followed by a chorus of laughter.

Some boys stopped when Aaron looked at them, and closed their mouths, embarrassed. Others showed their teeth in louder laughter. Some merely smiled. But not one had the courage to give him a sympathetic glance. He counted them without counting, remembered those who didn't laugh, felt contempt for those who turned away, and forgot all of them when the Buzzer popped his gloved fist into his gloved palm, like a pistol shot, by Barneyway's bed.

"Sting some,
        sting, sting, sting some
                tonight."

Barneyway stared vacantly into the rafters and ignored the Buzzer, and Aaron, who was sweating for him, recognized his courage, for he didn't fight but he didn't show fear. But it was courage without hope, submission to the most terrible insult he could suffer without a struggle; it was accepting defeat while he still had a chance to win, even if a remote, improbable chance. And Aaron wanted to scream at him that peace was not worth this price, that he should get mad, act scared at least, show some proof that he still cared what happened to him.

But the Buzzer clapped his gloved hands over his snapping groin, spit out the word sting and, jut-jawed, marble-eyed, his neck streaked with tightened cords, arteries, and veins, then hopped a step with each snap, each sting until he reached Aaron's bed, where he shut his small eyes, sucked wind through his pursed lips as if to signify bliss, and sang:

"Bee-wrap some,
bee-wrap a flao-wa, me,
get me some
                punk-honey."

A single cheek-twitch betrayed Aaron's tension, and it was his only movement until the lights blinked and the clash of the gate stopped the Buzzer's song, until the Buzzer swaggered to his bed, where he popped his gloved fist into his gloved palm, and got under the covers. Aaron then slipped under his own blankets to a chorus of guffaws, with all his clothes on but his dungaree shirt, wishing he had the blade, and no longer concerned with who might get hurt with it.

The man was an undefined form of counting brown, quickly gone and quickly forgotten, as every boy in the dormitory except Barneyway, who peeked at Aaron with sorrowful eyes, from covers pulled up to his nose, propped himself up on a pillow and waited for the lights to go out.

A low-toned hum began with first darkness, rumbled, receded, then rose to a higher fluctuating pitch, with the snapping back of blankets, then broke into climactic song with the bodiless apparition of white shorts which appeared and hung motionless against the darkened wall, then suddenly ceased as the shorts bobbed steadily toward Aaron, with a patter of bare feet.

Aaron cried for the blade under his breath, swallowed hard down a constricted throat, doubled his legs under the blankets, not sure yet whether the Buzzer was headed for himself or Barneyway, but got prepared to kick in either case, relaxed when the shorts reached and passed his bed without slowing, and was caught off guard when they turned and leaped at him: a leather slap stung his face, the covers were jerked down, and the Buzzer grabbed his T-shirt.

"Take off your pants, pu-unk!"

Aaron caught a hip with a kicking heel, knocked the Buzzer away, dived out of his bed, bumped his knee against the concrete, scrambled to his feet, ran, limping, the knee buzzing with pain, into the center of the dormitory, ducked a punch the chasing Buzzer threw at him, and found himself with his fists up, his back to the washroom, no longer scared because he was already fighting, had already made the Buzzer miss a Sunday punch, had two hands for the Buzzer's two hands, had his shoes on and the Buzzer was barefooted, and had twice as much speed.

"Fuck you, Buzzer. I don't have to take your dirty shit. Fuck you. Fuck you. Fuck you," he cursed, and he cursed out of anger and to encourage himself, too, and he kept cursing as the black spectral figure, with its white slitted eyes, its grimacing white teeth, its menacing white shorts, threw wild punches at him and drove him toward the washroom.

But he safely hopped back a step with each punch, hands up, crouched, ready but not excited, cursing steadily to keep his anger and his courage up, ducked some more punches, cursed again, and, finally, made the Buzzer pause, made the Buzzer realize that he had a noisy battle to fight when the smallest noise could bring the man.

"Shut up! Shut you mouth, you little paddy pu-unk," the Buzzer said and started stalking Aaron with short, flat-footed steps.

"Make me shut up, you fucking black queer. You black queer!" Aaron shouted, anticipating every move the Buzzer made, for the white shorts were a signal flag of body action, and the eyes chinked and the gritted teeth widened with each punch, and although he regretted his T-shirt, he counted the indistinct blur of his own face as an advantage; and with his heart beat clenched in his tight fists, he felt the thrill of total disregard for what might happen to him, for he was making it happen, meeting it before the double row of faces, the half-moon of Barneyway's face, and the floating cone of Rattler's nightgown, several yards behind the Buzzer, and he felt glorious and cursed again:

"Fuck you, Buzzer."

"I'm gonna kill you, you little pu-unk," the Buzzer said in a guttural whisper, moving cautiously toward Aaron, both hands high, ready to throw the one bomb that would put Aaron down.

"What the fuck you waiting for, queer? Black queer!" Aaron taunted, for he had fought enough big men to know that if one lost control of his temper it made his own weaker punches but better skill that much more valuable, and taunting also gave him the advantage of the aggressor while backing up.

"You're the punk. You fucking punk. You fucking queer."

"I'll kill you for that. I'll kill you! I'll kill you!" the Buzzer screamed and pawed the concrete with his bare feet like a wild animal preparing to charge; and his yell sobered Aaron, made him tense, quiet; and his quick silence sobered the Buzzer as they both got ready for the final clash, the one that would settle everything; but in the unexpected stillness, heavy footsteps could be heard running down the road, then voices, the jangle of keys, the compound gate swinging, squeaking back, and banging against the fence.

"The man, Buzzer," Rattler warned and ran to his bed, to the frantic rustling and snapping of sheets and blankets, as everyone slid under their covers, leaving Aaron and the Buzzer facing each other for an anxious moment, a moment in which Aaron hoped the Buzzer would risk the hole for a chance to throw a knockout punch, for he considered both the hole and the punch together a small price to pay for getting the battle exposed, but the Buzzer hissed:

"I'll getcha, pu-unk," and hurried away.

And although Aaron stalled, pretending to act bad, but really hoping and trying to get caught, he was under the covers and feigning sleep, with his closed lids veiling the flashlight beam, when the man entered.

He listened in mock slumber to the rubber soles as they walked by him into the washroom, halted, waited, recrossed the dorm, waited at the door again, and were softened by the closed door as they recrossed the courtyard. He then heard voices, the squeak and clash of the gate, the jangle of keys, footsteps again, and silence.

## III

A coke bottle cap hissed. The gallon jug of Kool-aid gurgled. The moist frosting of the chocolate cake melted on the blade of a slicing knife. Food-packed paper plates and refilled paper cups balanced on the uneven surface of the picnic blanket, and the dim cluster of silverware and the crooked stack of white napkins diminished; but Aaron's fork was imbedded in the rocky hill of potato salad on his plate and the golden skin of a chicken wing was barely shredded from his nibbling bites.

For the delightful sight of his family seated around the red blanket, in the oak grove, enjoying with Barneyway and his mother, Juanita, the pleasure of a picnic and each other's company was marred for him because they took his own happiness for granted and because he realized that the happiness he did feel would last for only a brief hour or two, and they would then go home, and he would go back to the dormitory.

"Is there anything wrong, honey?" Nora asked, and tried to pull him close to the starched white bodice of her summer frock.

But he leaned away from her, irritated by a long, tickling strand of her dark hair, until his body was a muscle strain on one side, from his tilted head, through the wing of his back, his tightened thigh and calf, to his toes, bent against the sole of his brogan.

"Sure there's something wrong," Stanley said, speaking through closed teeth, pocketing the food in his cheek, stretching his full lips until he swallowed the food, then explaining: "He's in jail. That's what's wrong. And it'll stay wrong as long as he stays here."

He pointed accusing fork tines, sheathed with potato salad, at Aaron, who bristled with resentment, for although he didn't expect Stanley to sense his ache, being in jail should have been enough to get sympathy from a brother, even a fighter, who always had to hurt a little bit and who couldn't shake hands without squeezing so hard it became a duel.

"Sure, and he'll stay here until he learns to behave and act like a real man," Edwin D'Aragon said, and the crossed legs of the camp stool creaked under his heavy shifting weight, as he bent his bald head back, tilted a paper cup of Kool-aid bottom up, smacked his lips when he lowered it, and handed it to Nora to refill.

"It'll always be what's wrong, until you learn to behave, buddy," he added, clenching and reclenching his hand to hurry Nora, while Aaron took a tasteless bite of the brown flaked wing, unable to remember one word of advice from his father which didn't make him feel at fault.

"It's unfortunate that he has to suffer in this way. But, perhaps, it might help him to behave," John said, coatless, holding a drumstick in one hand, gesturing with the other, the gray plaid vest lending his bearing and his words a formal authority.

Yet the cultivated speech, so different from institute slang, had an almost feminine undertone to it which made Aaron feel uneasy and gave him the impression that something womanly lay beneath the correct manner, the too erect, military posture, and the graceful gestures of the slender hands.

"I just wish I had received my naval discharge in time to do something about him. I might have prevented this fighting spree. I—"

"Why don't you men leave him alone? You act like a bunch of nagging old women. We came here to cheer him up. Remember?" Nora cried. "Isn't that right, Juanita?"

"Yesh," Juanita said, holding a breast of chicken a scant two inches from Barneyway's open mouth, and whipping her head with an expert motion that removed the hennaed locks from her cheeks but obscured her view of Nora.

"Yesh, that's right," she answered and filled Barneyway's mouth.

The frilly lace of her slip and bra was conspicuously visible beneath her sheer blouse. For she had insisted on putting the jacket of her pin-stripe suit about Barneyway's shoulders in spite of the heat, and he sat, his eyelids sagging with contentment, like an infant cradled in one of her arms while she stuffed him.

Aaron detested him for allowing it and remembered with sarcasm the lonely dinners Barneyway ate at home: the pre-prepared, warmed-over food, the single plate, and, for company, the wooden back of an empty chair across an empty plain of oilcloth.

"Let's see yuh go, Aaron. I don't know if you got any spunk left. Barneyway can take this place better than you can. Come on," Stanley challenged, and Aaron jumped up from the blanket, stepped out of the shade and into a clear, sunlighted space, where he charged into Stanley without putting up his guard, eager to prove who had guts and who was a punk.

But Stanley pawed with his open palms as if he were dog-paddling and effortlessly tapped, tapped, tapped at Aaron, until Aaron, in frustration, took two of them in the face and snapped a jab to Stanley's stomach.

"That's it, think!" Stanley said, grinning, thick lips curling mischievously back from big teeth, and he side-stepped Aaron's next charge, met the next one with body punches, evaded the following one with an open-handed slap, then skipped away in low, fluctuating clouds of dust with every succeeding charge.

His balking tactics became more frustrating with the increasing heat, yet Aaron disregarded John's advice:

"Don't hide your face when you charge him. You can't see what he's doing," thinking, with malicious satisfaction, that John was smart, but no fighter, and might have become a Barneyway in the institute; and he charged again, but ran into three fast, stinging slaps; and Stanley moved away, warning:

"Do what he says. You gotta look at a man to beat him."

Aaron's right eye watered. His cheek tingled. He panted. The bright sun was unbearably hot. He tensed himself to charge a final time, to drop his guard and punch back with doubled fists, but relaxed with Nora's order:

"Stop it, Stanley. That's enough. His face is all red. Now stop it. You come here, Aaron."

Stanley lowered his guard, bright teeth big under a curled lip, and stepped toward the blanket as if he had stopped, but suddenly pivoted and sank a fast hook into Aaron's belly, doubled him up, grunting, more surprised than hurt, sucking breath in to fill the balloon of pain in his rib cage.

"You rat, Stanley," Nora cried and, standing, guided Aaron to the blanket, where she sat him down next to her, then slapped Stanley's shoulder.

"I'm just helping him keep in shape," Stanley protested, winking at Aaron, and was joined in laughter by the other men, while Barneyway pretended to be preoccupied with his mouthful of chicken.

"All you men are alike," Juanita said, and her pale eyes slanted like an unconscious coquette to look past a hindering lock of hair at Stanley.

"You've got to hurt people just to prove that you're men. And you're not satisfied unless you do. I hope my Barnham doesn't grow up to be that way."

"Well, you can't say he's not already on his way. He's in here for fighting," Stanley replied; and Aaron, whose eye still smarted, but who had regained his breath, felt like settling their doubts for them about Barneyway, and, in comparison, his own choice of the slaps—and more: a blade.

"Tha's just the trouble. He sees how the rest of you men act and he thinks. . . ." She stopped to catch her breath and blew out heavy whisky fumes. "And he thinks he's got to do the same, he—"

"Well, a boy has got to be manly," John interrupted, his raised eyebrow a chevron of authority, "but he has to learn that there's a difference between manliness and brutality, between a gentle *man* and a bully. The fighting these two boys did to get themselves put in here was nothing less than that of a pack of niggers."

"Worse," Edwin D'Aragon said, stuffing a piece of chicken into his mouth.

"No, not worse," Stanley said, "but they've got to learn to take it out in the gym, through sports, that's all. All boys are that way, really. They just gotta use it up in the right place or they'll keep ending up in jail."

"Can't you men leave them alone?" Nora asked, twin dimples of exasperation in her cheeks. "Do you have to keep punishing them?"

"Well, by God," Aaron's father said, as if Nora had not spoken, and grunted as he reached down to the blanket and pressed against his belly, grabbed a knife, a fork, and his plate of potato salad, set the plate, which was heavy with cubed chunks, egg yolk and egg white, mayonnaise, and pungent onions, upon his closed knees, then began to pry apart the fork tines with his knife blade, to help him spear more salad with each thrust, and said again:

"Well, by God. The sooner he realizes that about the gym the sooner he'll get out of here and stay out of here."

He shifted his weight, carefully, upon the camp stool and spoke to Aaron.

"In all my life, me, Edwin D'Aragon, I've never been to jail. I've outworked five men at a time, and I've been in every state in the country, and I've been in places full of crooks and bums and even murderers, and I've never been to jail. And I'm forty years older than you are, and I can still outwork most men walking, buddy, and I haven't done any laboring since I was a young man. Acting tough and getting tossed in jail don't make you a man. You take it from me. You listen to me and you won't get into trouble like this."

He stuffed a big forkful of potato salad into his mouth to signal that he was through, but Aaron resented what he considered a mouthful of food-thickened, self-praising words too much to risk even admitting that he had heard, for he wanted to call his father a belly full of fat in a starched shirt.

"Why don't you leave him alone?" Nora shouted and threw

her plate on the blanket, and the fork bounced off and smeared potato salad on the red nap.

"Don't you remember? We came here to see him and cheer him up! And all you men have done is pick on him. Leave him alone! Can't you see that he's almost ready to cry?"

She tried to put her arm around Aaron, but he pulled away, resenting her insinuation; and she appealed to John.

"Can't you make them leave him alone? And can't you stop it, too?"

"Late advice is useless," John said, "and we did come here to have fun with him. But remember," he glanced at Juanita, "although it never hurt anyone to be loved, overindulgence will only make them weak."

"Yeah, but every guy, no matter how rugged he is, likes to be babied a little," Stanley added; and Aaron began chewing vigorously on his chicken in order to endure their sympathetic glances.

He then didn't know which was worse: all the bickering over him or their awkward attempts to enjoy the picnic.

Their faces were mobile but not contented. Chewing mouths said nothing, but the uncomfortable topic was not closed. It hung in the still air like the hum of Sunday traffic. It floated above the picnic blanket in as disturbing and yet as distant a manner as the strains of jazz from a visitor's car, which passed on the main road. It filtered the sunlight like shading oak leaves, dappled his father's bald head, played tremulous shadows over the olive skin, spread appealing patches of dark color over the cheeks, and made it appear as if his father was pleading to be understood; and he wanted to speak to his father and break the spell. But time and distance and resentment were as solid as a wall between them. And he was startled when his father lifted himself off the creaking camp stool, with an agility that Aaron had forgotten he still possessed, and said, showing his strong teeth and smiling with mock bravura:

"Come with me, my leetle boy."

John started a conversation which faded out of Aaron's hearing along a haphazard trail of dusty shrubs and scattered oaks. But it was a conversation which Aaron would have preferred to the useless, uncomfortable one in which his father was going to try and justify his good intentions by a few simple unfamiliar words; and he, himself, was going to agree with too simple answers in order to get the ordeal over with; and his father was then going to feel better, and everything was then going to be exactly the same. He managed to stall and to keep it from starting for a while, but his father finally said, from a tight mouth:

"We're trying hard to get you out of here by the end of summer. We weren't going to tell you, because it's not sure yet. But your brothers and me have talked to the head of the Community Chest, and he says that because of it just being a fight and if you behave here, we might be able to get you out and put you in a private boarding school. There's one in San Francisco that might take you."

Aaron's heart palpitated, not with shame or surprise at the unexpected news, but because three months was too long, and the news was like all his father's promises: too far in the future to help when they were needed and too late to do any good when they were kept.

"It's the best we can do," his father said, shortening his steps, trying to stop. "You've got to stay here three months before the county will review your case, and you've been here almost a month now. We've tried, Sonny, but it's the best we can do."

Mournful syllables of "too-long, too-late," nearly formed in Aaron's mouth, but he could not break a long self-disciplined habit of keeping his business to himself, of asking as few favors as possible; and misshapened knife blades flitted through his thoughts in place of an explanation.

"We're trying to do the best we can for you . . . Son-ny," his father said and his voice cracked; and Aaron looked up and saw his father, truly, for the first time that afternoon.

Eye whites were yellow. The mouth was slack. And the fat hands trembled so badly that Aaron wanted to clasp them. But he no longer believed his father could suffer for him, that it was for him; and his inability to ask for help stifled his sympathy, a sympathy which he associated with women, punks, and Barneyway, a sympathy which would leave him too weak to stand off the Buzzer.

"Don't you have anything to say. . . ? Sonny?" his father asked, stopping. "Don't you see that's the very best we can do? We've tried, Sonnyboy."

Aaron stared at the tufts of grass at his feet to escape the yellow eyes. He then flattened one with his foot, and shook his head, and became aware of a big hand, half-raised, half-extended toward him, as if it were afraid to touch him, but then dared to touch him, and ran thick fingers through his hair.

"Try to understand, Sonnyboy . . . Sonnyboy."

But the rough massage only raised a tingling resentful shame to Aaron's scalp, for he didn't want affection, nor did he want to return it. He cleared his throat. He swallowed. He tried to say something which would stop his father. And he finally managed to nod.

But his father then hugged him against his fat belly, and pinned his arms to his sides, and kissed his forehead.

Aaron struggled, and started to cry out, to complain, then gave up, and suffered it, but mouthed silent cries for the blade, the blade, the blade.

## IV

Whispering blades of tall grass seemed to bend beneath the weight of Aaron's shadow, which pressed quickly ahead of him toward the creek hide-out, spread the blades, brushed swiftly off the compound wall, and vanished around the corner of the compound before he reached it.

He glanced back once before turning the corner, although he had already double-checked for stray guards and inmates before leaving the road, then side-stepped along the dirt ledge to the rusted extension of steam pipe which pierced the back wall, leaned gingerly upon the warm metal for balance, dropped into the creek bed, while searching the hedge of branches on its opposite side for a glimpse of blond hair, blue shirt, brown shoe, squatted down, still searching, pulled at the red limb of manzanita, duckwalked into the tunnel, and spotted Skip's feet hanging below the main pipe channel as the limb swung shut behind him.

He hopped easily through the intertwining branches, stepped on a hot-ashed butt Skip flipped down at him, and examined the flat face for an answer before the answer, found no answer in the stoical pattern of the face but in the spatula-tipped fingers which unbuttoned the shirt, exposed a black-taped handle, and drew out eight inches of rat-tail file ground into a shiny hatpin point.

"Wow!" Aaron said and reached for the knife, wanted to touch it, to claim it, to feel its rough-ground surface, both impressed and disappointed by its deadly lead color, its quarter-inch stiletto blade, which was too thin and too light for the sticky black tape of the heavy handle, and yet gave the knife a dangerously swift appearance.

But he forgot all reservations when he gripped the handle and felt its power surge into his arm, reach his shoulder, tighten his back, and spread through his body, down into his stiffened knees; and he stabbed at the air with vicious strokes, swung around and around, stabbed at leaves, pierced one, two, ripped them into ragged parts, knocked his knuckles against a hard manzanita branch and stabbed again.

"Easy! Easy!" Skip cried, covering himself with his arms. "Besides, you're not holding it underhand. Remember? Hook! Hook!"

Aaron made an underhanded thrust with an easy twist of wrist and hand.

"Hey! Yuh got control this way," he said, pleased, and did it again. "Jesus, this blade is so sharp and smooth it oughtta go into a guy's guts like an ice pick. The Buzzer'll never know what happened."

"Now you're with it," Skip said and slid off the pipe. "Better put it away now. Let's strap it on your leg. That's the only way to carry it if you're gonna have it on you all the time. It'll hold and rip right off. Up!" he said, and he pulled a small roll of tape out of his pocket, blunted the blade's sharp point with a black gob, bound the blade against Aaron's shin bone with two bands, bit and tore them with a ragged sound, smoothed them, then patted Aaron's calf, and said, "There she is, man."

Aaron eased himself off the pipe onto his toes, then his heels, slowly, carefully, until the cool, unbending strength and biting pressure of the slender steel, bound to his leg like a splint, felt part of him, until he was unbending, cool, and deadly, and shared its peculiar lead-colored beauty.

"Yuh like it, huh?" Skip said, biting on his tongue, proud, blond hair illuminated by a beam of sunlight which broke through the canopy of leaves.

"Yeah, thanks. Yeah. I like it," Aaron replied. "Just let the Buzzer mess with me now. I'll show him what it can do, alright. The first chance he gives me."

"Show him, then. Show him the first chance you get."

Aaron hoped for a chance as he stalked back through the long grass, and Skip had to hurry to keep up with him. He hoped for a chance as he scanned the courtyard through the compound gate, and every linked space was a telescopic lens. He hoped for a chance as he hurried across the courtyard, as he threw open the screen door, as he stepped into the dormitory, but was disappointed by the empty beds and the bare white walls. He still hoped for a chance as he rushed back to the washroom, hoping the Buzzer and lots of guys were inside, hoping he could rip the blade from his shin bone in front of all of them and stab, stab, stab, but there were only empty toilet stalls and the long yellow urinal, and Skip honked:

"You'll get your chance. Don't worry. You'll get your chance, but you've got to wait for him to start it. Take it easy. Let him start it."

Aaron stalked the grounds until dinner time, searching for the Buzzer, hoping to make the Buzzer start it. But the blade taped to his leg did something to his step, and he felt as if he were counting the paces around the boundaries of his own kingdom. He began to survey his fief from a duke's sight, from a tall, tall height. He grew and he swaggered, and he bounced into the gym, where he shouted instructions to a boxer, criticized a guy punching a heavy bag, gave the guy an example of how it should be done, mocked a guy shadowboxing in front of a mirror, and shadowboxed his way back out the gym door, grandstanding, and wishing, just wishing, Dominic could see him.

The whistle interrupted Skip's efforts to calm him down. But after dinner, Skip warned him again that he had to let the Buzzer start it, that he had to use both his speed and a surprise, that he was acting too bad, that the Buzzer was going to back away, do a little planning, and maybe show up with a blade of his own.

Aaron creeped through the gate at lockup, and he kept Skip's face in mind across the courtyard. But he let the screen door slam behind him, and it thrilled him, and he purposely slammed his locker door. Then he sang in a loud voice. And he laughed too loudly. And he hung around the Buzzer's bed. And he could barely keep himself from bragging about his blade, from making smart remarks. And he still overplayed it. And the black face was less annoyed than perplexed. And it remained silent and suspicious until lights out.

The garbage wagon was his royal coach around the grounds the next day. He hardly saw the Mexican kid who worked with him, and he felt as if he lifted all the cans himself. He waved to "regulars," at work on their daily jobs, he usually passed without a nod. He rein-slapped the old horse into a close gallop on every return trip from the dump, and he made every guy in his path jump out of the way.

He ate seconds at every meal, and he had a tug-o-war over the milk pitcher with a guy at lunch and made such a scene out of it that the guy let go. But the Buzzer, who, as cadet captain, could have stopped it, said nothing; and everyone at the table was astonished; and Aaron began to care less about getting the Buzzer than doing his time like a duke.

After dinner, he joined Skip and a crowd of boys on their way to the baseball field, just for a good time and the excitement of an overtime game, as their compound teams were deadlocked.

He noticed from his seat on the lowest bleacher that a lot of guys wore dungaree jackets, although the sun was an hour from setting. And, since even the cool air was a source of contentment to him, he felt contempt for them. He then felt contempt for Barneyway, who had to sit by himself on the top bleacher. And he felt contempt for the Buzzer, who trotted in so awkwardly from right field, kicking up puffs of dust with his heels, cussing under his breath because he had dropped a pop fly, then rudely tossed his glove at the feet of the colored fielder from Skip's team, who had been waiting for it, and replied:

"I don' give uh good gaw-damnn," when the kid mumbled something about the glove to him.

Aaron's contempt was so great that he watched the Buzzer stand before the bleacher and complain: "Ain't there no gaw-damnn room on this here bench for a player?" then threaten: "Move ovah an' make room, or *I* make room," without realizing the Buzzer meant him until the black hand flipped at him, as if to shoo him away.

His contempt was so great that he was more astounded

than insulted, and he had to recover from his surprise before he realized that his chance had finally come, then, conscious of the blade taped to his shin, the power that was his power, he hopped off the bleacher, and said evenly, "Start *making* any time, Buzzer."

He said it without raising his voice above a speaking level, calmed by the steely confidence of the blade, by the chance to use it in front of guys from two compounds, the chance to finish the Buzzer with an underhanded swipe to the guts, drop him to the ground with a bleeding belly, and be a duke forever afterwards.

Purple flamed into an amazed red on the wet underside of a hanging lip. Black eyes blurred with doubt and indecision, as if the stalemate on Friday night and Aaron's strange behavior at lockup were fresh in the Buzzer's mind. Angry lines creased the black face at being called by such a little guy in front of so many guys and because, Aaron knew, the Buzzer thought he could kill the little guy with his fists, not just whip him, but the wonder stayed in the mouth and eyes, and waiting seemed to cool the anger.

"The man be here in a se-con'. You safe out in the open, paddy boy. But you be dead when I get you ass alone."

"Pick your best shot," Aaron replied as the Buzzer sat down; and thrilled by the uplifted faces of awe and respect, more determined than ever to make the Buzzer go now, now that he felt like going and was sure he could win, he was prompted by the sight of the first batter standing away from the plate, watching through the wire backstop, bat hanging loose in his hand, to push his first true victory over his enemy to its limits; and curling his lips in a determined effort to copy Dominic's snarl, he said, "Any . . . time . . . *punk!*"

The Buzzer's head snapped around and sent a shiver over him, but no reply disturbed the warming murmur of wonder and praise which followed; and when he sat down on the wooden bleacher, he felt like a real duke on a real throne,

and he felt like one throughout the game, throughout a glorious lockup, throughout the following and very sunny day,
and until lockup time the next evening, when Skip, his face
webbed by the shadow of iron links from the compound gate,
argued:

"I know how yuh feel about it, Aaron. But lots of guys are
starting to say you're too wise. You already been nicknamed
'Big Man.' "

Moths fluttered and thumped against the protective cage of
the porch light behind Aaron, and he was grateful that the
boys who lingered in front of the open doors of their dormitories and as silhouettes along the lamp-yellow walls of the
porch could not hear Skip.

"Do you think I'm a wise guy?" he asked, remembering that
he had made sarcastic remarks to the hypocritical compliments
of the now flattering boys and that he had turned down Barneyway's attempts at friendship with a mighty word: punk!
But no one had complained to his face. They had even
laughed at his remarks as if they were clever jokes.

"Do you?" he insisted.

"No," Skip said. "I don't think so at all."

"Did any of these guys who are so free with their complaints
now try to help me when I needed it? Answer that!"

"Nooooo," Skip admitted.

"Well, if they don't like the way I'm acting, let any of 'um
try and do something about it," Aaron said, swinging the gate
open, and its webbed shadow shifted and narrowed and ran
off Skip's flat face. "You know I ain't no fathead, Skip, and
you know I consider you my only buddy."

"Okay, man," Skip said, backing away and waving good-by.
"Don't let the cat mess with you tonight, either."

Aaron crossed the courtyard with a bouncing step, soothed
by Skip's concession until he reached the porch, where he
stopped, jammed his hands into the pockets of his dungaree
coat, turned away from the screen door, and began to pace

about, reluctant to face Barneyway now, and bothered by his own excessive fondling of the blade the last two nights, although he hadn't prayed since Big Stoop had slapped him.

He could tell by the indentations ground into the steel what part of the blade he was touching, and he had squeezed the soft taped handle until it had hardened into grooves and ridges which fit the fingers of his right hand. He had also fallen asleep gripping it both nights and had dreamed of carrying it aloft through the dormitory and all over the institute grounds like a crusader's sword. Duke, bad duke, of the whole institute.

The tape edges began to irritate him, too, for they made his leg itch; and as he bent over to scratch it, he thought of the consequences he risked by carrying the blade: the hole, more time, Youth Authority, and all three if he used it; and he didn't want to use it anymore. For he had what he wanted: the right to do his own time, to do good time and—the way he felt now—even great time. Something he wouldn't give up for anybody, not even . . . Judith?

He tried to picture her expression if she discovered he had the blade, then if he stabbed the Buzzer. He pondered whether it would be one of awe or sadness or, maybe, one of disgust for a fool. But he saw only the dot on her cheekbone and saw it as proof that he had to be strong. For he now believed that the beauty mark looked sharp on her and gave strength to her plump face, and he tapped his chest with his fist and entered the dormitory, too pleased with the safety the blade gave him to allow himself to worry any longer, but faltered at the first sight of the pink envelope lying upon his bed and approached it cautiously.

The return address meant nothing to him and he didn't bother to read it, for he knew the letter was from Judith. But he studied his own name under the light bulb, while trying to prepare himself for the "be good" advice he expected to find in the letter.

"Aaron D'Aragon" looked strange in another person's handwriting. The letters seemed so big and bold for the soft pink background of the paper, and he had to check the dorm and satisfy himself that everything was quiet, that most of the guys were busy with their own mail before he could get the nerve to slide the pages out of the envelope and snap them open.

Dear Aaron,

I tried to write as soon as I got home from the visit, but the letter was so bad that I kept it a whole week, trying to make up my mind to send it, and now I've decided to write it over again. All the way back on the bus I thought about how to tell you how sorry I was for what I did to my face. I was sorry because you didn't like it. I still don't know why I did it, but I want to tell you *how* I did it anyway, just like you told me things last weekend.

The first paragraph was such a relief that he sat back against his pillow to finish the letter, with no more than a smug glance at Barneyway, who had a letter of his own.

I got home so early the day of the first visit that Mom thought I had come straight home from the show, and she was in such a good mood about it Monday morning that she made my breakfast for me. And I made the mistake of asking her if I could visit you. Then she started yelling at me and slamming the plates down and stomping back and forth in her bathrobe and making such a scene that she burned the toast, and then started blaming me for that, too. And she got me so mad that I left without finishing my breakfast.

All the girls were across the street from school at Pop's Place and one of them had the idea of cutting school to make me feel better. We walked around until I was sure Mom had gone to work. Then we went to my house. We listened to music in the morning but after lunch we got pretty bored and we started talking about different girls and the way they dressed and that. And, I don't know how, but pretty soon there we were with a bottle of India ink and some needles.

I did mine myself. I kept telling myself that it would just be a little one and that I'd hardly be able to notice it, and I put a drop of ink on my cheek and started poking the skin. It only took a couple of minutes and it barely bled, but afterwards, the skin around it turned all puffy and white. We compared them but you couldn't tell what they really looked like. So we covered them up with band-aids and we were all scared but we all felt like buddies.

Mom asked me why I had the band-aid on that night and I told her I had a pimple, and she was still in a huff about breakfast and didn't question me. But the next day she got suspicious and tore the band-aid off and the scab with it, and we had another big argument. I didn't really care about the argument. I was more disappointed because the beauty mark was too big and was blue instead of black. I felt better though because all the girls had them, and in a couple of days I was even sort of proud, until you saw it.

But Mom went on another one right away. She was still on it when I went to see you. There were beer cans all over the house, and I guess you know the way it must have smelled.

But I don't really care what she thinks, Aaron. I care what you think. So, I've made up my mind to save up my allowance and get it taken off by a doctor. And I'm going to try and get along with her so she'll give me permission to go see you. I'm going to do two things for you, and I want you to do one thing for me. Don't let those boys you told me about get you in trouble, that's all. Let's be good together, Aaron. And you can get out soon and we can start going together.

Promise me, and I already promise.

Love,

JUDITH.

He folded the pages with his promise, proud of the guts it took to put on the tattoo, which in a way was for him, and very proud of her promise to take it off, which was all for him. She was both and he could be both. For he had the blade and he had her, and he slipped the pages back in the envelope and slipped the envelope into his left breast pocket, and he thought of the letter until he went to sleep and dreamed of it in his sleep and thought of it before anything else when he awoke the next morning, determined to be as good as his promise.

With his eyes still closed, his head a wild, furred animal under the covers, he burrowed under the pillow until he touched the letter, pinched it between his fingers, dragged it carefully out, recited by memory those so tiny and important words:

"Let's be good together, Aaron," revived his confidence that he could do both, because he had both, the letter and the blade, then focused his eyes upon his name, and woke up, truly, to window frames of morning sunlight on the outside wall and a dorm full of sleepy tousle-haired boys, who busied themselves at get-up tasks.

"Let's be good together, Aaron," he mumbled and sat up, set the letter on the pillow, opened his locker without a screech, slipped his dungaree pants and his cotton shorts off the hook without snagging them on it, pulled them under the covers and put them on without a mistake, even speeding up the ritual of dressing that he had followed for two mornings now, because the blade could be seen below the hem of the nightgown.

"Let's be good together, Aaron," he whispered, patted the blade, scratched the binding tape, caressed the letter, stood on the cold concrete without a shiver, slipped the nightgown off in a single bending, pulling movement, hung it up without looking, fit his T-shirt on like a skin, slid his arm through his shirt sleeve while he lifted the shirt out of the locker, tucked the shirt into his pants while he buttoned it, bent down for his shoes and socks, and repeated:

"Let's be good together, Aaron."

"Let's be good together, Aaron," he said again, his mind full of his nighttime prayers, for he had said his rosary twice for the promise, and included every person he knew, including the Buzzer and Rattler, in the requested blessing. His knees had not hurt. His back had not ached. His heart had swelled with pride and enthusiasm, for he would do both. He could do both.

He flexed his calf muscle, strained the tape bands, set the letter on top of the locker, fixed his bed with brisk, efficient blanket-snapping movements, caressed the letter with a swipe of his palm, slid it into his left breast pocket, and marched to the washroom.

Green sparked eyes stared alertly back at him from the washbasin mirror. There was no morning puffiness to them, and his sallow complexion was also overtoned by a healthy tan. He took a deep breath, held it, prepared to duck his face into the washbasin water, when the Buzzer entered, and the breath puffed into a cloud of moisture on the mirror.

"Here, take this one," he heard himself say. "It's all ready."

He stepped back. He saw his own hand offer the washbasin, and he heard himself insist:

"No. Go ahead. Take it. Take it."

He saw the gold teeth glint with awe, and he even felt sympathy for the black eyes, crusted with twists of sleep in the corners, that shimmered with disbelief, and for the confused voice that mumbled an embarrassed thanks before the Buzzer obeyed and bent over the basin; and he felt the same sympathy, touched with pride, at count, when he responded to the Buzzer's command with such a military snap to attention that the man had to order the disconcerted Buzzer to come to attention himself.

He marched through the day with an exhilarated step, with

her tattooed beauty mark as a sign of her guts and her letter in his pocket as a sign of her love, and his blade taped to his shin. He went out of his way to be kind to the Buzzer. He offered him the chocolate pitcher at breakfast, and he filled his cup for him at lunch. He told him the answers to math problems in class and he cheered for him at the baseball field, he helped him clean the dorm and he repeated the command for dinner count to make the stragglers fall in line. At lockup, he even sat down on the Buzzer's bed and tried to join the conversation.

But the black creased skin fold was purposely, almost shyly, turned to him to avert the black face; and the benevolence which flooded his limbs with energy was disturbed by a premonition, like an undercurrent of fatigue, that his joy could not last, that the Buzzer would come to some decision about the confusing kindness and there would be trouble, but it was a premonition that he had to deny or taint and ruin his state of grace.

Guffaws accompanied sly comments about him all the next day, beginning with breakfast, when the chocolate pitcher was passed around the table and kept away from him. At noon count, the guys kept shifting the line, kept him out of formation, and got him reprimanded. He had to eat his lunch without salt, and every request was answered by a snicker. He went to the chapel afterwards, where he tried to magnify the beauty mark and pray away his bitterness. But wisecracks from the desks at the back of the schoolroom became outright threats before class was over, and the Buzzer shoved him out of line on leaving, and the state of grace was then forgotten in worry over survival without trouble: without the blade. The cackling laughter in the gym angered as well as worried him, too; but Rattler's cry of "kiss-ass" as he left, trying to control his temper, convinced him that his survival was impossible without trouble, nor worth it. And by the time he reached the compound gate he was ready to give somebody a lesson with his blade, ready to prove that there was a difference between kindness and fear; and cussing to himself, he forgot to close the dormitory door, then heard and purposely ignored the Buzzer's command to close it.

The center of his back was as sensitive as the transparent mass of a jellyfish, and his body bristled with anticipation as he marched by the tense boys, savoring the surprise he was going to pull, letting the Buzzer kindle his anger to a point past any possible fear; although he gazed on the slicing planes of sun and shadow before him, he felt as if he could see the Buzzer stand behind him and speak the threat:

"Peoples here born in barns, need some schooo-lin', an' I gonna be the tee-cha, an' maybe I give uh lesson ri-ight now!"

Aaron stopped in a square of sunlight, sunlight which encased the cold lucid anger within him in mild heat, sunlight which belied the anger as the attempts at goodness had belied his confidence and will, as his hesitation now belied his determination to fight, to forget now about get-alongs and concentrate on strong-arms and get-bys, to be cold if that was all that counted, colder than the Buzzer, as cold as his blade, and he spun slowly around, balanced on his toes, and spoke in a sharp-pitched, stylized voice:

"Don't nobody signify nothin' no time about me! Don't say nothin' no time and not right now! Come on, bad actor, if you think you want to, think you're big and bad! Come on. I've got an equalizer that will even all the odds!"

But a beckoning wave of his arm made the Buzzer falter, slow, and stop, made his enemy hesitate with confusion; for Aaron's anger, once released, now burst out of him, exploded. His head felt hot and light. Nothing mattered but his grievance.

"I'm not afraid to get hurt or even killed, Buzzer. I'm not going to let nobody push me around. Not nobody."

The sun seemed to spotlight him and dramatize his speech and actions.

"The trouble with all the punks around here is they're afraid. I'm not afraid, Buzzer. I'm not afraid and *you* better believe it. Whoever takes me on is going to have to pay for it with his hide, black, white, or Mex-cun brown, bad actor or punk.

"Punk," he repeated, and pointed at Barneyway, and started shouting, unable to dam or slow the torrent of angry words. Yet he was intensely aware of what he was doing. He watched himself do it. But he was beyond his own control, beyond the control of all the boys together, including the tight-lipped Buzzer.

"You want to kick each other's ribs in, bust on each other's skull, Buzzer? You want to cut on each other a little bit? Call it, Buzzer!" he challenged, and grabbed his pant leg to show his blade and prove he meant it; but he checked the motion, for the power of surprise, but only for that, because he believed what he said, and he welcomed the chance to fight with the blade, to see who would die, but die angry, die bad, die strong, strong, and full of heroism.

"I'll make one guy pay for all the crap I've taken, Buzzer. I don't care who it is. I don't care if it's Big Stoop," he said, believing it, thinking it really possible; and trying to attack something bigger than the man, he shook his hands at the ceiling, and shouted:

"I'll even go to Hell. Yuh hear? Hell! I'll roast in the flames for doing somebody in. It'll be worth it! Yuh understand? I'd stab God if he messed with me. Stab God, yuh hear? Stab God! Stab God! Stab . . . God! . . . Stab . . . God! . . . God! . . ."

His boast resounded in the dormitory, then passed, unchallenged, out of hearing altogether in the persistent quiet which followed, but it hung like a haunting echo in the guilty corners of his own mind.

He went out into the courtyard, but he could still hear it. He went back to the gym, but the aggressive noises he heard there seemed mild compared to the sound of his threat. He went to the baseball field, where the tiny competitive cries of outfielders emphasized how puny and yet how very serious was his own cry, which neither a silent count nor marching commands nor the boisterous talk at dinner could help him to forget. The echo sounded more blasphemous than ever in the chapel, because his intention to use the blade kept him from kneeling, and his attempts to fill the chapel with prayer sounds while standing ended in stutters. He then saw a flawed knot on the square face of the wooden Christ, which resembled a beauty mark so closely it distracted him. He studied it and decided that it was just a curlicue in the grain of the cheek-bone. He then guessed that it was a lumpy spot of congealed varnish, because it went away with the sunlight; but he went away, too, and without praying.

Dusk and unfrequented paths on the visitors' lawn helped him to keep busy and isolated but brought him no relief. He soon began to limp, too, for the blade was taped too tightly to his shin, and every time he sat down or leaned against something to rest, the letter crackled.

Only a bed-hugging speechless lockup and the wide berth given him by the other boys helped him to conceal his lost hope that he would ever be able to either keep his promise to Judith or be bad, let alone both.

But lights out brought many ghosts. Some were shaped like the blade. Some crackled like the letter. Others shriveled into tattooed dots at a glance. But all spouted blasphemy. All moaned over broken promises. All warned of coming battles. And a warm, sticky, multicolored current of blood and milk and ink spurted out of a thousand tattoos, and splashed over him, and awoke him, sweating, late at night.

# V

The oak tree spread crooked, moss-infested, leaf-clustered, swaying branches and a hushing shade over Aaron, as if warning of a family conspiracy; and he wouldn't give Judith his attention.

"I waited a week, Aaron," she said, but he still refused to answer.

For her beauty mark was a tattooed point of betrayal, and smacked, as well, of a little girl's annoying and faulty attempts at big girl make-up, which marred the brushed simplicity of her blond bangs and the natural hair fall and curl of her page boy and seemed in bad taste with the full skirt and feminine ruffles of her green summer dress.

"Aaron," she said, touching his cheek and irritating him with such a familiar act in front of his family.

Nora had opened the basket of sandwiches with the stealthy care of a thief, had spoken only to offer food, and had then sat next to him on the picnic blanket, with the petrified limbs, the dark beauty, and the empty gaze of an anonymous cover girl.

His father's bald head was the dull color of adobe, and he kept his cheeks fat with bites of baloney sandwich, finished two cokes in quick succession, and shifted nervously about on the camp stool without telling one tale about his adventures as a young man, which would have been a happy miracle to Aaron, if the behavior weren't so suspect.

Stanley now squatted on his haunches and appeared to be examining the oily liquid in his coke bottle, although he had shown the same, unnatural preoccupation when he had hugged Aaron, without smiling, in front of the office, had driven, without speaking, to the field, and had carried, without help, the blanket and the basket and the Kool-aid jug to the shaded spot of the previous week.

But his body was so muscular that, when he squatted, stretch lines creased like suspender straps between his sport shirt collar and his shoulders; and the barely suspended power kept Aaron on guard.

"I didn't tell them what you told me, Aaron. On my Mother's Honor, I didn't," Judith said and touched him again.

"I got scared, Aaron. I saw Nora and she said that they had been to see you and that you were real sad. I was sure that

the trouble had gotten worse. But I only told her that somebody was bothering you, that's all. On my Mother's Honor,"
she said and pulled on his chin and turned his face toward her.

The beauty mark then looked so out of place situated in
the center of such plump freckled innocence that he was over-
whelmed once again by all the confusion and misery caused
by his misinterpretation of it: his belief that it was somehow as
sharp and strong and suitable for her face as the point of his
blade for its handle, an example of both the good and the
gutty; and he distrusted a growing sense of gratitude toward
her and a rising belief in her loyalty. With the maddening
bleat of a cricket in the shaded grass behind her, which
shouldn't have been making noise in the middle of the day, he
tugged his chin free of her fingers and tried to escape his
burdens through the small consolation of rejecting her.

"Come on, honey, tell us what's wrong. We only want to
help you," Nora pleaded, pressing him against her, and rippling the bodice of her blouse. But the subtle movement of the
silk and glazed shadow implied some kind of scheme, and he
resented her affection.

He resented the massive, chewing jaw of his father, too,
which dropped, which pulled hollows into the cheeks, the
temples, which crunched closed, which expanded with muscle,
which then flooded the cheeks and temples with firm olive
flesh, and which made the shrug of his own shoulders in reply
to Nora seem so totally helpless.

"Somebody bothering you?" Stanley asked, leaning over the
blanket, using the coke bottle for a brace.

"Big guy, huh? Bully?" he said, balancing so far over the
blanket that his outstretched arm looked like the long left feint
of another boxing trick, which would later be joked about and
justified because it made a man out of a guy. Aaron didn't
answer.

"Why don't you answer your brother?" his father demanded,

getting angry, gulping down the last swallow of his sandwich, with a dough-white flash of bread.

"Do you think we're asking you for nothing? Do you think we came all the way out here so we could go home feeling bad?"

He picked the last half of his sandwich off the paper plate and brushed the plate off his knee.

"I'm not good for nothing, huh? All I'm good for is to pay the bills. Is that it?"

"Daddy, Daddy," Nora pleaded and motioned to him to be quiet, and he began to chew sulkily on the sandwich, for which Aaron was grateful.

"Listen, Aaron. Don't be a sucker. If I can't understand what's wrong, nobody can," Stanley said, handing the coke bottle to his father and bobbing closer to Aaron, while he balanced on his heels with the easy athletic grace that Aaron so much admired.

"Tell me, Aaron," he said.

"Tell Stanley, Aaron," Nora said. "You know he'll be able to help you."

"Tell him, Aaron," Judith said. "He wants to help you."

"Tell me," Stanley said.

"Tell him," Nora said.

"Tell him," Judith said.

"Tell him," both women said together, and he blurted out:

"The Buzzer! A great big colored guy! He beat Barneyway up and now he's trying to get me!"

But he hid his face in his hands, sure he had taken a step he was going to regret.

"Tell the superintendent, honey. Don't let that boy hurt you," Nora said.

"I can't be a dirty snitch," he replied and he shoved her arm away, already sorry he had told them.

"By God!" his father exclaimed, "I wouldn't let anybody pick on me if I could stop 'em. All we need is for him to get hurt here. I'm going up and tell the superintendent, myself."

He tried to raise his heavy body from the canvas seat, but he was clumsy because of the coke bottle and the sandwich, and Stanley kept him seated.

"Hold it, Dad! Let's figure this thing out," he said and quickly asked Aaron:

"Has he hit you yet?"

"No," Aaron mumbled. "He tried the other night though. . . ."

He stopped, recalled the slap, but disregarded it because of the struggle's outcome.

"What happened?"

"I held him off until we heard a guard coming. Now he's waiting for a good chance to get me. I tried to be nice to him afterward. After she wrote to me," he added, with scorn, pointing to Judith. "Then he thought I was scared. But I let him know that I wasn't. And I'm not and he won't get me, either. I'll get him first. I'll do him in!" he yelled, and his eyes flooded with tears, and the red blanket tilted and swam over the seated figures.

Nora's cry of "No-no, Aaron!" was a flash of light; and his father shot into a large, wavering size above him, then spread sidewards at the waist like an image in a curved mirror.

"By God, I'm going to stop this right now."

"Wait a minute, Dad. Wait a minute now! It's better he's got the guts to try and stop the guy than let himself get bullied around. He's got to live in the place."

But the bald head spun like a top, and Stanley's back bobbed and weaved before it, and Nora tore at Aaron's clothing, and he struck at her arms and sprang to his feet.

"You'll *all* help him kill me."

"Sit down," his father said. "Nobody's going to kill you."

"I'm not sitting down and he's not gonna kill me, either. I'll kill him first," Aaron shouted. "I'll get him before he gets me, I tell yuh."

"Don't talk like that. You'll end up in the gas chamber. You'll go to Hell, Aaron," Nora said.

"I'll slap your face. I'll teach you to talk like that," his father said and started around the blanket; but Stanley grabbed him, struggled with him, succeeding in stopping him, then asked, "How will you kill him, Aaron?"

"I'll kill him with my blade! I'll bury it in him," Aaron said, backing away and stumbling over a tree root.

"What blade? They don't let these kids run around with knives in their pockets. Who you kidding?"

"You don't think so? This blade," Aaron said and, with one practiced motion, bent and raised the pant leg up to his knee and exposed the black-handled knife.

"Oh, my God!" Nora screamed.

"Aaron!" Judith cried.

"Give me that!" his father said, struggling to free himself from Stanley.

"Dad! Dad! Let me handle this, pleeeeese!" Stanley pleaded; and his father stopped struggling again, glanced at Aaron, and then began to jerk angrily at his tie.

Stanley turned, once more, to a wary Aaron, and propped his knuckles against the thin indentation of his belt, with all the studied caution of an angry schoolteacher trying to control his hands.

"Nobody's going to try and take it away from you, Aaron. So come on over and settle down."

But Aaron kept his distance.

"Have I ever lied to you, Aaron?"

"No," Aaron replied, and it seemed that the admission lightened his crushing burden somewhat, cleared the dense, stupefying heat in his brain a little, tempted him to give up the blade and be freed of all the problems associated with it. But he couldn't forget how the Buzzer had treated him after two days of trying to be nice, and he still felt that Judith had wronged him by telling the family, by the tattoo, and by expecting the promise from him; and he kept the blanket and several feet of grassy turf between himself and Stanley.

"Then trust me and let me help you. Let all of us help you. We're on your side and we're not going to let you get hurt in any way—that means being considered a sissy by the rest of the guys or letting the superintendent know you had a knife."

Aaron still hung back, for although the words sounded good, they were unsupported, and he needed something more dependable, a plan that he could count on and use to clear his mind.

"We'll explain to the superintendent that he's not to question or punish anybody. We'll ask him to just transfer you to some place where the bully won't be around. How's that? Then you not only won't have to fight him, with or without a knife, you won't be bullied or thought of as a snitch, either. How's that? Think about it, fella. If you fight that guy with that blade, you'll never get out of here."

The growl of a passing diesel truck penetrated Aaron's stupor, accented the warning, and he fastened upon it, to focus his thoughts, and recognized that he still had to fight the Buzzer, that the blade was no guarantee of victory, and that he might lose his soul as well as his life.

He listened for the ripple of the truck's tires above the bubbling engine drone, but heard the restricted breathing of his father and his brother and his sister and Judith, as they waited in the shade for his response. He then noticed that Nora was standing next to the moss-fringed trunk, making speaking motions, and holding her arms out to him.

"Please, honey, we want to help you. You'll get in trouble by yourself," she said, and he replied:

"I'll give Stanley the blade, and that's all."

And her arms dropped to her skirt, with a tiny listless slap. But his mind cleared with the sound.

## VI

Sweat made a loose, uncomfortable wrinkle of Aaron's collar, dampened his hairline, his brow, plastered his T-shirt to him, but did not annoy him, for he liked working alone as a stable boy; and he dug the rusted rake tines deep into the thick muck on the cow stall floor. Nor was the muck offensive to him, for the old manure had dried and the mud gave off a clean smell, which mingled with the sweet pungency of hay. But he had detested everything about the big dairy barn, including the morning light which streamed through its high rafters like church rays filtered by colored glass, until a few days of familiarity, if not safety, with it had helped him shake his despair over Stanley's failure.

Monday morning work count had been such a time of hard-to-control exhilaration, it had intensified the despair which followed. For Mr. Handy had told him not to go out on the garbage wagon, and when the lines had broken and the boys had scattered, he had felt like singing. But Mr. Handy had then explained to him that the Buzzer, as cadet captain and straw boss of the dairy, would show him what his new duties were, and he had quickly learned that all the supposed transfer had done was increase his chances of getting hurt.

He thought of Stanley's repetitious and worthless reassurances as he raked the muck into a pile by the stall door. Stanley had started reassuring him so carefully, as he carefully pulled the black bands off, to prevent tearing the leg hairs off with them. Stanley had then reassured him so carefully, as he carefully explained how names would not be mentioned and how Aaron's reputation as well as his life would be protected. Stanley had then reassured him so carefully, as he carefully packed the picnic supplies into the car and drove carefully to the office, Stanley had then so *very* carefully reassured him, as he very carefully left him in the car with Judith and Nora, and went carefully into the office with their father.

Aaron leaned the rake against the splattered wall and shoveled the muck into the wide-bedded wheelbarrow with conscientious energy, an energy that had developed when he found that work lessened his fears, but fears that Judith and Nora had promised him would disappear, because he had trust in his family and, as Nora added, in a girl who liked him very much; and the beauty mark had lost its stark emphasis in the flood of color to Judith's cheeks.

He scraped the last loose lumps together, slipped the shovel under them with a quick slide, dropped them on the muddy brown pile in the barrow, laid the shovel on the pile and reached down for the slippery hose. A hose as slippery, he mused, ironically, as Stanley's promises when he had come rocking out of the office with his heavy-shouldered, short-stepping boxer's tread, when he had promised a transfer in the morning, and had guaranteed that nobody, not even Big Stoop, would ever know who the guy was. Nobody, not . . . even . . . Big Stoop, Aaron thought and looped some hose slack around his bare arm, streaked his wrist with mud, and twisted the iron nozzle.

The hose bucked and writhed, but much less fitfully than he had writhed on Sunday night, hoping that he would get transferred, that his faith in Judith's tattoo would be fulfilled, that Nora's intentions would prove to be as true as her beauty, and that Stanley would turn out to be as strong and persuasive with his tongue as he was with his fists.

But the hose hardened into a tight noose and pinched his arm, and he had to pry at it before he could free his arm and use it. And after he had washed the walls, loosened the muck that had pasted to the floor, and cut the spray, he threw it into the aisle as angrily as he had wanted to throw his death in Stanley's face after count on Monday morning. He then raked the floor as if he were digging furrows in the wood, scraped the mess into the doorway with a squeaking shovel blade, shoveled it into the wheelbarrow, and, lastly, washed the stall clean.

Wet floor boards glistened like varnish in two more stalls within the next hour, for Aaron worked fast and he worked as quickly every morning, and not only from anger. Working, also, kept him from thinking about the failure too much, and working kept him hoping that things might still work out. For his fit of rage and his threat of an equalizer had kept him lonely but unharmed, and he reminded himself of this after he emptied the wheelbarrow, started on the fourth stall, and felt the uneasy sensation of being watched.

Still, he kept working and lifted his eyes as he lifted the shovel, looking for the Buzzer, who had appeared at least once every morning, watched him without speaking, then disappeared. He took a long look behind him as he propped the shovel against the side of the stall, but he could see no one, let alone the black face of his enemy, and although he felt on edge, several days had hardened him and he was not scared.

He squatted down, dragged the rake under the metal belly of the food trough, dug the rusted teeth into the turflike muck, and had to pull and strain to break some of it loose. He concentrated upon this, grunting, forgetting his feeling of being watched, forgetting that he was supposed to be on guard, which was something he hadn't been able to do when he had the blade. He rose, raked the muck to the door, propped the rake against the wall, stepped out into the aisle, reached for the shovel, and froze motionless as he touched it.

An eye and a shiny black forehead protruded beyond the edge of the last stall!

His fingers clamped, slowly, around the wooden handle, and he pulled it slowly toward him, without panic, but as an act of sheer will, then swung it to his shoulder like a rifle, and held it there until the eye disappeared and shoes crunched on the straw-littered floor.

He listened for a few minutes in case they returned, trying to hear over the pounding of his heart, telling himself that he had nothing to fear, that he had the rake and the shovel, and that the Buzzer wasn't brave enough to risk getting hurt. But the stall walls could screen any crouching figure, brave or cowardly, and he went back to work without confidence.

He tried to forget his worry by working, by shoveling the muck into the wheelbarrow with greater and greater speed, and he tried to picture how a pleased Mr. Handy would compliment him for his good work and stopped! still bent over the shovel! For Mr. Handy had mentioned that he would be in the pastures all morning! The Buzzer was in sole charge!

He straightened up, listened, stared, and, because he was aware of how scared he must look, the mud streaks caked on his face and a shirt that was too big and loose for him now irritated him. But he could see no one nor hear anything within the hushed high-roofed building, and he bent down, shoveled the last two bladefuls into the wheelbarrow, and leaned the shovel against the stall side of the wall for safety.

He stepped into the aisle, looked carefully in both directions, listened again. Nothing. Only a manure- and straw-littered floor. He lifted the hose, undid the tight kink in it, dragged it into the stall, turned the nozzle without paying attention to what he was doing, and jumped when the hose bucked, slithered along his arm and shot a hard spray against the metal trough. He smiled at his fear and turned the spray onto the spots of mud and dung, straw and hay which clung like adobe to the wooden boards. But it made so much noise he worried that someone would creep up on him, unheard, and he softened the stream to a wide spray, climbed up on the round wooden stool, and looked around the barn.

Specks of dust floated in the sunbeams which pierced the cool, darkened and peaceful atmosphere. An atmosphere in which, in spite of the Buzzer and Stanley's failure, he was not tortured by the unwieldy power of the blade, he did not worry about losing his soul, he was not burdened by problems he couldn't solve. It was an atmosphere in which the summer heat had no effect, and the month of September seemed within a reasonable count, and he called himself chicken and stepped down from the stool.

He rested his squatting haunches on his muddy heels, turned the spray on full blast again, and shot it under the trough. He kept it directed there for some minutes, pleased by the ping of hard water pellets on the chalky blue belly, pleased by the manner with which the pounding spray ricocheted off the trough and the now-clean boards back into his face, pleased because it was cool, because it was refreshing, and, pleased, he smiled at the absent-minded way he had polished the small space beneath the trough; and glad of a chance to smile at himself, he leaned forward to catch more spray drops, and heard a deadened noise, as if someone had knocked something over in one of the darkened corners of the barn.

He twisted the nozzle and cut off the spray.

He held his breath and listened.

No sound.

He waited.

Still, he could hear nothing, and he stood and stepped out into the aisle, where he squinted his eyes and tried to define every shadow and every dark shape in every dark corner. He scanned the whole barn. He even looked into the rafters and onto the loft above the closed doors, with the large wired bundles of hay stacked upon it.

There was nothing.

He waited silently until he was completely satisfied that he was alone, then he returned to the stall and turned the hose on again, but he could not shake the feeling of being watched.

He tried to soften a corner section of the stall which was stiff with muck and prepare it for his shovel when he heard something slide on floor straw. But he was afraid he was getting overanxious, and he kept at his job until he heard the noise again. Only it was accompanied by a thump this time, and he was afraid to move. He heard it again as a faint rustle, and he cut the spray off and stood, with his pulse throbbing in his fingers, as motionless and quiet as his trembling would allow.

No noise.

He stepped out into the aisle again.

Nothing.

He stepped back into the stall again, and turned the hose on, and worked diligently at softening the muck, while he kept the stream to a medium spray, still apprehensive, still listening.

But as he began to clear the muck and get interested in the work again, an oppressive feeling gradually overcame him, settled like a chilling haze on his brain, and stretched slow pimpling tentacles of fear over his scalp and along the entire skin surface of his body. Yet he couldn't make his hands turn to cut the spray off, although he stared at them so intently he could have counted the drops of moisture upon them; and they stayed locked until he saw the hair rise on his forearms and the sight shocked him into wrenching the nozzle—to a noise outside the stall!

He balanced the nozzle like a billyclub and tried to build up the nerve to turn around and look into the aisle.

Finally, he pivoted, and listened again.

Nothing.

He then dared to step to and out the stall door, but tightened in terror at the crouched form of the Buzzer, all burred head and broad shoulders, a foot beyond the wheelbarrow, ready to tackle him.

"Got yuh now, pu-unk."

The nozzle struck the Buzzer across the face in a pure reflex action, for Aaron turned and started to run at the same time, and he was already several steps down the aisle when Rattler and two boys came around the corner of the stalls, and he pivoted on the next step, quick with panic, foot sliding on straw and wood, and started on a hard run back toward the Buzzer again, tried running around the spread-armed, spread-legged enemy who blocked the aisle, but saw two more boys behind him, and changed direction, charged directly at the Buzzer, caught him with the best right hand he could throw, leaped with the punch, felt the jolt of knuckle and cheekbone in his shoulder, but caught a hard fist to the forehead that knocked him back, clawing at the air for support, and bounced him off his buttocks, and he struggled for his feet and reached his knees, but caught a brogan toe to the forehead that knocked him down again, and he was kept down by a barrage of kicks and punches to his head, to his ribs, to his back, to his belly, to his arms and to his legs, kept down in a clamoring tumult of grunts and yells and curses and the thump and scuffle of brogans and fists, and kept down by a belly kick that drove a toe to his backbone, that dropped him in a sweeping faint when he tried to crawl to a stall.

But kicks brought him back to consciousness, to the grunting moans of his breath, to the empty, suffocating bellyache, and he tried to protect his face, made a feeble attempt to cover it with his hands, to push it into the muck, but his hands were kicked away, and a shoe toe crashed into his mouth, shot blazing splinters of numbness into his brain and into every bone in every part of his body, deadened every limb, each muscle, and he knew he was out, because he could hear the thud of the brogans and feel the jerks of his body but the kicks didn't hurt anymore, and soon the thuds became fainter, the jerks less pronounced, and they occurred less and less often, but he no longer cared, anyway, for all he wanted to do was rest on the floor, just rest on the mat of mud and straw, just rest and sleep, just rest and sleep . . . sleep . . . sleep . . . and soon there were no more kicks.

Wind whispered through the bare rafters at the very peak of the barn ceiling but in shifting currents of gossip, too brief, too high, and too thin to understand.

"We better wash that bloo-ud off his face with the hose. Clean him up a little."

Lifted, and then floating, and then his chest caved in, and then his squashed lungs squeezed warm, wet bubbles of breath out of his mouth with a rasping noise, like a thick-toothed file on wood.

Snoring.

He could hear himself sleep.

Hear a garbled wind gust:

"He look pretty bad."

Hear a pulsing, answering flurry:

"Probably still a wise punk."

Hot breath choked him coming out his mouth and nose, then stung like cold spray on his face.

"That good enough. Still bleeding. Can't stop it."

"Wonder what he looks like in the ribs?"

"Probably good and busted up, paddy-wise."

"Better pull off his shirt and see."

The sleeves plucked his arms off, leaving him stump-shouldered and cold.

"Ribs look like a tractah run ovah 'um."

"Close his eyes. Spooky, with just the whites showin'."

And a trapped breeze moaned in a barn corner.

But his legs were useless, too: hinged by bone-dry joints.

Although a brisk current could sweep low, muttering:

"That boy sure has got some white skin. Look at that belly."

And fitful gusts could then blow back and forth, before:

"Bet he got a pale ass, too."

And a blustering rush of wind broke into gales of laughter, howled over the stall, then receded into rumbling echoes:

"Bet a buck that boy got a sweet rump. He has. Hell. Unbuckle his pants."

Rumbling echoes of laughter.

But there was a sharp change of wind. Surging, icy billows began to roll back over the stalls.

He was cold! Where were his clothes? Where were his clothes?

"He fink now, they send us all to Lancaster and Preston anyway."

"That's a fact."

Cold blasts of wind blew over him. Where were his clothes?

"Why don' we get us some the-en?"

Cold gales of laughter.

"You're shuckin', Buzzer?"

"He-ell no, I ain' shuckin'. Watch."

Laughter.

"Not yet, Buzzer."

"Why not?"

"That little boy still got his prune, man. You'll tear your peter up."

Short flurries of cold wind blew in all directions, intersected, clashed, whirled around in brief skirmishes, then, suddenly, burst upon him in a violent, chilling squall.

"Got the butter, Rattler?"

"Ha, ha, ha . . . first!"

"You crazy, I first."

"Ha, ha . . . second!"

"Ha! Third, then. Ha! Third!"

"Fourth!"

"Ha, ha, ha, ha, ha, ha, ha, ha, ha, ha, ha, ha, ha, ha. . . ."

# Part Nine

# Put Down and Played for Shine

# Put Down and Played for Shine

## I

A drawn window shade deadened the total white of the room, muffled the clanking of the expanding steam pipe which had disturbed Aaron's dreams, and lulled his sleep-lazed mind. But the morning was filled with a strange, antiseptic smell, and although he rested between crisp sheets, the mattress was too level and wide beneath him. For the familiar hollow made by his own body was not there and his searching toes kept stretching until, with a start, he awoke completely, sure that he was not in his own bed, afraid that something had happened to him, and recognized a hospital room.

He ran his fingers gently over his cracked lips, the tender puffiness which narrowed the vision of his left eye, and the hard lump on the left side of his jaw. He tried opening his mouth and his jaw creaked with pain. He carefully raised his arm to feel the egg-sized lump on his forehead and winced from the twinge of pain in his chest and shoulder. He then lowered his arm, but very slowly, and felt the broad strips of tape that bound his chest like a cast, and experienced the terror aroused by the crouched Buzzer all over again.

He saw the grimace on the black face.

He saw the attacking figures of Rattler and the other boys.

Struggling to fight back, he recalled striking with the nozzle and kicked his feet into the top sheet with the effort, and

283

caught his breath at the pang it caused, but felt a tremendous delight, and let himself lay back like a king in state, crowned by the lump on his forehead.

His jaw twisted into a lopsided grin in spite of the suffering and the defeat, and his left eye burned with pride beneath its swollen lid. For although he couldn't place the nozzle whack or any of the incidents in sequence, and it couldn't have been too hard a whack or he might have escaped, he had tangled with the duke of his dormitory and four or five of his boys, bad actors in blue, and had made a knockdown, bust-em-up battle out of it. He had made them put him in the hospital and he still wouldn't kiss their butts and he still wouldn't let them treat him like a punk and he didn't even have a blade!

Now he wanted to talk about it! to brag about it! to show off his wounds! He wished that somebody would come into the room and tell him all the details of the fight and what all the guys were saying about him.

The blast of the morning whistle relaxed him, for someone would be in soon with food, and a sigh of relief that the fight was finally over passed through his cracked lips. No more worry! The score was even now that the Buzzer and Rattler had their revenge. They had saved their reps and he still had his. He had managed to do both, after all! He had proved that he could care for Judith and the family by giving up his blade, and nobody, not anybody, would mess with a little guy who put up the battle he did. He could be like the whistle: blast like hell, but announce good things like sunlight and breakfast and dinner and Sunday visits. He could swagger through a Saturday morning boxing crowd. He could be choosy about what records he wanted to hear on the chapel lawn, and then let some other guy, maybe the Buzzer, pick first. He could look forward to visits with Judith and the family, and he could buddy up a little with Barneyway and make things easier for him, and without fear, too. For the punches and kicks, with the exception of the one that had nailed his belly to his backbone, hadn't really hurt, not when he was busy fighting. All of his wounds, too, from the lump that ached on his forehead and drew the skin tight and must be discolored, to the eye that had to be black it was so swollen, to his cracked ribs, his puffed lips, his jaw, were banners of bravery!

The total white of the room, softened by the drawn shade, was soothing and suited his feelings, the perfect contentment that was settling over him, the flattering pictures he had of everyone: Judith's tattoo was a beauty mark of sophistication, Stanley was the Golden Boy in his boxing trunks, John was a great brain surgeon, a genius with a scalpel, Nora was the June Bride who walked down the church steps, under crossed swords, in a shower of rice, his father sat at the head of the Sunday dinner table, surrounded by the family, his belly braced by its edge, his broad napkin spread like an apron from his tie knot to the rim of his plate, Barneyway entranced an institute audience with boogie woogie from a grand piano in the very center of a stage, and the Buzzer grinned his appreciation, and Rattler's cross rocked with the rhythmic nodding of his forehead, and Aaron floated between the sheets, dozed for a short while, drifted off into mild, forgettable dreams in which there was only hospital good time until September: clean sheets and good food and reading and rest and no morning get-up, no work, no constant guard, no blades, no battles; and he awakened happily, to the pleasant sight of Buckshot's tan face and a breakfast tray.

"Hey, man!" he said, surprised by his hoarse voice.

"Okay, buddy. How you feelin'?" Buckshot answered, but his eyes were a woeful brown.

"Look like the Buzzer finally got me, alright," Aaron croaked, trying to make a joke out of his wounds and show Buckshot how brave he was; and he waited for some complimentary remark, for some flattering expression to disturb the flawless complexion of the round face. But he was kept waiting, and he finally brushed impatiently at the bedspread, and Buckshot said, "Guess you better sit up. If you can, that is. Then I can set this tray on your lap."

Bands of pain tweaked across Aaron's chest and hampered him when he tried to lift himself into a sitting position, and Buckshot set the tray quickly down on the enamel bedstand and wadded the pillow into a back brace; but after he placed the tray on Aaron's lap, he turned to leave without making a single comment; and Aaron asked, "Hey, man, why don't you tell me what happened? Stick around. Don't cut out. Let's jive a little."

Buckshot raised the shade, obviously stalling, raised it to shoulder height, decapitated his brown head from the silhouette of his trunk with its sharp edge, and exposed a shimmering square of iron bars and caged scrub brush through the window pane.

"All I remember, really," Aaron said, trying to start the conversation, "is that I got jumped by the Buzzer and some of his boys and got knocked out. I don't really know what happened. But I do know that I cracked him across the face with the hose nozzle."

"So that's how he got that mouse on his eye!" Buckshot exclaimed and looked directly at Aaron for the first time.

"Is it swollen bad?" Aaron asked, hopefully.

"Well, not bad. But he's got a good lump, and the lump is blacker than the rest of his ugly head, and there's a skinny little scab on it."

"Good. I only wish I could have done more. Did I get any of the others?"

"No, man. Not that I know of. But you did get the Buzzer so it shows. You know, man?" Buckshot said, and the shade cutting across the back of his neck made his cocked head look disconnected and wobbly. "You're surprising me how good you act. You been out a whole day, counting the shot the doctor gave you when you started screaming. You looked like you might die when they brought you in here. I'm glad you're getting well so fast."

"A whole day?"

"A whole day this noon. You looked real bad, like you got hit by a truck or something."

"Does the man know what happened?" Aaron asked and lifted himself slightly, for the pleasure of a chest pain.

But Buckshot pushed the corn flakes bowl into the middle of the tray, and set the spoon next to it, and shoved them both toward Aaron before he answered, simply:

"Yeah."

"Yeah, what, man?" Aaron said, irritably. "Man, you make me nervous! Why don't you tell me what happened? Mother's Honor, I don't know myself."

"I gotta go deliver some trays to the big ward, man. Those guys are gonna start squawkin'," Buckshot said and stepped back.

"Say, man, what's the big problem?" Aaron asked, worried, lifting from the pillow, disregarding the pain, for Buckshot's kinked curls glinted quickly past the window.

"Tell me, man! You got me scared. I'm not crippled or something, am I?"

The brown shadows on Buckshot's fat face sagged with pity.

"You gotta tell me, Buckshot. You gotta tell me. You gotta!"

But Buckshot's round-shouldered back concealed the opening door, and Aaron commanded, in a rasping voice:

"Tell me!"

Buckshot stopped again. But he didn't close the door. And he spoke to the door, slowly:

"They . . . gang-banged you . . . man."

A hot shock kept Aaron bent forward for an embarrassing moment, but tingled into a chill, as he let himself, while breathing heavily through cracked lips, while trying to deny what must be an undeniable fact, what even a fool would expect from the Buzzer, sink back onto the pillow.

"I gotta go, man," Buckshot said and closed the door behind him with a quiet click of the latch, leaving Aaron in a semi-stupor, the untouched tray on his lap, unable to get mad or even cry, unable to feel anything but shame, unable, also, to fit the splintered recollections together in his mind, for they were like some fragmented puzzle: cold and wet on the dairy floor, nausea, a dry smell of manure and straw, but nothing else, nothing else, and even these fragments were as unreal as the illusions of a dream; and the corn flakes turned soggy in the tin bowl as a thin layer of scum soon covered the chocolate.

## II

Black bars picketed the open space between the window frame and sill and a foot of barred sunlight slanted onto the floor. Aaron had watched the bars lengthen on the floor and increase in number, like extra sentries, as the morning had passed and the sun and his shame had risen higher.

Steel-rimmed glasses had sat like microscopic specks upon the large ruddy nose of the stocky nurse who had straightened his blankets, lifted his tray with one thick hand, folded and smoothed the sheet back over the blankets with the other, and who was as crisp and white and clean and antiseptic smelling as the rest of the room.

She had tried to coax him into eating the corn flakes and had lifted him by an underarm to a higher sitting position, while she placed an extra pillow behind him. But he had gasped at a sharp pang in his rectum, and she had then stared at him through the steel-rimmed glasses with such intense steel-gray eyes that she had intensified the pain and made him fear food, for it would have to come out, and he could not forget Barneyway's cry about the toilet paper spotted with blood.

Buckshot had picked up the tray, but had balanced it, to prevent spilling the corn flakes and chocolate, like a man on a tightrope, who could not risk a glance nor spare a word for Aaron.

Every set of footsteps which passed in the hall after he left revived the shame, for Aaron feared that each set would stop at his door, and the walker would enter to stare at the "new queen," the other Barneyway. He began to dread the day he would be well, too, for it might be Queens, Row for him or, just as bad, the main grounds with a ruined reputation.

Judith's tattooed dot was a nasty perforation now, an abscessed pore, and Nora was a navy-base chippy, and Stanley was a punch-drunk fighter who took dives; but it didn't help. Nothing helped, and all he wanted was help. And the heavy tread in the hall did not promise help. Nor did it walk lightly away, but slowed, and stopped, and the door latch clicked, and Big Stoop stepped into the room.

The sharp brim of the khaki cap shortened and strengthened his big head, but it was contempt which slanted his cold eyes, glazed the parchment dry skin of his broad cheeks, and crackled from his lipless mouth with the depth and sharpness of the loud-speaker:

"Woke up, huh?"

"Huh?"

"Gimme the names of the guys who jumped you."

"Huh?"

"The names . . . kid," Big Stoop said, eclipsing the window.

"I . . . I don't know."

"What?"

"I can't remember," Aaron said, mechanically, drawing back into the pillow, away from the big looming head.

"Don't give me that stuff. You saw who hit you, and it was

the same guy, and maybe some others, who was bothering you."

"I didn't see," Aaron insisted in a grating but level whisper, lying easily, without guilt, without fear of being slapped in a hospital bed, with resentment breeding a stubborn loyalty in his sickened body where there had been only a void, and beaten up and even gang-banged, he was no punk fink.

"I still don't know. I was in a stall cleaning, something knocked me down, and I woke up here. That's all I know."

"Gonna play hero, huh?" Big Stoop said, and Aaron could have thanked him, because his own half-shut eye had either blinked unwittingly or he had actually seen an involuntary waver of sympathy soften the harsh outlines of Big Stoop's face before he heard his voice. And he sensed by the hope the waver had aroused in him that if Big Stoop had shown a fraction as much concern for him as for the idea of catching someone and punishing them, he could have been conned into telling the whole story: names and everything.

"You really don't remember, huh?"

"No."

"You know that you got raped though, don't you?" Big Stoop said, and although Aaron didn't answer, he asked: "How do you know that and not who it was?"

"I was told."

"Who told you then?"

"The orderly," Aaron replied quickly and, as quickly, wanted to kick himself for getting trapped, certain Buckshot would get in trouble.

"You know," Big Stoop said, apparently satisfied with that part of Aaron's answer, without being taken in by it, "you guys don't have any sense. Here some guys have seriously beaten you up, have even raped you, the very worst thing that could have happened to you, outside of murder, and yet you protect them. You've got a twisted sense of honor, of what a man is, if you ask me. Nobody's ever really taught you what's right and what's wrong by planting a swift kick in your ass every time you even look the wrong way. There's some man in you, I'll grant you that. But it's so far off base, it'd be better if you didn't have any. Then, I might be able to get some sense into you, maybe. I bet a hundred bucks your old man spoils you, lets you have your own way. The way your brother did all the talking Sunday, I figured something like that."

"I've got a good father," Aaron said.

"Well, I'm your father now, kid," Big Stoop said, with a thin smile at Aaron's reply, "and you listen to me. You're gonna need me some time when you're here, maybe for a probation recommendation. You won't get it, kid. I don't care how good you act. You don't like getting raped and yet you won't help me put a stop to it. You got no sense, no sense, kid. Stay here in this goddamn hospital, and when you get out, go out on the main grounds and take your chances again with the same filthy bastards that got you this time."

He waited, evidently to see if the double warning had any effect; but Aaron, although scared, wanted to spit in the hulking face above him, hated it so much he would have sided with the Buzzer against it at that moment; and he wanted to shout his defiance as the face moved away on the towering frame, turned, and vanished behind the door.

But the door shut louder than the unspoken shout, and its white surface gave him nothing to hate, yet it stood before him like a blank promise of an uncertain future; and he watched it change shades with the passing hours, saw it deepen from a plain white to a somber tone, with the deepening of the day and his own spirit, saw it tint with pale tones at sundown, then finally blot and discolor with the black habit of the chaplain, when he had long stopped trying to defy it and there was only despair where there had been shame and then hate in his spirit.


The soft down on the chaplain's cheeks seemed to feather with the scrape of the chair he pulled next to the bed. And the twin suns on his rimless glasses, reflections of the burlap-textured shade, glimmered like silk screens over his gray, nearly colorless eyes.

"Your face looks pretty bad. It'll probably take about a month for the swelling and the bruises to go completely away," the chaplain said, smoothing the covers down in front of him, as if to remove all possible obstructions and allow a smoother flow of language, of feelings, and of understanding between himself and Aaron.

His words were so soft they seemed to seep through the dry and bloodless lips and pop apart in the harsh reality of air like bubbles of spittle, and Aaron, although he warmed to them, had to lean toward the chaplain in order to hear all of them.

The tiny bones and cords and slim blue veins under the transparent flesh of the chaplain's slender, almost deformed hands, reminded Aaron of Buckshot's story about how little the chaplain ate, how he picked at his food, and tasted this, and sampled that, and spent the better part of an hour in doing it, but how his blond and buxom, southern wife cleaned her plate and had seconds, too, and how her breasts and hips rippled with such unsatisfied, sexy undulations under her plain dresses that the guys in the officers' mess had a jack-off contest over her, while imagining how wild she was and how she scratched when she came.

"Do you pray, son?" the chaplain asked, swallowing with effort, the bony point of his Adam's apple bobbing up and disappearing into the meatless sack of his double chin, as if he had to squeeze the words up and through the strangle hold the banded collar had on his scrawny neck.

"Yes, but not like I used to," Aaron said, feeling guilty over the nights he had fondled the blade instead of the rosary, wondering if his wounds were a sort of penance for this sin.

"Your religion?"

"Catholic," Aaron replied, grateful for the chaplain's choice of a topic, impressed by the great difference between him and Big Stoop, guessing that a man as little and delicate as the chaplain had to be a chaplain just to get by in the world, and had better be a chaplain just to stay alive among the bad actors in the institute.

"Have you made your Holy Communion?" the chaplain asked, smoothing down his scalp-flat colorless blend of blond and gray hair.

"Yes," Aaron said, proud of the implied virtue of his answer. "And I've been confirmed, and I was an altar boy, too."

He shifted uncomfortably between the sheets with this partial lie, for he had only served mass twice before his mother died, and he had not returned after her funeral.

"Aaaah," the chaplain said, with an enthusiastic flicker of his lenses. "You have something most of the boys don't have. You have faith. You know what it is to put all your confidence in God."

The colorless eyes blinked in a monotonous, irritating manner, as if prompting Aaron to agree, and he nodded a noncommittal reply, partly because he really didn't understand what the chaplain meant and partly because he felt insincere, for he was no longer a good Catholic.

"Confession is a wonderful thing," the chaplain said, still blinking. "Though we Protestants don't practice it in the same manner as Catholics do, we realize how it can soothe the suffering soul and bring peace to the troubled person. Don't you agree?"

"Yes," Aaron said, feeling a tone of insincerity in the chaplain's voice now with the too gracious respect for his opinion, but he did really agree. "I do feel good after I've been to confession. But I'm always a little afraid I'll commit a sin before communion the next morning."

"Ah, yes, yes," the chaplain said, warming to his subject, sliding the chair closer to the bed, resting both clasped hands upon the bedspread.

"But after Holy Communion, you feel like a changed person, a much better person, I bet. Isn't that so?"

Half-moon hollows curved sharply down pale cheeks to a pinched mouth, which leaned so close with Aaron's nodded reply, with the black-sleeved elbows that now appeared on the bedspread, that Aaron could smell the sour breath when it opened to speak; and he held his own breath to keep from turning rudely away.

"I'm sorry that you're so seriously hurt as this. I know that you must need someone, an adult, to depend upon. And because of your good religious attitude, and since there is no Catholic priest here at the institute, I'd like you to count on me. Any time you need help, any time, no matter what it is, I want you to come to me, and I'll see what I can do for you. All right?"

Thin hands separated, smoothed a blanket fold, and reclasped. But the chaplain stayed at the same close, uncomfortable distance, waiting for an answer; and Aaron nodded yes, quickly, for he did truly appreciate the offer, especially since he had nothing else to depend upon; but he breathed with gratitude when the chaplain leaned back and smiled with false teeth and pale-orange gums.

"We're going to become good friends," the chaplain said. "Really, son, and I do mean this, under God, it's too bad we didn't know each other this well, had this understanding, I mean, before this other happened, or maybe. . . . The leader of those boys who attacked you. . . ."

Gray eyes drifted from a close unblinking scrutiny of Aaron's face into a wandering gaze.

"The . . . leader. . . ?"

Ivory fingers touched and prompted the bloodless lips.

"What's his name?"

"The—" But Aaron's answer was stopped by a bullet-swift glance, and a wave of disgust and anger swept over him as he clamped his cracked lips together.

"His name?" the chaplain asked. "His name? His name?" Aaron twisted his swollen face into the most obvious sneer he could manage, and the pinched mouth fell open, the half-moon hollows drooped into straight lines, and the twin suns reappeared on the lenses.

"I, I . . . I really must be going," the chaplain said, and the chair scraped, the bed quivered and rose with his frail black figure, and he walked with hurried and jerking steps out of the room.

## III

Aaron formed spectacles by touching his thumbs and fore-fingers together, limited his sight to small circles of the pimpled plaster ceiling, and tried to make a design out of the rings of light. He noticed, with disappointment, that the rings weakened in intensity as his gaze glided away from the center bulb to the ceiling corners. He then noticed that the corners were darker than the walls supporting them but were much lighter than the drab yellow of the drawn shade. But the whitewashed room was as monotonous to look at as the bleat of the crickets was to hear, and he wished that he was back on the garbage run and busy enough to evade all thought, then rejected this thought, too, because it included the complicated and fearful idea of appearing on the main grounds.

Two full days of twisting and sweating had taken all the crispness out of the sheets and all the energy out of his hate. The hot damp pocket of the pillow was a discomfort that kept him constantly aware of his swollen forehead, his jaw, and his eye. The tape, the flannel nightgown, and the covers encased his fractured ribs and heated his body flesh into steamy wrinkles. His loins were soft and slippery with sweat, and his rectum often itched, too, and rather than scratch it or rub it, he had devised a way of rocking his body and squeezing his buttocks together, which permitted him to ignore it for a while.

He lifted all the covers but the sheet and threw them back, with a flick of his right hand, upon his legs, and only the sheet covered him from the crotch up. The fingers of his left hand were bruised and stiff from some kick, and he wondered when he would be able to close it into a fist and whether he would ever be able to jab with power again.

But his body felt liberated, and he did not move until the aching numbness settled into his back and buttocks again. Then, although he tilted first to his left and then to his right side and held each position for a minute or two before settling once again upon his back, he could not forget *who* he now was nor *where* he was nor *why* he was there.

For the waxy face of the chaplain haunted the mental haze caused by the pain pills and the daydreaming. Aaron's thoughts kept revolving around and around a flickering tattoo, which kept reappearing and reappearing on the sallow cheek, and the sleepy bliss and the escape into laziness which he had expected to enjoy were completely poisoned. The struggle to keep himself clearheaded and awake was equally discouraging. For the idea of revenge as his only pass to the grounds festered upon his mind like a pimple beneath the skin: painful, but without enough pus in it to erupt. He then had to face the fact that he couldn't whip the Buzzer without help, and he couldn't expect help of any kind from any person, not even from Skip, for there was the lost blade to explain.

He pressed the smooth protruding button of the buzzer attached to the bed frame for distraction, and tried to think of something to ask the nurse for, in case she, instead of Buckshot, answered his call.

He never asked her for the bedpan.

He pressed the button again, then remembered that Buckshot had already picked up the dinner trays, his last job, and was gone. He tipped the pitcher to check it, saw a little liquid near the bottom, decided to ask the nurse for more water, and set the pitcher down as the door opened.

Barneyway stepped timidly in, but held onto the door knob, as if ready to leave. His large eyes were tremulous with anxiety and the cleft in his chin quivered with a tentative smile.

He then raised his hand in an awkward salute, and a compassionate pang tightened Aaron's throat, and he let his own jaw sag in a swollen smile.

"They beat you up bad," Barneyway said, lifting a timorous finger toward Aaron's black eye as he approached, and lifting it higher and almost touching the knot on Aaron's forehead when he stopped.

"They kicked you, huh?"

"They had to kick me," Aaron said; and Barneyway pulled his hand away, held it as if he didn't know what to do with it, then sneaked it down his side, below the level of the bed, and out of sight, in such a humble manner that Aaron tried to apologize.

"Sit down, Barney. You okay?"

"Okay."

"The Buzzer bother you any?" Aaron asked, with only a slight huskiness in his voice.

"No. He's been real quiet since you got hurt. He's afraid to try anything. Big Stoop has come around every day and even asked about his eye."

"What'd the Buzzer say?" Aaron asked, excitedly.

"He said he tripped, and Rattler backed him up and so did some other guys, and Big Stoop believed him because he's cadet captain."

Aaron let his head settle into the damp pocket of the pillow, disappointed, but tried to picture the Buzzer scared, peeking over his shoulder with pursed lips, and, unable to, he said, his voice quavering with emotion:

"I'm glad you came to see me, Barneyway. It took me this messed-up body and this face to really see what you been up against. I mean *really* see. I know what kind of pressure you were under when you didn't fight the Buzzer back. I'd like to stop fighting, too."

Tears welled up in Barneyway's eyes, and he lifted his hands as if to grab Aaron, to touch him at least; but Aaron shied away in distaste, and Barneyway hid his hands below the bed again, and sat back in the chair.

"We'll be friends again," Aaron said to make him feel better; but he was discouraged by Barneyway's weakness when he needed encouragement so badly himself, when he needed somebody, anybody, to give him a reason to fight; and trying to revive his own spirit, he added:

"And don't worry, either, because I'll figure out a way to make sure the Buzzer never bothers us again."

"What do you mean?"

"I don't know what I mean. But I know I gotta do it. Only power counts, man. If you're not big enough to be bad acting, then you gotta do what you can do. I don't know what I'm gonna do, but I know I'm gonna do something."

"Don't get in trouble, Aaron. It's not worth it. It's not. It's not."

"Why not?" Skip honked from the doorway and swaggered in, hopping with each step, as if hitching up his pants.

"Why not? Get in trouble, Aaron, and I'll get in trouble with you," he said and crushed all of Aaron's shame with his stubby hand.

"I'll help yuh get 'im, Aaron. We'll get him together. It ain't over yet."

He shoved Aaron's leg aside and hopped onto the bed, causing a small quake, but made Aaron's discomfort insignificant by his willingness to do battle for him, by the strength of his knuckle-battered face.

"You didn't have your blade when they jumped yuh, did you?" he asked, gruffly, and with complete confidence.

"Did you?" he asked again, and Aaron shook his head, feeling like a coward, and saw further proof of his cowardice in Skip's reply:

"Well, I'll get yuh another one, man. And I'll get one for myself, and we'll catch that Buzzer in a cross and nail him with two shivs instead of one. How about that?"

He brushed at a blond lock of hair on his face, but wiped it flatter instead, and noticed Aaron's glum expression.

"Let me tell yuh something, man. Regardless of what the guys might say or think, I know what kind of a battle you put up, and I know you didn't give in. I—"

Aaron's blush caused him to pause, and he looked from Aaron to Barneyway and back to Aaron again.

"I'm with you, man. Don't let this guy make you like him, man."

"I'm not, Skip," Aaron said. "It's not him."

"What is it?"

"I'm pretty messed up right now, man," Aaron said. "You know."

"I know that I'm gonna help you get even," Skip said and turned sidesaddle on the bed, purposely ignoring Barneyway, and ignoring Aaron's blush, too, he talked on.

"Every real guy gets even, Aaron," he said. "Every real guy, man. Look at Dillinger! He shot the guy to death that put the finger on him. Remember that movie with Laurence Tierney, man?"

He stopped and thumped a knuckle into Aaron's thigh, and forced him to answer.

"Yeah, I remember."

"Remember how he pulled out that wooden gun that he carved to escape from jail with and made the stool pigeon cringe?

"Remember?

"Remember that when the guy looked like he was gonna pee his pants, he showed him that it was just a play gun, handmade, and blackened with shoe polish?

"Thennnnn, when the guy starts to laugh and yet almost cry, he's so happy, Dillinger puts his hand in his pocket and shoots him with the real rod he had stashed there?

"Remember? Remember?

"Ain't that cold? Ain't it?" he said, gleefully, and slapped his thigh, and grinned at Aaron's lopsided grin.

"Did you see Paul Muni when he played Scarface? and shot George Raft down in the hotel for making his sister? and they were married and he didn't even bother to find out? Did him in in a silk bathrobe?

"All the real guys get even, Aaron. Al Capone! James Cagney! St. Valentine's Day Massacre! Pretty Boy Floyd! Edward G. Robinson! All of 'um, Aaron! All of 'um!" he shouted, making quick, finger-barreled, hammer-thumbed, trigger-fingered motions, throwing mock punches and jerking the bed so much that Aaron had to spread his arms and legs to lessen the jolts; but he was pleased and affected by Skip's excitement, and he nodded eagerly in reply to Skip's question:

"Man, you wantta really hear about revenge? I mean really?"

Skip scooted closer and knocked his knee against Aaron, but didn't notice it; and Aaron, although he flinched, didn't care, because he wanted to hear the story.

"Well, man, I knew some pachuco dudes once. You know, some real pachucos, Mexicans, bad actors with pachuco crosses on each hand. And this one pachuco, name of Hector, he used to wear a great big silver cross around his neck, and even had a six-inch cross tattooed on his chest, and he was the baddest, coldest, revenge-gettingest dude I ever saw. Man, listen to this," he said, and Aaron lifted his head higher on the pillow.

"Once I escaped from a foster home over in River County. They put me there after my second burglary job because my old man had taken off on my mother when I was about ten. Well, anyway, I was cutting across country to stay off the highways and clear of the highway patrol when these chicanos in a fruit-picker camp took me in. I stayed a whole week with 'em, and when I was there, I saw this Hector corner a guy who had given him the finger with both hands from a passing car full of guys from another camp. That was about a week before I got there, and he got this dude and slapped his face about ten times, and, then, talking some kind of fantastic Mexican slang, he made the guy kneel down and cup his balls in his hands without squeezing 'em. Do you know what that means?"

Spittle bubbled in the corners of Skip's mouth, but unwilling to pause for a long breath, let alone an answer, he gasped a whistling short wind and kept talking.

"Man, when you grab a guy's nuts, you gotta squeeze 'em or you're a punk, a bitch, a whore. And this guy practically cried. He begged and begged Hector, and said he'd do anything for Hector except that. But Hector, and, man, his arms were as big as tree branches from pickin' fruit all his life, man, Hector, he made the guy cup 'um or fight, and the guy lifted his hand right up between Hector's legs and held 'em, man, and when he did, Hector spit in his face for doin' it, man. Now, tell-me-like-it-is, man? Is that revenge, man? Now, tell me, Aaron? Tell-me-like-it-is? Is that revenge? and just for a guy giving you the double-barreled finger? Revenge, man. Wow!"

"That's revenge. Yeah, now that's really revenge, man," Aaron agreed, and the Buzzer was on his knees before him, pink palm upraised, gingerly cupping the crotch of his dungarees. "I'd love to make the Buzzer do that in front of everybody, and I'd love to spit in his face."

"Make him do it then," Skip said and slapped Aaron's leg. "I'll help yuh. We'll make that black queer bastard kneel down and cry."

"I'll get him," Aaron said. "I'll get him for me and Barneyway. That's the only answer. I've got nothin' else. Do it and all the way. I'll get him for both of us. For both of us, Barneyway!" he cried, filled with exuberant hate, although Barney-way sat in rigid silence on the chair.

"On my Mother's Honor, I'll get him for both of us," Aaron said and raised his fist; and Skip reached out and grabbed it with both hands and raised it higher, like a winning fighter at the end of a bout; and Aaron liked the test of pain that streaked across his chest.

## IV

Sunday visits were a muffled, saddening chaos through the hospital walls of voices, cries, laughter, the boiling rap of exhausts, car hum, and the static and crackle of names from the office loud-speaker; but pain pills had eased the numbed discomfort of Aaron's back and buttocks and allowed his brain to absorb these sounds as half-formed sensations, like those which occur midway between sleep and daydreaming; and he basked in an artificial calm of pride and lonesome boredom, lulled by the pills and by his decision to strike back at the Buzzer.

It was a decision which, with Skip's enthusiasm, had helped carry him through the lonely hours of doubt before sleep and the dull morning hours when the impulse to pray began to bother him. He had soothed the nerves that demanded relief in the sanctuary of a church with a memory of the chaplain and with a self-reminder that it took tough fists not prayer-clasped hands to make it in the institute, and he then tried to satisfy his spirit with glorious thoughts of revenge.

Steps and voices in the hall loomed upon his conscious mind like the pressure of touch, and he fought the desire for a visit that rose within him at the sounds by trying to absorb them, too, in his mental haze, and he was beginning to succeed, for he was starting to forget them, when the door pressed a block of air upon his swollen face, and he opened his eyes to the sight of his family and Judith filing into the room as if it were a sanctified tomb at the end of a grueling pilgrimage.

Nora came in first on slow, carefully spaced, spike-heeled steps, wearing a black gabardine suit which accentuated her somber carriage; her black hair swooped down to her cardigan collar like a mantilla worn for mass; her face had the pale, guilty complexion common to older girls awaiting their turn in the confessional booth; and she clasped her black purse like a prayer book in one hand and led Judith by the other.

The blue in Judith's eyes seemed to shrink to the size of her beauty mark with her first step past Nora, and she did not say hello, nor did anyone else speak.

Not his father, who waddled in and stopped at the foot of the bed, hat in hand, the ball of his belly snugged in a vest, suit coat hanging loose and heavy padded at his shoulders, light creasing across his olive-skinned skull.

Not John, who strode in with the arrogance of a naval officer until he, too, saw Aaron, then faltered with the shock that snapped across the taut skin of his face like an elastic band, and almost tiptoed into a corner.

Not Stanley, either, who entered last, and who closed the door with an almost reverent attempt to prevent a noise, and who, then, leaned against it as if cornered, broad shoulders clothed and magnified by a V-neck sweater, and the breadth of his chest intensified by a triangular patch of T-shirt at the neck.

A loud-speaker pronouncement of a name was nearly intelligible in the silence, and the promise of happiness it carried for some unknown prisoner mocked the unhappy beginning of Aaron's visit in the hospital room.

"It looks like a funeral procession," he said, making a joke and instantly clearing his mind, although incapable of laughing at it himself.

"Do I look that bad? It's been three days, you know. I

could barely see out of my eye at first. My jaw doesn't even ache when I open it now."

The frog was gone from his voice, which was both agreeable and regrettable to him, for although he wanted to shatter the thin layer of discomfort with frank speech, a cracked tone could have made his wounds seem more serious and could have punished them more.

"You look okay," Stanley said. "I thought you'd be in worse shape than that. Eye's still black, but the swelling's down. Jaw looks a little big yet. That bruise on your forehead will take longer to go away than that little bump it's on. There isn't too much wrong. I've looked worse after a four-rounder. Remember that battle I had in San Jose? You look pretty good, considering. . . ."

"Pretty good?" Aaron repeated, trying, but unsuccessfully, to prompt Stanley to continue, for the unfinished sentence left the deceptively mild atmosphere, in which the half-drawn shade filtered and softened the rays of the sun, tense and charged with his shame.

Considering what? he then wanted to say and force everything into the open, force them to admit what had happened, force them to confess what they had caused, and, most of all, force his father to speak and suffer. He wanted to *hear* his father suffer, as well as *see* him suffer. For the big man wasn't trying to bluff his way out of his distress as usual, but stood heavily by the bed and, finally, made a clumsy attempt to straighten the folded bedspread, when Aaron quickly attacked him.

"Too little, too late, huh?" he said, his voice wavering and unsure, but he didn't back down.

"Why didn't you do more sooner? I might not even be here if you did."

The bald crown darkened with an angry rush of blood, but bowed and turned, so that Aaron, who lifted himself from the pillow, tolerating the tender pressure in his buttocks, had to speak to the fan of dark hair below it.

"You let me down. You didn't get me transferred like you promised."

"Listen, Aaron," Stanley said. "Don't blame Dad. I was the one who should have made sure you got transferred. I guess I left too much of it up to the superintendent. You can't tell him what to do, you know. I guess since I was so vague about it and who the bully was, he didn't think it was that serious."

"Why did you, *you* take the knife? You're the guy who's always talking about how tough you are and how important it is to be a good fighter. I might have kept them off me with it. You took away my only protection. You let 'em get me."

"Do you think it would have been better if they had allowed you to kill someone?" John asked.

"I didn't want to kill anybody. I just wanted them to leave me alone," Aaron retorted, still propped on one elbow, using the sore strip in his side as justification for his lack of respect.

"Why didn't you tell them it was so serious then? Stanley thought it was just a fight and tried to prevent it from becoming serious. You weren't honest with them. How could you expect them to understand?"

"Do you think anybody would have believed me?" Aaron countered; and John's swiftly lowered face was a wide but sharply beveled plane of intense concentration—square boned, yet molded by lean flesh—and who, when he spoke again, spoke with a firm but very soft voice:

"You have to try and understand the family's position, too, Aaron. I, we, don't deny yours. They tried to help you last week. They didn't really know what was going on, and they have to suffer in their own way for what happened to you. But they're still interested in keeping you from turning into a savage dog, and if you keep up this self-pitying attitude, you'll destroy yourself. Do you understand that?"

"Do you know what they did to me?" Aaron shouted.

"Do you?" he said again, and John didn't answer, but this only increased his urge to whip them with himself, all of them, Judith, too.

"Do you know what they did?"

"I don't care what they did," John said. "You've got to forget what they did."

"Forget what they did?"

"Forget what they did," John insisted, "or you'll destroy yourself."

"They'll destroy me if I try to forget. Don't *you* understand that? If I don't get them for getting me, everybody'll try it sometime. The whole institute'll think I'm a weak punk. A punk! Do you know what a punk is? Do you?"

"Aaron," John said, and ignored the question. "You've got to be big enough, strong enough to live without thinking of revenge. I hear you tried to be nice to that boy, but you probably overdid it, and that's why he thought you were afraid. Now you're going to the opposite extreme. You've got to learn to compromise. We're not going to try and get that boy punished because we can't prove anything, and it won't do you any good. So, we're compromising, we're going to concentrate on getting you out of here. We don't care about revenge. We want to help you. But you've got to compromise, too. You've got to be bigger than the inmates here or you'll end up just like them. If I could only make you see that. You've got to make up your mind that you belong to a bigger world than the vicious one behind the barbed wire of this fence."

"I can't make up my mind, because I do belong here," Aaron said. "This *is* where I belong, in a reform school. And why should I believe you? What do you know what goes on here? Compromise! You've never had to fight in your life. Spent all your life in school with sissies, bookworms. Come around on holidays, with manicured fingernails and fancy advice. What do you know? You look like a judge right now, with that old man's vest. What do you know? You don't know nothin'! Nothin'!"

His father spun around, as if ready to reprimand, but hesitated at the sight of Aaron's face, then cried:

"Let's get out of here! He doesn't want to be helped. I can't stand this anymore."

"I know *you* can't stand it," Aaron shouted. "Yeah, I know you can't. Go on, get out! Get out! Get out!"

John started, and then snapped to attention, as if he were going to give an order, but his body slackened, and he motioned to the others to follow him, and left the room.

"Pray, Aaron, pray," Nora said and tried to kiss him, but he shoved her away.

"Pray? Look who's talking about praying? You haven't been to confession since Mother died! You spit on her coffin. And you been having a ball since! What if she saw you in that suit coat? V-neck. No blouse. You go pray. You need it worse than I do. Go on! Get out! Go pray! Go pray!" he shouted at her, and he dropped back onto the pillow and stared at the ceiling, while her high heels tapped out of hearing, hurt because they made him feel at fault when he believed they were at fault and because they didn't solve his problem for him, and then surprised when the chair scraped and he saw Judith.

"Why don't you go with 'em, stool pigeon?" he said, trying to stop her approach.

"I wanted to try and explain, Aaron," she replied and moved shyly but stubbornly closer.

Her features were extraordinarily clear to him, but framed as she was by the bright window behind her, shadows hovered like a premature age upon her face, creating slight cheek puffs below her eyes, and he wondered if she had been crying.

"I told them . . . Aaron . . . because . . . I wanted to help you . . . Aaron. I didn't know. . . . I would have never believed . . . that something like—"

"Just like you didn't know why you put on that tattoo,

huh?" he interrupted and made her wince. "Where are your
tight skirts? What are you doing with a pleated one on?
You're nothing but a paddy chick. I should've never let that
beauty mark fool me. Don't hide it."

The tattoo was disappearing behind her profile.

"I thought you were gutty. Promise together, hah!"

"That's not fair, Aaron," she said, but the tattoo sat like a
still target in the center of a blush spot, and her explanation
was feeble. "I wanted to help you. Don't you see that?"

"I sure do see. I see myself in a hospital bed. I see what a
weak bitch did to me."

"Bitch?" she said and her voice almost broke. But she
pointed at the tattoo, which trembled, as if it were imbedded
at the flabby base of the cheek puff, and stuttered: "I-I-I-I, I
should have never come to see you in the first place, and, then,
I, I, I wouldn't have thisssss."

But he repeated: "Bitch! Bitch!" trying to drive her away.

She bit her lips, but stayed. And there was a long pause in
which the loud-speaker crackled, and squawked, and obliter-
ated a name, and which she ended with her admission: "Aaron
. . . I don't know how to make up for my part, Aaron. I don't
know how to help. Everything I've done has . . ."

She looked around her as if she were trying to find the
answer in the hospital room, failed, and then faced him.

"Why don't you try and do what John said?"

"I can't. Don't you understand that?" he asked her, pacified
a little by her admission. "I've got to get back at 'em or they'll
never let me alone. Never. Never. I've got to get 'em. I'm
gonna get 'em," and he added, to put himself beyond any possible, weakening plea of hers: "I'm gonna make 'em pay."

"Don't say that, Aaron. Think about the consequences.
Think of what you're doing to yourself. They might kill you
next time, too. Think about getting out. Maybe if you behave
real good, they might let you out of here sooner just because
of what happened to you. They might—"

"Sooner?" he said, turning a swollen burning eye upon her. "Sooner? Ha, ha. Ha, ha, ha. That's a good way to get out. Just let yourself get. . . . Do you really know what happened to me? Do you? They treated me like a whore. Do you understand? Like a whore!" he repeated, getting a tremendous pleasure from the anguish he was causing her.

"What if we got married? We wouldn't know who was the woman. Ha, ha. Ha, ha, ha, ha, ha, ha, ha, ha."

And he laughed with a forced but unbroken and unceasing snigger until he realized she was talking to him, trying to make him listen to her.

"Huh?" he asked. "What?"

"How could you. . . ?" Her pale lashes were heavy with quick tears. "How could you be so bitter?"

"How could I be so bitter?" he mocked, his cracked lips curling in a stilted grin.

"It's easy, easy eeeeeeeeeessssyyyyyyyyyyyyyyyyyyyy," he said.


# V


The box of candy bars from Judith lay opened upon the bed-spread before Aaron, and yellow letters spelled out Mars with a big M and a yellow star upon each pale green wrapping. But each wrapping was so pale and so transparent that the choco-late-coated bar visible beneath it gave it a blended tone which was neither gray nor brown nor green, and he wondered if the fading afternoon light helped produce it.

*Toasted,* the smaller letters on a bar said, and *Almond,* and *chocolate,* too, which he hadn't noticed at first because it was written in brown. *Mars Toasted Almond,* with *chocolate* in letters of chocolate as an unnecessary afterword. Or was it necessary? And were the *Toasted Almond* and the *chocolate* part of the name or explanations?

He snapped the card with his thumb, as he picked it up

again, and read the "Get well! Love, Judith!" upon it, without caring for her love or the card or the candy bars. But he could comb his hair in the mirror without suffering from sore ribs now. He could sit straight up, too, and did most of the long day. He could also flap down the hall in his flannel slippers and his nightgown to the bathroom, endure the stare of any guy he met, do his duty, and walk directly back, in spite of his dread, and enter the blank white walls once again without shirking.

The puffy moon face of a stranger still looked back at him from the mirror though. Black masked the eye around the bright green iris and its bloodshot ring. The bruise remained, his lips were still scabbed, his tan was fading again, and his complexion was more a sallow yellow than any color, but he didn't care about that, either.

He picked up a candy bar and examined it, and either it was smaller than they used to be or when he was smaller they looked bigger. It was only two by four inches at most and only half an inch thick at the widest part, where the unseen almonds must be. There were enough words on the cover, too, in tiny, small, and medium-sized letters to confuse anybody, not just Aaron D'Aragon, who got confused about everything.

Maybe Judith wasn't trying to con him? Maybe he tried to make something out of her that she wasn't? Maybe he did that with Nora? and with his mother?

No!

He had crushed the candy bar.

He opened his hand and the bar rolled out with a tiny rustle onto his fingers, and he saw MARS in a brown circle with a yellow star on the bottom of the bar, and TOASTED ALMOND written below it, and nothing else.

Mars Toasted Almond was the name of the candy bar, but he had to see its opposite side by accident before he could figure it out. Otherwise, it was one extreme or the other for him, as John had said; and Dominic had been right because there wasn't any buddy-up that Sunday night; and Stanley, a champ, had taken away his blade; and his father *had* been a great working man and had never been to jail; and Barneyway *didn't* end up in a hospital room, boxed by four white walls and a white ceiling and a hardwood floor.

Could he bet that the floor was hardwood? Could he bet that the ceiling was darker than the white walls because it was still daylight, but there was no sun, and the center bulb wasn't on? The room was a lot better than Queens Row, or the main grounds, or the empty rooms of the big house that he used to fill up with buddies like Barneyway, anyway. Buddies? Was that why he was the leader?

He dreaded waking up in the morning most of all. For waking up to the daylight sounds of jail was. . . . He straightened up, for he heard someone in the hall and recognized Skip's voice before Skip's flat face poked around the door, with a conspiratorial smile spread across it.

"Guess what, man?" Skip said, and stepped in, then, very carefully and very quietly, closed the door, and tiptoed like a schoolboy in a spook movie, with his back hunched, his head hanging, and swim-stroking for balance, across the room to Aaron's bed.

"Guess! Go on, guess!" he said, and he looked so proudly and purposely foolish that Aaron smiled.

"Which hand?" he said and put both hands behind his back, fumbled with them, and held them out before him.

"I don't know," Aaron said, wearied by the play acting, but he slapped the skin-cracked knuckles of Skip's right hand, only to have Skip pull it back and put it behind him again.

"Guess!" he said and put the left fist out in front of him, and Aaron slapped that, too, but Skip pulled it back also, and Aaron said, crossly:

"Well, what is it?"

Skip then put both of his hands out in front of him again, said, "Guess!" once again, and turned them over and opened them, exposing empty palms, but he threw his left arm out before Aaron could complain, and a black-taped blade fell out of his blue sleeve next to the box of candy bars.

"There's your equalizer, daddy-o!" he said, his voice rising triumphantly to his honking nose, as Aaron sagged weakly into the folded pillows.

"How about it, huh? I told yuh I'd get yuh one."

The knife lay lightly upon the bedspread. Its taped handle tilted down with the slight incline caused by Aaron's leg, and its shiny blade bridged the spread from the handle to its pointed tip, which was propped up by a fold and touched the candy box.

"How about it, huh?" Skip said, squinting at Aaron.

"Yeah," Aaron said, but without enthusiasm, leaving it untouched. "It's a blade, alright."

"What's the matter, man?" Skip asked, wrinkling his nose.

"Nothing," Aaron said and laid his fingers on the blade. It was still warm from Skip's body. "Thanks."

"It's a good blade," Skip said. "I took my time with it. I polished it with emery cloth and everything. Take a look at it."

Aaron held it in his hand but didn't lift it from the spread. He examined it at arm's length and saw how smoothly the blade creased his hand, how there were no grindstone marks nor ragged file edges on it, and how polishing had given it a blue overtone. He then noticed how carefully the tape had been wrapped around the handle, making even quarter-inch ridges from the blunted end to its final wrap, where it tapered to the width of the blade; and he said, with genuine appreciation:

"It's a beauty. It's a beauty, Skip. It's as pretty as a blade can be. I'll keep it."

"Whatta ya think I brought it for?" Skip replied, but he was proud and he swaggered over to the window; and Aaron, to prove that he was grateful and that he wasn't afraid to accept the blade, held out the box of candy bars.

"Have a Mars, man," he said.

"Sure," Skip said and swaggered back and crushed a bar, with a brisk crackling, in his hand.

"Take another one," Aaron said, and Skip grabbed another bar and jammed it in his shirt pocket, and Aaron set the box down and looked doubtfully at the black weapon.

"Put it under the mattress, man."

"An orderly might see it when he changes the sheets," Aaron replied, although Skip had misinterpreted his glance.

"Put it under the candy, then."

"It won't fit, will it?" Aaron asked, but in such a listless manner that Skip stopped tearing at the candy wrapper.

"You could work it in, if you wanted to. What's the matter, man?"

"Nothing."

"Don't you want the blade?"

"Uh-huh."

"You don't act like it, man. You ain't ascared of that Buzzer now, are you?"

"No!" Aaron answered and added, quickly:

"Maybe the guys will think I'm hound if I use a blade?"

"They'll think you're hound if you don't try and get 'im, Aaron."

"I'm not afraid," Aaron said and tried to talk himself out of any implications of cowardice. "I was thinking the guys might think I was afraid of the Buzzer, if I . . . I was thinking I could get my rep back better if I chose him with just my fists. Sort of man to man."

"He's a duke, Aaron," Skip said, and bit off the end of the candy bar, and chewed as he talked.

"Nobody expects you to fight him fair. There ain't no fair to it. He stomped you with a gang of guys when he was bound to whip you by himself. You'd have to be real lucky to beat him, Aaron. But that ain't it, anyway. Beat him! Win! That's all that counts. Do-him-in! Besides, you already proved you got guts. You made him stomp yuh. You made him use all those guys. And he knows it. Now, he's goin' around saying that the reason they all jumped you was so they could all get some. Some guys believe him. But I don't. Most guys don't. You already got a rep. You just gotta keep it, and anything goes."

He wiped the chocolate off his lips with the back of his hand.

"Everything's fair in love and war, you heard that. He stomped you, man! If you don't hurt 'im, he'll try again, and he might kill yuh next time. But if you come on him with a blade in the belly, he's gonna be too scared to mess with yuh, and, by that time, guys'll be willing to help yuh, not just me. And, besides, if you do get 'im, he might settle for just being even. He got yuh so bad, he might figure a blade squares it."

"I don't wanta kill 'im, man," Aaron said. "I'm tired of fighting. I just wantta do my own time, that's all."

"I would'a never risked my ass to make that blade, man, if I thought you'd talk like that. Gimme it back," Skip said and held out his hand. His teeth were streaked with chocolate.

"I didn't say I wouldn't fight," Aaron said, feeling ungrateful. "I said I was tired of fighting."

"I could get Youth Authority for making that blade, Aaron. You got me leery now. I went to a lot of trouble."

Aaron rolled the blade under the bedspread, and Skip dropped his hand, satisfied.

"I'll get a blade, too, Aaron," he said. "And when you get out of here, we'll make a battle plan. We'll make it so cool, so smart, that every guy in the institute'll know who did it and nobody'll be able to prove it, and we'll get ourselves a reputation as great avengers, and even the man will give us the nod. How about it? I'll help yuh. I hate that Buzzer. I seen him whip on too many dudes my size. I wantta get 'im."

"When I get out?" Aaron asked, trying to keep the despair out of his voice.

"As soon as," Skip said, and he kept chewing as he described his scheme, splotches of chocolate on his lips, his teeth, and his tongue. "I'll start tailing him now. Just like they do in the movies, man. Clock his habits, you know. Find out when he's alone, everything. And when you get out, I'll already have some good ideas and we can plan our strategy.

"Great Avengers, man," he said and aimed the candy bar. "We'll get us a mob in here called the Great Avengers. That's what we'll do. And when we make probation, we'll continue on the outs, we'll shake down bookmakers and that for protection. Because they can't tell the cops," he explained. "But we'll begin with the Buzzer and we'll go on to Big Time. Okay?"

Aaron nodded wearily, but was careful not to show his disbelief, hoping that if he agreed, Skip would leave, and he offered the candy box to him again.

"Take another one, man," he said, and Skip, obviously surprised, glanced down for verification before taking one, then announced, quickly, as if wanting to take advantage of Aaron's consent before more doubts occurred:

"I better take off."

He hurried to the door, where he waved the candy bar, and repeated, before he left:

"Anything goes!"

Aaron set the box down on his thigh with relief, but he saw unhappy implications in the disorder Skip had made of the candy bars. For if Skip messed up with the blades as badly as he had messed up the rows in the box? then?

He backhanded the box off his thigh, but without energy, and it landed upright on the bed without losing a candy bar. He could then make out the form of the blade through the bedspread, and he felt like ripping it free and throwing it out the window.

The handle was bound so tightly and neatly that it had the general tapering shape of a blackjack through the spread. He tried to grip it, but the cloth rolled around it made it unwieldy, and he let his fingers relax and noticed that the sweat from his palm had slightly dampened the cloth. Still, he was impressed by the care Skip had taken with the blade, and it had taken guts to do it, in spite of the play acting, or was it because of the play acting?

He slid his hand under the spread, and as he tested the tiny point of the blade with his finger, the room light went on, and he could tell that the chocolate wagon was in the hall by the noise the guys from the big ward made, getting into line for their cups. But he was too concerned with his fear, when his daring had helped make him a gang leader, to care about chocolate.

Skip was a play actor, but maybe he, himself, had been playing a part when he had charged down the street against the beans from Santa Clara? He had been too carried away by the thrill to care what might happen, as he remembered, or to even realize that all his buddies had stopped running before it was too late. He then had to fight because he was trapped and couldn't back down in front of so many guys.

The clatter of a cup and the loud click of the dipper against the big pot told him the chocolate wagon had arrived at the next room, although he was preoccupied with whether or not he had been playing a part when he had risked a battle with the Buzzer in the dorm. Could anger or pride be the real cause? as it was in his fight against Rattler? He could remember now that against the beans, the Buzzer, and Rattler, he had really believed that he would win and that he wouldn't get hurt, although all the odds were against it, and he had felt no fear.

The door closed in the next room. Wheels squeaked with the start of the chocolate wagon, and it then rolled, with a tinny rumble, toward his door. Maybe you had to be play acting to risk? Maybe you had to pretend if you wanted to keep believing in things? in people? in yourself? Otherwise, you'd see nothing but nothin' and quit. The rumble stopped. A cup rattled. The door opened. But it didn't matter to him. They could throw away the chocolate for all he cared. And they could throw away the blade, too.

## VI

Potato rot blackened and dampened the lug box that Aaron had saddled with a burlap sack to protect his white trousers. And its rotten odor set an appropriate boundary of stinking taboo between his seat by the potato closet and the gossiping, smoking, white-uniformed boys on the opposite end of the shaded kitchen porch, who, like him, were taking advantage of the few minutes of rest before the dinner whistle.

A pale bruise, thickening his left eyebrow, and a bloodshot eye corner were all that showed of the beating, although he wore a padded cloth protector over his bruised ribs. But not even indifference had been able to protect his bruised pride. A week of silent treatment and harassment made him tighten now with every remark. All laughter seemed at his expense. Every unusual move made him suspicious. The dry grass and weeds which covered the sloping hill gave suspect ripples, for he could feel no wind. The eucalyptus trees which grew out of the gully on the opposite side of the graveled yard formed a giant fence and closed him into a blind corner between the side wall of the officers' mess and the back wall of the dining hall, where he couldn't depend upon the chance of a scuffle being seen to protect him.

His meek questions had floated unanswered in the chilly air. He had been forced to learn his waiter's job by himself. At least once a day, the salt, sugar, and pepper shakers which he had so carefully filled and wiped clean were replaced by grimy empty shakers and his clean hand-washed towels by dirty food-spotted ones. The nasty remarks had also become so numerous and so direct that his thin hope of lasting until September began to fade once more and he feared that he would never hope again.

Secret sounds were muffled by cupped hands in the circle of boys. But he could almost spell his name with the suspicious wrinkles of their white shirts. He could read the dirty writing in Bobby Shuck's crooked blond curls, too, although the cadet captain made a slouching question mark of his hunched back. He could trace the sly smile in the dark pimple-specks that scattered like freckles over Boomby's pitted cheeks, and it was a smile of the cheeks alone, for the big duke's mouth did not move, and his stony Mexican eyes lied.

Sticks and stones could break his bones, Aaron repeated to himself, but words, wisecracks, snubs, being put down and played for shine meant nothing, nothing, nothing. Nothing, he said again with the nigger slur of his name, and he knew that it had spilled out of a drooping corner of Bobby Shuck's mouth. He despised Bobby Shuck for imitating the Buzzer's drawl, for trying to copy Boomby's cold smile, for playing the part with a pachuco slouch, but only proving, with all his play acting, he was only a paddy.

The porch shade blended the dark pits into the dark complexion on Boomby's cheeks and made the smile harder to detect. But Aaron had learned to define it on his first day in the dorm when his box of candy bars had been stolen. The theft had been as ironic as the smile, for Aaron had cared as little about the candy as he did about the blade, which he had hidden and forgotten deep in the hospital trash, and he would have given the candy bars to anybody who asked for them.

But he did fear the smile. He feared it when he saw Boomby tease a little guy so bad he cried. He feared it because he only saw it when there was trouble, and he feared it because he was afraid that the smile combined with another obnoxious practical joke, like hiding his waiter's cart in the mop closet, or with a pummeling, like the little guy had taken, might force him into a battle that he could only win with a butcher knife or with a meat cleaver or with a lucky blow of a frying pan or a slashing tray, a loser's battle that he no longer had the guts to fight.

September and freedom were all that counted, he reminded himself, and tried to pretend that the smile wasn't for him, that he couldn't see the smile, that the smile wasn't on the smirking brown face, that it didn't even exist, and it suddenly didn't. For his heart leaped into pumping excitement, as the Buzzer and Rattler came trudging, loud-talking, and laughing around the corner of the office, into the graveled yard.

A blue cap flattened the Buzzer's head, lengthened the heavy droop of his lips, shaded his scheming eyes. He shuffled through the gravel, swaying, ungainly, hopped up onto the porch, and joined the group around Boomby and Bobby Shuck.

Rattler followed, but kept his bony limbs behind the Buzzer, and aimed quick glances with his tattooed cross at Aaron, although he helped stir the white mass of kitchen uniforms into a whirl of excitement.

Dinner count was due, so they had only come for trouble, but Aaron had already endured a week of their wisecracks in school, and leaving right away meant worse trouble later. They had driven him out of the gym once, though, and he now haunted the stacks in the library, where the enforced quiet protected him, and where he could also avoid Skip and his embarrassing gang war games.

"Hee-hee!" he heard and recognized as Rattler's cue for the Buzzer's snigger, which followed immediately and was followed, in turn, by a chuckle from Bobby Shuck, a giggle from another guy, and Boomby's smile.

He then waited for some remark, fearing a round of them.

"Rot-rot! Is that all that punk on that box there got?" the Buzzer said; and Aaron dropped his hands between his thighs with the trailing chuckles, let himself droop into a slouch, and told himself to relax, told himself that nothing counted but the short month until September, but Boomby added:

"He got more than rot./He got a sweet little knot."

And Bobby Shuck said: "Now don't tell me/that boy ain't dear./He got the cutest,/the smallest,/the whitest rear."

And Aaron got up to leave with the loud laughter, for the dozens were on, and the kitchen hall was a screened sanctuary beyond the swinging doors, but a sanctuary which he had to reach and tried to reach, as Rattler and Bobby Shuck both tried to drop a cap at the same time.

He heard them and he didn't hear them. He heard their voices but he closed his mind to the jumbled words: pussy and punk intermingled with little fat boy and clean old man. He didn't know who said what, and he didn't care, and he didn't look, but kept himself aimed for the screen doors, and almost reached them before the Buzzer, flanked by the white uniforms of Boomby and Bobby Shuck, blocked his way.

"Ha-ha, ha-ha," the Buzzer laughed, and Aaron turned to go around them.

But they shifted in front of him with a snigger.

He stopped, with an angry pressure in his chest, and turned back.

They shifted again.

He stopped again, as an impulse to strike quaked through him, but, grinning and dangerous, he knew they would ruin any chance of a go-home, and hurt him.

He turned again, but completely around, planning to circle the officers' mess and enter the mess hall by its front doors, listening to the Buzzer's drawl as he crossed the porch, but not grasping what it said until he leaped from the porch:

"Fu-ucked the son, li-ike to get the mama's cu-unt!"

And he landed with a flat-footed crunch on the crushed pebbles that jarred his entire body.

He heard himself say, "Go-home, go-home."

But he turned again, and snorting like a punch-drunk

fighter, he leaped up onto the porch and charged into the Buzzer, punching wildly with both hands, punching with all his power, but punching with punches that felt as light and as weak as fly swats, but he kept punching and he kept punching, and he kept screaming:

"You mother fucker, I'll kill you. You mother fucker, you mother fucker, you mother fucker," until his voice was a screech, but he screamed it as Boomby and Bobby Shuck each grabbed a handful of his hair and jerked him to the concrete floor, screamed it as they twisted him over on his back and held him down, screamed it when the Buzzer dropped on his bruised chest and knocked his breath out of him and pinned his arms to the porch with bony straddling knees and Boomby and Bobby Shuck kneeled on his legs, screamed it when the Buzzer began to slap his face back and forth between both palms, screamed it when Boomby started running a hand along the seam of his crotch, screamed it when Bobby Shuck pinched the cheeks of his butt and Rattler swung an arm in wide circles and poked with a finger and sang:

"Ro-ly, Po-ly, tickly my Ho-ly!" and he screamed it as Boomby warned:

"Don't hurt the little punk, Buzzer. Don't hurt him. Don't hurt him. Get goodies, instead. Cop a feel, Buzzer. Cop a feel," and he screamed it as the Buzzer reached back and crushed his balls in a black hand, and he screamed it until the curse changed to a shout of pain, then one prolonged screeching cry of anger, of frustration, of hate, and, finally, a stomach-deep sob; and then, unable to shout or scream, he began to spit, and still sobbing, he spit in the Buzzer's face; his voice a wounded croak, he spit on Bobby Shuck; his lips a white froth, he spit on Boomby and tried to spit on Rattler and made them all duck and get mad and threaten to hit him; but the dinner whistle blew and resounded like a siren along the porch, and they let go and ran, disappeared in a sweep of white pant legs, a quake of hustling footsteps on the concrete floor, and a rapid beat of footsteps across the gravel, leaving him alone, but still sobbing, still spitting, still croaking, and stamping his feet, stamping his feet, stamping his feet.

But he suddenly stopped. He stopped stamping and stopped croaking and stopped spitting, and his sobbing settled into a quavering whimper; and he jumped up, his hair falling in his eyes, his white uniform dirty and wrinkled, his face burning with concentration, for he knew how to get them and right away, and if he couldn't whip them, he'd kill them.

He staggered drunkenly through the swinging doors, while hot tears streamed out of his eyes and ran salty into his mouth and mucus stuffed his nose; and although a door snapped back and struck him across the ankle, it did not slow his reeling lurch down the empty hall; and he pressed on, almost toppling forward, and stubbing each shoe toe with each reeling step.

Hot blood fired every muscle, heated every inch of vein and artery, flooded his head, and drowned the clamor in his ears of the voices, the pans, the carts, and the last minute instructions from the main dining room.

Hot blood enlarged the pumping need of his heart for compensation for the wronged good will, for the spurned friendship, for the ruined reputation, and speeded the palpitating tempo of its demands for revenge for almost two months of punishment, mutilation, and despair. Hot blood churned through his body with the hot rage of a body that wanted to die destroying, but die, ease, free all pain of mind and body in one stupendous self-destructive act.

Yet, as he staggered down the hall, whimpering, sniffling, eyes hot and blurred, his mind was separate from his body and very lucid and very cunning and yet divided. One part, the controlling central part, self-consciously directed his walk along the hall toward the supply room door and watched to see that he was not seen, although he did not care if he was seen, would have liked to be seen so someone, anyone would try to stop him, and he could explode into immediate suicidal action. This part held the memory of the delivered supplies, the skull and crossbones on the rat poison cans, which he had helped to put away upon the supply room shelves a few days earlier, when the idea had first registered that it might be a clever way to get revenge without getting caught.

The second part of his brain hovered above the other and kept warning him, telling him what he was doing. It did not try to stop his entering the supply room door, nor slow his beeline path through the darkened musty shelves, nor tell him to stop when he grabbed the foot ladder from the back wall, set it next to the shelf he wanted and climbed, stumble footed but surely, up its steps, and reached, reached for the small circular cans, dropped one to the floor with a clatter, jammed another one under his shirt, climbed down, picked up the fallen can, put it, too, under his shirt, and was conscious of the sagging weight.

It did not try to stop any of this. It only told him exactly what he was doing and where it would end. It did not say *stop!* it said *look!* It said, "Now you close the door, still crying, sniffling, not caring. Now you turn and stagger down the hall, into the main dining room, where everyone turns to look at you and, then, self-consciously, turns away, avoiding you, giving you a clear path. Now you stagger straight down the main aisle of the dining room, all the way to the end, through the heavy odor of clam chowder and its steaming transparent clouds. You look around you once, although you don't care if you are seen, then jerk open your shirt, and pull out a can with sweating hands. Somebody must be looking at you!"

The other section of his mind self-consciously takes control, and he turns his back, conceals his actions by holding the can carefully in front of him, still crying but slightly, still whimpering but softly, still sniffling but less so, but still desiring revenge, still wanting to explode in a fit of suicidal rage, but also wanting to win, to win, to win.

The reflective brain continues:

"Now you are using your shirt for a better grip and twisting the tin cap loose. Now you are dumping the heavy powder into the clam chowder and taking a step you will never be able to retreat from. This is murder and suicide, and you say you don't care. You don't stop with one. You even leave the can lying by the pitcher and move down the table to the second pitcher, but return to the first because you remember that the Buzzer sits at this end of the table, in the same spot, as cadet captain, for every meal. You are repeating the same suicidal process, killing yourself with them. You twist the cap loose, lift the can and dump the white powder into the thick hot spicy soup, stir it with a fork even, a cunning act. You've done it, and now you and they will be destroyed, destroyed, destroyed."

But the other portion of his brain takes control again, and he picks up the cans, stuffs them into his shirt, leaves by the front doors of the dining room, runs crying and at a trot around the officers' mess, through the crunching graveled yard, onto the porch, where he flattens each can with a single stamp of his heel, and carefully jams them into a large trash can.

He moves stealthily now that it is done and enters the washroom. He splashes water on his face and blows his nose, but he is not refreshed. He looks in the mirror. The whites of his eyes are a rabbit pink. His lower lids are as heavy and dark as coffee rings. His lower lip trembles. He cannot really look into his own eyes, the faded green of the iris or the deadly black of the pupil, for he is afraid to see the change in himself.

"It is over," the reflective mind continues, "and you go out into the changed hall, changed forever by yourself. You have done it. You have poured rat poison into the Buzzer's soup. Two cans of rat poison. You may get more than him. It is strychnine. You know that. You have seen its quick effects. You have seen the carcasses of field rats lying in the dairy, where they had eaten the poisoned grain, unable to escape from the man's trap before they died in it."

Sweat trickles all over his body. The thought of the skull and crossbones makes him dizzy, but it is too late. He walks slowly out to his place at the food counter and picks up the bread spatula. He usually likes the fresh bread odor, but now he cannot even smell it, let alone care about it. He knows all the guys are looking at him. He also knows that none of them will let him catch them at it, for they are afraid of the scene he will cause. He looks around him and sees only profiles and the backs of heads. He doesn't care, anyway. He's done it and he's going to win, any . . . way.

The wait for the sound of marching feet seems much longer than usual, and then he hears it: an explosive sound of thick-heeled brogans striking rhythmically against the asphalt. A quarter of an hour then seems to pass before the first two boys reach the wide double doors and both lines swing into the dining room and down its opposite sides to the twin food counters. The lines bring noise in with them. Happy noise. Dinner time noise. Trays clatter. Voices laugh, loud talk, hurrah. Shoes scrape. Lines stretch thin and close. And the sound of the marching feet continues in a rhythmical pattern.

Sweat flushes break out on Aaron at short intervals, tingling, tingling all over him. He itches and wants to scratch the slow slide of sweat drops, but he mechanically begins to slip the spatula, with a practiced motion, under two, only two slices of bread, and lifts and drops them into the corner pocket of each passing tray. He does not look at the trays nor at the boys pushing them. For from his position at the end of the food counter, he can see straight down the middle of the dining room to the front doors, and he watches and waits for the Buzzer and Rattler to enter with the last company. The last and final company, he thinks and sees them.

Twin shadows in the doorway, they part inside the doors and move down opposite lines, and the Buzzer, luckily, will get his bread from Aaron. Aaron will serve the Buzzer his last helping of food, at his last supper, on his last Friday. A final meal of clam chowder and fish. Clam chowder mixed with two cans of strychnine. A perfect seasoning for a nasty bastard. Poison chowder, hah!

"Poison chowder, hah! Poison chowder, hah!" Aaron keeps chanting to himself, letting the monotonous beat build up the pitch of his feelings, wishing the smell of poison chowder was all over the room, hanging in steamy odorous clouds above all the tables, and adds, when he notices Barneyway:

"Die, too, you little gutless punk. You might as well be dead, dogging it the way you do.

"Die, die, all of you die," he repeats under his breath, wishing it was in everyone's soup, the officers', too, and he envisions the two mess halls as one, sees a dining room full of bodies, sees stiffened and intertwined limbs of blue, white, and khaki sprawled all over the tables, the benches, and the aisles, sees them until he sees the Buzzer only two boys away from him, sliding his metal tray along the counter.

One boy away and their eyes meet. Victory shines in the Buzzer's eyes like the dull glow of shoe polish. He waits for his bread. Aaron scoops with the spatula, lifts high, reaches, pauses, then twists and dumps the bread into the soup bowl with a cackling laugh, and continues to cackle, as the Buzzer, lips contorting but making no sounds, backs away, then turns and hurries to his table, where he turns again, looks curiously at Aaron before sitting down, looks once more from his seat, and, as if no longer bothered by the strange behavior, jerks the soup pitcher out of another boy's hand and pours the thick creamy liquid into his tin bowl.

Drops spatter over his tray as sweat streaks down Aaron's face.

Aaron tells himself that he doesn't want to commit a mortal sin, that he doesn't want to kill, that he does not want to go to Hell. He then tells himself that it is not his fault, that all he wants is to be left alone, to do his own time, and go home in September. He has to wipe the slick handle of the spatula. The bread box is almost empty. Queens' Row is now before him, but he does not see the faces nor the trays.

He watches the Buzzer. He can distinctly hear the click of the Buzzer's spoon handle as it hits the edge of the tin bowl for a first spoonful of chowder. He can feel the Buzzer's breath as the Buzzer blows upon the hot soup, feel the metal spoon against his own teeth, taste the thick soup, detect the minute grains of undissolved powder upon his own tongue, and feel them scratch down his own throat. His Adam's apple bobs with the Buzzer's. He does see Rattler's head hovering an inch above a bowl, too, shoveling the soup down, hurrying for seconds. But his eyes are fixed upon every lifting spoonful of soup the Buzzer takes, upon the raised and motionless spoon when the bowl is empty, upon the pitcher as the Buzzer jerks it away from another boy, upon the pouring soup, and upon the final creamy dribble.

The din of silverware against metal trays, the clamor of voices, the heat from bodies and warm food and steam tables which fill the room bring Aaron close to a faint, for his need to protect himself now that the deed is done weakens him and quells an impulse to break into hysterical laughter at the Buzzer's greedy rush to self-destruction. He gets dizzy, and he has to hold onto the bread box for support. He feels feverish. His tongue is thick. He waits for something to happen and he is afraid that something will happen.

The Buzzer finishes his soup and starts on his tray. But nothing happens. Aaron is the only person left at the food counter. The others have gone to the cool shade of the back porch to relax. Yet, nothing happens. Open mouthed, he eats the breaded filet of sole bite by bite with the Buzzer. And nothing happens. He watches for some sign of pain, of discomfort, of nausea, of vomit, and he watches so long, with such expectation that nausea rises in his own stomach, and he has to look away to keep from vomiting. Still, nothing happens.

He looks for signs of sickness among the other boys at the table. But he sees nothing.

Fish and salad finished, the Buzzer starts on his cake. He is in the middle of his first bite, gold teeth upon chocolate frosting, when he notices Aaron's anxious stare, and the lack of hate in it seems to confuse him. He pulls the cake back and looks curiously at Aaron, then stuffs the cake into his mouth, gets up from the bench, lifts his tray, and goes to the scullery counter, where he drops the tray upon the stack with a clatter, deposits the silverware in a wire rack, the cup in its rack, the bowl in another, and steps to the door. He looks back at Aaron for a long obviously confused moment, steps aside for some other boys, and disappears in the direction of the gym.

Aaron stays at his station until every member of the dairy crew has gone, then hurriedly gets his cart from the kitchen and rolls it out to the table. He picks up the pitcher and stares inside. A thin film of soup scum coats its metal dents and hollows. He sniffs at it, trying to detect some odor of poison, but there are only the sharp smells of spices and clam. He begins to doubt that the poison will work. For it got the rats before they could get back to their holes, and it should have got the Buzzer before he left the table.

He then feels strangely lightheaded, almost buoyant. The pitchers lift from the tables like bubbles. His shakers stack themselves on the cart. His damp cloth wipes cleanly and freely, hardly touching the table tops. His cart rolls before him with the slightest push, and he returns it to its proper place in the kitchen before any of the other waiters are through with their jobs, and goes out into the cool air, the long shadows of the late afternoon.

But the gym's shadow stretches across the visitors' lawn and near to the compounds, whose yards and roofs are squares and rectangles of concealed black which hide the answer his strained nerves quickly demand to know. Yet he moves away from the compounds, toward the gym, and, head down and his hands tucked into his back pockets, he begins a compulsive, fast-stepping pace to work off the restless fear that begins to churn in his stomach again. He had jumped to conclusions and he realizes it now. A human being cannot be judged by a rat.

He changes direction and zigzags along the gravel paths which crisscross the visitors' lawn, with its scent sharp and irksome to his nostrils, wanting something to happen: good or bad; but since he no longer wants to kill the Buzzer nor die himself, he begins to hope for a compromise: stomach-aches and no deaths, pain without serious injury.

He scans each knot of boys he passes without leaving the gravel paths, stares at the boys who stand in front of the compounds, the pairs who pace the gym ramp, and the loners who move about on solitary routes, searching for a member of the dairy crew to see if any of the effects of the poison show.

He crosses and recrosses the lawn several times without success, but with a pictured dorm of blue corpses, overturned beds, and a vomit-smeared floor gradually taking on the set and unshakable outlines of a tableau; and he stops, and decides to risk going to the dorm, and finds himself in front of the chapel.

He starts toward the dorm, but stops, and takes another step, but stops, and turns, and hurries across the road to the chapel, without a plan or any idea of what he is going to do.

In four steps he crosses the porch and opens the heavy door, and he is several benches down the aisle, head lowered, still worried about a dorm full of dying boys, when a wheezing moan stops him in midstep, and his gaze freezes on his brogan toe.

Another moan makes his head lift, and his gaze shifts from his toe to the floor and shoots down the aisle to the altar, to the Buzzer on his back below it, twitching with the spasms of a headless chicken, and reaching with spread fingers for the angels.

With another moan, the sight vanishes, for Aaron turns and runs to the door and claws for the handle before he realizes what he has seen, before he realizes that the Buzzer is down, hurt, helpless, maybe dying, that this is what he has been planning and hoping for, that this is what he used the rat poison for, that he is running away from the victory he has dreamed of, that he is letting panic cheat him of the pleasure of winning, and of winning now!

"He's down! He's down!" he repeats to himself and keeps repeating until his fear gives way to hate, hate to rage, and rage gives him the nerve to turn around, to start down the aisle once more, back toward the altar, slowly toward the twitching body, but still careful, still not sure the Buzzer is really helpless, still suspicious of a possible trick, of a practical joke, still expecting the dark pimple-specks of Boomby's smile to pop up between the benches, the bloated cheeks of Bobby Shuck to appear by the altar, and Rattler's cross to come out of the chaplain's office, or all three foes to come from the front door behind him; and he stops again and looks back at the door, truly fearful that it will spring open and that they will charge at him; and he does see their ghostly forms run down the aisle toward him, as if it were the dairy, through the flood of discolored light from the stained glass windows; and he tightens for a clash that never occurs, which a chilling moan from the altar stops, which snaps the tension; and with a shout of fear and elated rage, spurred on by his cry, he charges down the aisle and kicks the Buzzer in the ribs with all the force of his unslackened momentum and trips and almost falls and has to grab at the altar rail; and yet the soft thump of his brogan toe is disappointing, and the Buzzer's shriek and sudden convulsion is so frightening that only the rail keeps him from falling, and only one-legged hops sidewards help him escape the backward snap of the muscular body and the wild jerking and twisting of the arms and legs.

He then holds onto the rail to keep from collapsing, but holds on entranced as the body bends back, arches off the floor, rolls on its side; and the bulging eyeballs pinpoint him for a horrible instant, then puff bigger with another wheezing moan, another suffocating gasp for breath; and Aaron shouts to avoid them and starts kicking at the exposed belly, kicks when it sucks in for air, kicks while it stretches and shivers and snaps as if it will burst, kicks it as he had wanted to kick it in the darkened dormitory, in the tumult of the dairy, kicks it with the fury and hate of those hospital visions, kicks it and kicks it and kicks it until he can't lift his leg, until he, himself, is gasping for breath, until he notices that the convulsing body and the twitching arms and legs are insensible to his kicks, that the grimace on the Buzzer's face is frozen with internal pain, that his kicks are as weak to the Buzzer as his punches on the kitchen porch, as the crack of the nozzle, as ineffectual as all his threats, as the blade he never used; and a scream rumbles as deep as a growl within him and splits his lips; and he kicks the black head back on the rigid neck, and balances on one foot, and growling and cursing and wishing he had a blade to stab with, drives his heel into the gritting teeth, lifts it to drive it down again, but screams with shock at the sudden wild shudder and limp collapse of the convulsing body, at the blood-flecked foam that slobbers out of the mouth; and he staggers back, afraid to look, whining with fear at his murderous crime, sure he is surrounded by accusing witnesses; for the bench rows swim in dizzy waves, silence crackles like malicious gossip, stained windows burn as bright as cop-car lights; and an eerie beam from a pale-glass pane spotlights him, but it paralyzes him, too, at the foot of the altar, and it holds him captive, and it holds him for the chaplain to burst through the door and condemn him for murder with a bullet-swift glance, for the angels to behead

him, for God to strike him dead; and he moans and drops to
his knees to beg forgiveness, to prove that he is sorry, that he
didn't want to kill, to pray for the Buzzer's soul, to pray for
his own soul, and to pray for everyone's soul; but the button-
size pupils then seem to dilate with recognition of him; and
another wheezing moan whistles past the jeering teeth and
through the foaming mouth, mocking him, mocking his fear,
mocking his prayer, mocking his remorse, mocking his pity,
mocking his poison, mocking his kicks, mocking him now as
always in the past; and he jumps to his feet, and angry enough
to kill but too tired to kick, determined to prove he can't be
mocked but too tired to shout, he begins to taunt and to taunt
as if an audience of boys sat on the benches, to taunt because
it's all he can do, but to taunt with pleasure, to taunt slowly
and relish the satisfying hate in every single taunt, to taunt
and drag his victory out:

"Need help, Buzzer? Ole buddy?" he taunts and pants for
breath.

"An equalizer?" he taunts and pants again.

"A doctor, maybe?" he taunts and pants.

"A month's rest in the hospital?" he taunts while he pants,
for he cannot pause, and he continues to taunt and pant, but
taunt, taunt:

"How about a prayer?

"That's what you came for, huh?

"Or should I pray for Barneyway?

"Or me?

"Or you get what you deserve?

"How's that?

"How about a good punking?

"I'll pray those bull-dike angels ball you with their swords.

"Up your big black ass!

"How's that?

"Ram yuh, Buzzer, while you're moanin' and groanin'.

"Like you, Buzzer.

"Like you.

"How's that?

"Jerk your goddamn pants off!

"Buzzerrrrrrrrrrr!" and he grabs the Buzzer's wrist, inspired by the taunts, raging and strong again, but shudders at the touch of icy skin, and fears he's been taunting a dead man, for there is no pulse, then fears he is losing his mind, for there is a pulse, although feeble and tiny, the second he thinks of one; and then he is sure he is losing his mind, for his touch seems to start the horrible convulsions all over again; and the arm starts snapping, violently, angrily; but he can't let go, and he can't let go because, somehow, his grip is all that convinces him the Buzzer really lives, that he, himself, lives, that keeps him conscious, and because he senses that if he lets go. . . ? that together, they'll. . . ? And he starts kicking again, and he kicks to prove that it is the Buzzer who is dying, kicks to prove that he wants him to die; and he kicks until the motion of kicking finally frees his hands; and although the body collapses again and the wheezing moans stop and he wants to run, his legs buckle beneath him and he falls back on the altar rail, where his useless legs will not only not carry him away, he is too tired to even turn away from the sight of the bright sweat oozing out of the black skin before him, too tired to clap his hands over his ears and shut out the weak groans and the short gasps that bubble through the foaming lips; too tired to deny that the gold teeth still jut out, that they still offend him, that they have jeered him from his first day in the institute and that they will jeer him until the last day of his life, that they will jeer him in Hell, even in Hell; and because he is too tired to deny them, all the jeering memories crowd for attention in his mind; and he sees them one after the other, one imposed upon the other, and many at once: the "Ha-ha, ha-ha" with the grotesque dance and the taunts in the school and the crouching menace in the dairy; and he sees them as he sees the jeering teeth; and he hears them as he hears a tiny squeak; and he hears them and he hates them, but the squeak is so pitifully little to come from such a husky bully that it arouses a sympathetic tremor in him; and the memories are so unbearable that he fastens upon the teeth as he waits for another squeak, and he lets himself succumb to the sympathy; but the teeth still jeer, the memories still crowd into his mind, and his own pity doesn't help him; and he bursts into a rage at his own weakness, at his need to feel pity for the Buzzer, when he is finally defeated and dying beneath him, and he shouts:

"Remember what you did to me when I was down, Buzzer? Remember?" and he grabs the balls and crushes them in his fist and twists with all his strength, and he twists harder at the Buzzer's shriek, twists although the shriek is faint, and he uses his free hand like a wrench on his own wrist for leverage, and he twists still harder as the body starts convulsing again, aware while he twists that the trembling is different this time, that it is still strong and horrible but smoother, as if the muscles are somehow contracting together, in one unbroken movement now, not separately and wildly as before; but he is afraid he is imagining this and he denies it as the body arches backward so severely that he swears the heels will touch the head; and he denies this as he denies that it is his own voice that is yelling and cursing, that it is his own voice that is trying to convince the Buzzer of how much he is hated, of how good his dying is, of how good his suffering is, of how much more it, his voice, would like him, the Buzzer, to suffer; and he denies this as he denies that he can no longer understand his own words, that they are not as angry as his grip, and that they cannot be angry enough to really express his hate and his anger; and he denies this as he denies that he is not even making words but only a hoarse, growling sound; and he denies this as he denies that the crotch is rising in the air as if his grip is lifting it; and he denies this as he denies that the foaming mouth is gasping for breaths it can't breathe anymore;

as he denies that the convulsions have gone on for an un-
countable amount of time and have not lessened in intensity
as before; as he denies that the body is flipping about in angry
contractions while suspended a full foot above the altar floor,
arched from head to heels and kept upright by his grip; as he
denies that the suffering will go on as long as he can grip;
and he denies all of this and keeps twisting and shouting and
crying until his arm cramps with pain, until the fingers of both
of his hands ache with a numb stiffness, until he can no longer
even feel the balls, until he no longer wants to see the convulsions, until they torture him as much as the Buzzer; and he
jerks his hand loose and jumps back but croaks as he pulls
the back-bent body over on its side toward him; and he croaks
as he bumps into the altar, screams at the carved anguish on
the crucified Christ, ducks at the sight of the grotesque angels;
and trips backward over the Buzzer and falls to the floor,
where he starts screaming at the touch of the convulsing body;
and he screams as he scrambles to his feet and runs down the
aisle, the icy sweat still sticking to his fingers; and he screams
as he fumbles with the door handle in his clumsy haste, but
he stops screaming when he throws the door open and bounds
across the porch, and he has stopped screaming before he
jumps the steps to the sidewalk and starts running down the
hill, and he is no longer screaming when he runs past metal
shop windows as screened and sin-haunted by the murderous
blade as the dark-screened, sin-haunted lattices of confessional
booths; and although he is no longer screaming, he runs from
a chapel as haunted in his stricken brain as his mother's hospital bedroom, as haunted as if the blood-flecked foam spewed
from his mother's emaciated grin, as haunted by the carved
altar cross as by the scratched pachuco cross in the isolation
cell; and, haunted, he runs past fields of dead weeds and dry
grass, runs with a heart that pounds in his chest with all the
force and deafening panic of beating, praying fists, runs into
a wind that whines as hauntingly as the electric trains on those

lonely nights, that murmurs like the unhappy memories in that empty house, that throbs as deeply as all the sobs of all his family at his mother's coffin, that cuts his throat and sears his lungs; and, haunted, he starts running faster, although he cannot run faster, but runs faster, runs from every haunting fear and every haunting misery, runs from every fight and act of forced courage, runs from every humiliation and shame, runs from guilt, from the blade, from the chaplain, from Big Stoop, from Barneyway, from himself and from that tattooed beauty mark, runs from that tattooed beauty mark, and, running from that tattooed beauty mark, he runs past the baseball diamond and from the boys playing on it, runs toward the blurred brown fields, runs madly, blindly, runs to hide, to escape, to obliterate himself forever, somewhere, soon, runs, runs, runs, runs until he stumbles and almost falls, staggers, with dragging steps, crouched, but still running, completely across the road, and discovers, while still running, that he is exhausted, that his legs are pulpy, that each breath sucks his insides dry and that he is running toward the dairy compound! that he has unwittingly turned back with the curve in the road and is heading back toward the main grounds, where he will be caught! but he doesn't stop running because he can't stop running! fear and momentum carry him toward the compound with the unescapable force of a skidding car! toward an inevitable crash with a group of boys in front of the compound! but he can't stop running! and he can't go back! and he zigzags with confusion, breaks his plunging speed, and slows to a trot, but can't change direction; and his will-less body runs on, carries him with it, gulping air to soothe his seared lungs, to ease the side pain that splits his ribs with every jarring step; and though his feet finally begin to drag and the jolting heels to brake his speed a little more, he fears it will be too late, that the boys ahead will capture him; and they grow to Big Stoop's size before him, while each knee bends less and less sharply, lifts less and less high below him, and each foot kicks forward with less and less energy and covers less and less ground; and he sees the pavement come into focus, and he recognizes strange color variations in the asphalt, a shallow darkened pool where rain water had stood, and molten tar layers from the summer heat; and he steps on an ash-white high spot that shortens his step and snaps his knee-cap and slows him to a walk; and he walks now with plodding steps, each shoe lifting robot slow below him, lifting with a trembling effort of all his muscles, and slapping, flat-footed only a short space ahead of him; but he plods on, still unable to stop, still unable to turn, still unable to change direction; and he passes the smooth, calm dormitory windows, windows which conceal his murderous secret; and he sees that the group is still another compound away, but that the boys in it are close enough to notice how his white shirt trembles from his pounding heart, how his chest heaves, how he gasps for breath, close enough to see the guilt in his eyes, to be able to tell that he is a killer! but he still cannot stop because he might collapse if he tries and really attract attention; but he is so close to them that he is positive they can see how his hands tremble; and he jams his hands into his back pockets to hide them, and he squeezes his arms against his sides and binds his shivering body with them, and he squints his eyes to hide any expression in them, and he forces himself to take half breaths so he won't gasp, and he tries to appear nonchalant by making himself walk right past the boys and prove that there is nothing wrong with him, and prove that he is not scared, and prove that he is not a killer! but the word is so chilling that it stops him; and he begins to tremble badly again, and he has to walk to avoid a collapse and to hide his shaking; and he walks past the dairy compound, past the field between the compounds, and straight toward the group of boys, straight toward them because, decision or not, he cannot change direction, because he is incapable of any thought but the immediate one of somehow getting past them; and he walks toward them as toward waiting cops, walks as if to his death, walks toward them and almost to them when the smack of running feet behind him stops him, and stops him, he is sure, forever, stops him with his hands still clenched in his back pockets, stops him so he may be grabbed, stops him and keeps him stopped while his last feeble strength ebbs away with the smacking sound, too weak and too afraid to discover the source of the sound, yet positive that it can only come from the only dormitory behind him, and just as quickly positive by the rapid and unflagging sound that he will not be grabbed, but just as positive, grabbed or not, that he cannot possibly take any more misery, that he will drop dead if anyone else besides the Buzzer is sick, and positive that he will drop dead, he stands with the dead ache of a heart that has already died inside him, a heart that can't be hurt any more or any worse than it has been, as the quiet colored boy who replaced him on the garbage wagon runs by with a high-stepping panic, soles flashing behind him, and side-steps the group and the good-natured grab of another boy, and speeds beyond the group, without slowing, and cuts across the visitors' lawn, and climbs the hill, body slanting forward, fists and arms and knees churning, and runs into the office, and lets the door slam behind him; and Aaron stands motionless, with that dead ache of a dead heart inside him, hands clenched in his back pockets, as the station wagon backs up behind the office in a cloud of gravel dust and burning rubber, swings forward and down the service road next to the eucalyptus trees, then onto the paved road, siren wailing, tires rippling, motor grinding in second gear, whizzes past him, khaki caps in the front seat, the colored boy in the back, and screeches to a halt in front of the dairy compound, where the doors swing open, the two men and the boy jump out, the men grab stretchers, and all three of them disappear through the gate; and Aaron stands motionless, with that dead ache inside him, although he can hear yelling and Big Stoop shouting orders, although he knows what is going on and what can be seen inside the dormitory; but he continues to stand motionless, with that dead ache inside him, as boys run toward the compound from all over the grounds and mill and shout in its courtyard and in front of its gate, and more men run to the compound and push their way through the crowd, a crowd that swells, in what seems seconds, to riot size; and, with that dead ache inside him, Aaron finally begins to drift toward the crowd, drifts toward it with as effortless and motiveless and strong and incomprehensible a pull as an iron filing toward a magnet, drifts toward it without curiosity or panic or fear or even remorse, drifts toward it with an ache so dead within him that his pounding heart has no effect upon his winded body; and he reaches it, with that dead ache inside him, as Big Stoop and another man come out of the dairy dorm, carrying someone on a stretcher between them; and he lets himself, with that dead ache inside him, be pushed into the excited crowd, lets himself be pushed so far forward that he catches a glimpse of the stretcher; but he lets himself, with that dead ache inside him, be pushed still farther back and then forward again, and, then, back, and forward, and back again, and he begins to feel hot and giddy, but lets himself be pushed around because he doesn't care if he is shoved, because he doesn't care if he can see or not, because he doesn't care if anyone else is sick or dying, because no care can help the dead ache, but because he doesn't care, it all seems so stupid, he feels an urge to smile, because he doesn't care, it all seems so useless, he feels an urge to chuckle, because he doesn't care, it all seems so hopeless, he feels an urge to laugh loudly, to laugh desperately; but the urge diminishes as the crowd thins before the gate in order to allow the stretcher to pass, and a numb expectant horror grips him instead, and his dry tongue swells and grits against the ridged roof of his mouth, and his blood pounds into pain in his temples, and though he slaps his hands to his mouth to stifle a scream at the sight of Barneyway's puny body flipping around on the stretcher like a hooked fish, at the bulging eyes, at the peeling lips, at the gums and teeth putting out in a jackass's grin, he cries:

"Barney! Barney! Oh, Barney!" as the figures around him spin by, as he wobbles, bumps against a boy next to him, spins completely around once, and falls, headfirst, to the pavement.

# Part Ten
# Good Time

# Good Time

## I

Harsh fumes burned Aaron's nasal passages. But strong fingers gripped the back of his neck and forced him to inhale. And he awoke, with a frightful jerk, to a world of white, white blur, white streak, and found a wavering focus for reality in the steel-rimmed lenses of the nurse. He lined his eyes up with them. And the bottle of smelling salts was withdrawn from his nose. And the strong fingers let his head lay back upon the gurney.

A pimpled, pocked surface, shadowed by twilight, formed an empty sky of stale white. Figures, objects hovered on the edges of his vision with the distant, shifting, now looming, now receding emphasis of dream forms. Sound passed through antechambers of echo and reflection: voices sputtered like wet matches. Shut doors flashed yells in the darkness and blotted out low moans. Footsteps clapped bright and brighter and brighter and burst into ribbed tubes of fluorescence upon the ceiling, and, totally awake, his memory returned with a jackass's grin, and he asked the hovering pointed brim of the nurse's cap:

"What happened to Barney?"

Broad hips belled out of a pinched starched waist, but there was no answer.

"Tell me."

Huge busts then ballooned with a deep sigh, and she said, simply:

"He died."

Sucking air dried his parted lips, lips still marked by the red welts of new skin, but he didn't sob. Waves of pitying tears for his dead friend rose up in his eyes and spilled over the shallow brims of his lids, and his nose ran heavily with mucus, but he didn't sob. The tears ran in silent curving trickles into the ridges of his ears as a cabinet door opened, a plastic vial top popped with suction, and the nurse's big face swelled between mountainous busts above him, a paper cup and two capsules in her hands, but he didn't sob.

He swallowed the capsules with the water and undressed in front of her without shame, put on a clean nightgown, then padded barefoot behind her to a private room, entered as if he had not been absent for a week, and, as she locked the door, climbed between fresh sheets, and settled into them, while still breathing through his mouth, and with tears still streaming down cheeks now smarting and sensitive from them. But he could not sob nor could he shut out of his mind the image of Barneyway's twisting, flopping body and the silent bray of his open mouth.

Drowsiness came and blurred the visions of a dying Barneyway, slurred Aaron's mumbled pleas for that final penance, that unbroken sleep, dried the streams of tears, the damp blots on the pillow, and dropped him into a long and relieving and untroubled sleep, from which he awoke, without fear, to the stern face of Big Stoop, hovering over the bed.

A strange hue neutralized Big Stoop's ruddy complexion, and Aaron could not tell whether it was caused by the pale light of morning, which cast a blank tint over all the white objects in the white room, or the blank sleep.

"I'd like to ask you some questions," Big Stoop said; and Aaron sat up but made no attempt to brush the strands of hair away from his eyes.

"Did you have any idea that anything was wrong before you heard the siren?" Big Stoop asked and cleared Aaron's mind with the question but disgusted him; and he shook his head, lying in a simple defense against a con-job and the severe, microscopic examination of him, but disgusted with himself, too.

Big Stoop's blunt features seemed to sharpen with superiority, as if he knew he could turn any answer to his advantage; and Aaron could tell when he was ready to ask the next question by the tightened knife-edge of his lipless mouth.

"When did you know they died of strychnine poisoning?"

"They?" Aaron gasped, tongue caught on his lower teeth, stuck where the word had ended, and remembered that he had dumped two cans of poison into the soup, that the white powder had dissolved into the thick creamy liquid twice. And the knife-edge became loose and dull and Big Stoop added, reluctantly:

"Three boys died: Barnham Aragon, Oliver Wiley, and Thomas Rodriguez. Three others are in bad, though not critical, condition. They'll pull through."

"My God! My God!" Aaron cried and hid his face in his hands, wondering how he could have possibly forgotten the Buzzer's twitching body, those jeering teeth; and his shoulders rocked with his shaking head, and he scraped his fingers down his dry face and pulled his eyes, his cheeks, his mouth into distortion, but he didn't cry.

"Are they the boys who jumped you?" Big Stoop asked, his mouth tight again.

"Not Barney," Aaron said. "The Buzzer raped him, too."

"Are you sure?"

"Yes."

"How?"

"I saw it," Aaron said.

And Big Stoop straightened up, took off his cap, and ran his hand over his gray hair, which had been flattened by the cap's pressure, and then rubbed the red cap line which marked his forehead.

"Do you see what you've done to those boys and yourself for not telling me who attacked you?" he asked; and the explanatory tone of his voice brought Aaron closer to tears than the news that he was a multiple murderer, for he could not pity himself, and he did not want pity, and sympathy from Big Stoop would be unbearable.

"You know, sometimes I may seem cruel, and I might be cruel. I don't try to be a Good Joe, my job's too hard. But I'm a guard, a cop who's taken an oath, and my job is to keep things like this, what you did and what was done to you, from happening, and it takes being cruel sometimes to do it."

Aaron wanted to shout at him to stop and just ask if he, Aaron, did it, so he could confess and hopefully drop back into the blank sleep, but found himself denying what he wanted to admit in defense against another con-job.

"Now, you're going to have to do a lot of time for this, years, and maybe they'll try and give you the chamber, it's not out of the question, and I could probably help you get a better deal from the judge if I could tell him that you co-operated with me, that you were really sorry for what you did? Do you follow me?"

Aaron pursed his lips to keep from speaking and shook his head again. He didn't care if he got the chamber, and he wasn't going to let Big Stoop scare him.

"You don't, huh?"

Aaron shook his head.

"Well, let me make it clear for you then," Big Stoop said and flipped his cap on and fitted it down tight on his forehead.

"If you don't give me all the facts now and without any nonsense, before the sheriff shows up again, I'm going to toss you in the hole, and I'm going to keep you there on bread and water until you do talk. Do you follow me?"

Aaron didn't answer, and he expected a slap, which he would have welcomed.

"Those boys are gone forever, wise guy, and you'll have to spend the rest of your life with their lives on your conscience. No punishment's going to be worse than that! Your life's ruined already, and if you'd co-operate, you might be able to get some mercy."

"Mercy?" Aaron said.

"Mercy," Big Stoop repeated, leaning down with a sharp mouth again; and Aaron could have laughed just to disturb the mouth, to loosen it a little, and to make the welcome slap follow, let alone laugh at such a thought as "mercy," but he shook his head.

"You're a tough guy, huh, kid?" Big Stoop said, and Aaron tensed for the tightened lip, the betraying blink, the slight lift of an elbow which would signal that a slap would follow, so he could roll instinctively with it, roll but not from fear, roll only to make Big Stoop miss.

The huge hands did lift but only to slap against the huge thighs, and Big Stoop stepped to the doorway, where his cap almost touched the upper frame, and he hesitated there, with one shoulder, a hip, a leg pinched in the narrow opening, and warned:

"This is your last chance, kid."

"Go to Hell," Aaron answered, with a calm that completely concealed the thrill he felt.

## II

Discolored streaks and hollows erupted into scabrous, cracking bubbles of old varnish on the walls and ceiling of the courtroom antechamber, where Aaron sat on the edge of the varnished bench seat and away from the back rest so his feet would touch the tile floor.

He sat with a studied disinterest in the tall frosted window behind him, with a studied disinterest in the shadow ribs of bars behind its sheathed surface, and with a studied disinterest in the traffic noises of the free people on the street.

He sat in a new blue uniform but with a studied disinterest in the cool antechamber he had been locked in for over two hours. He sat with a studied disinterest in what was going to happen in that courtroom behind the locked door, where his family and the judge and his future were supposed to be.

He sat with a studied but unsuccessful disinterest in the shrunken and mummified vision of a Mexican mother in black veils, who had haunted his dreams in the place of an unseen, although dead, Rattler. He sat with a studied but unsuccessful disinterest in the nightmare vision of a Bible-spouting Mrs. Wiley, who had flapped with wide black sleeves over flickering glimpses of the squeaking Buzzer. He sat with a studied but unsuccessful disinterest in the beer-bloated and lipstick-smeared face of Juanita, and with a totally unsuccessful disinterest in the flopping stretcher-bound body of Barneyway.

Prayers had failed as usual and had only quickened his despair, and he could no longer force himself to even try and recite them. The sense of weightless peace that he had prayed for and that used to accompany unburdening his soul on bended knees in the dark cubicle of a confessional booth was an unfulfilled promise he now reserved for his death.

Still, in spite of his studied disinterest, he often caught himself listening to and trying to understand the muffled voices behind the varnished door; and approaching footsteps made him tense, and he stiffened into a military posture when he heard the sound of keys, only to slump into a question mark when the noises passed, disappointed because he stayed locked in the solitude of the chamber and relieved because he didn't have to cross the threshold of the doorway and begin the excruciating experience of the hearing.

He scraped a brogan over the tiles with a small but certain

satisfaction. For it was an inmate's brogan instead of a dress shoe because he had refused to put on the new suit and shoes that Nora had brought him. He had also refused to do more than let her embrace him, and although she had bound his arms so tightly to his sides that he could smell the broadcloth of her suit, he had refused to let her sniffling weaken him into crying.

He had refused to tell John or Stanley or his father or the lawyer, as well as the sheriff, what had happened, too, and he had torn Judith's letter up, unread, and had flushed it down the toilet, had watched how its ragged edges had lighted on the enameled pool, how the lined paper had dampened and darkened and smeared with ink before disappearing in a whirl of suction and crashing water.

Footsteps near the door made his hands clammy.

Keys!

He sat up and held his breath as a key scratched in the keyhole, rattled for position, settled with a scrape into place, and turned with a heavy click.

Door panels vibrated.

Voices, more than murmurs, less than normal speech.

The door knob gave a small squeaking turn and the varnished panels gave way to a fat bailiff in a blue uniform, and Aaron set his feet to stand up. But the round face turned away, spoke again, turned back, and announced, curtly:

"Visitor," and Judith stepped through the doorway.

Sun-bleached hair framed a plump tanned oval, on which the beauty mark looked less dark and conspicuous but which was hesitant with light intimations of freckles and doubt. Her hands were clasped self-consciously at the midriff of her charcoal dress, and the heavy strands of her light-brown lashes veiled her eyes.

The door shut behind her and he heard a key lock it, but he made no attempt to rise from the bench, and she seemed afraid to move closer.

Finally, she took one step, hesitated in a walking position for a moment, as if making sure the floor was safe before bringing the second patent leather slipper even with the first, and said, "John says that there's a chance if . . . if . . ." then added:

"We're all with you, Aaron. . . . I'm with you, too."

But she said it, thickly, as if her throat were coated with phlegm, and looked evasively into the blind corners of the chamber.

"John says. . . . He says. . . ."

She stepped closer, while her words echoed as loud as shouts in the boxed chamber, deafening him, weakening him; and her broad starched collar rose noticeably with her breasts, as she twisted her clasped hands.

"John says that if you'll only co-operate, the case can be transferred to juvenile court, where you'll get Youth Authority, and—"

"And they'll send me to a state reform school instead of San Quentin until I'm twenty-one, and then send me to San Quentin," he said, huskily, hating her for helping them, but using the hate to put himself beyond her pleas.

"No, John says—"

"John sent you, didn't he? He told you to write, didn't he? I wondered how I got a letter so quick," he said and rejoiced at the rude burn of her tanned cheeks.

"Well, let me tell you something. I'll get Youth Authority, anyway, because of my age. And let me tell you something else. Because of my age, they can't put me in Que."

"Que?"

"San Quentin, and let me tell you something else. They can't snuff me, either."

"Snuff you?" she asked.

"Gas me, baby! They can't give me the gas chamber. And let me tell you something else," he said, but his throat was dry and he had to swallow before he could continue.

"Do you know that I've got a great rep now? Do you know that all the guys in the DT come around to my isolation cell and talk to me through the window? Do you know that all the guys in Whittier and Preston have heard about me and are hoping that I'll get sent to their joints? Do you know—"

His lips twisted and his cheek flickered as he struggled to say more, but her mouth sagged and her lower teeth showed as if she might cry, and a disturbing and weakening pity started rising in him, but keys jangled and one scraped and rattled in the lock and saved him, and he shouted at her:

"Do you know that I'm Big Time now? That nobody will mess with a killer? Do you know that no matter where I go, I'm going to do Good Time? Good Time? Good—Good—Good—"

He stuttered as she withdrew in revulsion, for a facial expression as cynical as Dominic's, which actually made her look like Dominic, centered in her tattoo, and disconcerted him.

But when he stopped, her eyes suddenly widened and softened, and her mouth fell open in a silent sensual exclamatory cry of pity, a cry punctuated by the beauty of the mark.

But he shut her mouth with a final shout of "Good Time!" and his sentence ended with the cynical period of her dot.

But the vibration of the opening door caused it to tremble with beauty again.

And then tighten as he stood at attention.

Then softly fade into her tan with his first faltering step.

Then pinch and harden on her face as he marched to her and past her.